Douleurs terribles dans les membres.

LE SOIR

60 Cmes

Mardi 9 novembre 1943

17 HEURES

EN PLEINE ACTION

ANNIVERSAIRE

Raymond DE BECKER

UN DOCUMENT

NOUS SOMMES EN PREMIÈRE LIGNE

Léonce JACQUEMIN

RECTIFICATION

NOUVELLES DU PAYS

Cinq cents grammes de pain à partir du 11 novembre

Il n'y aura plus de tabac

Deux catégories de tabac : le KROTIN A et le KROTIN B

La Conférence de Berlin

« Capitulation sans conditions »

L'arrivée de M. Mussolini

A la Wilhelmstrasse

L'avenir de l'Europe

Stratégie Efficace

Berlin admet que la situation est des plus sérieuses.

DDR. PART BERLIN.

Communiqué allemand

LA SEMAINE INTERNATIONALE
Du décrochage à la victoire défensive

par Julien VENPLAETSE

UN FAIT entre 1000

Das habe ich...!

THE
VENTRILOQUISTS

A novel by

E.R. RAMZIPOOR

PARK ROW BOOKS

PARK
ROW
BOOKS

ISBN-13: 978-0-7783-0815-7
ISBN-13: 978-0-7783-0925-3 (International Trade Edition)

The Ventriloquists

ParkRowBooks.com
BookClubbish.com

Printed in U.S.A.

To Sherry Zaks. I made you a book.

THE
VENTRILOQUISTS

"All art is propaganda."

—W.E.B. DU BOIS

THE VENTRILOQUISTS

The Jester—Marc Aubrion

The Smuggler—Lada Tarcovich

The Gastromancer—David Spiegelman

The Saboteur—Theo Mullier

The Professor—Martin Victor

The Pyromaniac—Gamin

The Dybbuk—August Wolff

The Scrivener—Eliza

YESTERDAY

The Scrivener

THE OLD WOMAN'S neighbors said there was something peculiar about her. She walked about the city in the company of night, and she kept her umbrella closed in the rain. When the door to her flat opened, which it rarely did, a glimpse inside revealed the woman's eccentricities: she'd covered her walls in newspapers from her era, the color of weathered bone. If they listened closely, her neighbors could hear the whispers of old words.

"That's how I knew it was you," said the girl to the old woman. "You couldn't possibly be anyone else." The girl was standing in the hallway; the old woman held open the door to her flat, but would not invite the girl in. The lessons of war—the locked doors, dead bolts, averted eyes, the secrecy—had become habit, as immovable as fingerprints.

"Age makes us all peculiar," said the old woman.

"But the newspapers—"

"Many people read newspapers."

She leaned on her walking stick and watched the girl's smile fade with disappointment. Rarely did the old woman travel without her walking stick, but she refused to call it a cane: people carried canes as they neared death, and though the world had aged, she was not prepared to age with it. It was a walking stick. Aubrion had taught her that: the importance of words and names. And strange as it was, the tempest of emotions that blazed from the girl's eyes—amusement and curiosity and improbable beliefs—resembled Aubrion with a clarity that made the old woman's legs weak.

"Come with me," said the old woman, and closed the door to her flat. The light that returned to the girl's eyes lifted the old woman's heart to a height that was unexpected, perhaps inexplicable. Together, they took the elevator down and stepped into the nascent morning.

All was quiet, save their footsteps and the early cries of the city. A few of last night's stars clung stubbornly to the sky. Enghien gleamed with rain-dark asphalt and OPEN signs began to blink awake. Age was not so terrible, not really, but the old woman could not abide this feeling: that she was a foreigner in her home, that her country belonged to someone younger.

"What's your name," asked the girl, "now that the war is over?"

The astute question gave the old woman pause; this girl knew something. "Helene is the name my parents gave me," she said. "And what is yours?"

"I'm Eliza. Where are we going, Helene?"

"To a building with blue doors." Eliza nodded, as though she understood. Perhaps she did. Helene studied her wide, earnest eyes and asked, "How long have you been searching for me?"

"Twelve years," said Eliza.

"And how did you find me?"

"Victor left behind documents, records of what happened. He sent them to my parents, who gave them to me before they died."

"Martin?" said Helene.

"Professor Victor."

"Ah, yes. I suppose I'm not surprised."

"I've been piecing together the story—everything from beginning to end," Eliza said hesitantly, as though she wasn't used to saying it aloud. "I've gotten a lot further than I thought I would, to be honest. It turns out you can find anything, if you want to."

"I'll not deny that," replied Helene.

They walked in silence. Helene smiled as they approached the building with the pale blue doors, pleased the occupants were still painting it the same color, that it had been blue in the forties and was blue now—a small honesty in a world of half-truths. She took a key from her pocket and unlocked the door. Since Helene moved to Brussels in the late 1980s, the city had converted the old photographer's laboratory into a museum, replacing the tables and photo-chemicals with uniforms, polished guns, bullets, framed documents. These were just *things* when Helene was a girl. People called them relics now, organizing them into exhibits.

"Are we allowed in here?" said Eliza. She lowered her voice as though they were passing through a cemetery. "It seems like we'd need permission."

"I know the museum curator. He won't mind."

Helene led her companion into a back room—a closet, really—with a lightbulb hanging on a string between two chairs. She pulled a string to turn on the light. The chairs bracketed a foldup table. Eliza's brow furrowed at the austerity.

"It's not much, I know," said Helene. "But how can this museum compete with the—oh, I don't know what the tourists are seeing these days—the Magritte Museum, I suppose, or the Museum of Natural Sciences? They have no money."

"It doesn't bother me," said Eliza.

"Well, it bothers me."

The old woman sat, instructing Eliza to do the same. Helene watched the girl settle in her chair. She was young, impossibly young; at that age, everything had meant so much and so little. Helene remembered.

"Before we talk," said Helene, "I want to know a bit about you. You asked me earlier about my name now that the war is over. I assume you know a bit of my history, then."

"I do," said Eliza.

"And you've come to me because you want something, correct? But you wouldn't be here unless you had something already."

Eliza placed a leather notebook on the table between them. It was an anachronous thing, irritable with creases and stains. "I've used Professor Victor's notes to assemble most of the story. It's all in here, everything I know, laid out day-by-day as it happened. I know what became of Tarcovich and Grandjean, Mullier and Victor, Noël and Spiegelman—even August Wolff. You remember them, don't you?"

Helene tucked her hands beneath the table to hide their tremor. She had not heard those names spoken aloud in so long that she'd come to regard them as dreams. Listening to the words fall from Eliza's lips was like peering through a window at a different life.

"But I'm missing something," said Eliza. "The story has a skeleton, but no flesh, and no soul. It has an outline, but no colors. When the Nazis took Belgium, it wasn't like I learned about in school. They took lives, of course, but they took our words and thoughts, too. *Le Soir* was one of the first casualties. *Soir Vole*, the Belgians called it, for the Germans stole the most important newspaper in the country and turned it into a cheap propaganda mouthpiece." Helene was surprised at the bitterness in Eliza's voice. "That's why *Faux Soir* was born. In 1944, the secretary general of the *Front de l'Indépendance*—that was one of the major resistance groups during the war—"

"Dear God, is this a dull classroom lesson?" interrupted Helene. "Do not try to impress me, Eliza. You have my attention without all of that."

"I'm sorry." Eliza blushed.

"Go on with you."

"Right, then. So, when the Allies liberated Brussels, the secretary general of the FI feared people would forget what happened with *Faux Soir*. In the first issue of *Le Soir* that was released after the occupation, he wrote a eulogy for *Faux Soir* memorializing the artists and their work. Victor kept a clipping." Eliza laid a yellowed slip of paper from her notebook on the table before Helene.

The old woman leaned forward, too frightened to touch it. The newspaper clipping was old, like Helene; the world had left it wrinkled and frail. At the top of the page, the words *Le Soir* still held their post, soldiers who'd never gone home from battle. Helene did not buy newspapers any longer, but every once in a while, she'd stop at a newsstand just to hold a copy of *Le Soir*—still among the most popular papers in the country, still breathing. The paper was in color now. Its photographs were polished. And young boys no longer sold it; instead, the papermen came from faraway places, as different and new as *Le Soir* itself. Helene would hold the paper and stand in the wind, delighting in the idea that no one would ever guess—no one would have the slightest clue—that this old woman had such a role to play in its history.

But *this* paper—Eliza's paper—this was the *Le Soir* Helene remembered. She wanted desperately to touch it.

"Read it," Eliza whispered.

Helene read aloud. "'Let us never forget that, even in battle, we are men: no strangers to our own humanity. Let us preserve a tradition of laughing through bloodshed—not only of the soldier, but of Gavroche and Peter Pan. With his humble slingshot, David killed Goliath. So too shall we crumble the colossus with feet of clay.'"

Eliza kept her hands on her notebook, as though drawing strength from its pages. "Does that mean anything to you?" she asked.

"Yes." Helene brushed her fingers across the page. When she had fled Toulouse, shortly after the German occupation, she had followed an army train passing across the border to Spain. The men had pointed at her, skinny and bulky, wearing all the clothes she owned. "How do you do, Gavroche?" they had called. She had been small for her age, in those days; the dirt on her face had become part of her, a second layer of skin. Helene touched the name *Gavroche*, and her breath caught.

"I have the story of David and Goliath." Eliza tapped the cover of her notebook. "I want to hear the story of Gavroche and Peter Pan."

Helene covered her face with her hands. The room's wretched cold set her bones aflame. She could not recall the moment when she became an old woman with aching bones, but there must have been such a moment. Last she remembered, she was crouching under a newspaper stand with a match in her cupped palms, ready to fight, to die, to live: ready for anything.

"I hadn't expected to tell anyone," Helene said, taking her hands from her face. "After it all ended, I wanted to die in obscurity. I felt it was what I needed, what I deserved. You're young, with your notebook, and your ideas. You wouldn't understand. I wanted to fade, like mist. But Aubrion..." She laughed, shaking her head. "By God, there is nothing he would have wanted more than for people to know."

"I know this is sudden. If you're not ready, Helene, you do not have to—"

The old woman slapped her hand on the table. "This has nothing to do with Helene."

For a moment, Helene thought Eliza might recoil from this

outburst. But Eliza simply tilted her head and asked, with gentle curiosity, "What do you mean?"

"Nothing." Helene paused, oddly ashamed. "It's a nonsense tale."

"I've come for a nonsense tale."

She smiled. "Have you?"

"It's what I've been searching for."

"Then listen." Helene leaned back in her chair with her eyes closed. "I have your missing piece, Eliza, but if you are to receive it, you must forget the name of this old woman. This is not a story about *grown-ups*, you understand. It's not about anything you've learned in your travels. This is a story about the beings that live in our dreams, the *gastromancer* and the *dybbuk*— a nonsense tale, you see. It's about dreamers, about children, and what happens to us during wartime."

2 YEARS BEFORE
FAUX SOIR

The Pyromaniac

I KNEW IT, just by the looks of the fellow: he wouldn't be buying a paper, not him. Here was a man who was too good, too bright, for the workingman's paper. But I'd not sold a paper in hours, nor eaten in three days. I was so weak I could no longer make a fist. Half-mad with hunger, I put my hand in the man's pocket.

The man whirled, unkempt hair flying. "What the devil—?" His eyes fell on me. They were wide and bright, as though spinning tall tales everywhere he looked. "Are you trying to pick my pocket?"

"No, monsieur." I was. "I'm collecting payment for the paper you're about to buy." I slid over a copy of *Le Soir*.

He laughed, surprising me. The man had a good, loud laugh that the alley could not contain. Smiling, he dropped a handful of coins on my newsstand. "Keep the money," he said, "and the paper."

"Thank you, monsieur!" My stomach tightened at the prospect of apples and pastries.

"My pleasure."

The man prepared to walk away. I remember that I did not want him to go, this strange little man who was so loose with his coin. So I said, "Where have you come from, monsieur?"

"Hmm? Oh, church, if you can believe that." He pulled a face. "I've been going regular with a girl who won't come to bed on Saturday night without repenting for it the Sunday after."

"What was it about, monsieur?"

"Well, I met her at a barbershop—"

"The sermon."

"Haven't the slightest."

"You mean you sat through it and you don't know?"

"It was quite boring." I got the impression he felt this way about a lot of things. He looked at me, his eyes softening. I'd set up my table—just a stack of crates, really—where the smallest alley in Anderlecht kissed the longest street. As the man lifted his face to the sun, I watched passersby marveling at the pair of us. "I do recall this one bit, though. I rather liked it—a good bit of theater. The minister got to the part where Christ was being carried away by his followers. Have you heard this? His body had been pierced by a spear." He mimed throwing a javelin. "As his disciples carried him off, they tore at their clothes and dipped the cloth into his blood. Isn't that extraordinary?" The man shook his head, laughing.

I, too, cared little for sermons (before the Nazis came to Toulouse, my parents had wielded all manner of threats to get me to attend church). The man smiled down at me, asking me to forgive him his interest in theater over morality. I did. He held out his hand, and we shook. "My name is Marc Aubrion," he said.

Since fleeing Toulouse for Brussels, I'd found it easier to live as a boy. Scabby-kneed lads were part of the landscape; orphaned girls kicked up clouds of attention wherever they walked. But I was prepared now, for reasons I could not articulate, to introduce myself—my real self—to Marc Aubrion: "I'm—"

"Don't tell me."

I froze, off-balance. "Monsieur?"

"People with names die in this war. Haven't you seen the papers? The lists of fallen soldiers grow longer each week."

To my knowledge, I'd never spoken to anyone on either side of this war, content to walk the space between Nazis and resistance fighters with my head down. But I knew then that Marc Aubrion must be part of the resistance, for I saw in him something that could not be contained, not even by his own will. Even then, I saw little reminders of everyone I had ever loved in him: my mother's quick laughter, my father's reverence for the pedantic, my sister's pigheadedness, a boundless joy I had not seen since my schoolyard friends.

This odd, joyous man—Marc Aubrion—looked around my alley. His eyes went to the bed of old papers I'd made behind my newsstand, and he said to me, "You are like the rats, the alley cats, the cockroaches. They're the ones who stay alive."

"I'm not sure I want to be a cockroach, monsieur," I said.

"Sure, you do. Cockroaches were alive long before we were, and they'll be alive long after. They come out to do their job when it's required of them, but they return to the ground when it's over with. They stay alive." Marc Aubrion put a hand on my shoulder. "Trust me when I say this. You are *gamin*, like the boldest things on this earth."

Let me tell you something about my friend Marc Aubrion. Though I have known many writers who were given to stage fright, Aubrion would have found it difficult to define, let alone to experience, that feeling. It did not matter whether the audience laughed at his jokes, or at him: if they were laughing, they belonged to Marc Aubrion. That is not to say that he wasn't afraid, in the days of *Faux Soir*. To be alive was to be afraid. Although not every day of the occupation brought us pain—it is easy to forget that now—unpredictability bred our fear. We were trapped inside an arrhythmic heart, holding each other between tremors. Marc Aubrion *was* afraid, but he was our *bouffon*, our jester. When the lights went off, he lit a match with a joke.

As you might imagine, Aubrion's path to the resistance was fraught with crooks and digressions. Soon after Belgium surrendered to the Germans—when good King Leopold took the crumpled wad of our country out of his pocket and handed it over like money for sweets—the Germans issued a summons. Every newspaper editor in the country was to attend a meeting to discuss "the future of their most noble profession."

Upon their arrival, the editors were escorted to a ballroom and shot.

Paranoid about martyrs, the Nazi High Command ordered the bodies to be cremated behind a courthouse. Aubrion, who had supported his playwriting habit with newspaper articles and theater critiques, was unemployed overnight.

Then the libraries closed, the fruit stands went away, and the caramel wind no longer blew the carnivals in from the east. The Germans boarded up the playhouses and pubs that had hosted Aubrion's performances; they took the galleries, the museums, the bookshops. Only the smallest, poorest venues escaped their notice.

On the outskirts of the city, one such venue—a third-rate art gallery—was hosting an evening show. This gallery was quite run-down, with an ancient curator who often forgot to charge entry fees. The art was not good, but the ticket stubs and flat champagne were evidence that people were still making things, people were still alive. Aubrion went often.

Even so, he almost decided not to attend this particular show. Some artist or another had made his debut with a new exhibit: *Sketches of a Rough Life*, simple drawings of farmers with their livestock and plows. That sort of thing infuriated Aubrion. The Nazis permitted artists to work their trade as long as their pens were dull, their canvases simple and muted. Aubrion despised those pallid stories and drawings so popular during the war. But as I've heard it told, he'd just had an article rejected by the new resistance paper *La Libre Belgique*, and he did not want to be alone with himself. So Aubrion walked to the third-rate gallery.

Although I cannot remember who told me this story, I remember what they said: Aubrion was standing before a painting as large as his body, an oil-on-canvas temple in a land of geysers and mist. And Aubrion was looking at the painting when the air raid siren began to wail.

How do you imagine an air raid? They are nothing like that. I experienced so many of them I could sleep through the sirens by the war's end. I witnessed air raids alone, in the company of friends, with strangers. And it was always the same. You see, an encounter with an air raid is like an encounter with God: they are as mysterious, as unknowable. We accepted these encounters with the same grim finality with which people accept the afterlife. We never tried to run, and we never hid; there were no screams. When the siren wailed, I would look up at the ceiling or sky, as would everyone else, and I would wait. So it was with Aubrion.

But then it was not the same. If the bomb found him, Aubrion realized, it would find *all* of them, every piece in the gallery. It would find this painting of the temple, these drawings of the farmers, those sketches, those prints. The bomb would find every mistake the artists tried to cloak in thicker, bolder oils; it would find every triumphant stroke of yellow and green. With each siren's call, Aubrion knew what the Germans were doing—or rather, what they were undoing.

I'd often catch Aubrion staring at the piles of brick and concrete that had once been buildings. "The Library of Alexandria dies here every day," he'd say. But he did not die that day, nor did the painting of the temple, or the sketches of the farmers, or the artists, or the curator. I do not know how Aubrion contacted the *Front de l'Indépendance* to pledge his service; there were a variety of channels you could use. I only know what the records say: that Marc Aubrion's service to the FI began a week after that air raid.

The Nazis may have burned the editors' bodies, but there is more than one kind of martyr. And some things are much harder to burn.

20 DAYS TO PRINT NIGHT

The Dybbuk

THE *GRUPPENFÜHRER*'S HANDWRITING was not beautiful. His peers used to say he wrote letters like old clowns told jokes. Because of this trait, which had embarrassed him since childhood, *Gruppenführer* Wolff preferred typewriters to pens. And so the music that accompanied his evenings was the *click-click-click-click-snap* of mechanical words.

October 21, —43, he typed. *Contacted four targets: Tarcovich, Mullier, Aubrion, Victor. Locations: south Namur fish market, Le Lapin, Great Brabant Theater, Old Church Library. No obstacles. On schedule.*

He slid the paper out of the typewriter. This was a new model, more efficient than the previous. But the typed letters were no more beautiful than Wolff's penmanship. Wolff studied the thick *A*s and *N*s, the pitiless curve of the *G*s. Even so, the typewriter was Wolff's shield: the Gestapo's psychoanalysts were known to pick through officers' files, examining their handwriting, pulling apart the officers' beliefs and insecurities.

When forced to make handwritten addenda to his files, Wolff did his best to hide them.

The *Gruppenführer* deposited the paper in a folder labeled Memos. Officers of the Reich were expected to keep detailed notes. And so Wolff's folders swelled dutifully. But because Wolff had seen the consequences of truth-telling in the Gestapo—the whispers, the men carried away in the night, the mysterious suicides—his lies happened compulsively, like a facial tic.

On that particular evening, however, the *Gruppenführer's* memos were more truthful than usual. He had indeed contacted four targets that day, of the names Tarcovich, Mullier, Victor and Aubrion: the smuggler, the saboteur, the professor and the jester.

The lies started with the locations of Wolff's targets. Aubrion, for one, was not in the Namur fish market, but was instead at the once-famed Marolles Theater.

The Jester

Marc Aubrion had a joke he used to tell. "I am not an honest man," he would say. "I swore I wouldn't be caught dead at the Marolles Theater—and I almost was!" It's a terrible joke, and not in the charming way that English weather is terrible, but actually terrible. We knew that, obviously, but we laughed whenever he told it. Repetition gave it life. Or we were blessed with low standards; I don't know.

Speaking of such: the Marolles Theater. Aubrion was sitting in the back row, so if anyone had asked him whether he'd been there that evening, he could have replied, "I popped in for a second to see if I liked it, but had every intention of leaving." Before the war, the theater had been renowned throughout Belgium for its *zwanze* plays, of which Aubrion was especially fond. *Zwanze*, at its heart, is nonsense, treachery, farce; I believe the literal translation from the Dutch is *drivel*. *Zwanze* is to the Belgians what Dada is to the Swiss and the Americans. But when the Nazis invaded Belgium, taking our printing presses, our radios, our books, our language, our schools, they erased the line between sense and nonsense. A style of art and humor that had meant everything now meant nothing. And so the Marolles Theater stopped performing the plays Aubrion loved and started performing everything else: shoddy slapstick, poorly done Shakespeare, romantic comedies that seemed to combine the two.

Aubrion sat with his feet propped on the seat in front of him, watching some adaptation of a *Tintin* comic strip. It was halfway through the play, so Aubrion was halfway through a bottle of whiskey. Mind you, Aubrion did not drink unless the situation demanded it of him, and in *his* view, only two situations demanded it of him: unbearably poor plays, and unbearably good ones. When Aubrion worked as a theater critic before the war, he had mostly been plagued by the latter; since he started writing for the resistance paper *La Libre Belgique*, it was largely the former. But he felt quite strongly that it was his duty to continue supporting the "ill-destined" Marolles.

In any case, *Gruppenführer* Wolff directed his men to stand guard at the exits, then took the seat next to Aubrion's. Onstage, the orchestra struck up a tuneless dance number. Aubrion was trying to figure out how to compose a scathing review of the play that did not betray the fact that he'd actually watched the thing, so he did not notice the *Gruppenführer* at first.

When he did, Aubrion said: "Oh, dear God. Is this some sort of immersion-theater gimmick?"

"I beg your pardon?" said Wolff, unbuttoning his overcoat.

"Oh, no, no, no. It is, isn't it? Have we really sunk so low?"

"I don't know what you mean," said Wolff.

"You're clearly an actor." Aubrion took a sip from his bottle, then waved it toward the stage. Patrons who turned to glare and murmur were swiftly deterred by the *Gruppenführer*'s uniform. "Nazis don't watch plays, so you must be in it."

"I need you to step outside with me, Monsieur Aubrion."

"Look, pal, why don't you go immerse someone who will actually appreciate it?"

Sighing, Wolff pulled his handgun from its holster. He pressed it into Aubrion's stomach.

"Fuck." Aubrion felt all color and heat drain from his cheeks. "This isn't a gimmick."

"Stand up slowly, please, monsieur."

Aubrion followed Wolff's instructions. "Whatever it is, I didn't do it. Unless you're with the papers, in which case I did it really well."

"I am with the papers. Come outside, Monsieur Aubrion."

The Smuggler

Lada Tarcovich was with her fourth customer that afternoon when the Gestapo came to call. Shadowed by a dozen men in black uniforms, *Gruppenführer* Wolff applied his boot to the blush-red door of the brothel, splintering it open. He grimaced at the cloud of dust and shrieks of old wood. A sergeant held his rifle aloft. "Everyone on the floor! On the floor!"

The *Gruppenführer* stepped around his soldiers as they rounded up half-clad men and women in scanty dresses.

"Wait!" cried a bald man with a red nose, silenced by a gun barrel to the chin. The *Gruppenführer* moved aside as a soldier grabbed a young woman by the arm.

"Stop," Wolff said. The soldier let go of the woman—scarcely more than a girl, with plain features and brown hair. Death shone in her eyes. "Where is Madame Tarcovich?"

"Why do you want to know?" But the child's defiance shattered like glass. Lowering her eyes, she said, "Madame is upstairs."

Wolff's men began mounting the staircase. He waved them back down. "Arrest the men," he said. "Let the women go."

Gruppenführer Wolff found Lada Tarcovich entertaining a bearded man upstairs. Upon seeing Wolff, the man quickly lost interest in his activities and ran from the room. Tarcovich, a small woman with porcelain features that pointed toward an oddly squarish jaw, stood up with no regard for her nudity. She went to a dresser and took out a thin shawl, which she wrapped around her shoulders. Thus clad, Tarcovich sat on the bed, blinking up at Wolff with almond-shaped gray eyes.

"I knew you'd come," she said.

"But you did not run," replied Wolff.

"That's worked quite well for everyone in Europe, hasn't it?" Tarcovich glanced around Wolff with exaggerated surprise. "You didn't bring any men?"

"Downstairs. There's no place for them here."

"I agree, but your *Führer* does not seem to share my opinion."

"Soldiers are for battle. You and I are here to talk about war."

Wolff reached into the leather bag slung around his shoulder, pulling out a newspaper—a resistance paper, Tarcovich realized. Her eyes widened. The paper was a charred, crumpled thing. Someone had tied it up in twine, and the unevenness of the sentences and paragraphs made it seem as though the paper was trying to squirm free of its bonds. The *Gruppenführer* held it out to Tarcovich.

"You do know what this is," said Wolff. "Don't you?"

"No." The word was very small. She tried again. "No."

"Do you not?"

"Honest to God."

Wolff shook the newspaper. "Take it."

Tarcovich took the newspaper. It came apart in her hands.

"What does it smell like?" asked Wolff.

Tarcovich closed her eyes and inhaled the newspaper's remains. She shuddered. "Fire," she murmured.

"Yes." Wolff took it from her, tossed it to the carpet. "Let's talk, shall we?"

"What do you want to talk about?" said Tarcovich.

"Your trade."

Tarcovich's lips curled. "You came all the way from Germany to talk about fucking? I'll admit I'm flattered, *Brigadeführer*, but—"

"*Gruppenführer.*" The four syllables tugged themselves free from Wolff's mouth before he could stop them. His rank was new, and he still cared about it, which embarrassed him. "Be smart about this, madame. The Gestapo has records of all your activities from the past three years."

She arched an eyebrow. "That must be exciting for them."

"Two years ago, we had enough information to put you away for a very long time. Now we have enough information to put you away forever. Do you understand?"

A breeze stirred the red drapes. "What do you know?" said Lada.

"Since 1940, you have aided in the proliferation of over two hundred and fifty underground publications—the most recent of which is *La Libre Belgique*." Wolff stepped on the newspaper. It crunched into the carpet under his polished boot. "You run the largest book smuggling ring in Belgium. You are a trespasser, a rabble-rouser, and you write disgusting erotic stories about the English."

"That is not true. I write them about the Americans." Tarcovich pulled the shawl tighter, her skin cold and prickling.

She allowed her attention to drift to her bookshelves and cupboards. Whispers of Tarcovich's identity glittered among the stocky paintings and plain oak brothel furniture: jewelry she'd smuggled from Germany, ivory and jade, old books, things that should not have existed during wartime—the lives she had saved. A cigarette smoldered in a gold ashtray. Aubrion himself had passed many hours among the treasures and spoils of Tarcovich's trade.

The smuggler gathered herself and spoke: "You want me to do something, don't you?"

"Yes," said Wolff.

"For you. Or you would have shot me already."

Wolff nodded. His face was lined with premature wrinkles. Tarcovich had seen her girls age before their time, working a trade that chipped away at their souls. She had seen their lips crack and their skin grow thin. So it was with August Wolff. But her girls had not asked for this war—men like Wolff had begged for it.

"What do you want me to do?" Tarcovich asked him.

"There is a matter you're going to help me with. A matter of words."

The Saboteur

Contrary to what August Wolff would type that evening, Theo Mullier was not at the restaurant *Le Lapin* when Lada Tarcovich and the *Gruppenführer* found him. Instead, Mullier was ending his shift at a Nazi print factory. From the back of a gray Mercedes, Wolff and Tarcovich, now clothed in a collared dress and defiant red scarf, watched him shuffle out the door, dragging his left foot. (Wolff had planned to bring Aubrion along for the ride, too, but Aubrion annoyed him so much that the *Gruppenführer* dropped him in a cell.) Mullier glanced down the narrow street. Dusk had painted everything an inky blue: the lampposts, Mullier's brown jacket and short trousers, the high buildings with their sightless windows. The Germans must have hosted a parade yesterday. Flags stamped with swastikas had been draped over windows and awnings.

"Is that him?" the *Gruppenführer* asked, rolling down the window of the Mercedes.

Tarcovich nodded. "He looks like a peasant, I know."

It was far worse than that: he looked like an invalid. Theo

Mullier moved with the uneven gait so common among prisoners of war—shuffling, his shoulders drawn together and sloped. In those days, the Germans made no secret of their devotion to perfection: the *Übermensch*, the sculpted army.

"I've never actually met him, to be honest," Tarcovich went on, "but I've been a fan for ages. I used to read about him in between customers. That bit with Goebbels…" She shook her head. "Horrible."

"Brilliant," said Wolff. He addressed his men, restless and smelling of shoe polish in the airless car. "Hold off. We must wait for the street to clear." Wolff asked Tarcovich, "Isn't he a printer, as well?"

"Editor, printer, writer. He doesn't look like much, but that's part of his charm, as I've heard it."

Mullier hobbled to the poorhouse next door. There, he waited. He was soon rewarded by a shout that carried down the street and into the car: the factory director, screaming at his workers in Flemish. Mullier did not smile—he rarely smiled, that man—but permitted himself a nod of contentment. The next day's paper would report that a pair of factory workers discovered a half-naked girl in the director's office. She was distraught, filthy and American. The director would be disgraced, his perverted loyalty to the Allies exposed.

Wolff asked, "How many times has Mullier performed that operation?"

"I can't say." Tarcovich's eyes were on Mullier. "Girls with passable English are a cheap investment these days."

"To be sure."

"It's a fantastic scheme, isn't it? If you want to destabilize a Nazi print factory, convince the higher-ups that the director is not a Nazi. People see what they wish to see, and your type is especially paranoid. Such is the secret of sabotage."

"Indeed."

"*Indeed,*" Tarcovich mocked. "Don't be so sullen, *Gruppenführer.*" She laughed shortly. "I suppose no one suspects a scrubby man with a clubfoot to be a leader in the *Front de l'Indépendance*, do they? Let alone an editor of the infamous *La Libre Belgique*." Tarcovich reached into her dress pocket. The soldiers in the front seat of the car whirled, going for their handguns.

Wolff leaned sideways to shield Tarcovich with his body. "Gentlemen, *please*. We have already searched her."

"Don't be afraid, boys." Tarcovich removed some lipstick from her pocket and unscrewed the top, waving it in front of the soldiers' faces. She held their gaze, applying the makeup as slowly as she could.

"Wait until he's turned the corner, then surround him," the *Gruppenführer* told his soldiers. "Take a lesson from Monsieur Mullier, gentlemen, and do it quietly."

The Professor

The coffeehouse was mostly empty that evening. People did not gather anymore, you understand, unless they were trying to start something, and if they were trying to start something, they certainly did not gather in public. There was none of the prattle and push from before the war. Martin Victor sat hunched over a small table, his suit a clump of tweed and chalk dust. Three young men with self-conscious leather notebooks and a pair of older women sat at adjacent tables. Victor was joined, shortly, by a second man in a long coat.

"I was starting to worry." Victor took a notebook and a pencil out of his pocket. "Did you run into trouble?"

The second man sat across from Victor. The two were separated by a table engraved with the fingerprints of the day: pen-scratches, beer stains, blood. Though it had been a week since the last German raid, the coffeehouse was still heavy with the memory of it.

"I thought I was being followed," said the other man, "so I took a different route."

"Good, good. You're based at the French outpost, aren't you?"

"Yes. If you don't mind, I will leave my coat on. It's rather cold in here."

"Devilishly cold."

"Should we exchange names?" asked Victor's contact. "Or does that violate protocol?"

"We could exchange code names, of course, but they're rather ridiculous, I find. Would you like to order anything? I'm having coffee—"

"I think we should get to work."

"I agree." The professor brought his chair closer to the table. Victor's voice carried, a teacher's curse. He tried to talk softly. "My paper has received word that the Nazis have formed a new Ministry of Perception Management that's administered by the Gestapo, specifically a man named August Wolff. We're trying to do a profile on this Wolff character."

"Understood."

"Here's what we know about him so far. He's in his early forties. Young for a man of his rank. We think he's at least a *gruppenführer*. He was in school for journalism, somewhere in Berlin, but he didn't perform very well. The man can't write to save his life, we hear." Victor shuffled his notes. "Before he was put in charge of the Ministry of Perception Management, he was the Germans' number one man for book burnings. There's a rumor—mind you, we don't know whether it's true—that he keeps a book or a paper from every burning he's assigned. And..." Victor glanced through his notes again. "And I think that's all. What intelligence have you gathered on him?"

"His primary interest is propaganda. Particularly black propaganda."

Victor tapped his lip with his pencil. The professor was fairly certain he'd heard the term before, but devil take him if he could remember what it meant. "How would *you* define black propaganda?" asked Victor.

"Propaganda is 'black' if it is supposedly from one side, but is actually from the other," said Victor's contact. "If you create a false Nazi publication full of misinformation—about Hitler's illnesses, say, or German war crimes—that is black propaganda."

"Ah, I see. The German people would believe this information because the newspaper would seem to have been written and published by the Nazis."

"When, in actuality, the Allies are writing it to sway public opinion. The small resistance presses have done this sort of thing before, but Wolff is interested in something much larger."

"Then he's an idiot," said Victor.

"Why is that?"

"It's not possible. The resources and talent you'd need, not to mention the funds—"

"How long have you been a journalist for the underground?" interrupted the man in the long coat.

"Since the war started."

"And in all your years, you've never seen a large-scale feat of black propaganda?"

"No, never."

"You don't believe it can be done?"

Victor thought, then decided: "I don't believe the Nazis can do it."

"Neither do I," said the second man, opening his coat to expose the swastika on his sleeve. As the German stood, the patrons traded their coffee cups for handguns, which they leveled at Martin Victor. Silent, the professor raised his hands above his head.

"I beg your pardon for the circumstances of our meeting, Professor Victor," said the German. "I am *Gruppenführer* Wolff."

The Jester

Back at the Nazi headquarters, Wolff's men deposited Aubrion, Tarcovich, Mullier and Victor in a room furnished with a low, square table, handcuffing them to their chairs. Two soldiers with machine guns paced in front of the door. The combination of stone walls and heavy furniture warped the sounds of their footsteps, shading them in hushed, dreamlike tones. Shortly, Aubrion grew bored. He turned to Theo Mullier, who was rubbing a bruise over his left eye.

"What is that?" Aubrion asked, pointing at a patch on Mullier's jacket.

"This?" Mullier craned his neck to look at it, like he'd never seen it before. The patch depicted a lion reared back on its hind legs, bordered by the letters *F* and *I*. "Our insignia."

"We have an insignia?"

"The *Front de l'Indépendance* does."

"Since when?" Leaning back in his chair, Aubrion put his feet up on the table. He noted with some pleasure that his shoes were filthy, and that the guards were scowling at him from below their hideous mustaches.

"A while now." Mullier ran a hand through his beard. It was mostly white, streaked with ink from the printing presses. "Some months, maybe."

"Why the hell," said Aubrion, "does a secret organization have an insignia?"

"Oh, here he goes," groaned Lada Tarcovich.

"But I'm serious!"

"I've no doubt of that."

"That's rather like hanging a sign above a refugee shelter that says 'Jews Hidden Here.'"

"We're not really a secret organization any longer," said Victor.

"I wonder why," retorted Aubrion. "And what kind of a typeface is that anyway? Mullier, you should be ashamed of yourself."

Mullier spat on the carpet.

"It was necessary," said Victor, too loud in the close room. "For legitimacy. The insignia, I mean." The professor wiped his glasses on his coat. His handcuffs complicated this process.

"Given our goals, it is important that the people perceive us as a viable entity."

"A viable entity that is currently discussing policy initiatives in front of their captors," said Tarcovich.

Aubrion laughed. "We are doing a better job sabotaging ourselves at this moment than Mullier ever could."

"Amusing," said Theo Mullier.

"I just hope someone is smart enough to screen our teams for Nazi informants when we don't report in on time," said Aubrion.

Tarcovich's makeup was smudged, just a little, so it looked like she had a mostly-healed black eye and a slightly bloody lip. Aubrion wondered why his theater pals never thought to use lipstick for stage effects; it was far cheaper than fake blood. Now *there* was an aphorism, he thought: lipstick is cheaper than blood. He'd have to work it into an article sometime.

"We'll report in on time," said Tarcovich.

"How do you figure?" said Aubrion.

"If they wanted to kill us, they would have killed us."

"And so?"

"And so, they obviously mean to turn us loose. Our people will never know to check for Nazi informers. It will be as if nothing happened at all."

"You seem to know a lot about these matters," said Mullier, trying to maintain a neutral tone. But because Mullier had the subtlety of a rabid boar—at least according to Aubrion—he sounded as though he were launching an interrogation.

"Oh, shut up." But Tarcovich had paled. In the years he'd known her, Aubrion had rarely seen her so rattled, even in the direst situations. She knew what became of women who fell to the Nazis, particularly women of her ilk. "I'm allowed to speculate," she added thinly.

"Perhaps the Germans only want information." Victor shifted in his chair as though he found this theory unlikely.

Aubrion glanced around the room. "I don't see any thumb-screws."

"Maybe they mean to hold us here until we die?" offered Mullier.

"I do not see any corpses, either—" Aubrion again.

The door creaked open, emitting August Wolff and a man in a suit.

"Oh, hang on—there's one now," said Aubrion, and his companions laughed. Though Wolff could not have been over forty, he had gray hair and the frail bones of the old or recently ill. It seemed odd that a man of his rank should look so fragile. Aubrion had rarely met a German who was not obsessed with physical vitality, and he had never met an officer of the Gestapo who did not radiate health.

Gruppenführer Wolff dismissed the guards at the door with a wave and instructions to wait outside.

"Good evening." Wolff and the second man joined the others at the table. "I am *Gruppenführer* August Wolff. This is my colleague, Herr Spiegelman. Please allow me to apologize for the way you have been treated. We had no alternative. Is there anything you require before we get started?"

"May I smoke?" asked Tarcovich.

"Certainly."

Wolff motioned to his colleague—Spiegelman, whose impeccably tailored suit, trimmed beard and graceful movements were at odds with the dark circles under his eyes. Spiegelman took a metal case from his pocket and handed Tarcovich a cigarette and a match. She took it with some difficulty, pulling at her handcuffs.

Mullier's clenched fists shook on the table. "You'll take cigarettes from a Jew who's whored himself out to the Reich?"

Saying nothing, Tarcovich took a drag on her cigarette. Aubrion watched Spiegelman's face; the man didn't flinch, not exactly, but his eyes narrowed, and he stared down at the table.

"Now," said Wolff. "Is there anything else?"

"May I drink?" said Aubrion.

"I believe you've had quite enough to drink today, Monsieur Aubrion," said Wolff.

"I liked you better when I thought you were a stage prop."

"Let us get to business, if you please. Herr Spiegelman?"

Spiegelman placed a copy of a newspaper on the table. The title page shouted *Colère!* Though far from the most widely-circulated paper at the time, the Communist publication had a loyal following. Like the other paperboys, I loved *Colère*. It always sold out.

"This is one of the last surviving copies of your separatist paper *Colère*," said Wolff.

"Hang on," said Aubrion. "Last surviving?"

"We burned the factory last week."

"You fucking pig."

The *Gruppenführer* carried on as if he hadn't heard Aubrion. "I've singled out *Colère* not because it's particularly well-written or crafted. It is not. It's long-winded for a revolutionary paper. The people like simple, catchy sentences. You'll corroborate that with a great many theories, I'm sure, Professor." He nodded at Martin Victor. "However, there is something unique about this paper." The *Gruppenführer* turned it over and flipped to the third page. "This column here. *Dispatches from the High Command*. What can any of you tell me about this column?" No one replied. "Anyone?" Even Aubrion remained silent. "Oh, come now. Must I resort to crude threats?"

"It was written by a Nazi turncoat." Tarcovich took a drag on her cigarette. "A former *oberführer*, I think. It was mostly information about military movements, and the like."

"As you know, that sort of column is very much in demand," said Professor Martin Victor. He attempted to smooth his tie—a nervous, compulsive movement—but it tangled in his handcuffs. "After I returned from my investigations at Auschwitz back in '41, and I wrote about—what I saw there…" Victor paled. "After that, the Belgian people were clamoring for more information on the atrocities, the horrors—the numbers. It's always the numbers that get them. One hundred thousand refugees. Twenty-two thousand casualties. You know. There became a great demand for information about what Germany has been doing, what its goals are."

"And the column was born," Mullier supplied.

"All we needed was a Nazi willing to sell himself." Tarcovich smiled.

Wolff nodded. "Except that there was no Nazi traitor, was there? He is a fiction."

Spiegelman spoke up. "He was a literary invention, a tool for the editors of *Colère* to control what people believed." His voice was high and gentle. "When the *Front de l'Indépendance* was having a bad week, the turncoat's column assured everyone that the Nazis were frightened, that the Resistance Front was doing its job. When the people grew afraid and began cutting off their support to the rebels, the turncoat wrote about how the Nazis would march across any village that did not do its part to help the cause."

"He was a brilliant invention," said Wolff, "and the column was one of the greatest tools of propaganda I have ever seen."

Tarcovich said, "So it was beautiful, and you burned it. All of Nazi history written in a single sentence." Her cigarette had gone out. Spiegelman leaned over to relight it.

"Yes, what more is there to be said?" asked Mullier.

Wolff folded his arms on the table. "A great deal, as it turns out. I have studied the column, and I mean to use it as a template. We've made great strides in controlling public opinion, to be sure, but we could do better. The people of Belgium, and all of Europe, really—they are not fond of us, let's say."

Aubrion snorted. "That is what happens when you kill them and take their things."

"Everyone knows the Allies are beginning a concentrated military push into German-held territory," said Wolff. "We cannot turn them back now, nor do we need to."

"What we *do* need is to make it so that Europe does not want them here," said Spiegelman, "so by the time the first American boot tramples through Brussels—"

"—Brussels will be ready to hamstring the soldier who owns it." Wolff nodded at Aubrion. "You four have done much for the *Front de l'Indépendance.* You represent everything one needs to run a successful publication—"

"Drunks, layabouts and whores?" laughed Tarcovich.

"Writers, journalists, distributors," said Wolff. "Herr Spiegelman, if you please."

Spiegelman picked up a paperweight and placed a copy of a different newspaper, *La Libre Belgique,* on the table. The paperweight slipped from his hands and fell to the floor with a rambunctious clatter.

Victor jumped, a thin cry breaking from his lips. Aubrion and the others did what we always did around Victor, pretending not to notice his shame. In truth, Aubrion did not know Victor before his mission to Auschwitz, where he was among the first Allied researchers to gather intelligence on what happened there. He had only seen photographs of a much taller-looking man. Victor's notebooks weathered the encounter with the camp better than he did; many emerged from the experience intact. Aubrion sometimes imagined the professor holding the leather to his chest against the gaunt barbed-wire smells of the place.

"You mentioned the power of numbers earlier, Professor," said Wolff. Victor's hunted animal eyes would not leave the table. "Do you know how many people read this paper each week?"

"Forty thousand," the professor monotoned.

"You are wrong. Seventy thousand people, Professor Victor— and that is only counting the Belgian readership. This paper is a weapon to rival any missile. That is why we are recruiting you to create and distribute a copy of *La Libre Belgique* that looks like all the other copies, that *sounds* like all the other copies, but that portrays the Allies *unkindly*. Do you understand?"

"You want us to help you build a propaganda bomb," said Mullier, bluntly.

"The largest propaganda bomb that has ever been dropped," Wolff confirmed.

Tarcovich gave a curt nod. "It makes sense. Belgians read *La Libre Belgique*, learn about how the Americans and the English are defiling churches and raping young girls, and they tell their friends and families throughout the continent—"

"Then a foundation is laid." Victor shook his head. Sweat had plastered the remains of the professor's hair to his skin. "It would be easy, after that. You could infiltrate other publications in a similar way. Turn all of Europe against the Allies."

"Your connections to *La Libre Belgique du Peter Pan*, as the Belgians insist on calling it, will prove crucial here," said Wolff. "Monsieurs Aubrion and Victor, you already know how to write in the style of this paper. Madame Tarcovich, you are familiar with the myriad channels your kind uses to distribute the paper. Monsieur Mullier harbors a great many talents. And we have reason to believe that one of you is—or was at one time, we aren't entirely sure—that one of you is the editor of the paper, 'Peter Pan' himself."

"How impressive," said Tarcovich, and she was not being facetious, at least not entirely. To preserve our anonymity and spread our risk, the *Front de l'Indépendance* rotated editors-in-chief. Through procedures that remain cryptic to me, the FI selected a new editor to manage the production of *La Libre Belgique* each year. The year's procedures and the editor's identity were guarded so closely that even I did not know who had been appointed Peter Pan that year. And if I had known, I might not have lived to see my thirteenth year; this is neither paranoia nor exaggeration.

"However, I will not flatter you," Wolff continued. "None of you represents the best the FI has to offer. But that is to our benefit."

"I am so relieved you could benefit from our mediocrity," said Aubrion.

Wolff took Aubrion's joke at face value—always an error, in my experience. "You *should* feel relieved. Because of your standing within the organization, your activities are more likely to go unnoticed. You know better than I how the FI monitors the activities of its 'heroes.'" He snapped the word in half like a shattered bone. "But of course, that is not the sole reason I chose you—"

"Oh, you clever bastard," interrupted Tarcovich. "We're all odd ones, in some way or another."

The *Gruppenführer* smiled thinly. "That is one way of phrasing it. You all have something to hide, as it were."

"How is it going to be done?" asked Aubrion.

"Aubrion, stop this," hissed Mullier. "Are you turning your back on our cause so easily?"

"Don't be a dolt. We have no choice but to listen," said Tarcovich.

Spiegelman said, "I am somewhat of an expert, I suppose, in linguistic ventriloquy. I will offer training and guidance throughout this endeavor."

"And I will coordinate," said the *Gruppenführer*. "You can, of course, refuse this assignment, but you will have to be terminated, and we will seek out someone else to play your part. I certainly hope it doesn't come to that. It would be a lot of unnecessary trouble."

Aubrion leaned back in his chair. "All right, let's say we agree to help build your bomb. If it works, and the FI finds out what we did, we'll be useless to them and to you. What will become of us then?"

Wolff produced a folder. "This contains documents signed by

the *Führer* assuring you that, after you've done your service to the Reich, you will be granted safety and immunity in a country of your choice."

"What laws are in place to ensure that your government keeps its word?" asked Victor.

"If you'd like," said Wolff, "I can walk you through them."

"Is there a precedent for such things?" asked Tarcovich.

"For the legal protection of defectors? Of course."

It was here the idea came to Aubrion. All this talk of documents and legalities had infected his mind with a fog, until he happened to think of a joke. This was nothing new for Aubrion; his brain was a receptacle for countless jokes. But this joke was different from all others. Unlike all others, this joke had not yet been told.

"I suppose we don't have a choice," said Aubrion.

The others stared at him, trying to detect insanity or drunkenness, and probably seeing both. He stared back, willing them to play along.

"No, we don't," said Mullier, looking squarely at Aubrion.

"You have my support, *Gruppenführer*," said Victor, avoiding Aubrion's gaze.

"And mine," said Mullier.

Tarcovich shrugged, adjusting her scarf. "Mine, as well." Spiegelman passed her an ashtray. She stubbed out her cigarette, smiling at Aubrion through the tail of smoke.

19 DAYS TO PRINT
EARLY MORNING

The Pyromaniac

JUST OUTSIDE THE ALLEY, shops and carts and newsstands were waking up. Shopkeepers stretched sheets of tattered, yawning burlap across the tops of their carts. Men with aprons and tousled hair came outside to put signs in their windows: fresh sausages, beautiful glassware; the longer the adjectives, the more likely that they were false. Whores wandered home, their eyes red from the night's labors. A breeze picked up the smell of roasting meat, perfumers' wares, wet dogs, sick men sleeping and dying in the gutters. The night had deposited an uneasy layer of snow on the rooftops and streets. When morning began to feud with night, the snow turned into rain. It was then that the city froze over, trapping the cobblestones and windows under panes of milky glass.

I watched Aubrion and his companions walking toward me, ducking into an alley bordered by chapped brick buildings. Just inside the alley, I stood arranging stacks of papers on a newsstand. I was around twelve when I sold papers in Enghien—a part of Hainaut that Aubrion described as "storybook" at his kindest and "dull" at his least. This was two years after my first contact with Aubrion and the *Front de l'Indépendance*.

"Hello, Gamin," Aubrion said, calling me an urchin, a stray. And so I was Gamin in those days, a child whose birth name had been penciled over by Marc Aubrion.

"Monsieur Aubrion!" I said, waving. "What are you doing in Enghien?"

"I'm wondering that myself," he said. I recognized his companions from wanted posters and Aubrion's stories—the saboteur Theo Mullier, the smuggler Lada Tarcovich, and Professor Martin Victor. As they looked on, perhaps a bit irritated with Aubrion, my dear Aubrion told me the most extraordinary story of his capture. When the tale was done, Aubrion gestured toward me. "Everyone, meet Gamin—Gamin, meet everyone. Gamin is the only newspaperman in the country with a conscience."

"Oh, but Monsieur Aubrion, how would you know?" Tarcovich said, smiling.

Mullier leaned against a wall to take some weight off his clubfoot. "Isn't he the lad who burns things for money?" he asked, nodding at me.

"So does every waffle-maker in the city," said Aubrion, stepping between me and his companions.

I clutched at a newspaper, taking sudden interest in the appearance of my shoes. Though Mullier was wrong—I never burned things for *money*, and no one at the FI had ever requested that I do so—I was not about to correct him. My reputation was widely known by that time, a fact that filled me with equal parts shame and pride. When one of my fires spread to a Nazi supply outpost, the FI became far more tolerant of my presence around Aubrion and their official business. I told the FI that I'd burned the supply outpost intentionally. Only Aubrion knew the truth: although the fires did not make me feel whole again, they eased the pain of what I had mislaid.

But Aubrion did not know the truth of my identity. Like Mullier, like everyone, he believed I was a boy; I had never told him otherwise. I had donned my new identity after my parents died in Toulouse, cloaking myself in the anonymity of the streets: just another lamplighter, another urchin, another messenger, another newspaper boy. And in the two years I'd known Marc Aubrion, my identity mostly had not mattered. I was his soldier regardless of what lay beneath the armor; he was my hero regardless of what he knew.

"Gamin," said Aubrion, "how much for a copy of *Le Soir*?"

"Forty-eight centimes, monsieur. But, if you please, why waste time on that rubbish?"

"I'm a writer, aren't I? I should read what my competition has to say every now and again."

Aubrion tossed me a few coins. I unbundled a stack of *Le Soir* from the pile at my feet, handing him a copy. Handling fresh newspapers, still warm and wet from the mouth of the presses, is a holy thing. I felt this as I passed the papers to Aubrion, and I could see that he felt it too: he unfolded *Le Soir* with a hunger that bordered on indecency.

"Marc?" said Tarcovich.

"Hmm?"

"Marc, what are you doing?"

"I am reading." Aubrion snapped the newspaper shut. "Gamin, how many copies of *Le Soir* will you sell today?"

"I don't know, monsieur. I never counted."

"Guess."

I calculated, embarrassed at how long the multiplication took me. I was educated until I was about nine, but then the war started. And so, while I have learned to handle words, I still find numbers slippery. But Aubrion showed no impatience. "Maybe a thousand."

"Did you all hear that? Maybe a thousand, at this one newsstand in an alley in Enghien."

Groaning, Victor leaned against a brick wall. "We know, Aubrion. Many, many people read collaborationist papers."

"But how many read *Le Soir*?" asked Aubrion.

"About three hundred thousand." Victor nudged my stack of papers with the toe of his shoe. "That is our best guess. It was, after all, the country's most popular paper, before the war. By some estimates, it is even more popular now that the Nazis have their hands on it."

"Three hundred thousand traitors," said Aubrion, not quite seriously.

"Don't joke that way," said Tarcovich. "Why wouldn't they read *Le Soir*, the only source of news for people too scared to buy papers from the underground? And besides, they have the likes of Hergé writing about—about Tintin's adventures, and that nonsense, every week. Cartoons during wartime." Tarcovich shook her head. "We can't compete with that sort of thing. It makes the people feel like nothing is wrong, Marc, that Belgium can breathe easy. Who can blame them for wanting normalcy, even if it's a lie?"

"Soir Vole," spat Mullier.

"Stolen indeed," said Victor.

"Gamin, let me ask you. How would you like to help me with something?" said Aubrion.

"I'd love to!" I said. Anyone at my age would have said the same. Marc Aubrion was dark-haired, always a little unshaven, with eyes that were wide with the entire world's secrets—even the unexplored parts of it. When he started giving me errands for the FI, and then jobs, and then *assignments*, I found eager lads at the workhouses to help me with my tasks. Aubrion soon discovered my little army, how we used to gather to dream about his next caper. By God, he loved us. There were secret messages to deliver, or politicians to spy on, or books to smuggle— and afterwards, Aubrion weighed down our pockets with food, candy, pastries and comic books. I'd heard about the others, too, as had the workhouse boys: about the saboteur Theo Mullier, the smuggler Lada Tarcovich, the professor Martin Victor. And now they were here, standing around me, these men and women from the underground newspapers and back-alley rumors. I was bewitched.

Aubrion gave me a playful whack with his copy of *Le Soir*. "I knew I could count on you. Tell me, what day is it?"

"The twenty-second of October, monsieur."

"Damn, we haven't much time. I need to see René."

"René Noël?" said Tarcovich. "Marc, I love you—which is why you must believe me when I tell you that René Noël doesn't want to see you."

"Oh, yes he does. He just doesn't know it yet."

"I do not want to see you," said René Noël. The director of the *Front de l'Indépendance* press department looked Aubrion up and down, as though Noël could not believe the man was still alive, and started to close the door on him. Aubrion put out a hand to stop him. I'd walked Aubrion and the others through the city, leading them through neighborhoods and passages the Nazis did not know. Confident no one was tailing us, we'd finally approached the headquarters of the *Front de l'Indépendance*; the building was disguised as a small meatpacking factory and had thus far evaded German notice. Noël, who seemed able to sense when Aubrion was dangerously near, had accosted us at the door.

"René," tried Aubrion. "I have—"

"—to leave." Noël tried once again to close the door, but Aubrion blocked him. The director's sigh was akin to a curse. "Fine, come inside—but do it quickly. People will hear."

The director barred the door after us. He wiped his hands on his trousers, smearing ink across the green; Noël insisted on wearing a contrived uniform with oversized trousers and the *Front de l'Indépendance* crest on his shoulder. The director was a stocky tree stump of a man, bearded and gray, with spectacles and a thicket of hair streaked through with ink. He looked as though he could handle himself in a fight, which was a lie that saved him a fair amount of trouble. "And you brought a child?" said Noël. "What the devil is the matter with you?"

"Gamin is hardly a child," said Aubrion.

Noël scoffed. "That means little, coming from you," he said, hurrying past skinny oak tables where men and women sat with typewriters and notebooks, clicking and scratching words into existence. We followed Noël down a staircase and into the basement.

Though narrower than the room upstairs, the basement was equally frantic. People bustled about, some in uniforms and others in filthy aprons, doing the work of the resistance. Words like *death* and *hope* decorated blackboards and papers. With a thrill in my heart, I glanced over at Aubrion. He winked at me. An exchange of feelings passed between us, far grander than any words I could use to describe them. Aubrion had previously told me the location of the base in case I needed a quick place to hide, but I had never stepped inside. And now this "errand boy," this nameless urchin who sold papers and went to bed hungry, this child of the streets—*I* was standing in the FI headquarters with the likes of Theo Mullier and Martin Victor and Lada Tarcovich, names I had read on wanted posters and in newspapers, characters from my most fanciful make-believe games.

Only years later did I recognize that they were not *quite* what I had believed them to be. I had built these people into monuments. As Wolff himself had said, they were not the FI's finest; they weren't even the FI's average. But to me, standing among them was a great, sacred dream.

My smile faded. I was "a man of the resistance," as Aubrion put it. If the Germans captured me, I would be treated as such, for my youth was no longer innocence.

A woman left her typewriter to hand Noël some papers. He looked them over. "I hate the last paragraph. The rest is fine."

With a look of disgust that was probably directed at Aubrion, Noël tried to hurry away. But Aubrion persisted: "You don't understand. I have an idea."

"All the more reason for you to leave. Do you know what happened the last time you had an idea?"

"Yes, we—"

"Lost two percent of our readership."

"You have no evidence that it was my fault."

"A column on how the war is affecting breastfeeding? Aubrion, what on earth were you thinking?" With another shake of his head, Noël tried unsuccessfully to leave the tiny room.

"René," said Tarcovich, blocking Noël's exit, "Marc is leaving out some valuable backstory."

Victor hung his tweed coat on the back of a chair. "We were contacted last night by August Wolff."

Noël's eyes widened. "*The* August Wolff?"

"God, I hope there's only one," said Tarcovich.

"What did he want?" asked Noël.

Tarcovich said, "He wants us to co-opt *La Libre Belgique*, to use it for a black propaganda campaign against the Allies."

"And you agreed to this?" said Noël.

"Obviously," replied Mullier.

"Oh, God." Noël looked startled, perhaps just noticing that Theo Mullier, the renowned saboteur, was among us. Though I am not sure the two had ever met before, there wasn't a resistance fighter alive who would not have recognized Mullier: a short man with ordinary features clustered in the middle of his face, grubby beard, hands knotted with muscle and wear. Mullier's presence lent us some credibility, I think, which says more about us than it does about him. Noël said, "This could be—"

"Wonderful." Aubrion sat, stood, unable to keep still. "That is what I'm trying to tell you, René. It's the perfect cover."

"For what?"

Aubrion threw his copy of Le Soir on the table. "What if—what if—while Wolff is watching us prepare a black propaganda campaign using La Libre Belgique, we instead carry out a counter-campaign using the Nazi mouthpiece Le Soir?"

"I am lost," said Mullier.

"Me too," said Tarcovich.

"As am I," said Noël.

"Let me back up." I watched Aubrion take a breath, trying to capture his thoughts and order them. "If not for the occupation, Belgium would've celebrated the twenty-fifth anniversary of the German defeat in the Great War on November eleventh of this year. I say we celebrate anyway: by putting out a fake copy of Le Soir on November eleventh. It'll look just like the regular Le Soir, just your ordinary collaborationist swill, until you start to read it. Then, my God, there'll be jokes, puns, anything we can think of—all in the voice of Le Soir."

"To what end?" asked Tarcovich.

We expected him to trip and fall into some madcap justification for this scheme. But Aubrion did not do that. I saw him travel somewhere far from buildings scarred by German mortars, far from our shamed, false city.

"I think, Lada," he said, "that people are losing hope. This war has been dragging on for a long time. If we can make light of the Nazis, just for a day—hell, for an hour—it will remind people we've beaten them before." He smiled. "I know how this sounds, but..." Aubrion held out his fists as though begging someone to remove his handcuffs. "You've seen them, great crowds of refugees fleeing France and everywhere else, leaving everything behind, leaving their dreams on the roadside with their carpetbags. Somehow, we have a chance to give it all back."

Everyone was still—everyone but Noël, who had fallen prey to so many of Aubrion's foolish ideas. "My God, Aubrion," the director said. "It's brilliant."

"*Zwanze*," I said.

Aubrion ruffled my hair. "That's exactly what it is."

"It's suicide," said Victor, pushing up his glasses. Sweat gleamed on his upper lip. "Do you even comprehend what you are proposing?"

"You might think me bold for saying so, but yes, I do comprehend my own idea."

"No, no, take a moment to *think* about it. For an ordinary print run, let us say fifty thousand copies of this newspaper, just to be generous—for an ordinary run, we shall have to secure about fifty thousand francs. With *four* zeros. Assume for a moment that fifty thousand francs materialize out of the air."

"Why, Victor," said Aubrion, "I never knew you had such a splendid imagination."

"Once we have the funds, we will have to secure printing presses, probably two hundred thousand sheets of paper, two hundred barrels of ink, additional funds for bribes and goods, additional funds for *transporting* the ink and paper to a print factory, we shall have to—"

"That seems correct so far." Aubrion was doing the math on a chalkboard behind the professor.

"—recruit printers, photographers and editors who are perfectly comfortable with the idea that this funny little newspaper is their last will and testament, as well as carriers and vehicles to transport the thing. I might add that we will be operating under the strictest surveillance. After all, August Wolff expects us to produce a paper for *him*, as well—"

"That's right," said Aubrion, as though this was all very reasonable.

"—but assuming we are able to do *all* of that, which is the most irresponsible assumption I have ever indulged in—" Victor, who had gone red in the face, paused to catch his breath. "Even if we succeed at all of that, we are still talking about *eighteen* days. That is how long you have given yourself to print this newspaper. And even if we *do* manage to accomplish all of this in under three weeks, the Nazis won't allow the paper to run for very long. It might reach a few hundred people, at the most, and then we're caught and executed."

"We're already caught," said Tarcovich, "and halfway to executed. Do you truly think they'll grant us asylum? As much as I might hate to say it, Marc is correct. If we write this paper, our deaths will mean *something*."

Victor turned to the saboteur. "Mullier? Surely you see the sense in what I am saying."

But Mullier shrugged. "We have done mad things before. It will not be easy, but it is not impossible. War changes the rules."

"It does indeed!" said Aubrion, surprised at Mullier's amenability. He'd met Mullier toward the beginning of the war, when Marc Aubrion was a junior writer for *La Libre Belgique*. Noël had received word that a man who'd been sabotaging reputations since the first Great War—who'd gone nameless throughout the entire affair, executing daring feats without accomplices—had recently joined the FI. Intrigued by Mullier, Noël had instructed Aubrion to interview the fellow. Aubrion had taken the assignment, excited to meet this singular character. But he'd regretted it almost immediately. Before the days of *Faux Soir*, Aubrion had expected to survive the occupation and would accept nothing less. Thousands of us had been shipped off to camps, shot in the streets, taken in the night—but not Aubrion. After meeting Theo Mullier, though, Aubrion's perspective on "survival" changed: while Theo Mullier's body had survived the Great War, someone put a bullet in his sense of joy, in the organ that turned tragedy into laughter. Survival meant nothing if he was not whole, and Mullier was not; he had not been whole in some time. And so Aubrion too was astonished at Mullier's support.

The professor echoed Aubrion's surprise: "I cannot believe what I'm hearing." Victor looked at each of us as though he'd never seen us before, or might never see us again. "You lot are acting as though this foolishness is our only option. Why don't we run?"

Noël said, "Security has tripled in the past month. You'll be dead before you reach the border."

"We have an idea," said Aubrion. "Let us focus next on production, and then we can worry about distribution, and then execution."

"If only you were that funny on paper," said Noël.

"Are we all agreed, then?" said Aubrion.

"I am not sure what I'm agreeing to," said Victor. "Are we agreeing to die for a joke?"

"Yes." Aubrion realized that everyone had stopped typing and writing, chalking and printing. The room, which had been full of the sound of words, was now silent. "That's right."

Tarcovich took a pen from her pocket, then spread open Aubrion's copy of *Le Soir*. She drew a copy editor's carat between the words *Le* and *Soir* and wrote *Faux* between them. Aubrion's pulse quickened. The word sat there like an elegant intruder in a couple's bed.

"*Le Faux Soir*," said Tarcovich. "I rather like it."

<u>YESTERDAY</u>

The Scrivener

THE OLD WOMAN'S voice changed colors, like clouds darkening before a hailstorm. Eliza leaned forward. She hadn't lifted her hands from her notebook since Helene's story began. Every now and again, she would take up her pen to make a note.

Magicians and con men used to walk the streets of Toulouse, spinning tales for anyone with time to spare and coin in their pockets; Helene would beg her mother to stop so she could listen. They had a peculiar rhythm to their speech, these men. They spoke as though they were trying to recall something they'd read long ago. As she went on, Helene heard herself slipping into a similar cadence. It was musical, light; the air used to feel that way, before automobiles and paved roads. Helene played her words for Eliza, and the girl listened.

LONG BEFORE
FAUX SOIR

The Gastromancer's Tale

DAVID SPIEGELMAN'S GRANDMOTHER was an accomplished woman. She had been a skier, a rower, a naturalist (back when being a naturalist still meant discovering things that were not yet discovered), a published writer, and a mother six times over. Then, at the age of eighty-two, she decided it was time she settle down and contemplate her life while she still had some left. Her son and daughter-in-law, Leib and Ruth Spiegelman, had a modest home in Hainaut, and Spiegelman's grandmother liked how everyone in the neighborhood always kept their windows clean, so she moved into an apartment nearby.

It was there David Spiegelman used to visit her, at the age of eight or nine, when his hands were still curious enough to touch things that didn't belong to him. He used to wander through his grandmother's study, running his fingers across the covers of her books when he thought she wasn't looking. "Keep your hands to yourself, David, if you care a thing for your grandmother's heart," she'd tell him, which meant that Spiegelman learned patience as a small boy, waiting until his grandmother was out of the house to begin exploring her books.

On one such day, Spiegelman pushed a chair next to his grandmother's shelves and stepped up, holding onto the shelf for balance. Careful to listen for his grandmother's footsteps, young Spiegelman studied the titles on the top shelf. It was then he caught sight of a fat, leather-bound volume, unremarkable except for its blank spine.

Spiegelman sat cross-legged, turning the book over in his hands. It had not aged well, the spine creaking and the cover spotted with grease. Faint letters spelled out *Amazing Stories of Far Off Lands*. He cracked open the book. "It was a sort of encyclopedia, a catalog of strange customs, rituals, religions and the like, from places I'd never heard of," he confided to Aubrion, in the early days of *Faux Soir*. "I remember it was arranged alphabetically, from Ayyavazhi to Zoroaster. Being a contrarian, I started from the end."

The book taught Spiegelman many things his grandmother (and parents) did not want him to know: about opium and morphine, about people who ate pork and enjoyed it, what women looked like naked, what men looked like naked with other men, about cults, secret societies, children who eschewed their parents' advice and became artists or religious figures instead of lawyers or clerks. He took it in, all of it—but it blew over him like a strong wind, making a strong impression that was nonetheless forgotten quickly. That was until he saw the photograph in the back of the book, the image of the man with his puppet.

In the photograph, a man with slicked black hair and a suit sits with a puppet propped on his knee. The man has his hand on the puppet's back. When Spiegelman recalled the photo in his later years, it was difficult for him to remember what he saw in it. He had to imagine himself eight years old again, untouched by tragedy or responsibility, before the photograph's meaning revealed itself once more: the playful mystery in the man's eyes, the way he leaned into the shadows that touched his face and hands. Of course Spiegelman, a tiny Jewish boy with asthma and scrawny hands, would want to be that man, that magician.

For weeks after, Spiegelman practiced ventriloquy with his brother's wooden puppet. He would sneak out of the house when he could—"He's found himself a little girlfriend, maybe," his parents laughed—or he would slip into his parents' basement when he could not. Then, when he was ready to show himself for what he was, Spiegelman called his parents and grandmother to a conference.

"What I'm about to do has a long and interesting history." Spiegelman sat in front of his parents and grandmother with his brother's puppet on his knee. His brother squirmed in his mother's lap. "Let us start with the name itself. The word *ventriloquy* is Latin."

"Have you been teaching him Latin?" his father whispered to his mother.

"No, have you?"

"Not that I can remember."

Spiegelman went on. "It means *to speak from the stomach*. The ancient Romans—" he faltered "—no, the ancient Greeks did this in their religion. They would—they were called oracles—they would 'throw' their voice and make it sound as though they were talking out of their stomachs, and then these oracles would try to interpret the sounds, like the sounds were coming from the gods. It was supposed to help them tell the future or figure out what their ancestors wanted them to do to solve a problem. The Greeks called it *gastromancy*."

Adjusting his sweaty grip on the puppet's back, Spiegelman said: "Hello, I am the puppet. Nice to meet you. Today I am going to—"

"We can see your lips moving!" said Spiegelman's brother. He spoke with exaggerated authority, like a barrister exposing a lie on the witness stand. He was six.

Spiegelman blushed, pressing his lips together more tightly. "Today I am going to—"

"Son, what is the point of all this?" asked his father.

"It's—interesting. Isn't it? It has a long history." David Spiegelman added that last part in a desperate attempt to appeal to his mother.

"But what can you *do* with it?" said his mother.

"Is this why you've been sneaking off?" His father waved his hands like he was conducting an orchestra. "To play with dolls?"

His grandmother said: "A boy's got to have a hobby, Leib," and Spiegelman's heart leapt.

His father said: "He's not going to be a boy much longer," and Spiegelman's heart fell.

"Oh, Leib, go easy on him."

"He's nearly ten years old. Do you know what I was doing at ten? I was working in my father's shop six days a week, and studying on the seventh. He's got to think about his future."

"Next thing you know, he'll be practicing magic." Spiegelman's mother shuddered.

"Can you imagine? Our son practicing magic? What would everyone say?"

"We'd be the laughingstock of the temple," said his father.

His brother shrieked, "I want my puppet back."

And that was the end of David Spiegelman's career as a ventriloquist.

Though he never again tried to speak through the mouth of a puppet, Spiegelman continued reading about ventriloquy under the pretense of studying history. Relieved that their son had decided to become a scholar rather than a magician or, heaven forbid, an artist, his parents encouraged him, buying him books and sending him to study under the most famous historians in Hainaut. But *gastromancy* pursued him, haunting him like a disease. It followed him even as he slept: he dreamed in strange sounds that he struggled to interpret upon waking.

A few years after the puppet show, Spiegelman and his friends were playing in a park an hour before school. The school had a bell, an old cowbell that the teachers rang when it was time for the students to go inside. Somehow, Spiegelman and his friends did not hear it. They kept playing until an older boy realized they were an hour late for class. After some debate about the relative merits of slinking in tardy or avoiding school altogether, the friends slipped inside, braced for chastisement. Spiegelman, however, stayed behind.

"You're going to be even later," his friends warned.

"Go on ahead," he said. "I'll be there soon."

Spiegelman took some paper and a pen from his book bag, settling under a tree. Without giving much thought to what he was doing, he licked the tip of his pen and wrote:

> *Mr. Thompkinson,*
>
> *Please forgive David's tardiness. My youngest son spent the better part of this morning ill with the croup. With his father gone to shop, David had no choice but to stay behind and help me tend to his brother. I shall, of course, ensure he completes his schoolwork.*
>
> *With respect,*
> *Ruth Spiegelman*

He sat back to regard his work. Though it was David Spiegelman who put pen to paper, it was as if his mother had spilled the ink. The handwriting, the curious bend to the letters (she was born left-handed, but her parents forced her to write with her right, as was the custom)—it was his mother's voice. The polite but firm phrasing—it was his mother's voice. Even the way the words were positioned on the page, the paragraph starting halfway down the paper and meandering slightly to the left—it was exactly how his mother would have done it. Breathless with his work, Spiegelman went inside the schoolhouse.

"David, you're tardy." Mr. Thompkinson gave a pointed

glance at the clock, his eyebrows coming together in advance of a lecture. Spiegelman presented the letter to his teacher. As Mr. Thompkinson read it, the boy held his breath.

"Oh, I see. Oh, dear. Is your brother any better?"

David Spiegelman's friends muttered. Praying for them to shut up, the boy managed, "He's fine. Thank you."

"Good. Give my regards to your mother."

Spiegelman's identity changed that day. He was no longer that forgettable boy who read strange books. Now, he was a con artist, a master of deceit. Everyone had a physicians' note that needed to be written, a parent's signature that needed to be forged, a letter that said they'd been to class, or church, or that they hadn't been to Brussels with that girl. His classmates brought him samples, and under the watchful eye of his grandmother's bookshelves, David Spiegelman's pen became them all.

Soon, the demand was too high for Spiegelman to keep up. The enterprising young man that he was, Spiegelman began charging for his services, convincing his parents that he'd started a small newspaper business so that he could afford candy and books. After a year of paid labor, David was buying his parents tickets to the theater, to operas; his father, who owned a little shop, saw *Cyrano de Bergerac* on opening night, at *La Monnaie*.

This went on for about three years, an eternity for a boy Spiegelman's age. The inevitable happened a few months into Spiegelman's fifteenth year. A girl in another grade, someone he didn't know very well, asked him to write a letter from a teacher to her parents, informing them that she was making satisfactory progress in her courses. There were two problems with this plan: first, the girl was failing, and second, the teacher no longer worked there. Two days after the girl paid for the letter, Mr. Thompkinson asked David Spiegelman to speak with him after school.

Mr. Thompkinson held up a slip of paper covered in even, straight words. Spiegelman's mouth went dry.

"How many of these are there?" asked Mr. Thompkinson.

"Just the one, sir," said Spiegelman.

"You know what I mean. How long has this been going on?"

"I don't—"

"How many letters like these have you written, for how many students? Is it only teachers? Are you pretending to be their mothers and fathers, as well? Businessmen? Shopkeepers?" Mr. Thompkinson crouched so that his face was level with young David's. The yellow light overhead reflected off his pallid skin. "You could be in a great deal of trouble for this."

"I know, sir, I'm sorry, I didn't know, I—"

"Legal trouble, even."

Spiegelman clamped his mouth shut. His parents had taught him, from a very young age, to revere lawyers almost as prophets.

Standing, Mr. Thompkinson tore the paper to shreds, then deposited it in a trash bin. "No one knows about this but me. We can keep it that way, if you'd like. Your parents will never know, the law will never know. Would you like that, David?"

"Yes, sir." Spiegelman sensed something was wrong, that he was about to be drawn into something from which it would be too hard to escape.

"You're very young." Mr. Thompkinson paced, his hands clasped behind his back. "You don't know this, David, but sometimes, things are complicated for adults. Do you know what I mean by complicated? I mean that there are certain things that happen to us that are difficult to fix. Bad things, even when we aren't bad people. Are you understanding all this?"

"I'm not sure, sir."

"Take me, for example. I'm not a bad person, but my wife doesn't love me, and I'm a man, like any man, so what was I to do? I found a woman who does love me, only she's found out about Bette, and... Do you see what I mean, David? Complicated."

"Yes, sir." Spiegelman had no idea what Mr. Thompkinson meant.

"Sit down." As Spiegelman sat at a desk, Mr. Thompkinson fetched a sheet of paper and a pen. He laid them in front of the boy. "I want you to write a letter to me, from my wife, saying she's leaving me. Say she's having the divorce papers drawn up. Here's my wife's handwriting." Mr. Thompkinson placed two scraps of paper—a grocery list and a note with instructions to a milkman—on the desk. The simple intimacy of the grocery list (eggs, flour, pickles) made Spiegelman ill. "I mean to give it to my—to the other woman, so that she will come back to me."

Spiegelman licked his dry lips. "Is your wife leaving you?"

"Why does it matter?"

"It matters if it's not the truth."

"You lied for them." Mr. Thompkinson pointed out the window, at Spiegelman's friends playing in the yard. "And you didn't care, did you?" It had been fun, writing letters for the other children, becoming someone's uncle or teacher or minister. No one had gotten hurt; no one was sad, or angry. But adults were different. Adults did not lie, in Spiegelman's experience, unless they wanted to cause pain.

"I don't want to do this." Spiegelman pushed the pen and paper away from him. "I don't like it."

Mr. Thompkinson picked up the paper and slapped it back down. "I don't care what you like, you little shit."

The boy stared down at the instruments of his trade, the tools of the *gastromancer* that had brought him so much pleasure. His eyes grew warm with tears. "I'm not going to do it."

"Write the letter."

"No."

"Write the goddamn letter."

"I don't want to."

Spiegelman pushed back his chair and stood up. Mr. Thompkinson caught his arm, squeezing until the boy cried out.

"Write the letter," he said, "or everyone will know how you look at that lad Douglas van der Waal."

"What?" whispered David.

"I've seen it. You're an odd one, David, and you thought no one knew, you thought it was a secret that you kissed that boy Thomas last year in the park. But I know, David, and everyone else will know, too, unless you sit down in that chair and write that letter."

His whole body numb, Spiegelman lowered himself into the chair and picked up his pen.

"Good boy," said Mr. Thompkinson, as Spiegelman began to write.

So commenced Spiegelman's five years of servitude. Thompkinson passed the boy's gift and his secret on to another man, who passed him to a friend, and Spiegelman threw his voice into the mouths of adulterers and thieves. It might have gone on forever, if the war had not broken out.

David Spiegelman's grandmother died the day Hitler invaded Poland. Her father was from Poland, and her heart couldn't stand the news of what had happened there. After his brother Abraham disappeared, Spiegelman tried to arrange for his parents to flee Europe, but he couldn't get the visas in time. They died next. Shortly thereafter, the Nazis came for David Spiegelman.

The Gestapo found Spiegelman sitting on a chair near his grandmother's bookshelves, the same chair he'd used to climb up and reach *Amazing Stories of Far Off Lands*. He'd been running, sleeping behind old buildings; he'd dug his parents' grave. But Spiegelman was finished living with fear in his chest and dirt in his hair. So he went home to his grandmother's books, to join his family in more welcome lands. As the Gestapo leveled their guns at him, Spiegelman clutched a tattered copy of *One Thousand and One Nights*, trying not to tremble. But they did not fire. Instead, a man with tired eyes held out his hand to Spiegelman.

"David Spiegelman? I am *Brigadeführer* August Wolff."

Spiegelman shook his hand. It felt stiff but hollow, like the cheap wood the toymaker had used to make his boyhood puppet.

"Would you come with us, please?" said Wolff.

Spiegelman stood on unsteady legs. "Where are we going?"

"To the capital."

"What for?"

"I have a letter for you to write. I am told you are quite proficient at such things."

And that was the beginning of David Spiegelman's career as a ventriloquist.

18 DAYS TO PRINT
EARLY MORNING

The Jester

AUBRION SPENT THAT night drawing up a list of materials we'd need for *Faux Soir*. The list went through six drafts, five of which were scrawled on the chalkboards at the *Front de l'Indépendance* headquarters, the last of which was penciled on the back of yesterday's *Le Soir*. When he was satisfied with the results, Aubrion instructed me to send a telex to Wolff asking him to meet that afternoon. By then, it was too late to sleep but too early to do anything else, so Aubrion pulled on his battered coat and gestured for me to follow him.

We stepped outside, shivering. Though the air was damp, it wasn't quite raining; Belgium refused to commit to anything in those days, whether it was the Allies or precipitation. The run-on quiet of the streets was punctuated by the footsteps of Nazi patrol units. Aubrion could hear lamplighters running through the streets, or halfhearted songs trickling from alehouse windows. These sounds were scarce, though. The city had been imprisoned in a comma that divided the first days of the occupation from the last.

Morning came slowly, and as the streetlamps guttered, Aubrion bought coffee and pastries. We ate on a bridge that creaked under our weight, feeble from the last air raid. When our meal was done, I parted ways with Aubrion, who took a cab to the Nazi outpost in west Enghien. There, Wolff and Spiegelman awaited him in a conference room.

"Let's keep this short," said Aubrion, pulling out a chair. The mendacity of the room frightened him. It was unsettling—dysphoric—to think of generals tallying casualties on the plain wooden table, or pasting lists of concentration camps to the clean walls. The air held a faint stink of ammonia. "I do not wish to be here any longer than I have to."

Wolff sat across from Aubrion, flanked by Spiegelman. "As you like," said the *Gruppenführer.* The skin under Wolff's eyes looked bruised.

"You might want to take this down." Aubrion paused. This was a tricky thing, to communicate exactly what he needed for *Faux Soir* while selling—but not overselling—his commitment to co-opting *La Libre Belgique.* Wolff and Spiegelman waited.

"What we have in mind," began Aubrion, "is a four-page issue with a print run of fifty thousand copies. About one hundred copies per newsstand, assuming we distribute the paper to about five hundred newsstands across Belgium." That much was true. "It should be easy enough for us to do." That much was false. "We'll need about 200,000 sheets of paper, 200 barrels of ink, and 50,000 francs for bribes and goods—the old francs, not the new worthless shit you lot are squeezing from our mother's teats. Over and beyond these costs, we'll need materials to build a few small incendiary devices. We probably won't need a distraction—" quite false "—but in case we do, we should be ready."

"What do you consider a 'small' incendiary device?" asked Wolff.

"And why would you need a distraction?" said Spiegelman.

"Like a Molotov cocktail, but a tad bigger. You know." Aubrion spread his arms to indicate the size he had in mind. "If the FI learns what we're up to and tries to disrupt our distribution lines, we'll need to be armed, won't we?"

"You would fire on your own people?" said Spiegelman, who spoke without irony.

"That is an interesting question, from you."

"We are not discussing me."

"I said it was for a distraction, didn't I? Obviously I don't want to kill anybody. But if the FI figures out what is amiss, they're not going to afford me the same courtesy. I might need to get away. I might need to make people run in a different direction so I *can* get away."

"Is that all?" said Wolff.

Aubrion counted on his fingers to make sure he'd gotten to everything. "I think so."

Wolff and Spiegelman shared a glance.

"What?" said Aubrion. "What is it?"

Wolff said, "If you were to scale down the operation—"

"To what?"

"Make it smaller."

"I know what 'scale down the operation' means. I thought you wanted the largest black propaganda campaign ever."

"We do."

"And I thought that meant the *largest* black propaganda campaign ever."

Wolff rubbed his eyes. "The Ministry of Perception Management is still relatively new, Monsieur Aubrion, and unproven. They've given us a budget of five thousand francs—"

"Five *thousand*?"

"—to carry out this operation."

"I can't do anything with five thousand francs."

"You can," said Wolff. "You can raise another forty-five."

"What about paper? Ink? You do want a *printed* paper, do you not?"

"You must do what you can."

"Damn." Aubrion's fists trembled. "You know, if you were smart, Herr Wolff, you would keep 'rebel' print factories instead of burning them to the ground. Then perhaps you would be able to print something when you wanted it."

To Aubrion's surprise, Wolff looked down. "The decision to burn them is not mine." If it was not quite regret in the *Gruppenführer*'s eyes, it was something akin to that.

"Well, put a suggestion in the bloody suggestion box."

"We all do what we can, monsieur. Will that be all?"

"And what kind of a name is the 'Ministry of Perception Management' anyway? Who among you has been reading too many comic books?"

"Will that be all, Monsieur Aubrion?"

Aubrion took a breath and stood, his attention already elsewhere. "Yes. That's all."

"I expect weekly reports on your progress," said Wolff.

"Weekly?" said Aubrion. "I am to work in handcuffs, then?"

"Do not be so melodramatic, Monsieur Aubrion."

Wolff stood, but Spiegelman remained seated. "I'd like to have a word with Monsieur Aubrion about the mechanics of the project," he said. "You did grant me permission, *Gruppenführer*, at our earlier—"

"Yes, yes." Wolff consulted his wristwatch. "I have a meeting in four minutes."

"I'll debrief you this evening." Spiegelman glanced at the soldiers by the door, motioning Wolff closer. "This is a sensitive matter. Perhaps the guards could wait outside?"

The *Gruppenführer* hesitated. But he said, "Make it quick," and left them alone.

The Gastromancer

The door creaked—a rusted question mark—as it closed on Wolff's and Manning's footsteps. Spiegelman opened his mouth to say something, but of course, Aubrion was quicker.

"Let me hear your opinion on this," said Aubrion, resuming his seat, "because I already know my own. Which of us is the greater sellout?"

"Aubrion—"

"Worse sellout? Greater? I am not sure which adjective is appropriate."

"Monsieur Aubrion, let me—"

"Which of us has more of his soul left? I suppose that's the question to ask."

"Would you *shut up*?" Panicked, he glanced around to ensure no one was watching them. Of course, the room was empty. He sat slowly, leaning in to whisper, "I want to help you."

"That's hardly a secret, isn't it?"

"I'm not stupid. I know you're doing something else."

"I'm sure I don't know what you're talking about."

"A different project, something other than *La Libre Belgique*. You must be."

"You're right. I'm trying to decide whether I want to be buried alongside my mother or stepmother. That is my other project."

"Oh, God," said Spiegelman, the cry of a man who'd just received word of a death. He put his face in his hands, too overcome even to weep, trapped in his grandmother's study again. His world became her perfume and the musk of old books; he was clutching *One Thousand and One Nights* and ready to die. Did Aubrion see him for what he was, for what he needed? Spiegelman suspected he did not, that Aubrion could not understand his soul even if Spiegelman picked it apart and laid it clean. Spiegelman imagined his future, as he often had: a land bordered by concrete walls made of repugnant, infeasible options—pledging his services to Aubrion, this little fool with his feet on the table, this strange man who did not seem to comprehend the bullet that awaited him—or Wolff now, Wolff tomorrow, wearing himself into shreds with a letter to *this* general, a letter to *that* governor, knowing they would die because of something Spiegelman wrote with his own hands.

But the air around Marc Aubrion's body crackled with something unspeakable and new.

"Listen to me," said Spiegelman. "You can believe me or not. I'm a Jew—"

"Who works for the Nazis," said Aubrion.

"You think everything is so simple."

"You work for the Nazis, yes?"

"It's not."

"Do you, or do you not?"

"I do, but it is not that—"

"All the more reason for me not to listen to you."

"I had no choice but to do what I did! They killed everyone I knew. I'm a Jew and a homosexual." Spiegelman's heart fell a thousand meters to land somewhere forbidden, the nameless cell where he locked up and banished everything he wanted most. "Do you know what that means? A death sentence. They killed my family, my parents. I have one skill I've used all my life to get by. I am not proud of what I am or what I've done, but I am trying to work with what I have."

Aubrion took his feet off the table, ran a hand across his face. "All right."

"All right?"

"Yes."

"Does that mean—"

"Is this room bugged?"

Spiegelman shook his head. "It's one of two rooms in the base that aren't."

"Tell me what you want from me, Spiegelman."

"I want to give you my skill."

"Linguistic ventriloquy."

"Yes." Spiegelman shivered, though the room was warm. He felt racked with fever. "Yes, that's right."

"I've read some short pieces," said Aubrion, and the passion with which he spoke was like standing naked in a storm. Spiegelman felt he must catch the rain in his hands or drown. "But I've never actually seen anyone do it."

"I can show you. Please, give me a chance to show you."

"Are you any good?"

Spiegelman's eyes were clear. "I am the best there is."

17 DAYS TO PRINT
FIRST SIGN OF MORNING

The Pyromaniac

WE SAT AROUND a table in the basement of the FI head-quarters, all six of us, plus René Noël, who sat at the edge of the circle and feigned skepticism. I knew, even then, that Noël thought it important to remain skeptical at every stage of Aubrion's plans: not quite blunting Aubrion's creativity, but not allowing it to leave the house unsupervised, either. Nevertheless, even the cautious Noël felt that something tremendous was happening here.

Before our meeting, he'd asked the men and women of the FI who normally wrote in the basement to take their work upstairs; though everyone knew we were doing something dangerously mad, Noël did not want to trouble them with the details, nor to give them information they could reveal under interrogation. But I believe that was not his sole motivation: indeed, I think Noël felt a bit possessive of *Faux Soir*. He'd sent his daughters to America before the war; it was the way of things, you know, and he would never see how tall and bright they might be—

come. This caper—this mad, mad plan—might prove his only chance to watch his child grow up. He might only have a day, just a minute's pride before the German bullet, but that would be enough for René Noël.

Noël was not alone in his excitement. The immensity of what we were about to do was an almost visceral presence in the room, sitting among us like a kingly companion. I leaned backward in my chair, watching the others, eating a pastry Aubrion had bought me: a peach tart, the likes of which I hadn't tasted in over a year. Tarcovich was chain-smoking cheap cigarettes; Victor kept scribbling on the notepad in front of him; Mullier was eating an apple; Spiegelman was still, fighting to disappear. To the rest of us, David Spiegelman was somewhat of a curiosity: the twice-turned-traitor, the homosexual Jew, the man who spun magic with his pen. In a room of misfits, *he* was the oddest of the bunch. And even though he sat quiet and unmoving, he was as eager as any of us. We had done nothing, not a *thing* in our lives to rival what we were about to do here. I watched the others, and so did Aubrion, who was not sitting but pacing with a bit of chalk in his hand.

"I am going to start with some bad news." Aubrion rolled the chalk between his hands, dusting them in white. The room was darker than usual, one of the sparse lightbulbs that hung from the ceiling having burned out last evening. On the floor above us, the men and women of the resistance, journalists and propagandists, tapped at their typewriters. Their *click-click-click-snaps* bounced off the walls like chattering teeth. "The bad news is—"

"Germany has invaded Belgium?" said Tarcovich.

"Well, yes."

"Oh, so compared to what you're about to tell us, that is the good news." Tarcovich blew a smoke ring. "Comforting to know."

"Let him talk." Mullier punctuated this grunt with an enormous bite of his apple.

"The bad news," Aubrion continued, "is that August Wolff could only commit to five thousand francs—"

"Five thousand?" said Victor.

"Damn," muttered Tarcovich.

"—so we will have to procure most of the supplies ourselves." Spiegelman's voice was soft. We looked at him, and he shrank under our scrutiny. Aubrion had warned us that Spiegelman would be there, promising we could trust him. Secrets were the only reliable currency, in those days, and Spiegelman had filled Aubrion's pockets with a great many. But we were still measuring him, still on our guard. I think Spiegelman detected our unease, for he kept his eyes down.

"The good news," said Aubrion, "is that we will have to procure most of the supplies ourselves. If Wolff is buying us fewer things, we're giving him fewer opportunities to keep track of how much material we're using or to breathe down our necks." He tossed the chalk into his other hand. "August Wolff," he said, mimicking the voice of the *Radio Bruxelles* announcer. "Doesn't he sound like a villain of something?"

"He is a villain of something," Tarcovich said flatly.

"So!" Aubrion made a note on a chalkboard. "To start, we'll need forty-five thousand francs, two hundred thousand sheets of paper, two hundred barrels of ink, and a print factory. Any ideas?"

"To *start*," said Tarcovich, shaking her head.

"I used to work for a man," said Mullier. "Name of Wellens."

"Ferdinand Wellens?" said Victor.

"Yeah."

"Who is he?" asked Aubrion.

Victor pulled off his glasses and answered for Mullier. "He owns several of the larger presses in Belgium, and one in France, too, I believe. He's a businessman, mostly."

"Not a good one." Mullier scratched his chin, calculating. I wondered—as did Aubrion, I'm sure—whether Mullier had sabotaged the man's reputation. "But he might know how to get paper and ink."

Aubrion wrote his name on the blackboard. "We have seventeen days, Theo. We need to do better than 'might.' Is he sympathetic to the cause?"

"He's not against it."

The professor explained that Wellens was Catholic. "There is a warrant for his arrest which has never been filed. We can use this vulnerability as leverage, if the need arises."

"And this is someone you know?" Aubrion asked Mullier. "Who knows you?"

"We...know each other," said Mullier vaguely, and what should have been the simplest of sentences was somehow the most mysterious thing I had ever heard him say.

"Contact him and let me know what he says, will you?" Aubrion said.

Mullier nodded and took another bite of his apple. A chunk landed in his beard. I formed a compelling theory on why Mullier had never married.

"Anyone else?" asked Aubrion.

"I have an idea about where you can get the funds," said Spiegelman.

The others looked at him with some suspicion. I'll admit that I did the same.

"Where's that?" said Aubrion.

"There's a judge by the name of Andree Grandjean. She's known as a puppeteer, someone who knows which strings to pull. She's raised thousands of francs for orphans, refugees, the like. I've heard rumors that she has no love for the Nazis."

"What evidence do we have?"

"She hasn't taken a political prisoner since 1940. She sends them all to a courthouse in northern Brussels."

"Good enough." Aubrion pointed at Victor with his chalk. "Do you know anything about her, Martin?"

"Why would he know?" asked Mullier.

Tarcovich laughed. "We've found the only person on the continent who hasn't read Victor's file. His whole business is to know things."

"Andree Grandjean sounds vaguely familiar, Marc," said Victor. "I can write a report."

"Yes, do some digging." Aubrion wrote her name on the board. "See if you can find anything. If she hates the Nazis, she has reasons, and if she has reasons, she has secrets."

"Indubitably," said Victor. Martin Victor was the sort of person who said "indubitably."

"In the meantime, Madame Tarcovich..."

Tarcovich lit a cigarette. "Can I help you?"

"I want you to pay a visit to Madame Grandjean and see what you can do with her."

"I'm sure I can do a lot with her."

"She might listen to a woman," said Aubrion.

"But what am I to say to her?"

"Give her a brief sketch of what we're doing and see if she's interested. She's a judge, isn't she?"

"That is correct," said Spiegelman.

"A woman judge. That means she's ambitious. Frame it as a fun challenge. You know how it goes."

"A fun challenge," Lada said, flatly.

Aubrion grew defensive. "Lada, we are planning to light the brightest fire Belgium has ever seen—"

"Yes. And then to snuff it out immediately."

"Excellent! You've come across a fantastic way *not* to pitch it to her. Offer her money, recognition, anything. I have faith in you." Aubrion rocked back and forth on his heels. "What am I missing, what am I missing?— Oh, yes. Distribution points. Victor, do you have any ideas on how to get a list of all the distribution points in the country?"

"You mean newsstands?" said Victor.

"I mean newsstands, kiosks, stores, shops, carts. Anywhere that anyone can buy a paper. I need to know who's getting what, and how they're doing it."

"That information is tightly regulated by the Germans."

"I know it is."

Victor tapped a finger against the table. "A black-market auction is happening next week. It's invitation only, the best stuff in Belgium, things we couldn't even imagine. If such a list exists, we might be able to purchase it there."

"No Nazi presence?" asked Tarcovich.

"There might be a few German officials, but no one will be checking identification papers. I attended a similar auction a few months ago. It wasn't as secure as you might think."

"Spiegelman!" said Aubrion. In his enthusiasm, he dropped his chalk, which broke into three pieces. "We need an invitation to the auction."

"Done," replied Spiegelman, eager to solidify his commitment.

Aubrion turned to me, smiling. "I have a task for you, as well, Gamin."

My heart gave a cry of excitement. "What is it, monsieur?" In truth, I had not expected him to include me. I'd been flattered that Noël had not kicked me out, and astonished that I hadn't been dismissed when the meeting began. But *participation* had seemed unlikely.

"At the end of all this," said Aubrion, "when everything has been put in motion, we're going to need a fire." I stood tall and brave in the company of my heroes. "A big one."

17 DAYS TO PRINT
AFTERNOON

The Saboteur

"MONSIEUR MULLIER!" SAID WELLENS, embracing Theo. Theo Mullier accepted the gesture the way a child accepts an oversized sweater at Christmas. Still grinning, Wellens turned his attention to Aubrion. "And who is this fellow?"

"I am Marc Aubrion."

"Pleased to meet you, sir, pleased to meet you."

The three were in Wellens's office, at the largest print factory in the country. Earlier that day, Aubrion had volunteered to accompany Mullier to Wellens's factory "to be of help wherever needed"; the truth of it was that Aubrion, a shameless voyeur, could not pass up a chance to see these two men attempt to hold a conversation. Wellens smiled at Theo Mullier as though he were seeing someone else entirely, not this gaunt, unsettling specter. Mullier, who was not one for smiling, watched Ferdinand Wellens with clinical suspicion. It unnerved Aubrion, the way Mullier's eyes moved in his impassive face, as though his skin were molded from some immovable clay and only his eyes were human.

Wellens shouted to be heard over the mechanical groans of the presses outside his office door. "It's been years, hasn't it, Mullier?" Wellens clasped Theo's hand. "So many years."

"It has," said Mullier.

With a start, Wellens stepped back, blinking at Mullier and Aubrion from behind his large, round eyeglasses. "Remind me, how many years has it been? And, come to think of it, how do I know you in the first place?"

As Aubrion later discovered, Theo Mullier had not been entirely truthful when he'd mentioned that he once "worked" for Ferdinand Wellens—poor Wellens, who was desperate even for business with the FI. They knew each other because Mullier had sabotaged Wellens's reputation.

We have intelligence reports, an FI agent wrote to Mullier at the start of the war, *suggesting that a man by the name of Ferdinand Wellens is doing business with the Nazis. Your task is to make him unattractive to these clients.*

Mullier was just as good at making others seem unattractive as he was at appearing unattractive himself. For two weeks, he followed Wellens wherever the man went, taking note of whom he saw, what he did, what he ate, where he slept. Mullier was thorough, obsessive, keeping track of how long it took Wellens to bathe, counting how many steps he paced. He watched Wellens botch two deals with potential customers because Wellens couldn't remember who wanted the pornographic leaflets and who wanted the candy bar ads; he watched Wellens close a third deal because the customer felt so sorry for Wellens that he couldn't help but do business with the man. *I can see why the Nazis like him*, Mullier wrote to Noël. *He's an idiot.*

But he was an idiot with a chronic problem: Catholicism. Ferdinand Wellens was profoundly religious. He went to church every Wednesday and Sunday. It was the only thing Wellens did well, sneaking out of his apartment to escape the Nazis' notice and returning before anyone realized he'd been gone. Of course, the Nazis didn't forbid Catholicism, not exactly, but they frowned on it, particularly among their more public devotees. Wellens was just public enough for it to matter.

So, three weeks after the FI's assignment, Mullier followed Wellens to church. When all the congregants had gone inside, Mullier hobbled around to the back, where Wellens and the priest always exited after mass. He took a bucket of soapy water from where he'd hidden it in a patch of shrubbery. Careful that no one saw what he was up to, Mullier poured the bucket across the church steps. Then, he waited.

The priest walked out first, as he always did. He turned around, said something to Wellens, laughed, hiked up his priestly robes, and performed a maneuver Mullier had not seen outside the Royal Brussels Ballet. Wellens watched, eyes widening behind his round spectacles, as the priest slipped, his leg rising so that his foot was above his head. With a shout, Wellens reached for the priest, grabbing his hand just as the man began to fall.

Armed with a camera, Mullier sprang from the bushes. By that time, the priest's foot had been returned to its proper place on the ground. A viewer who was aware of the backstory would have seen the photograph for what it was: a panicked congregant preventing a man of the cloth from meeting an undignified end on a set of steps. But without backstory, the photograph looked entirely different: it seemed to show a tender moment between Wellens and the priest, the former having reached out to grab the hand of the latter, perhaps in a moment of religious fervor. Mullier snapped the photograph and ran, leaving the two, blinking and nonplussed, on the steps of the church.

The next day, the photograph was mailed in a perfumed envelope to the Nazi High Command. The Nazis stopped doing business with Wellens hours later. Wellens was spared a bullet by a German bureaucrat who was raised Catholic, who thus "forgot" to file Wellens's warrant. The photograph, for its part, still hangs on the wall of the FI headquarters.

Aubrion cleared his throat. "Um, Monsieur Wellens—"

"Wellens, the *Front de l'Indépendance* wants to do business with you," Mullier interrupted. "We are in the middle of a propaganda campaign against the Nazis."

"Oh, a *campaign*." Lines wrinkled Wellens's high forehead, like em-dashes on old paper. "That is exciting. What kind of campaign is it?"

His wary gaze never straying from Wellens's face, Mullier sat at the businessman's desk. Wellens had, as I mentioned, worked for the Nazis. That did not bother Aubrion much, for many people accepted German coin for their labors; even the Belgian government itself collaborated, you will recall. But Mullier, who was not so forgiving, suspected more nefarious motives.

The office was not furnished for three, so Aubrion had to stand near the door. It was there he watched Ferdinand Wellens, this odd, tectonic figure of a man, the sort of character Aubrion couldn't write about for fear of no one believing he existed.

"We are printing an anti-Nazi newspaper," Mullier said to Wellens.

"Interesting." Wellens pronounced each syllable individually, pausing before the next, as though the word were a sentence. "How many copies?"

"Fifty thousand," said Mullier.

Wellens whistled.

Aubrion added, "We have need of supplies."

"Let me think." Wellens rubbed his forehead. He was dressed in a gray suit and black coat, even though the factory was warm with the breath of the presses. His clothes were a size too large for him, and his shoes scuffed the floor as he paced. *He paces three steps in front of him, turns, and paces four steps the other way*, Mullier had reported to the FI, years before. And it was still true. Theo Mullier cataloged *everything* about his potential targets; a hairline fracture could become a chasm in the right hands. "You will need around two hundred thousand sheets of paper," said Wellens, "and two hundred barrels of ink?"

"That's what we figure," said Aubrion, surprised.

"How—" Wellens stretched out the word how so that it had two syllables "—do you propose to get it?"

"That is where you come in," replied Mullier.

"I see." Wellens snapped his fingers to indicate that he had an idea. Aubrion did not know anyone who did that besides play-actors. The businessman's whistling and snapping and pacing—all were accessories to his character, and Aubrion loved them, found them sublimely amusing. But Mullier's lips never twitched at Wellens's antics. "The only department that has that kind of money these days is the Nazi Ministry of Education." The businessman grinned, triumphant.

"And so?" prompted Aubrion.

"Why, don't you see? It's so easy. The FI can become a school."

Mullier blinked at the naked stupidity of that statement. "I do not understand."

"All right, all right, listen a moment. Here is what we can do." Though there was no way anyone in the factory could hear them, Wellens lowered his voice. "We can pose as a group of pro-Nazi Belgians who are building a school to train Hitler youth. We can put together a curriculum, draw up lessons, everything. Then, we can take our plan to the Ministry of Education, pitch our curriculum, and ask them for the supplies we need to open the school." Smiling, Wellens spread his arms wide. "Good, no? We will need someone with experience in education to help us draw up a convincing curriculum, to justify the funds and such. But if we have that, it can be done."

Mullier and Aubrion were too astonished to speak. It was a stupid plan, something that should not have worked at all, so haphazard that it looked dangerous, like a condemned building fashioned into a public library. The Nazis would never, in a thousand years, expect it.

"Yes," Mullier finally managed to say.

"It can be done," agreed Aubrion.

The Smuggler

Lada Tarcovich never spent as much time in courthouses as her twin professions might suggest. She had never been caught smuggling, not once. And prostitution was not illegal in the days of *Faux Soir*, though it was a useful excuse to accost suspicious-looking women from whom the Gestapo needed information; whenever she took a girl into her care, Tarcovich instructed her on how to avoid attracting unwanted notice. So, on the twenty-fourth of October 1943, Tarcovich walked to a courthouse for the first time to demand an audience with Andree Grandjean, judge at the Court of Appeals.

It seemed an odd tack to take: throwing good sense over her shoulder the way her superstitious grandmother would have thrown a pinch of salt, marching up to the judge, and asking her to take part in their mad plan. But whenever Lada Tarcovich doubted the wisdom of Aubrion's schemes, she recalled a conversation they had at the beginning of the war.

This was before the occupation, before the three weeks of blood that preceded the king's surrender. The pair sat in Lada's room in the attic of the whorehouse. Aubrion was hiding out. Aubrion was often hiding out in those days; his brand of satire rankled the sensibilities of wealthier compatriots. It was 1940, that year when politicians were dusting off *neutrality* and *capitulation* to hawk like stale bread from their podiums. A small but vocal paper had just released a satirical story called "Please Step Over My Henhouse, Thank You Very Much"; in the story, a chicken that learns of a war between neighboring lions asks politely, in several languages, whether it can remain neutral. The author, one Marc Aubrion, had included a somewhat on-the-nose portrayal of a warthog named after a local governnor. The governor was not pleased. And so Aubrion was hiding out with Tarcovich until the incident faded from public memory, as he had done before and probably would again.

Aubrion threw a newspaper down on Tarcovich's nightstand. "Look at him," he said, nodding at a photograph of King Leopold taking a pen to paper. "What the devil is he writing?"

"I don't think he's writing." Tarcovich lit a cigarette. "I think he's signing."

"Signing what?"

"His declaration of neutrality, I assume."

"But his pen is poised in the middle of the page. Look there. He doesn't even have the backbone to pick a side on his own document."

Tarcovich laughed. "Don't be too hard on him, Marc. He's got a handsome uniform."

"He's an earthworm. He's less than an earthworm. At least earthworms are *useful*."

Shaking her head, Tarcovich put out her cigarette in a porcelain ashtray. Her attic, where she passed the time between customers, was a slant-roofed cavern of treasures. The shelves were warped from carrying gold-trimmed books, and jewelry boxes, and sculptures. Busts with famous noses and chins occupied each corner. A painting that had been reported stolen from a castle in Germany hung on a crooked nail.

"Remember Belgium," Aubrion murmured. The room had little space for furniture: just two chairs and a malnourished nightstand. Aubrion sat backward in one of the chairs; Tarcovich stood leaning on the other. He said again, "Remember Belgium," taking on the voice of a radio announcer.

"Don't be dramatic, Marc," said Tarcovich. "It's not dead yet."

"No, no, the propaganda campaign—"

"Oh, from the Great War?"

"'The rape of Belgium!' I hear the posters caused a magnificent stir in America. Do you think the Americans even know where Belgium is?"

"I wonder sometimes whether Belgians knows where Belgium is. Declaration of *neutrality*." The word was oily with contempt. "What the fuck does Leo think he's doing?"

"Do you think his mistress calls him Leo?"

"She doesn't."

Aubrion blinked. "You're joking."

"I don't joke about business," said Tarcovich, flatly. She picked up Aubrion's newspaper, the evening copy of *Het Laatste Nieuws*. "How long, do you think?"

"I give it three years until Hitler comes knocking."

Tarcovich nodded. Her eyes were somewhere far. "So we have three years," she said, "to get out."

"Yes." Aubrion walked over to a globe on Tarcovich's shelf and gave it a spin. "What king's globe am I defiling?"

"That? I took it from the king of Monaco."

Aubrion laughed. "I have an idea for a play."

"I'm not writing another play with you," said Tarcovich.

"It's a two-act farce about four heads of state who try to trick the others into entering a horse race, only the race is rigged. They all think they are the one who will win, so they all enter eagerly, but in the third act—"

"You said it's a two-act."

"That's the beauty of it, Lada. It's a farce. Didn't I mention that?"

"When was the last time you finished a play, Marc?"

"Well, we have three years to work on it, don't we?" Aubrion grinned, and Lada knew he would walk—he would skip—to the map's edge, and that she would follow him there, even if there were monsters.

"And who are you?" asked the clerk in the courthouse foyer, snapping Lada out of her reverie.

"A concerned citizen." Tarcovich was suddenly aware that her neckline was too low for a concerned citizen. In this vapidly formal building—oak chairs, a small waiting area, windows that had been papered over to protect the glass during air raids—Tarcovich looked out of place, to put it mildly.

The clerk sighed. He was a balding caricature of a man, the kind of person who became a clerk after being told, since childhood, that he looked like a clerk. "We all are. What do you want?"

"To speak to Madame Grandjean about a possible fraud."

"May I see your forms?"

Tarcovich faltered. "I'm not sure I feel comfortable sharing such confidential information with someone other than Madame Grandjean."

"Then you will not be sharing this information with Madame Grandjean, either, I'm afraid." The words *I'm afraid* came half a second after the rest of the sentence, to ensure Tarcovich knew he didn't have to be polite, but was doing so out of chivalry. "Is there anything else I can do for you today?"

"I'm sure there isn't." With a nod, Tarcovich left the courthouse.

She stepped out into the noncommittal fog, which was punctured by a sudden shriek. Tarcovich glanced to her left. Two policemen were dragging a woman up the courthouse stairs. Even from twenty or thirty meters away, Tarcovich could see the woman's wrists purpling around her handcuffs. As the woman and her captors disappeared into the building, Tarcovich realized—with dread, but with excitement, too—what she needed to do to gain an audience with Andree Grandjean.

★ ★ ★

As I recall it, the hard part was coming up with a crime. "It can't be something violent," said Tarcovich. "No assaults, definitely no murders. No thefts—I wouldn't do that to a poor shopkeeper. These times are difficult enough." I watched Tarcovich smoke, thoughtful. "I also do not want to be involved in some dreary protest."

Aubrion had been sitting on a table in the basement of the FI headquarters, which the *Faux Soir* group had held colonized since our first meeting. Our brothers and sisters of the FI were forced to cram themselves into the rooms upstairs, knocking their elbows together as they worked. Aubrion leapt to his feet, pacing. I watched him from my perch atop a broken printing press. He had not slept or eaten in hours; I hadn't the faintest idea when he'd last showered. No one could work himself into a fit like Marc Aubrion. I often saw him, pacing and muttering and writing, from night until morning. At first light, I'd step across moats of blotting paper to place a mug of coffee on his desk.

"Why not smuggling?" he said.

Tarcovich recoiled as though she'd been slapped. "I have never been caught smuggling. I am not about to start."

"You're about to die," Aubrion said, laughing. "What does your reputation matter?"

"I am about to die. My reputation is all that matters."

Mullier ambled into the room. Aubrion taught me to handle words carefully like glass, so I do not use the word *ambled* thoughtlessly. Theo Mullier never walked or jogged or trotted; he ambled everywhere, like a lost old man or an inquisitive toddler.

"Monsieur Mullier?" said Aubrion.

"Mmm?"

"A question."

"Mmm."

"If Lada were to commit a crime, what would that be?"

He considered. Then: "Automobile theft."

Aubrion's face lit. "Perfect."

<u>YESTERDAY</u>

The Scrivener

THE OLD WOMAN PAUSED, paused, her eyes glittering but downcast—and suddenly, like a thunderclap, or a change of heart, Eliza *saw* her: the character from the story, Aubrion's friend, the little roach, the urchin with silver in her pockets. Her face changed; the years that Helene had worn on her forehead and cheeks smoothed over in an instant. It felt like a trick of the light, an optical illusion, and in an instant, it was over. The old woman came back to herself.

She would not speak, and seemed embarrassed. Eliza asked her about it.

"Not embarrassed," said Helene. "But—"

"Reluctant?"

"Perhaps. I have not spoken of this, really."

"Of what?"

"I don't know. Whatever it was—what I did." Helene closed her eyes. "The fires."

"Oh."

The old woman sat and breathed, and then she spoke. "This

is what I will do. As I told you before, this is not simply a tale of men and women, but of creatures, as well."

"Creatures?" Eliza would not say so, but she wondered whether the horror of the war had shaken loose something in the old woman's mind. But it could not be. She would not believe it.

"I will tell you about the fires, and about the *dybbuk*. It took me some time to realize it, I'll admit, but he and I had more in common than I'd wished. This is my story, and what David Spiegelman, the *gastromancer*, told me."

IN THE TIME OF FAUX SOIR

The Dybbuk and the Girl

WHEN I WAS YOUNG, my parents lived six blocks from the University of Toulouse, across from the students' dormitories. My memories of this time feel secondhand. Every fall, the students would arrive with their carpetbags, and every summer, they would go back the way they came, dragging their bags, stained from the semester, behind them. When the students left, the university sent teams to repair the damage they'd done to the dormitories, and men would blanket the buildings in scaffolding, climbing the wooden skeletons until dawn. On the day they finished, I would come home from the market with my mother, and I'd look up at the dormitories in awe of the transformation: the scaffolding gone, the buildings suddenly new again. One year—1940, to be exact—the University of Toulouse did not send construction workers to repair the dormitories. The Germans saw to that.

Three months later, my parents were trampled by a crowd of refugees fleeing Toulouse.

I know nothing of what truly caused the stampede. When the Nazis occupied France, they organized bread lines to distribute rations, and my parents and I queued in our line every morning. But one morning—and this will puzzle me until I die—my parents asked me to stay behind, leaving me on a hill overlooking the town square. It was there I watched the line of filth and skin fracture in the middle, a hairline split that bloomed into chaos. The crowd rushed the Germans at the front of the line, and then they were running for the city gates, pushing, mud in their mouths and on their faces. Someone cried, shrill— "They're coming!" I think—and when it was over, my parents were gone. I searched for my grandfather, who was supposed to care for me if my parents died; I never found him. But four months later, I found fire.

Blame *L'Ingénue* for the first fire I started. It was a popular paper in Toulouse before the Germans came to call, one of those magazines my parents never let me touch and the shopkeepers hid in the backs of their stores. The front of the paper, I remember, looked like a dull finance magazine, and my father was constantly impressed with the editors' ability to come up with boring headlines ("Are taxes to blame for the rising price of steel?"). The back of the paper betrayed the magazine's true intentions; as I recall, it featured rather evocative photos of young women who became sartorially sparser as the winds grew colder. Shortly after the death of my family, I was wandering the streets of Toulouse near the Spanish border. I was half-mad with hunger in those days, limping from a bad gash in my leg. The sky made promises that the clouds couldn't keep, swearing that the rain would stop and the sun would dry my rags. But it rained, and a copy of *L'Ingénue* blew past me. I followed it toward the river Garonne.

The rain had dyed the bricks of my city a deeper crimson. I have seen many orphans and refugees in my time, their identities articulated by the holes in their shoes; I was no different. My feet were soaked. Shivering, I leaned against a wall to catch my breath.

A flicker of orange caught my attention. I squinted. In the distance, someone had built a campfire beneath the wounded stone roof of a church. Closing my eyes, I heard their voices: a strange, otherworldly peal of laughter in the deserted city. Of course, the only people who had occasion to laugh in my city were the people who had destroyed it, but I was too ill to contemplate such things, and I started toward the campfire. *L'Ingénue* joined me.

When I was close enough to see their uniforms, my heart froze in my chest. The men who sat laughing around the campfire wore the same boots and patches as the men who'd marched across my home. I did not know them as Nazis, not yet. But their identities would not have mattered to me. They were beasts that spoke in an odd tongue and put their hands where they did not belong. I crouched behind a headless statue, watching the men gather armfuls of discarded paper to feed their fire. The evening was so cold that even from such a distance, probably two hundred meters, I could feel the warmth. The flames struck me as beautiful: clean and bright, with no mistakes.

I became aware of a pile of supplies behind the men, nestled up against the church. They had packages of food, barrels of water and wine, guns and bullets, and red canisters I had seen them pour onto buildings before dousing them with their flamethrowers. *L'Ingénue* sidled over to their camp, whispering for me to follow. I waited for the men to be distracted, to laugh again, then I sprinted from my perch, throwing myself behind the supplies. Dizzy, I clutched at my chest, waiting for my heart to slow. To my welcome surprise, the men showed no sign of having noticed me.

Breathing hard, I lifted one of the red canisters, staggering under its weight. It could not have weighed that much, now that I think about it, but I was a child, you see, and so hungry. As the men sat with their backs to me, I crept over to *L'Ingénue* and poured kerosene across the pages. Then I ran behind the camp and back to the headless statue, kneeling behind the stone.

I did not wait long. One of the men, who had the characteristic gait of the nearly drunk, picked up *L'Ingénue*. Someone made a joke. As they all laughed, the almost-drunk man answered with another—I can still hear the words: *Wenn ich besaß eine frau!*—and threw *L'Ingénue* onto the flames.

I do not know what I expected to happen. I knew there would be fire, or rather more fire, and I knew that was what I wanted. I wanted my parents, and my bed, and the sandwiches my father used to make, the ones with eggs and cheese, and I wanted the smells of my city, and because I couldn't have any of it, I wanted these men to hurt. But beyond that, I am not sure that I had a concrete idea of what would happen once they fed *L'Ingénue* to their campfire.

Have you seen those films, those time-lapse films of a tiny bud blossoming into a rose? Imagine that, the explosion of color and power and will, magnified a thousand times so that it is so much faster and so much more powerful than anything you have ever witnessed. That was what happened on that cold evening. The men threw *L'Ingénue* onto the fire, and then it was ten or twenty more fires, enveloping the screaming men as they struggled to get away. I watched them, smelling their burning flesh, half blinded by what I saw.

I turned away to wipe the sting from my eyes. When I looked again, the men were gone, and so was the church. In their place were skeletons: the coal-black remains of the scarred church, the still-life bodies of men who had done me harm.

"Want to know why the Nazis are so dangerous?" Aubrion said to me once. I thought I knew why: they made people so scared that they would trample their neighbors to get away—that they would step on the bodies of children who went to school with their sons and daughters. "Everything they do, every goddamn thing, is propaganda." Aubrion was slightly drunk when he said that, I remember. "When they invade a country? That's propaganda. The order in which they invade? Propaganda. Shooting a traitor in the back? Propaganda." Aubrion often spoke to me this way, in broken lectures. It wasn't often that he reminded me of my father, but he did when he grew especially passionate; my father had been renowned, in his time, for treating pubs as lecture halls, but when I try to recall such things, it is not my father's face that appears, but Marc Aubrion's.

And so, Marc Aubrion told me, August Wolff was taught to use fire as propaganda, a weapon that purified as it killed. It is hard for me to discuss the Nazi relationship with fire. I've spent my life, from the moment I became conscious of myself, defining myself as *not* a Nazi, and yet the Nazi relationship with fire mirrored my own. I came to fire as a child running from the Germans; fire came to August Wolff as a young man training for the Gestapo.

The first time I saw the Germans take a torch to a home—my friend Baptiste's home, where he lived with his grandparents— the fire emptied everything that it touched. *Fire purifies*, August Wolff wrote in his memos, and I remember feeling the same, the delirious ache in my body as my perception of things changed. *It cleanses*. The house was new again, remade in ash and soot. *It is beautiful*.

"Wolff thinks it's all shit," Spiegelman confided in me one evening. Just the two of us were awake. Even Aubrion slept. "All of it. The whole Nazi business."

"He said that, monsieur?" I asked.

"There were so many times he let it slip—small confessions about his guilt, his sense of duty. I believe I was invisible to him after a while. He said things around me that I don't think he would have said to anyone else. He wanted to be a writer, you know. He likes the idea of building things out of words. The Germans are good at that, I don't have to tell you. But Wolff doesn't think they're doing enough."

"What else does he want them to do, monsieur?"

"I don't know." Spiegelman rocked back and forth. I'd seen

orphans do that, alone on cast-off roads. "Perhaps he wants them to pause and appreciate what they are destroying." I shook my head, confused. "Listen," Spiegelman said. "August Wolff often makes me think of a story from my childhood. My grandmother told it to me. My parents never held to the superstitions of the day, so Abraham—"

"Your brother?" I said.

"Yes, my younger brother. Abraham and I got our stories from our grandmother. 'This is a sad tale, David,' she told me. I was around eight or nine, too big to sit on her lap, but she pulled me into her arms anyway. Grandmother spoke, and I pocketed each word. 'A sad tale, David,' she said, 'not a scary one this time. It is about a spirit called the *dybbuk.*'

"The *dybbuk*, she told me, is a wandering soul, divorced from its body." Spiegelman's voice was paper-thin. "We all must die sometime, of course. When most of us go, we are mourned by those who love us. But some of us are not so fortunate."

"What happens to them?" I asked. My breath felt cold in my chest. "The less fortunate souls, I mean."

"They roam the earth, searching for a body to inhabit. They pick the bodies of women, most of the time, or young children. Often, they live inside a soul for years. They peel away the voices of these stolen bodies and trap themselves beneath their skin."

"Do they stay there forever?"

"Not forever. Only until they complete their task."

"What task does the *dybbuk* have to complete, monsieur?" I asked Spiegelman.

Spiegelman leaned back, rubbing the bridge of his nose. "It can be different things. Some want to find their families, the ones who did not mourn, and force them to account for this crime. My grandmother told me about *dybbuks* who took a body because they never felt at home in their own. They leave when their voice becomes stronger.

"But the weight of the *dybbuk*'s task is often too much for them to bear." Spiegelman shrugged. "They're quite human, in that way. They want to relieve some of the pressure, release some of that burden—they want to share their stories, to be free from guilt, to achieve their wishes, to shake off the chains of their obligations. They are constantly scrabbling to share and to win, Gamin," said Spiegelman. "That is who they are."

"Can people help them?" I wondered.

"A good question." Spiegelman put his hand on my shoulder, a rare and strained display of affection. "People often help them without knowing it, or so my grandmother believed." He nearly laughed, the way I've laughed at jokes told at my own expense. "Most of the time, they don't find out that they've helped the spirit until its task is done. The *dybbuk* is sly that way."

The Dybbuk

The building in front of them was short and slender, with a broad face marred by dirty glass. Wolff's diaries—the ones from his youth, not the false diaries he kept during his time with the Nazis—speak of an experience he had as a boy, about seven years old, watching a colony of ants devour a rat carcass. Whenever the *Gruppenführer* saw his soldiers running toward a print factory in their dark uniforms and their dark rifles and boots, he thought of those ants: so orderly and complete, every part of them dedicated to the business of undoing.

Half the soldiers went inside the building, while the other half poured kerosene around the perimeter. Soon, the morning was thick with the smell of it. Wolff turned away, struggling not to cough.

"I've been told you get used to it," said Herr Manning, fanning the air in front of his face. "But I haven't."

"You don't," Wolff replied, and that was true. He felt as though his body were elsewhere, as though he were watching the conflagration from behind glass.

In the distance, Wolff could hear the shrieks of the factory workers—many of them women, most of them unaware they'd been printing papers for the underground. That was the way of things. Though many underground printers, typesetters, operators, and linotypists were volunteers, it was sometimes the *foremen* who volunteered without their workers' knowledge. The foremen broke up the workers' tasks so they never saw exactly what they were printing, just fragments of an unseen whole. They did not discover the true nature of their task until they heard the words: *On the floor, on the floor!* Their ignorance could not stop the bullets.

"What is this?" said Manning. "The third—no, second rebel factory we've found this month? The year is far from over, and we're on track for a new record."

The shrieks grew closer, and then a woman burst from a door at the rear of the factory. She ran, stumbling, tripping over her simple dress and clogs, almost falling. All the while, of course, she screamed. Wolff learned early in his life that a certain kind of scream lies dormant until death, when it is drawn out in a fevered rattle—a rattle that rang coarse and hollow over the sounds of gunfire.

October 25, —43, Wolff would write, later that evening. *Precision operation on print factory responsible for rebel publication* La Barrière. *Eradicated all traitors. Burned the papers. No survivors. Our banner marches on without delay, wiping the stains of their rebellion from this earth.*

"How many do you think worked there?" asked Manning.

Wolff's eyes itched. "Worked?"

"I beg your pardon, *Gruppenführer*?"

"About a thousand. That was our last estimate."

Wolff's next comment was cut off by a sound—a roar, from the dancing fire that smelled of kerosene, the fire that continued to roar long after Wolff and his men had gone.

16 DAYS TO PRINT
MORNING

The Gastromancer

HIS ASSIGNMENTS USUALLY began with an envelope, sealed with the stamp of the Gestapo: an eagle bearing a swastika beneath its outstretched wings. Spiegelman opened three envelopes that lay in a pile on his desk, one after the other, setting the contents aside like organs during a transplant. The first envelope contained a letter from a museum curator to his mistress; the second from the mistress to the curator; and the third from the curator to his wife. Spiegelman's palms grew clammy as he picked through these lives and misdeeds.

He got up to wash his hands at the basin in the corner of his living quarters. The Nazis did not disaggregate their work and their lives, and so most offices on base contained a cot, a washbasin, and a trunk for personal effects. These amenities were tucked behind the office space, as though the Germans were embarrassed that they had to pause their duties to sleep or tend to their morning or evening ablutions. Spiegelman's quarters were relatively spacious; Wolff had seen to that. The basin was white porcelain, the walls barren and clean. Wolff had permitted Spiegelman to order a plain blue rug, which muffled Spiegelman's footsteps as he returned to his envelopes.

Spiegelman almost didn't need to read them. He'd found the pattern in mistresses' writing years ago, selling his skills as a boy. They all wrote the same way: the pleading insecurities, the shocking language, promises turning into bribes that later revealed themselves as threats. Even the handwriting was similar. It was forced, often curly, as if each letter were trying to make more of itself than was possible, given its low birth. Mistresses always put too much pressure on their pens, which made the letters look juvenile and thick. And then, of course, there were the spelling errors, the overwrought language.

Someone knocked at his door. Spiegelman put aside his work.

"Come," he said.

The *Gruppenführer* entered and closed the door. "I hope I am not disturbing you."

"I am just starting the Schoenberg letter."

"Remind me." Wolff took a seat in front of Spiegelman's desk.

"A curator who displeased the *Führer* by refusing to house Nazi artifacts in his museum."

"Oh, yes. It should be simple enough, no?"

"It'll be done before the day is out."

"The letter?"

"The relationship."

Wolff's mouth crumpled up, the closest he came to smiling. "You are that confident?"

Spiegelman said, without humor, "I have ruined more marriages than all the distilleries in Belgium."

"I almost pity them."

Spiegelman shifted in his seat. He dreaded these meetings with the *Gruppenführer*—not just because the man was despicable, but because Wolff was pathetic, and his Midas hands turned everything he saw into a cowardly husk. Spiegelman struggled to hold himself up in the presence of Wolff.

Wolff said, "I've come to speak to you about *La Libre Belgique*."

"What about it?" Spiegelman picked up a pen, fidgeting with it.

Wolff leaned in. "I am telling you this in confidence. I do not have a good feeling about it. Aubrion and the others agreed far too quickly."

Spiegelman's heart raced. "Perhaps they understood they didn't have a choice," he said.

"Perhaps."

"You don't believe that."

"I am not sure." Wolff rubbed his eyes. "I have a feeling, but no evidence, that they're planning something."

"What could that be?" Spiegelman could feel himself sweating through his shirt. He hoped Wolff would attribute this to the room's warmth.

"Counter-propaganda, possibly. Or simply something that jeopardizes the project. I don't know. It could be anything. Regardless of what they're doing, it is important for me to keep them on a leash."

"Absolutely. What would you have me do?"

"Exactly what you have been doing." Wolff handed Spiegelman a blank sheet of paper. "Be my leash."

The Smuggler

"Your Honor, the accused, Lada Tarcovich, stands accused of automobile theft." The barrister said those last three words with the air of a man who didn't get to say them very often, the way a surgeon might've said "heart transplant" at the time, or a politician might have said "invade Russia." Surely this would be the trial that made the barrister's name a household presence. (The next day's paper did not even mention the fellow.) The barrister paced in front of Tarcovich, pausing every now and then in case someone in the audience wanted to take a photograph of him. The courtroom was mostly empty. Tarcovich stood flanked by two policemen, her hands chained at the wrists. She kept her head down, playacting as a chastened prisoner, but her eyes were fixed on Judge Andree Grandjean sitting above them in her white wig and robes.

"Is the accused represented by anyone?" asked Judge Andree Grandjean.

"I am representing myself, Your Honor," said Tarcovich.

"Do you have any prior experience representing yourself in a court of law?"

Tarcovich enjoyed the woman's voice. It was low and firm, the way few women's voices were. "No, Your Honor."

"Then I recommend the court adjourn until you can secure the services of—"

"I am confident I can do what needs to be done, Your Honor."

Grandjean's mouth clamped shut. She was obviously not used to being interrupted. "Very well," she said. "You may continue, barrister."

The barrister inhaled audibly, then posed, as if this were some impressive feat only he had mastered. "Your Honor," he said, "earlier this afternoon, the accused was spotted loitering near a Nash-Kelvinator model 600."

On the morning of her arrest for automobile theft, Lada Tarcovich did not know how to drive a motorcar. To her credit, she could remember reading about the car in one of Professor Victor's books. She just couldn't remember what it was called. Cursing herself for being such a pitiful car thief, Tarcovich sauntered around the vehicle, because car thieves did not, in general, saunter, and she didn't want anyone to know that she was a car thief, at least not yet.

The car was parked behind a church in northern Charleroi. She peered through the windows. It was a bulbous thing, pudgy with strange lights and lines that formed an old man face at the front. More importantly, the car was unlocked.

"She then proceeded to use a blunt instrument to shatter the rear windows."

Lada Tarcovich had calmly opened the door on the driver's side of the vehicle and climbed in.

"Miraculously, she was not bloodied by this barbarous display of barbarism."

Tarcovich stiffened at the barrister's redundancy—not to mention the alliteration. She'd expected him to exaggerate, of course, but she had not expected such linguistic carelessness.

"Encouraged," the barrister went on, "the accused began to tamper with the motorcar's ignition system."

Tarcovich had studied the keyhole to the right of the steering wheel, remembering that one required a key to start a motorcar. "Damn," she'd whispered, for the driver had not been dumb enough to leave his key in the ignition. Tarcovich felt around the driver's seat. Nothing. She felt around the passenger's seat, breathing quickly now, inhaling fresh leather and cigar ash. Nothing. She turned around, saw something glinting in the back seat. Her heart pounding, Tarcovich leaned back and grabbed the key. She'd laughed, insane with triumph. Humming "Ode to Joy," Tarcovich jammed the key into the ignition—forgetting, of course, to *turn* the key.

Judge Andree Grandjean was twirling a pen as the barrister spoke. Tarcovich had never seen anyone look so bored, and she'd once walked in on her former lover having sex with a *man*.

"Her speed and sophistication," said the barrister, "are likely a testament to the number of cars she has stolen in the past."

Unsure what else to do, Tarcovich had grabbed the key and twisted, certain she was going to break it. The car rumbled to life.

Tarcovich screamed, then realized the motorcar was supposed to be making that sound. She grabbed ahold of the steering wheel, fiddled with the clutch, remembered at the last second to put her foot on the pedal, realized her foot was on the wrong pedal, switched pedals, and then pushed on the accelerator, hard.

The barrister posed for a moment before continuing. "The accused then attempted her getaway."

The citizens of Charleroi had set up a poultry market across from the church where the car was parked. Tarcovich, who had taken hold of the steering wheel but had not thought to use it, sped toward the stalls. Ahead of her, people scattered, yelling at her to stop, stop, for the love of God, stop!, throwing their children out of the way. Screaming, Tarcovich accelerated into a flailing mass of wood, tarp and feathers. But the car swerved, and not even the chickens were hurt.

"Your Honor—" And here the barrister paused, his head bowed. "I cannot even guess at the number of lives lost as a result of this tragic display."

Rolling her eyes at the barrister, Tarcovich decided now was the time. "Your Honor," she said, meeting Grandjean's gaze. "May I approach the bench?"

"Your Honor!" the barrister snapped. "This felon cannot be allowed to interrupt—"

But Grandjean was bored, which made her curious. "No, no," she said, waving Tarcovich forward, "I'll allow it. Not another word, barrister, or I'll hold you in contempt."

Tarcovich felt the policemen's eyes on her as she made her approach. She knew she should think of a speech for Judge Grandjean, lies and pleas that would fall into place like keys into locks, but her attention had been pulled to the judge herself. Though Grandjean's eyes were bloodshot with exhaustion, there was an honest curiosity to them that Tarcovich could not ignore. Her lips were lovely, too; makeup was scarce in those days, so women overcompensated when they *did* have it, painting themselves up like cheap canvas—but not Grandjean, not the judge with her pale sardonic lips. Lada admonished herself for noticing such things.

"All right, you're at the bench at last," Grandjean said. "What on earth is it?"

Tarcovich leaned forward and whispered, "The *Front de l'Indépendance* has need of your services."

Grandjean's eyes widened. She looked past Tarcovich. "Guards, take this woman back to her cell."

The policemen seized Tarcovich from behind, their cruel fingers digging into her skin. "Grandjean!" she said. "Grandjean, you are a woman, and I am a woman, and we know what happens to us in the end! Please, I'm begging you, the Germans—"

"If she says anything more, take her behind the courthouse and shoot her," said Andree Grandjean.

Lada's chains shook, the metal digging into her wrists. After all that, after all *that*, it would end this way—and Lada would rot in a cell for Marc Aubrion's foolish joke, for a theft that had meant nothing. Grandjean's gavel came down, the judge's words chasing Tarcovich out of the courtroom. "Case dismissed."

The Pyromaniac

After the morning shift at my newsstand, I visited the boys at a nearby textile mill, playing my usual games: dancing between the machines, pulling faces at the overseers. Someone raised an alarm, and the manager chased me out with a broom, so I waited outside until my friends' workday ended.

My work as a paperboy spared me the factories. I do not know the true scope of the horrors, but I have heard the tales, and I have seen the ghost-eyes and bruises. Children did not look like children back then. They came out of the factory at dusk, smoking cigarettes, their faces shining with sweat, their backs bent from hours spent crooked over a sewing machine. The only thing that betrayed their youth was their fingers. They had child-size fingers that they poked at each other, laughing until they coughed up grime.

I should note, I think, that all my friends were boys. That was just the way of things: boys took jobs during the war, and girls found it more difficult to do so. It often preyed on me, rousing me in the night: the realization that if these lads knew they'd been following a *girl* from one caper to the next, they would turn on me with the violent cruelty unique to young children.

"What are you doing here?" the boys asked me.

"Marc Aubrion wants us to steal some explosives," I said.

One of the boys spat tobacco. "From who?" he said.

"The Germans."

"People who steal stuff from the Germans get dead."

"Maybe they do, maybe they don't."

"You said it's Aubrion's job? What does he need stuff stolen for?"

I'd been present for all the FI meetings, and I knew it had something to do with *Le Soir*, though the Nazis thought they were doing something different with *La Libre Belgique*. But my knowledge ended there. It didn't matter to me, the fact that I didn't understand, but I was smart enough to realize that it would matter to my friends. So I said: "Something big."

My friends traded glances. Despite their cigarettes and bent backs, they were still kids—kids who couldn't afford comic books and were desperate for masked crusaders. When Aubrion started using the lads for jobs, I became his field commander. I translated his frantic blueprints into terms the kids could understand. "Deliver this message to our spy in the pub," he'd tell me, and I would assemble my forces to dress his assignments in promises and stories. I wonder now whether he knew what these assignments meant to me—to *us*—whether he understood that having a purpose was as important as the food in our bellies. I wonder if he knew what I would have built for him. As the boys smoked, watching me gravely, I'd spin adjectives for

Marc Aubrion; I would do what I always did, turning him into a comic-book hero.

And these kids would've done anything for him. I could see it in their faces, even then, the adoration, the hope: "A big job, huh?" they asked me, probably imagining gold and capes and tall buildings. "Damn, lads, Aubrion's pulling a big job. What is it?" And, then, inevitably, the childishness would give in to a bit of pragmatism ("What does it pay?") before they were back to being kids again ("Will the whole world know about it?"). My God, Aubrion would've loved it. He would have put on his superhero mask with both hands.

15 DAYS TO PRINT
LATE MORNING

The Dybbuk

HERR MANNING WAS SPEAKING, and August Wolff could hear none of it. Though Manning was not Wolff's superior—he had no official rank—the High Command always sent him to deliver Wolff's orders, reciting instructions in an insipid monotone. But Wolff's hearing had stopped at the word *library*. The *Gruppenführer* interrupted him.

"A library, Manning?" said Wolff.

"Yes, *Gruppenführer*. A library of perverse works." Manning shifted, displaying the perspiration stains on his shirt. "These are the orders. Himmler was explicit."

And Himmler *was* explicit, so there was no arguing with the orders. Wolff gathered a battalion, commanded them to pack their flamethrowers, and set off to Brussels.

The Library of the Covenant of the Three lounged between a haberdashery and a boarded-up toymaker's workshop. The library was a small, one-story affair: modest architecture for

Brussels. Wolff ushered his men forward, noting the squat roof and grimy windows.

"Evacuate them first," said Wolff.

Wolff's officers hesitated. One of them said, "Himmler's orders were to fire with everyone inside."

"So they were." Wolff's mouth was sandpaper. The officer had not addressed him by his rank. "My mistake." The officer tilted his head. Wolff cursed himself, for he never admitted errors in front of his men. That was suicide. "You may fire when ready."

It was a better fate, in a way. If they were evacuated first, if the intellectuals and deviants and homosexuals and tiny lads with large books were ushered out of the building in chains, they would likely be sent to a camp or prison, maybe to Fort Breendonk. Wolff had toured the fort only once, at Himmler's invitation. He'd felt ill for weeks after. Perhaps even *this* death—which Wolff had begun to hear, the screams of those being burned alive—perhaps even this death was more humane than that one.

That night, Wolff would type a brief note and place it in his memos folder. He was already composing it in his head. *October 26, —43. First of what promises to be many library fires this month. Library of the Covenant of the Three in Brussels. Contained a wealth of perverse and illegal works: books on Jewish cultural thought, lurid poetry, several books on homosexuality and the mind of the cross-dresser, at least a dozen tomes glorifying deviant behavior. The fire destroyed all.*

Wolff's men carried out books by the armful, depositing them in a pile in front of the library—then the flamethrowers, and the smell. August Wolff had not been raised with a religion. He was a good German lad who did his lessons and loved his mother and his country. He read books. He was taught that words were the rain that watered all things. "That boy will be great someday." They all said it: his teachers, his scoutmasters. The boy with the ugly handwriting would do beautiful things.

The Jester

Aubrion lifted his eyes to the thick-bellied morning clouds. Their snow would pave the dazed and mumbling streets that night. Belgium's homeless would die in it. Rooftop tiles and broken glass ran in the streets like ruined makeup. There was nowhere to shelter from the cold, and the Germans used farmers' wheelbarrows as carts for the dead. Men who had been wounded during the invasion used tree branches and plywood as crutches, too weak to stand; Jews huddled together in doorways; refugees spoke to each other from within torn, colorful rags. But it was always the ordinary people whose faces broke Aubrion's heart. Their clothing wasn't torn, and they looked well-fed, but there was nothing behind their eyes. Aubrion kept crossing the street to avoid them, big groups of them walking together and saying nothing.

Aubrion had not wanted to meet Spiegelman for precisely this reason: the smell of gunmetal like the taste of blood in his throat, the look of the world—it made him feel as though he was in the early stages of a fatal illness and could do nothing but wait for his symptoms to appear. But Spiegelman's telex had insisted he could not stray far from the Nazi outpost in the city. So, here he was.

He walked alongside a canal lined with trees clinging desperately to October. Winter had begun to exhale on their branches, threatening them with snow and ice. Still, the trees blushed their happy orange. Aubrion jumped up to pluck a little red leaf from a branch.

A vagrant with a crooked spine paced in front of a boarded-up butcher shop. Aubrion was fascinated by his feet, elephant-swollen and cracked like the road under them. As Aubrion looked on, the man began to trace shapes in the air, his veiny arms trembling with the task. Laughing, Aubrion wondered if that was how *he* would look when *Faux Soir* was all over, just another madman spinning words out of nothing.

Aubrion arrived at the coffeehouse to find Spiegelman sitting in the back, taking nervous sips from a mug. With a nod of greeting, Aubrion joined him and said, "Quickly, now. It's bad enough that we're talking about this in public at all."

"Agreed," replied Spiegelman. He rubbed at his red eyes with the backs of his hands, like a little boy up past his bedtime.

"What's the matter with you? You look worn to the bone."

Spiegelman stiffened. "Should we get on to business?"

"Fine, fine." Aubrion tilted his chair on its back legs, holding up his hands. "First things first. You got the invitation to Victor?"

"Yes."

"Good. The auction's not for another few days, but I didn't want to delay. Second, Victor, Wellens and Mullier are putting together a curriculum. You should speak to them." Aubrion waved a hand. "Find out what they need."

Spiegelman paused with his mug raised. "A curriculum? For a school?"

"A fake school."

"But is the curriculum real?"

"No, it's also fake."

"What makes it fake?"

Aubrion massaged his forehead. "I suppose the curriculum itself is not technically fake."

"But the school is?"

"Yes."

Spiegelman tilted his head.

"As I said, talk to Victor, Wellens and Mullier."

"Does Mullier talk?"

Aubrion laughed shortly. "Don't interpret that laugh as a compliment. I was mostly surprised you made a joke."

"I've learned to make light of things," said Spiegelman, allowing a smile to escape.

"Don't give yourself that much credit, either." Aubrion waved over the barman and ordered a coffee. "Another for you?" he asked Spiegelman.

"No, thank you."

Aubrion settled back with his mug. "We should begin talking about the content of the paper."

"I agree." Spiegelman leaned in as Aubrion spoke, and there was hunger in his eyes. His hands closed around each new mad scheme like they were the last of his rations. Aubrion reveled in it. That was what he liked best about his work; the men and women of the FI, former shopkeepers and teachers and builders, people with nice furniture and reasonable salaries—they could have done nothing, could've kept their heads down and gone about their business. But they didn't. Those who could have done nothing instead did *everything*. They put their whole selves to work for the cause. So it was with Spiegelman. Every bone and muscle in Spiegelman's body was prepared for this task.

"I want the paper to mimic the tone and layout of *Le Soir*," said Aubrion. "If you're a humble salesman picking up his evening paper on the way home to mama and junior, you won't even notice anything's amiss—until you start reading more closely. Do you know how *Le Soir* always has that obnoxious feature where they report on how the German army is doing? What's it called again?"

"I believe it's called 'How the German Army is Doing.'"

"Something like that, right? Where they go on and on about how the Storm Battalion and the War Hound Battalion marched valiantly in lightning-fast-turtle position or whatever it is, to defeat the Allies in some battle that didn't actually happen."

"I think I know what you're talking about."

"Our *Faux Soir* will have the same sort of thing, you see, except that it will be *zwanze*. We'll have some nonsense about a campaign that didn't really happen."

Spiegelman nodded, though he looked befuddled. "Anything else?"

"I also want photographs of Hitler."

Several coffeehouse patrons turned in awe.

"Whatever for?" Spiegelman whispered.

"Think about it, Herr Spiegelman."

Spiegelman's jaw clenched. "Don't call me that, please."

"But think about it! The people never see photographs of Hitler in *Le Soir*—or in any paper. Do you know who else they never see? God, that's who. Hitler has become this untouchable, unseeable, unbeatable *thing*. If we have a photograph of him, maybe doing something ridiculous, like fleeing from his own army, the people will know he's not a god."

"Is there a photograph of Hitler fleeing from his own army?"

"Why does it matter?"

"It matters because you want one." Aubrion stared at Spiegelman, who added: "Right?"

"Anything can be made to look like anything else. You of all people should know that."

Spiegelman leaned back in his chair as though all the air had been knocked from his chest. "Let me back up a step. There's something that isn't quite right. You and the Germans want the same thing."

"I don't—"

"Let me finish. You want the same thing—to sway public opinion." Aubrion watched Spiegelman's eyes move back and forth across his face, the way one might read a book. "How is *Faux Soir* any different from what the Germans have done with *Le Soir*? Why is one lie more or less ethical than another?"

Aubrion felt his hands curling into fists. "I do not understand the question."

Spiegelman enunciated: "What separates you?"

"You've read Victor's reports from the camps?"

"My family lived it, Monsieur Aubrion." Spiegelman's voice was so low Aubrion could hardly hear him. "I did not need to."

"The Allies have no Auschwitz. That is the difference."

"But you would use *Le Soir* to lie to people, same as the Germans would."

Aubrion poked his finger in Spiegelman's face. "Not the same as the Germans would. The Germans use *Le Soir* to take the people's hope. We will use *Faux Soir* to give it back."

It was all so simple when put that way, and Spiegelman stared at the table, absently flattening his hair with his palm. A pause took shape between the two.

"I will begin looking at past issues of *Le Soir*," Spiegelman said finally. "I'll report back with some ideas."

"Good, good." Aubrion tapped the rim of his mug, oblivious to how irritating it was. "Write up a few columns, if you can. If our plans for production and distribution fall into place as quickly as I want, we need to be ready to typeset and ship out as soon as possible."

"I understand." Spiegelman finished his coffee and got up to leave. He put on a blue fedora that matched his suit. "Until next time, Monsieur Aubrion."

Aubrion, who did not own any fedoras or matching suits, responded: "For the love of God, Herr Spiegelman, try to be funny, will you?"

YESTERDAY

The Scrivener

"YOU'LL WANT TO know what they were feeling for each other," said Helene. "But even now, it is difficult for me to characterize their relationship."

"What do you mean?" said Eliza.

"Let me see." The old woman leaned back in her chair to contemplate. Then: "In some ways, Aubrion and Spiegelman understood each other better than anyone. In other ways, they understood each other not at all. Looking into another man's face and seeing a mirrored version of yourself can be exhilarating, as I saw myself in Aubrion—but it's never really a mirror at all, you see, but a murky pond, with wavering and uncertain shapes. Aubrion had dirt under his fingernails. Spiegelman did not. And yet they seemed to be driven by shared desires, animated by the same hopes. It baffled them both." Helene smiled. "It baffles me even now."

15 DAYS TO PRINT
AS EVENING FELL

The Smuggler

TARCOVICH'S FITFUL SLEEP was interrupted by the jingle of keys. She opened her eyes to see Andree Grandjean opening the door of her cell. The judge was nearly unrecognizable without her wig and robes, her auburn curls coming down in fits across her shoulders. Grandjean put her hands in her pockets.

"Come to execute me yourself?" Tarcovich said dryly. It was not the best quip, but she was half-asleep, so she forgave herself. She threw her legs over the side of her bunk. The green trousers and work shirt suited the judge, holding her softest places in firm, gentle hands. The quirk in her lips betrayed an amusement that—Tarcovich was unhappy to admit it—reminded her of Marc Aubrion. But Grandjean shared none of Aubrion's smugness; hers was an easy, well-worn smile. Only Grandjean's hair felt improbable: childish curls making up their own minds about where they would fall and where they wouldn't.

Grandjean stood to one side of the cell, beckoning Tarcovich toward the entrance. Her every movement was strictly economical. "Are you going to ask to approach the bench again?" The judge's eyes brightened.

"Very amusing." Tarcovich felt her attention slipping, landing somewhere in this woman's curls. She knew she must be imagining it, the slight twist of Grandjean's lips, teasing her—flirting with her? Knowing the truth was impossible, even dangerous. Tarcovich had lost count of the miscalculations she'd made over the years, women whose friendliness she had mistaken for something else, and then angry suitors, strange run-ins with police.

"The FI is a blunt instrument, Lada," Grandjean said. "You drive cars into poultry markets. I prefer to work with a bit more finesse." The judge smiled. She had a small gap between her front teeth. "The way you and the FI do things is a crime, but I'm not going to be the one to punish you."

"How comforting. You should read bedtime stories to children for a living."

And then, like the last trick in a magic show, Grandjean's smile disappeared. "I would if there were any bedtime stories left to read. Now, please leave. Your superiors will want to know that it didn't work."

"It didn't work." We looked up, startled to see Tarcovich back at the FI base so soon. Sinking into a chair, she pulled off her scarf and tossed it onto a nearby typewriter. I'd been helping René Noël fix one of the printing presses in the basement of the FI headquarters, and at his nod, I fetched Tarcovich a glass of brandy. "We will have to try something else."

"So we're to understand," said Mullier, his voice low and dangerous, "that she let you out with no questions at all?" The last part of his sentence dissolved into an exhalation.

"I don't know. What do you want from me, Mullier? I did not ask, but she obviously had her people check up on me." Tarcovich drained her glass. She put it down, rubbed her swollen eyes. I could see, and everyone else could see, that Tarcovich was exhausted. "I know it's hard for you, but be smart. This is a woman with countless resources. If she had any reason to suspect I might be with the Germans, I would be decomposing right now."

"Damn." Aubrion got up from his perch at the table, picking up a broken piece of chalk. He rolled it around, a misshapen tooth in his hand. Though it was early in the evening, and I could still hear people typing and yelling to each other upstairs, we were worn out, wound up. The tension made me shift in my seat. Aubrion said, "Did you find anything on her, Victor?"

"Grandjean? Nothing." Victor flipped through his notebook like a magician showing his hand of cards after a trick that didn't work. Above us, a lightbulb flickered and went out.

"I thought we replaced that," said Aubrion.

"With what budget?" Noël retorted.

Victor wiped his glasses on his coat. "We will have to start exploring other avenues to raise money. That is my recommendation. Whatever Grandjean is engaged in, she's doing a masterful job keeping it secret—or she's not actually engaged in anything. I had a colleague before the war who studied the contexts in which people feel compelled to keep secrets. There's a paper on it, if any of you'd like to read it."

"I'm sure we're all clamoring for a copy," said Tarcovich.

I sat up straight, a rare occurrence for me. "Um, monsieur?"

Everyone looked at me. I blushed at the attention. I was conscious of their irritation at having been interrupted—except for Aubrion, of course, who addressed me the way he would've addressed anyone.

"Yes, Gamin?" he said.

"Are you talking about Judge Andree Grandjean?"

Aubrion's brow furrowed. "We are. Why?"

"Well, monsieur, I was just thinking—you were talking about the stuff she's doing, you see, and vulner—vulnerability—"

Aubrion pointed at me with his chalk. "Do you know something?"

"It's just—there's some talk—she's been helping the odd ones get out of Belgium."

"The odd ones?"

My blush deepened. "You know." I glanced at Tarcovich, regretting it immediately.

Aubrion put down his chalk and climbed back onto the table. He sat back, looked up in thought, then started to laugh the way he did when he had an idea. The laugh possessed him, taking over his body like a fever. "Oh, God. The fates are so kind."

"I am lost," said Mullier.

"Elaborate?" said Victor.

"She helps the queers," I whispered.

"We can hear, you know," Tarcovich said dryly.

"Do you happen to know whether she is one herself?" asked Aubrion.

"A queer? Everyone assumes so, monsieur."

With my words, I had a child's sense that I had done something wrong, and this was jarring, for I had not felt like a child in some time. An apology formed on my lips, never quite materializing. A crushing desire to expose my secret filled me up until I was bursting with it.

"It's so perfect." Standing up, Aubrion went to write something on the blackboard, then seemed to realize he didn't know what to write. "Isn't it? It is so perfect."

"Some of us do not understand why it's so perfect, Marc," said Noël.

"It means Lada can try again."

"Well, I think I am going to retire for the night." Tarcovich stood up, off-balance. She looked around with prisoner eyes as though she needed to get outside, desperate to go somewhere that wasn't here. "Good night, all."

"Lada—"

"Yes, Marc?"

"I just—"

"Do not start any sentences with 'I just' right now," said Tarcovich, furious with sorrow, folded up between her duty and her desires, a flower pressed into a book but left there too long. "I can assure you they aren't appropriate. I'm finished."

"With the job?"

"With this part of the job. Find some other way to get your funds."

Aubrion looked puzzled. "Are you upset?"

"Oh, Marc." Tarcovich's eyes had turned to glass, and she laughed. Shaking her head, she walked over to Aubrion and kissed his cheek. "I love you. I know you do not understand what you're asking me to do, so I'm giving you the benefit of the doubt. Please don't make me regret that."

"You have a chance to help us," said Aubrion.

"Marc, let it go," warned Noël.

"You do *not understand!*" The sentence started out innocently enough, but broke halfway through, splintering into a shriek. Tarcovich struggled to collect its ashes. "You can't be arrested and executed for what you are, Marc."

"Of course I can. They'd kill me for being part of the FI—"

"You weren't *born* a part of the FI! I was born to be arrested and executed, don't you see? They are putting the Jews on trains to death camps, for God's sake, and even being a Jew is better than being what I am. At least the Jews have each other, a community, a people. They have someone to hold hands with as they're led off to die. What do I have?"

"You—"

"If you wanted to go out and fuck someone tonight, Aubrion, if you felt like having someone's skin against yours one more time before we're all executed for this farce, you could do that. A Jew could do that. Gamin is a child and *he* could do that." I blushed, praying to disappear. "But could I? Could I ever?"

Tarcovich stopped only because she ran out of breath. Gasping, breathless in the stale air and the *click-click-click* of fresh words, she crumpled in her chair.

I have stored this memory in my pocket for decades. The words that passed between Tarcovich and Aubrion have always stayed the same, but their meanings have sharpened as I have aged. To love is to brave something uncharted; I have never had such courage, so I cannot comprehend how delicate it must be to love, or how beautiful, like watching the sun set fire to the stained-glass windows of an old church. And for Lada, it was different, because every act of love was a decision and a risk: whether to touch her lover's hand in public, whether her whispers brought her too close to the woman's ear, whether to allow herself those feelings in the first place. To make such decisions at *all* must have felt impossible, much less in the face of her own death. I'd never seen Lada Tarcovich cry; it was clear she didn't want us to see her cry then. But we are no match for ourselves, I've learned, so she put her face in her hands, her shoulders trembling.

Our sudden quiet accentuated the noises of the room: the hum of the lightbulbs, the typewriters overhead, someone upstairs shouting about an idea they'd just had, a leaky pipe gurgling behind the stone walls. The resistance breathed around us.

When Aubrion broke the silence, it startled everyone. "You have a chance to turn this into something good."

Tarcovich looked up, her face and eyes wretched with sorrow. "It is something good, to me." She clutched her chest. "That's what I am saying. You want me to use it as a deception, a weapon."

"All right, all right." René Noël stood between Aubrion and Tarcovich with his hands raised. "It is late. We're all overwhelmed. Let's adjourn this meeting and think things over for a while, eh? What do you say, Marc? Lada?" Marc nodded; Lada did not. "All right, then! Everyone out. Go on, go on." Noël shooed us from the basement like a put-upon mother. "Let's all get some sleep, shall we?"

We left the basement, all of us except Tarcovich. I remember so clearly that I was sad and afraid, though I could not articulate why; I could feel that the others were, too. So we let Noël herd us along, treating us like children. At that moment, I think, it was a welcome change.

14 DAYS TO PRINT
SHORTLY BEFORE DAWN

The Dybbuk

WOLFF SAW MOST clearly with the lights off. He lay flat on the wooden floor of his office with his head pillowed by a stack of books, letting the dark wash the sting of yesterday's fire from his eyes. Smoke from the print factory still clung to his hair. His watch ticked. Breathing slowly, the *Gruppenführer* slid the watch from his arm, then rubbed his wrist like a prisoner freed from his manacles. His mouth tasted of ash; he would never be rid of it. Upon returning to the base, Wolff had drunk whiskey, sherry, water, beer, anything to cleanse the black chalk from his throat, filling himself until he was ill. But it lingered. Each time he inhaled, the taste of books accused him of murder.

The *Gruppenführer* welcomed the discomfort, breathing through the ache in his bones on the floor. It shielded him from his thoughts. *To be thoughtless is to be caught off balance*, he wrote in his memos that morning. But he wanted the world to tilt a little, to let him slide where he pleased. The neat rows of paperwork and black boots—the neat piles of jewelry after the executions—had begun to tire him.

Spiegelman, who never knocked, opened the door without preamble. He switched on a light. The *Gruppenführer* rolled over and shielded his eyes.

"You sent for me," said Spiegelman. He paused, then said, "Are you quite all right?"

"I did. I am." Still rubbing his eyes, Wolff stood on shaky legs and ambled over to his desk. He released his body into his chair. "I wanted to speak with you. Do you know the last recorded incident of a member of the *Schutzstaffel* lodging a complaint with the Party?"

"I'm sorry?"

"Do you know—"

"I believe that's something you should ask Manning."

The spots cleared from Wolff's vision. Spiegelman was standing near the doorway, his arms close to his body, his back stiff. Wolff never liked how the man walked, his gait crooked with guilt. It made Wolff feel as though he too had sinned.

Wolff gestured at the chair across from him. "Please, have a seat."

"I'd prefer to stand."

"Very well." He held out his hands. "How long since the last complaint? Surely you can guess."

"I don't know. Four months ago? Six?"

"It was three years ago. *Obergruppenführer* Wilhelm Hausser was leading one of the, ah, the death squads." The name always seemed unnecessarily vulgar to Wolff. "He complained that his soldiers were committing suicide after being ordered to fire on Jewish women and children. Do you know what he was told? To outlaw suicide."

Spiegelman flinched. "Do you have an assignment for me, *Gruppenführer*?"

"It is not that people don't have complaints, you see. Just that we do not complain."

"*Gruppenführer,* I do not think it's appropriate for me to—"

"Please do not talk." Wolff was surprised at the desperation in his voice. "Listen to me."

"Fine," Spiegelman said cautiously. Keeping his eyes on Wolff, he sat down.

A headache was blossoming behind Wolff's eyes. The *Gruppenführer* wanted nothing more than to switch off the lights again. His own words felt slippery, greased with hidden meanings he could not detect.

"Not many people know what Heinrich Himmler studied as a young man at the *Technische Hochschule,*" he said. "I can't quite remember whether it's classified information, but I believe it is. Himmler studied agronomy."

"Plants?"

"Yes."

"He is nothing but a glorified farmer?" Horror spread across Spiegelman's face. "I beg your pardon, I did not—"

Wolff didn't address the slight. "While it is true that he studied plants, what is more important is *how* he did so. Himmler was interested in how we might use biology and physiology to breed superior crops. He became obsessed with the idea of engineering perfection. We destroy what we consider imperfect. It is true for people, and for print factories."

"That's what this is about?" Spiegelman leaned forward, his lips white. Wolff noticed a carnation in his breast pocket. He wondered where a man might buy a carnation during wartime. "You plan to lodge a complaint with Himmler about your orders to destroy rebel print factories?"

"Is that so unthinkable to you?"

"Of the two things you just mentioned, print factories are what you've decided to complain about?"

"Arguably, we can't repurpose people—not *most* people—but we can repurpose—"

"*Gruppenführer,* I cannot listen to this." Spiegelman was trembling. "Do you hear what you're saying to me? Have you forgotten who and what I am?"

"Never. Not for an instant."

"Then why did you bring me here? To torture me with this discussion?"

"Why do you think I've chosen to confide in *you*? You have no voice, Spiegelman." The words were not meant to be unkind; Wolff spoke matter-of-factly. "Regardless of what you could say, no one would believe you. You would be executed for my treason."

"Are you committing treason?"

Manning put his head in the room. Wolff's heart jumped, for there was no doubt Manning had heard part of the conversation. The officer next door to Wolff had been carried away last night, stoic and righteous to the last, and it was always men like Manning who made the call, bureaucrats with trimmed nails.

"*Gruppenführer,*" Manning said, "with respect, *Reichsführer* Himmler is waiting."

"We will continue this conversation at a later date," Wolff said to Spiegelman. His face wrinkled into a bitter smile, a sheet of paper that had been marred and scratched before its time. "*Reichsführer* Himmler is waiting."

The Gastromancer

When David Spiegelman first heard about Heinrich Himmler as a young boy, he laughed in his brother's face. "Even if he were real," Spiegelman said, "which he's not, because people like that don't exist outside of your comic books—"

"I don't read those comic books anymore. And Grandmother

told me about him." Abraham curled in on himself as he said this bit, hesitant to cite an authority like Grandmother.

"Grandmother doesn't know everything," said David Spiegelman.

"She knows most things."

"Even if Heimler were real—"

"Himmler."

"—how could he hope to exterminate an entire race? You can't fear that, Abraham. It's like fearing a Martian invasion. You're good at mathematics." David Spiegelman had mussed his brother's hair, a tad too roughly. "So, tell me. What are the odds?"

It was this conversation that convinced David Spiegelman, a devout unbeliever, that hell must exist. He'd been dragged in to meet Himmler three times since he'd been pressed into service for Wolff, and each time, he remembered. *Even if he were real,* his younger self sang, *which he's not, which he's not, which he's not.* And then, his brother's voice, high and delicate: *Grandmother told me about him.*

"Did Himmler say why he wanted me to come?" Spiegelman whispered to Wolff, who walked with him, behind Herr Manning.

"No. Simply that he wanted you to be present, as well."

Spiegelman slowed his pace to walk behind August Wolff. Regardless of how far apart they stood, Spiegelman always felt as though Wolff were too close to him, that he was constantly thrashing against the current of Wolff's presence. "The *dybbuk* lives just beneath your skin," his grandmother had said, "thinking your thoughts, dreaming your dreams."

Manning led Wolff and Spiegelman into a prim conference room. Spiegelman always expected so much more black and red than there was, but Himmler made up his surroundings to look like a corporate office. Indeed, an observer might have referred to the conference room as *businesslike* or even *boring* but never *sinister*: just a long table, straight-backed chairs, a moat of filing cabinets. Aides carried clipboards and paperwork here and there.

Spiegelman took a seat next to the *Gruppenführer*, who nodded at the bureaucrats and commanders already installed at the table. Himmler was cleaning his rimless spectacles at the head of the table, and Spiegelman was struck, as usual, by how young he looked. His face was pleasant, which is to say that it was unremarkable: unlined, pale, with dark blue eyes that blinked searchingly from behind his lenses. Spiegelman watched as Himmler patted down his close-cut hair and opened the file in front of him. Licking his fingertips, Himmler pulled a document from the file, scanned it, then ripped it in half, a wet, predatory noise that seemed to wrench the room in two. Himmler went on like that for an eternity, licking, pulling, scanning and ripping—placing each dismembered page in a pile.

"Shall we get started?" said Himmler, his words colored by a polite Bavarian accent. He did not smile, but he did not need to; the accent smiled for him. "As you all know, I am here to ensure the continued progress of our newly founded Ministry of Perception Management. First, I wish to thank all of you for the work you do here. Managing public perception is an integral part of our broader mission—to ensure the health and happiness of decent working people throughout the state.

"But, of course, this ministry is still young." Himmler paused, looking at each of them in turn. Spiegelman forced himself to hold Himmler's gaze. This was just a man. He was a powerful, evil, foul man that burned what he didn't know; still, he was just a man. God knew Spiegelman could look at another man. "Much remains to be perfected. So, if anyone among you sees something wrong, or inefficient, let him come to me. Let him speak to me personally. I welcome new ideas and am only too glad to correct mistakes." Himmler put a hand on his heart like he was swearing an oath. "Now, in the spirit of new ideas, does anyone wish to open our meeting with a thought?"

"With respect, *Reichsführer*," said August Wolff, so much quieter than Spiegelman had ever heard him, "there is a matter I wish to discuss."

"Please, by all means, *Gruppenführer*, ah—"

"August Wolff," Wolff said stiffly.

"Wolff, yes. You were recently promoted."

"By the grace of the *Führer*."

"What would you like to discuss?"

"*Reichsführer*, over the past two months, my men and I have made remarkable strides in seizing rebel print factories. No doubt you are aware of the harm these newspapers can inflict on our people, and of their disturbing popularity."

"No doubt," said Himmler, and each word was a land mine below the feet of August Wolff. Spiegelman felt viscerally conscious of the man's restrained, persistent energy, like the pressure of a needle about to break through the skin. The man's face looked like Spiegelman's natural handwriting: plain, with no distinguishable characteristics, prepared to be molded into anything.

Wolff went on. "However, *Reichsführer*, many of these newspapers represent extraordinary feats of ingenuity, both literary and technological. The factories themselves are often impeccably organized, while the papers are creative and well written. In fact, the Ministry of Perception Management has begun to explore the possibility of imitating some of the rebels' endeavors. The *La Libre Belgique* project that you approved is a recent example."

"What is your point, Wolff?" asked a man at the table who Spiegelman didn't recognize, another *Gruppenführer*.

"It is our policy," Wolff said, selecting his words with care, "to destroy rebel factories once we discover them."

"To cleanse them," said Himmler. "We do what has always been done in the face of plague. We burn away the sores."

"I understand, of course. But, with respect, *Reichsführer*, it is my belief that we are wasting what could possibly be a valuable resource. To borrow your analogy, instead of burning them, we need only to drain the sores, and then to—"

"I am going to interrupt you, *Gruppenführer*," said Himmler, "to ask the identity of the man on your left."

All eyes turned to Spiegelman; historically, this state of affairs had not been good for him or his people. His shirt was sticking to his back. Spiegelman felt ashamed at his own fear. This was how it went, he thought, how they burned away your dignity until there was nothing left.

Wolff inhaled. "His name is David Spiegelman."

The others did not murmur, dared not murmur in Himmler's presence, but their silence was almost too loud for Spiegelman to bear.

"He is one of your aides?" asked Himmler.

"Yes, *Reichsführer*."

"May I ask how Herr Spiegelman came to work for you, *Gruppenführer*?"

"He is renowned throughout Belgium for his skill as a linguistic ventriloquist."

Himmler's eyes flickered with recognition. A nauseous tingle spread through Spiegelman's stomach and face. This creature had heard of him, had possibly even admired his work. Spiegelman rebelled at the idea that he'd spent even a *second* in Himmler's thoughts. "So he is the one who writes the letters," said Himmler.

"He is."

"But he is a Jew."

"Clearly, *Reichsführer*." Wolff's tone inched a tad too close to mockery. Spiegelman felt his pulse in every pore.

"Were you aware of this when you took him on?"

"Yes, *Reichsführer*."

"But you were also aware of our policies concerning the Jewish race?"

"Of course."

"We have these policies for a reason, Wolff." Himmler took on the tone of a lecturing parent. "Only a week ago, I read a heart-breaking report of a Jewish man—a homosexual, actually—who raped a young woman and her brother. Who knows what drives them do to these things? Witnesses say he went into some kind of frenzy. It's horrible to think of it. I've since seen pictures of the siblings—beautiful, beautiful people. The man could have been my own brother. The woman could have been your sister or your wife, Wolff.

"What we want is simple—the safety and happiness of our people. The Jewish race poses a danger to our way of life. They are an infection, and to take them into our ranks is to allow that infection to spread."

Spiegelman became aware that he was breathing too quickly. Did Himmler know he was a homosexual? Did it matter? Himmler's hatred for the homosexuals was legendary, almost pathological. Two guards stood at the exit ahead of him, and there were at least two additional guards at the exit behind him. In other words, if Heinrich Himmler ordered him executed on the spot, he would be executed on the spot. *Forgive me, Abraham*, he thought.

"But, you represent the best of the Fatherland." Himmler gestured around the table. Spiegelman felt, somehow, that Himmler's gesture did not include him. "I trust you to do what you feel is right for us."

Wolff paled. "Thank you, *Reichsführer.*"

"No, no, thank you. However, I must warn you that your proclivity for choosing imitation over destruction can only take you so far. For example, *La Libre Belgique*. That is a project that balances imitation and destruction. That is why I approved it." Himmler paused so Wolff could say:

"And I must thank you again for doing so." The resentment in his voice was far too palpable.

Himmler waved away Wolff's thanks. In doing so, he knocked

over half the pile of ripped-up paper, sending it fluttering in inky snowflakes to the floor. "You may keep your Jew to help you as you see fit. As I mentioned, I've heard of his work and am aware that he has his uses. But do not allow this proclivity to define everything you do. Is that understood, *Gruppenführer?*"

"It is understood."

"Your mission is to stamp out rebellion in Belgium, not to celebrate it. Burn the factories, August Wolff." Himmler leaned back as though satisfied after a large meal. "Now, what is the next item on our agenda?"

14 DAYS TO PRINT
FIRST HOURS OF MORNING

The Pyromaniac

MORNING CAME QUIETLY, its hands raised for surrender. I'd slept in the FI basement that night, as I did most nights. I rose without speaking; so did Aubrion, who'd slept nearby, and Noël, who set up a cot upstairs. As I've mentioned, our base was housed in an abandoned meatpacking factory, so it wasn't designed for the comforts of men. We slept where we could, then went about our rituals: weak tea, stale toast, washed faces.

When Victor came in, I was watching Aubrion teeter on the edge of electrocution. He was standing on a chair, trying to repair the burned-out lightbulb in the basement with copper wire, pliers, a pocketknife and a candy bar wrapper; I don't think any writer could have come up with a keener metaphor for the *Faux Soir* endeavor. Martin Victor looked up at Aubrion and started to speak.

"Shit!" said Aubrion as an electric crackle whipped the air. He jerked his fingers away from the bulb, shoving them in his mouth. Victor tossed Aubrion a file. Aubrion barely caught it.

He took his fingers out of his mouth and read: *"Schule für die Erziehung von Kindern mit ewige Liebe?"*

"That's correct," said Victor.

"But what is it?"

"The name of our fake school."

Ferdinand Wellens descended the staircase into the FI basement, bellowing: "School for the Education of Children with Undying Devotion!" He launched the word *devotion* like an ungainly missile.

Clinging to the chair, Aubrion looked at Victor, who said: "It was Wellens's idea."

"I could tell. Undying devotion to what?"

"The school, presumably."

"Isn't that tautological?"

"Devotion to Hitler," said Wellens, pronouncing it *Hit-lah*, the way Churchill did. Wellens was dressed, improbably enough, in a suit that appeared to have at least three lapels. "That shouldn't be too hard to sell, eh?"

"We'll see about that," grunted Mullier. He took an apple from the pocket of his ink-stained coat, rolling it around on a table. I still wonder how Mullier had managed to procure so many fresh apples in a country that hadn't seen an apple farmer in three years.

"Where's Lada?" said Aubrion.

"She said she's not coming today, monsieur," I said.

"She told you that?"

"This morning."

"Christ. If I hadn't—"

"Leave it, Aubrion," said René Noël, who took a seat under one of the room's ubiquitous chalkboards.

"What about Spiegelman?" said Aubrion.

"There was no telex from him this morning, monsieur," I said.

"Is everyone planning on being fashionably late today?"

"Maybe if you provided coffee and pastries, people might

look forward to the occasion," Wellens said through his mustache. "I always provide coffee and pastries at my meetings. It's just good business."

"With what budget?" muttered Noël.

"Gamin, erase the board, would you?" said Aubrion.

"Certainly, monsieur." I set about my duties.

"Let's start with the Nazi school project." Aubrion pointed a piece of chalk at Theo Mullier. "What do you have to report?"

"Talk to Victor," said Mullier.

"Victor? What's the news on that?"

"I have assisted Mullier and Wellens in the creation of a curriculum for Nazi schoolchildren. It is based on three principles: loyalty, devotion and commitment."

"How are those any different from each other?" asked Aubrion.

"They're not," said Mullier.

"I was surprised to find," said Victor, "that most Nazi schools have redundant mottos. That says something about the nature of Nazi education, don't you think? There was joy, laughter, happiness, um, future, growth, destiny—"

"This is all very interesting, compelling, fascinating," said Aubrion, "but what else have you done?"

"The curriculum is organized by week, with a total of forty-three weeks." Victor held up a sheet of paper outlining the curriculum. "Each week has a theme. The theme of the first week is discarding the past, the second week is looking toward the future, the third week is devotion to the Reich, the fourth week is—"

"Well, if nothing else, you'll bore them into submission," interruped Aubrion.

"It's all very convincing," Wellens said, unconvincingly. "We plan to pitch our school to the Ministry of Education thusly: I shall act as the director of the school and present our vision,

Victor will present the curriculum, we'll have two people acting as instructors—"

"We're thinking Tarcovich and Spiegelman," said Mullier.

"Won't the Ministry know Spiegelman by looking at him?"
asked Aubrion.

Victor shook his head. "The ministries of the Nazi government are very insular. They hardly ever communicate with each
other. Certainly, anyone at the Ministry of Perception Management would know Spiegelman, but Education? It's highly improbable."

Mullier held up a finger. "I don't trust Spiegelman to do this."

"Why not?" asked Aubrion.

"He's working with the Germans."

"Was."

"He's not here now, is he?"

"He can't be here whenever we want him here. We don't
have any reason not to trust him. Until we do, I'm not going
to hear any more about it." Aubrion tapped his fingers on the
chalkboard. "Monsieur Wellens? Anything to add?"

Wellens said, "We will need Gamin to play our pupil." He was
pacing, turning on his polished heels every time he reached the
end of the room. "And we'll need props. Investors love props."

"What sort of props?" asked Aubrion.

"Obviously, the purpose of this exercise is to convince the
Ministry that we need paper and ink," said Victor, "but no pro-
spective school would ever go to the Ministry with nothing in
hand. We will need about a hundred fake textbooks."

"A hundred?" sputtered Noël.

Victor said, "They need not have anything in them. A hundred agricultural manuals covered in swastikas and made to look
like textbooks would be fine."

"Of course they'd be fine," said Noël, "if we could get our
hands on a hundred agricultural manuals."

"Bibles?" said Mullier.

"Perhaps pulp novels," said Victor. "My point is that if it's in print, it shall work."

"But there isn't a hundred of anything," Aubrion said softly, like he was reading a eulogy. "Not in print, and not in Europe. They've burned it all."

"That's not true." We all looked up to find Lada Tarcovich at the bottom of the stairs, unwrapping her bright blue scarf. "They didn't burn the pornography."

"I thought you weren't coming," Aubrion said, the end of his sentence slightly truncated when he realized what she'd said.

"So did I." Tarcovich took a seat apart from the others. And then she said, with the tone of someone reciting a grocery list, "When I'm not smuggling things out of the country or into politicians' trousers, I write erotic stories about the Americans. Some of them have been published. It was how I've been able to afford an apartment all these years. I am not, as my clients would attest, a very good prostitute—but I do have a finger on the *throbbing* pulse of the Belgian pornography market."

Aubrion was not quite sure how to respond, and neither was anyone else. I remember my cheeks burning far hotter than any of the fires I'd started.

"If you wanted them," added Lada, "you could have a hundred pornographic novels on your desk by tomorrow evening."

"What would it cost?" asked Aubrion.

"Only your dignity."

"Sold. Wellens—" Aubrion turned to the salesman "—have you been working on your sales pitch?"

Wellens drew himself up to his height. He was shorter than Aubrion, who was barely taller than me. "I have."

"Let's hear it."

Mullier crunched on an apple, a testy period at the end of Aubrion's request.

"Gentlemen of the Ministry, have you ever wondered what it would be like to be educated at a school that emphasized loyalty, devotion, erm, uh, loyalty, and commitment? Well, wonder no longer. Today, on this momentous day, we present to you—um—erm—"

"You don't remember the name of the school you invented?" groaned Aubrion.

The businessman was indignant. "Well, do you?"

Victor recited, *"Schule für die Erziehung von Kindern mit ewige Liebe."*

"Schule für die, erm—die Kindern mit ewige Liebe die Erziehung," said Wellens.

"Close enough," said Aubrion.

Wellens stood before the chalkboard with the posture of a marble statue. "Gentlemen, our mission is public enlightenment, and our method is to enlighten the public. Through our award-winning curriculum—"

"Don't say 'award-winning,'" said Aubrion.

"They'll ask which awards we won," explained Victor.

"—we forge the minds of the youth in the furnace of our classrooms." Wellens smiled. "Indeed, gentlemen, the Nazi aim is a noble one—"

"What on earth," said Spiegelman, who had arrived unnoticed, and who blinked at us from the bottom of the stairs, "did I miss?"

"Not as much as he did," muttered Tarcovich.

Aubrion said, "Monsieur Wellens, a little more practice never hurt anyone, isn't that right?"

"Of course, of course."

"Have we set a date to meet with the Ministry?"

"The third," said Victor.

"Of November?" said Aubrion. "Christ, that's five days from today."

"Four," said Tarcovich.

"That's four days from today!"

"Do you want *Faux Soir* to be finished before the eleventh of November, or don't you?" said Victor.

"Fair, fair, but—for God's sake, coach him a little, won't you, Martin?"

"I will do my best."

"Spiegelman." Aubrion turned to Spiegelman, now seated on a low stool, rubbing his eyes. His hair, normally so neat, stood up in protesting curls. "Have you started working on the content of *Faux Soir*?"

"I've finished the first draft of a column."

"Just one?"

"I was delayed last night." Spiegelman's eyes, which I remember as auburn and unnaturally bright, were a shade too dull this morning. He looked like a shell of himself, a bony ghost that had been forced into Spiegelman's tailored suit. "A meeting went on too long."

"What meeting?" said Mullier.

Spiegelman made an empty gesture. "A meeting."

"Who with?"

For a long instant, Spiegelman did not say anything. Then he lifted his head, exposing us to his pale, unshaven face and the twin hollows beneath his eyes. His eyes were red; they reminded me of an image from my past, from Toulouse, of dead animals the Nazis left in the wake of their tanks. "Himmler," said Spiegelman finally.

"Oh, God." Noël lifted his eyes in prayer.

"You met with Heinrich Himmler?" said Aubrion.

"I didn't have a choice."

I saw Mullier's hands curl into fists, calloused from decades in the bodies of printing presses. "Ask for an autograph, did you?" he grunted.

Spiegelman was up and in Mullier's face more quickly than I believed possible. "Fuck you," he snarled.

"You would, now, wouldn't you?"

David Spiegelman, who I didn't think capable of violence, seized Mullier's collar. Mullier swatted his hand away, then shoved Spiegelman to the floor.

"Theo!" said Tarcovich, and "God's sake!" cried Noël.

Aubrion and I ran to help Spiegelman to his feet. "I'm fine, I'm fine," he kept saying, leaning on me for support, but he was trying not to weep, jaw clenched against the pain. This moment comes to me often. It is strange, isn't it? Nothing happened; this was a minor incident, a footnote in something far greater. But think of it. Many people blamed the war for the terrible things they did, as if the war were a ringmaster leading us through a show—but I have never held the war responsible for the blood I spilled, or the friends I lost. I am responsible and no other. When the burden of my accountability becomes too great, though, I think of the time I rushed to help David Spiegelman. No one asked me to do it. It was an instinct. My instinct was to help, not to hurt.

When Spiegelman was steady again, Mullier advanced on him with raised fists.

"Stop it," snapped Tarcovich, getting between them. "Theo, don't be an animal."

"He's one of *them*."

"Don't be a child, either," said Noël.

"Fuck you," Spiegelman repeated through tears. "I do what I do because I have to."

"It's all right, David." Aubrion squeezed his shoulder.

"It's not."

"It's all right. Really. You do not have to justify anything. We've all made our choices."

Spiegelman shook Aubrion off him. "Clearly I do." He sat— collapsed—on the floor.

Tarcovich knelt by Spiegelman. He started to sit up, but she rested a hand on his stomach and whispered something in his ear. "Yes," he said. "Yes." We all watched as his eyes fluttered closed, a smile rising up to meet them.

I have long speculated on what Lada Tarcovich said to him. But the words are unknowable and unimportant. Only their quiet exchange of compassion matters for this story. Tarcovich's gift was for Spiegelman, not for me. All I can do is tug on the ribbons in wonder.

14 DAYS TO PRINT
AFTERNOON

The Smuggler

EARLIER THAT MORNING, Lada Tarcovich had made
an agreement with herself. She would visit Andree Grandjean
again on two conditions: first, Lada would not tell Marc Aubrion where she had gone until she damn well felt like it, and
second, Lada would not bring up the *Front de l'Indépendance* unless Grandjean did first. The problem with that second condi-
tion, though, was that it invited the question of why Lada was
visiting Andree at all if not to talk about *Faux Soir* and the FI's
need for funding. But Lada rarely concerned herself with why.
"'Why'," she often said, "is a bookmark that keeps falling out
of the novel."

According to Martin Victor, who had been observing Grandjean's activities, the judge received a delivery of wine every Saturday at one o'clock; Grandjean was known for getting people
to do what she wanted, and a lot of that involved getting them
drunk. Lada watched, eight blocks away from Grandjean's courthouse, as men from the Wouters Wine Distribution Company

loaded open crates of wine into a horse-drawn carriage. The men handled them easily, tossing the crates from hand to hand without regard for their contents.

Tarcovich kept her distance, walking past the factories and workshops on the outskirts of Enghien's industrial district. Sawdust crackled beneath her shoes. Dozens of empty apartments had been hollowed out and repurposed since the start of the war, their colorful awnings replaced with Nazi flags. Through the windows and wide-mouthed doors, Tarcovich saw people at work over sawhorses and benches, using whatever materials they could find. Metal was scarce, of course, as was wood. Everyone used tools that had belonged to someone else, probably someone who had died in the war. Snow flurries fell like a gentle veil around the shops.

The men of Wouters Wine Distribution Company took a break, an activity that largely involved telling foul jokes and urinating on a footpath. When that was done, they walked over to a metalworker's shop down the main road. Tarcovich ducked behind a stack of barrels that reeked of sulfur. The men chatted with their friends—two of them, a short man with a bent back, and a blunt-faced fellow. Quickly, while they were distracted, Lada darted over to the carriage.

Her heart thudding, Lada Tarcovich examined the crates of wine sitting beside the carriage. They were open, but covered in tarp. She threw aside the tarp to unpack one of the larger crates, stashing wine bottles behind a bush. With one last glance at the men to make sure they were occupied, Tarcovich climbed into the crate, covering her body in a greasy cloth.

She remained like that for a while, breathing grease and old grapes. When she finally heard the men's chatter, Lada held her breath, sweating with the effort it took to remain still.

"Wouters is an arse," she heard one of them say—and then she was lifted into the air. She bit her tongue to keep from crying out in surprise, tasting iron. "He thinks he can marry off that daughter of his?"

There was a brief sensation of weightlessness— "I once had a cow with a prettier face than hers," said the second man—and Tarcovich's crate hit the bottom of the carriage. She bounced, clutching at the tarp, then settled back into the wood with a coccyx-shattering *thunk*.

For all her foresight, Tarcovich had not planned on what to say when, a few hours later, Andree Grandjean unpacked one of the crates delivered to her office to find it stuffed with a failed, partially suffocated prostitute. And so Lada settled on: "Hello."

Grandjean, for her part, settled on: "Jesus fucking Christ!" She drew a pistol from somewhere, leveling it at Tarcovich. "Don't move."

"I don't think I can," said Tarcovich, who was still crumpled up in the crate. "My legs fell asleep three hours ago."

"I told you not to come back here."

"I'll admit I don't know you very well, but I have a feeling neither of us is particularly good at following directions." Bracing herself on the sides of the crate, Tarcovich tried to stand.

"Don't move, Lada." Grandjean cocked the pistol. "I have shot people before."

"We are in the middle of a world war. Shooting people is not as unique as it once was." Perhaps it was three hours of airlessness, but Tarcovich was flattered that Grandjean remembered her name. The judge was dressed in navy trousers and a tight shirt, and the color of her eyes deepened with fury; they matched the snow-riddled sky. Standing slowly, Tarcovich held up her hands. "What can I do to persuade you I mean no harm?"

"The opposite of everything you are doing now." Grandjean's hands were shaking. It was becoming increasingly apparent that she had never shot anyone before.

"Oh. Apologies."

"Why on earth did you come back?"

"May I step out of the crate?"

"Answer my question."

"Answer mine."

"No. Fine. Yes." Grandjean stepped back, her grip on the pistol wavering. "But do it slowly."

Her hands still raised, Tarcovich lifted one foot and then the other, easing herself out of the crate. Her right foot felt smashed, her back felt bruised, both her hands felt swollen, and her left leg no longer felt anything at all.

"Why did you come back?" Grandjean repeated.

"I wanted to approach the bench again."

"What?"

"I had a question."

"What about?"

"About why you've taken such an interest in the queers."

Grandjean's eyes widened. Tarcovich searched their depths for meaning. "I freed you last time," said Grandjean. "I can't do it again, do you understand? You'll have to remain in prison. It's your own doing."

"Are you one?" said Tarcovich, hardly able to believe she'd said it. The air around Tarcovich and Grandjean seemed to glow, the currents of something new humming between them.

"Am I one what?"

"A queer."

"No, I'm not a queer," said Grandjean—but did she hesitate, or was that Lada's hope? The judge's pulse was visible in her throat.

"Then from whence comes the interest?"

"What?"

"In the bloody queers, that's what."

The judge hesitated, and then: "My mother was one. But no one knew about it. She remained married to my father for many years, enduring everything he saw fit to give her. I watched and told no one. All the dignity of a human being, stripped away." Grandjean dropped the pistol and looked down at her hands, shocked at the confession that had fallen from them. And then it showed itself suddenly, catastrophically: the realization that Lada *wanted* her. The pistol lay vulgar on the floor. "I have some power, not a great deal, but some," said Grandjean. "I use it how I can, to help who I can. They've never harmed anyone, you know."

Tarcovich took a step forward to kick the pistol out of the way. Grandjean did not seem to notice.

"But you're not a queer?" said Tarcovich.

"Why do you keep asking?" Grandjean whispered. Her lips quivered. She was not wearing any lipstick, Tarcovich noted, and she did not need it. Her lips were red-soft and plump.

"I'll stop once you've answered." Lada took another step forward.

"I already answered."

"Say it again."

"I am not."

"Not what?"

"A queer."

"You're quite certain?"

Andree Grandjean looked up at Tarcovich, who was suddenly close to her, so close she could smell the sweetness of her breath.

"Yes," she said, but Tarcovich silenced the word with her lips.

14 DAYS TO PRINT
EARLIER THAT AFTERNOON

The Jester

THE OTHER MAN—what was his name? Renard? Lenard? It couldn't have been Tenard, because that was Aubrion's school-teacher, the one with the permanent black eye—the other man, whatever his name, tossed Aubrion a crate. "Wouters is an arse," Not-Tenard said. "He thinks he can marry off that daughter of his?"

Aubrion hoisted the crate into the carriage, then bent over to rub his back. His muscles were protesting harder than the French. "I once had a cow with a prettier face than hers," he said, and then Aubrion was worried, because it wasn't his *best* line. But Not-Tenard, a watery-eyed man who cared little for tasteful humor, grinned and slapped Aubrion's sore back. Aubrion made a sound he'd hitherto only heard from roadkill.

"Come, it's already half past the hour. Grandjean will have a fit."

Still rubbing his back, Aubrion climbed into the carriage alongside Not-Tenard.

He'd left the FI headquarters shortly after Lada, welcoming a change in the air after the confrontation between Spiegelman and Mullier. Though Tarcovich had urged him not to follow her, assuring him she did not require supervision, Aubrion was never one for listening. "But what if something goes wrong?" he'd insisted.

As he and Not-Tenard rode off, Aubrion scanned the countryside for anyone vaguely German-looking. Earlier, when he was just a few blocks from the FI headquarters, he'd noticed the whispered footsteps and retreating shadows of men following him through Enghien. This was to be expected, of course: he would have been more surprised if Wolff had *not* assigned soldiers to tail him. Aubrion was due to meet with Wolff today, to update the *Gruppenführer* on *La Libre Belgique*, and Aubrion wanted to disappear for a while before he had to be in the same room as that man: hence, a slapped-together disguise consisting of a false mustache, a peasant's tunic, hair dye, and a walking stick. As far as he could tell, Aubrion had lost his followers hours ago.

"Let me ask you," said Aubrion the laborer, "do you read *Le Soir*?"

"I don't read much," said Not-Tenard.

"But when you do read—"

"It's shit, but what else is there? My father read the paper every day of his life. He was a baker. Didn't ever do much schooling, but he read the paper." Not-Tenard glanced over at Aubrion. "What'd you ask for?"

"The quality hasn't been so great lately."

"What'd you mean, 'quality'?"

"It's not very good. It used to be better."

"Sure. As I said, it's shit."

Clearly agitated by Aubrion's questions, Not-Tenard whipped at the horse. When Aubrion worked for an art critic's journal, back when there was still art worth critiquing, his audience looked like him. They were men and women who loved art and who had the knowledge—or who believed they had the knowledge—to think meaningful thoughts about it. The war had repainted his audience: now, it was Not-Tenard, or rather men who looked, sounded, thought and smelled like Not-Tenard. Something like panic grabbed hold of Aubrion's heart, for what did he know of men like Not-Tenard? Marc Aubrion had not grown up wealthy, not by any means, but he'd resided in that comfortable pause between rich and middle class. When he was a boy, he had books and fresh milk in the icebox. Aubrion got his professional start as a comic, touring pubs between university courses. His jokes were pretentious by design, almost by necessity, and certainly by default. If Not-Tenard saw a photograph of Hitler running away from his own troops, would he laugh? So preoccupied was Aubrion that he did not notice when Not-Tenard drew the carriage to a halt. Aubrion blinked. In his absence, they had arrived at Grandjean's courthouse.

"What's the matter with you?" said Not-Tenard.

Aubrion looked into Not-Tenard's face, the man's nose streaked with alluvial veins and broken blood vessels, his eyes reddened by last night's bottle. He ached to ask the laborer what made him laugh—or, better still, what made him cry. The key to knowing what a man finds funny is to find out what he fears, Aubrion always said. He trembled with his desire to pin the man against the wall and demand a catalog of his favorite one-liners, his least favorite puns. Instead, he said: "Nothing. Nothing at all."

The Dybbuk

"What do you have for me?" Wolff asked Aubrion, who'd entered his office at the Nazi headquarters without knocking.

Aubrion handed Wolff a slip of paper. "An update on *La Libre Belgique*, with compliments from the *Front de l'Indépendance*."

Smirking, Aubrion bowed. Then he threw himself into the chair in front of Wolff's desk, his legs sprawled out in front of him.

A faint outline was visible through the paper's skin, the evidence of a drawing on the other side of the paper. With bile rising in his throat, Wolff turned it over and held up the paper, disgusted to see that he was trembling—for Aubrion had written his note on the back of an FI propaganda poster.

I remember the poster well. Eight thousand copies were distributed around Belgium before 1943, pasted on buildings and handed out at alehouses. It was a simple drawing of a German soldier thrusting his bayonet into the stomach of a young child, while a banner dances above him, proclaiming: *"Für Gott und Vaterland!"* The artist had imitated the style of the era's comic books, with thick lines and primary colors.

Wolff was hardly amused. "Do you think this is funny, monsieur?" he said softly.

"You would not let me send you a telex. Since I had to be here anyway, I thought I might bring you a small gift."

"We do not *telex* state secrets."

"Which is why I wrote *your* state secrets on *my* state secret."

Still trembling, Wolff crumpled the poster. Aubrion appeared to find this even funnier. He bent over, laughing, pushing his hair out of his eyes. Perhaps, the *Gruppenführer* thought, he had been misguided: Himmler was right to think that they should destroy rather than repurpose what these small, untidy men had built.

"Where did you go this afternoon?" asked Wolff.

"Oh, here and there."

"I'm going to give you one more chance to answer my question, monsieur."

"Christ, Wolff, did you have a bad night? All right, all right, don't look at me that way. I was only having a little fun. It gets tiresome to be followed everywhere."

"I will have my men do it more discreetly."

"Why don't you have your men not do it at all?"

"I'm afraid that's impossible. Where did you go?"

"Just down to the courthouse. I needed a bloody walk. Is that a crime?"

Wolff pointed at the balled-up poster. "You will sit in this office and rewrite everything that was on that paper. Then you will give me an oral update on your progress. You will not leave until I have deemed everything you've done satisfactory."

But the *Gruppenführer* took no pleasure in watching Aubrion take a sheet of paper and pen and begin replicating his note. Aubrion was too happy, there was no other way of putting it. He did not walk with a gallows gait, as Wolff had expected. Something was wrong here, Wolff knew—and he knew he must yank Aubrion's rope, or lose him like a stray balloon.

14 DAYS TO PRINT
EARLY EVENING

The Smuggler

LADA TARCOVICH LAY beside Andree Grandjean in bed, watching a group of refugees from her window. When Europe finally woke up to the Nazi threat, it did so in excess, putting every scrap of metal, every stray paper to use against Germany. As a consequence, the newspapers that traveled on the wind, those urban tumbleweeds of the pre-war days—they were gone, replaced by dull-eyed women and men, the homeless, refugees. Those below Andree's eighth-floor apartment collected their carpetbags. Lada watched until the wanderers were out of view.

"What are you looking at?" muttered Grandjean, her eyes closed. "If it's not me, then it's not important."

Smiling, Lada leaned into Andree's body and kissed her. Groaning with pleasure, Andree's lips parted, taking in all of Lada: her tongue, her smile. Lada's hands tightened around Andree's waist, pulling her closer. They broke away gasping.

As Lada's head fell back on the pillow, she allowed herself a bit of nosiness at Andree's apartment. Lada herself divided her time between the FI base and her whorehouse, so she had not lived in a real flat since the occupation. Andree's room was dense with leather texts, heavy furniture and that tasteless but expensive brand of minimalist art so fashionable those days. Hers was an apartment engineered to receive clients and bureaucrats.

Lada rested her head in the crook of Andree's arm. "Hello," she said.

"Hello?" Andree laughed. She had a throaty, unashamed laugh. "Is that all you're going to say?"

"Perhaps that's all that needs to be said."

"You talk far too much for me to think you believe that."

"Damn." Lada rolled over onto her back. "You've never had a woman before?"

Andree looked offended. "How did you know?"

"Well, you did tell me you weren't a queer."

"Right."

"And the first time was terrible."

"No!"

"Yes."

"Was it really?"

"It was, really."

"I didn't hear you complaining the second time."

"No." Lada kissed her. "I was not complaining the second time."

Andree went quiet. Then she said: "I've always known, I suppose." Andree Grandjean looked at Lada without seeing her, perhaps seeing a dozen other women she'd befriended a tad too closely, friends she'd hated once they took their wedding vows. "I've never spoken to anyone about it—or thought about it much, either. I suppose I was frightened of it. It was always a part of me that I knew was there, but never touched."

"A great tragedy."

"Hmm?"

"The lack of touching."

Andree smacked her. "You are incorrigible."

"And you are encouragable." Lada twisted Andree's nipple.

"Stop that," said Andree, and the two laughed and kissed again. "Have you always known?"

"I suppose. Lord knows I tried to beat it out of myself, though."

"How?" Andree rested her hand on Lada's stomach, just below her breasts. The familiarity of the gesture almost made Lada Tarcovich weep.

"I'm a prostitute," she said plainly.

"You're—?"

"You heard me."

"For...men?"

"If there's a prostitute for women, I'd love to meet her."

"How long have you been a—" Grandjean tripped on the word "—prostitute?"

"Seventeen years. Though I'm not very good at it."

Andree Grandjean's eyes hardened—and there was the judge who Tarcovich had seen on the bench two days prior. She'd forgotten that the two were the same person. Grandjean took her hand from Tarcovich's stomach.

"But, why?" she asked. The question was wide and open, with nothing more to it.

"My mother and father were wealthy, so I had suitors before I knew what the word meant." Lada's voice turned to steel. She had not thought of this in many years: how her parents had paraded her child's body before teenage boys, how they spoke of her to the gray-bearded men who thought they had a chance because they still had their hair. "At first, when I turned them away, it was all in good fun. 'Oh, Lada's just being difficult,' and such. But as I grew older, my parents became suspicious. I could not bear the thought of tying myself to a man. And so, I sold myself to a whorehouse—partially to prove to my parents and myself that I was not a queer, and mostly to get away from my suitors." Lada shrugged. "When I was young, it made sense in my head."

Grandjean took Tarcovich's hand. "Oh, Lada."

"I did that for years—also wrote erotic stories."

"About what?"

"Americans, mostly."

Grandjean shuddered. "Do you still have them?"

"They're terrible." Lada brushed Grandjean's hair from her face, kissed her chin. "Needless to say I did not prove anything, except that I wanted to fuck women."

"Why did you keep doing it?"

"Fucking women?"

"No, you fool."

Lada flashed a mischievous grin that Grandjean extinguished with a kiss.

"I don't know. It became different, after a time," said Lada.

"Seeing men?"

"Yes."

"How so?"

"I take no pleasure in it, and like I told you, I am not good at it. But I can do something—I can fuck powerful men who don't know what I am, who are passing laws that make it impossible to be what I am—I can have that. That is my gift." Lada laughed softly. "It is an illness, I know. Someone close to me—who was close to me—has been trying for ages to persuade me to see a psychoanalyst."

Andree Grandjean held her close. "Life passes too quickly for psychoanalysts."

Because they could, and because the alternative was so much uglier, Lada and Andree spent the rest of the afternoon in bed. There, the entirety of their world was the cool shock of each other's skin. Church bells rang every hour or so, accompanied by the crackle of firearms shot into the air. Fog obscured the sun; Grandjean switched on a light, washing the ceiling and floors in shades of cream. These background clues that time was passing, night was falling—it was all a very strange, very *zwanze* counterpoint to whatever was growing in that bed.

In the early evening, they both realized they were starving. Lada and Andree Grandjean got up to dress.

"I want waffles," said Tarcovich, "but also herring."

Grandjean buttoned up her shirt. "Why not both?"

"When was the last time you had either?" Tarcovich slipped her dress over her head. "I think that cafe on Avenue du Vieux Cèdre still has waffles."

"If they do, that means it is run by Germans or collaborationists."

"Shit, you're right, aren't you?"

"Inevitably." Andree Grandjean finished with her shirt and began buttoning up her trousers. She leaned in to turn off the light.

"Don't." Lada shook her head. "I'll miss you."

Grandjean whispered that Lada was a fool, which she was, and kissed her. "Lada, you haven't asked," said the judge, "but I've decided to help you."

Tarcovich looked at her. Andree's hair was sticking up, her shirt half tucked into her trousers. Starving or not, Lada wanted to climb back into bed with her and never leave. She'd always thought people were exaggerating when they talked about love—to say nothing of love at first sight. Love was *this*, love was *that*...not so, not to Lada. Love was not hating them *most* of the time; that was what she believed. And now, to feel this way only weeks before Lada Tarcovich would die, a feeling so expansive, but so small, infinite, but only hers—it was incomprehensible. Andree was alive in a way that made Lada feel alive, not just as a whole, but in every instant.

"Don't do it because of this," said Lada, directing her gaze toward the bed.

"I am not."

"You are, though."

"Perhaps." Andree tucked in her shirt. "But I am not going to be stupid about it. I want to know nothing about the FI's operation—just the part of the operation for which you need my help. If you are caught, I will not be implicated."

Lada nodded.

"What would you have me do, then?" asked Andree.

"We need money," said Lada.

Grandjean laughed. "Is that all?"

"You have not asked how much."

"How much?"

"Fifty thousand francs."

"Is that all?"

"You have not asked by when."

"By when?"

"Next week."

"Damn." Andree paced the room, pushing her hair out of her face.

Lada finished dressing and sat on the bed. "Is it possible?"

"It is not impossible," said Grandjean, which was the best they could hope for.

Lada and Andree selected a table under an awning for an early evening meal. Though the restaurant was vacant, the owner and his daughter were arguing loudly in the kitchen, so Lada and Andree had to lean close to hear over the row and the light rain. Shortly, their meal was interrupted by an old woman who approached their table as though she knew them. Wordless, Andree removed an envelope from her pocket and handed it to her. The woman accepted it, then withered into the crowded streets.

"What was that all about?" asked Lada.

"I'm buying an auction house." Grandjean shrugged.

Lada's fork clattered against her plate. "You're what?"

"Well, she's buying it." Andree gestured at the old woman's frail back with her spoon. "I'm simply paying for it."

"How much?"

"About ten thousand francs."

"Why do you need an auction house?"

"I don't." Andree licked the custard off her spoon. It was the most unglamorous thing Lada Tarcovich had ever seen, which was saying quite a bit, considering the nature of her profession. "But I do need somewhere to host our fund-raiser."

"Is there some reason you can't simply rent a ballroom?"

Andree Grandjean leaned back in her seat, regarding Lada. A light rain dusted their silverware and plates, plastering Andree's hair to her forehead. Tarcovich's skin prickled.

"I'm not sure whether you've heard, but the Gestapo just formed a Ministry of Perception Management," said Grandjean, "led by a man named August Wolff. Its goal is to turn the tide of public opinion, away from the Allies."

"I've heard," said Tarcovich, perhaps dryly.

"Have you? Good. I have slightly more faith in the FI than I did before. We fight wars with bullets and guns, Lada, but we win or lose them with propaganda."

Lada recoiled, half expecting Marc Aubrion to peel off Grandjean's face and laugh at her for failing to detect his disguise. "You're starting to sound far too much like a man I work with," she said.

"He seems wise." A pale-faced waiter with bloodshot eyes refilled Lada's coffee cup. Grandjean held up a hand. "None for me, thank you."

When the waiter had gone, Lada whispered: "An actor, do you think? In his spare time?"

"How else could you explain those eyebrows?"

"True."

"My point is that doing things is less important than *how* we do things. I *could* have just rented out a ballroom for our fund-raiser. But by renting out a building, a two-story building previously owned by the *Ahnenerbe*—"

"Was it really?"

"—I set up the expectation that this is going to be the event of the century, so grand and so large that I need an entire mansion to accommodate it."

Lada nodded, absently taking a bite of her veal pie. It had gone cold. "It's smart."

"I know." Grandjean smiled. Lada leaned in to kiss her, stopping herself at the last second. The two shared a heavy glance, then looked away.

Lada said, "What is our next step?" to shatter the sudden quiet.

"That depends. I'm not sure what kind of resources the FI has these days—"

"What do you need?"

"I'll need someone with connections at a newspaper. And someone who knows how to wreck a reputation. Oh, and do you happen to know anyone who can print some posters?"

14 DAYS TO PRINT
EVENING

The Professor

MARTIN VICTOR USED to say that no one ever accused a punctual man of lying. And so he planned to arrive at the auction sponsored by the *Ahnenerbe*—that group of thinkers who concocted absurd stories about the superiority of the so-called "Aryan" race—twenty minutes before its start. Victor's purpose, of course, was to steal a booklet containing the list of locations at which *Le Soir* was distributed throughout the country: every newsstand, shop and cart in Belgium. Victor twice tried to hail a cab, but drivers grew sparse as evening fell, going home to avoid German soldiers en route to whorehouses and pubs. The professor was forced to walk on shaky legs.

He had not slept the night prior; I know because I'd heard him moaning from his cot. Sleep had been a hard-fought battle for Victor since the Auschwitz assignment. "I close my eyes," he'd once confessed to René Noël, in a rare moment of intimacy, "and I'm surrounded by those faces from the camp, their pale lips. They're wordless—with pain, maybe, or perhaps they simply forgot how to speak."

He paused to wipe the sweat from his face and catch his breath. In his youth, Victor could work half the day and night without stopping, could juggle twelve projects without pause. His wife Sofia had teased him for it. The night before their wedding, he'd stayed up past sunrise working on a paper, thinking she wouldn't notice his exhaustion through the next day's excitement. When they reached the chapel, though, she'd chastised him soundly.

A piece of Victor, one that he'd spirited away after Auschwitz, wondered how his wife would have felt about *Faux Soir*, whether she'd think it brilliant or reckless, a waste of Victor's time and efforts. Though Sofia believed in heaven and hell, of course— the staunchly Catholic Victor never would have married her otherwise—she always said it would be a bitter afterlife indeed if it were tinged by earthly regret. Nothing upset Sofia more than a wasted hour, a squandered drop of sweat. It was perfectionist nonsense. Victor had loved her for it.

Marc Aubrion, who had agreed to meet him at the auction house, did not share Victor's views on punctuality. He appeared fifteen minutes late in an ill-fitting suit. *"Guten Nachmittag,"* said Aubrion.

"You're late," said Victor. "I instructed you to arrive twenty minutes early."

"Who arrives twenty minutes early? And when did you instruct me?"

"Last night," Victor said through gritted teeth.

"I was not awake last night."

"That much is evident. Come." Victor produced Spiegelman's forged invitations. "We're already behind schedule."

"Let's see," said Aubrion, "whether our friend David is as good as his reputation."

Aubrion and Victor joined the other latecomers in front of

the auction house. It was a well-dressed bunch, and a stern wind threatened their hats and bow ties. In his baggy blue suit and gray fedora, Aubrion looked misplaced, "like a human-interest story in a finance magazine," as he put it later. He shifted uncomfortably as he handed the usher his invitation, holding his breath as the man's eyes swept across the embossed paper. The man returned the invitation to Aubrion, giving him directions in German.

"*Danke,*" said Aubrion, tipping his fedora. He strode into the auction house, pursued by the usher's admonishing eyes.

Martin Victor appeared at Aubrion's side moments later. "Well done, David Spiegelman," he murmured.

"I'll remind Noël to give him a raise," said Aubrion. "What did the usher say?"

"He said refreshments are on the left, the water closet is on the right, and the main room is straight ahead."

"To the left we go, then."

"How are you planning on asking for refreshments, with your accent?"

But Victor's irritation was halfhearted, for his attention was elsewhere. The auction house had been turned into a temple to pseudoscience, an unholy museum for the *Ahnenerbe's* spoils. A rage as deep and cold as his wife's grave took hold of Victor's bones. Beneath the banners with their eagles and their swastikas sat pieces of stone carved with prehistoric inscriptions, a chunk of rock with a Nordic pagan symbol etched in the body, a pile of scrolls, a Medieval painting. Some of these things were up for auction, while others were there simply to show the reach of the German archaeological arm. Victor studied these things at university; though he was a sociologist by trade, he was a historian by training. *This* was truly why Martin Victor had joined the resistance: he knew that any civilization built atop a mythology of lies and thefts must be a civilization of sin. The swastika would forever symbolize evil. That itself was a crime.

Victor realized he'd followed Aubrion into the main room, where rows of chairs had been arranged before a low stage. It was all so Teutonically precise that it was nearly a parody. Aubrion made a joke about how the Germans had occupied the chairs. The professor didn't hear it. His mouth had gone dry. This was how his fits usually began, with a blank mind and a dry mouth—but Victor forced himself not to think about it, to think of nothing but the mission.

"Everyone has a champagne flute," said Aubrion.

"*No, Marc.*"

"Hey, pal, no need to snap. I'm just wondering where the *Ahnenerbe* buys party supplies."

Victor stopped, curious, in spite of himself.

"A good question, right?" said Aubrion. "I wonder whether the Reich has a supplier in each country, or one large supplier in Germany that exports at a discounted rate."

"Perhaps some combination of both. Or maybe they've signed a contract with—" Victor pulled off his spectacles. "Why do I let you drag me into these bloody stupid things?"

Aubrion laughed as Victor made his indignant way to the second row. Rather than following him, Aubrion took a seat near the back. It was a vibrant crowd: the air was humid with German, streaked through with Russian and some French. Pulling off his fedora, Aubrion propped his feet on the seat of the chair in front of him, prompting uncharitable comments from the surrounding patrons. He looked out of place anyway; there was no reason *not* to tempt fate.

The first item up for bid at the auction house was the auction house. As the auctioneer explained, the *Ahnenerbe* "desired some charitable contribution" from the "community's upstanding members" as a "show of their devotion" to the Nazi cause. It was all a roundabout way of saying rent was high and the *Ahnenerbe* no longer felt like paying. To Victor's surprise, and to the clear surprise of the auctioneer, an old woman eagerly bid on the red building.

"*Danke*, madam." The auctioneer's gavel connected smugly with its gold plate.

With the venue sold, the auctioneer proceeded to the next item up for bid. "Lot 002 is an antique—" he said, but Victor could speculate on the identity of Lot 002, for the auctioneer was interrupted by a shout. The professor turned around, clutching at the pistol tucked away in his tweed.

"Get your hands off me!" said the man—said *Aubrion*, for two men in Nazi uniforms were throwing Aubrion against the wall, dashing his forehead against the wood. Aubrion cried out as they snapped handcuffs around his wrists, the tears in his eyes visible even from the front of the room.

As the shouts grew louder and less coherent, Victor had to clench his teeth to keep from drawing his weapon. "Everyone remain calm," said the auctioneer, which, of course, caused more patrons to rise from their seats in alarm. Though he was taller than most, Victor had to crane his neck to see over the blur of panic.

The professor's fist closed around the handle of his pistol, still concealed in his coat. They had a plan, and this was not part of it, this was not meant to happen. For a second, Martin Victor, the first man to visit Auschwitz and return alive, contemplated rushing the Nazis. There was an alleyway behind the auction house with a gate, a sewer entrance most people wouldn't notice. If he and Aubrion climbed into it and walked for a bit, they'd emerge eight blocks east of the place. No one would suspect the paunchy fellow in thick spectacles and tweed; he could take them out, put his bullets in the Nazis' brains before they knew what they were about, kill them now among the artifacts and dreams they'd stolen and sold and lost.

Instead, Victor let his pistol go, feeling it sag against the fabric of his coat, as heavy and wretched as Aubrion's screams. It was not worth compromising the mission. For *Faux Soir* to proceed—Victor found himself mouthing these words, reminding himself of his mission, as he always had—for *Faux Soir* to proceed, he had to get the distribution list. He and the others could go on without Aubrion, Victor knew; Aubrion had put in motion something that could not easily be stopped. And so, as the Nazis dragged Aubrion out of the auction house, he locked eyes with Victor, and Victor, ever a good Catholic, turned the other cheek.

The auctioneer struggled to restore order to the room. "Ladies and gentlemen," he said, "please, there is no cause for alarm!" As the ladies and gentlemen (who believed there was, in fact, cause for alarm) made for the doors, men in Nazi uniforms appeared at the exits. Though they seemed unarmed, their presence reversed the trajectory of anyone who tried to leave.

Gradually, the room quieted. "Thank you," said the auctioneer. "We received word earlier that a member of an underground organization had infiltrated the auction." Victor snorted. They never mentioned the *Front de l'Indépendance* by name for the same reason that the *Front de l'Indépendance* had started wearing those stupid uniforms with the insignia patches: it legitimized them to a dangerous degree. "But the man has since been removed. Come, come, ladies and gentlemen, let's not allow a bit of rabble to disrupt our auction."

That did the trick. Victor watched everyone return to their seats, more flushed and disheveled than they'd been before. He drifted over to his chair in the second row, lowering himself on shaky legs. Mopping at his forehead with a handkerchief, Victor removed a flask from his jacket's inside pocket. He took a gulp to steady his nerves, aware he was conspicuously pale and sweating. Victor tried to remember a prayer; there must have been a prayer for such moments of weakness. But he could not summon one.

"Now," said the auctioneer, "Lot 002 is a fine piece of Roman pottery—" the vase was Carthaginian, Victor noted "—from the eighth century before the modern era." Victor shook his head; it was about six hundred years younger than that. "Do I hear twenty francs?"

"Twenty francs," someone called out from the back of the room.

The vase was sold for seventy francs, and then the auction was off: a parade of gold and dust the likes of which rarely escaped the historian's imagination. Clutching the bottom of his seat, Victor begged himself to focus, to listen to the auctioneer. The world separated itself from him, or so it felt, as though Victor were viewing things from behind a fogged glass. Despite his growing dissociation, Victor was horrified at the way these artifacts were being handled. Victor grew apoplectic as a couple, delighted with their purchase of the old Bible, began flipping through the pages as if it were a penny dreadful. Though he was raised a Catholic, fact-gathering was Victor's religion. In his youth, he would write down anything that interested him—overheard conversations, trivia, odd facts—in his notebook, trapping them like a hunter in the forest. No wonder, he thought, this auction was sponsored by the institute for the occult sciences: it was as false and unholy as anything Victor had ever seen.

He felt his palms grow clammy, his tongue turn to lead in his mouth. "No," he murmured, "be calm, be calm—" This was years before anyone had given post-traumatic stress disorder a name, before anyone recognized it or studied it. Furious at his own cowardice, Victor clutched his wrists—

The bow ties become tattoo-scars, the wristwatches become chains, and Martin Victor is standing on a hill overlooking Auschwitz, staring down into the worst humanity could do. It's the smell of the place, the sharp pang of urine and the tinge of blood and unwashed bodies and antiseptic and oh Lord in Heaven, he is just an academic, just a man of paper and pens, why have they sent him here, him of all people, and why did he agree to go? Martin Victor shut his eyes—"feeble-minded bastard," he whispered—willing himself back to the auction house.

"Lot 044," said the auctioneer, "is a list of locations where the six most prominent newspapers in the country are sold." Victor's blood pounded in his ears. This was the purpose for which he'd come. *My mission, my mission*, he may have whispered. "This sale has been graciously authorized by our friends in the German High Command. Think of what our enemies could do with that sort of information! We should try our hardest to keep it out of their grasp, shouldn't we? Do I hear sixty francs?"

The room took a breath. Then an older man in the back called out: "Sixty francs!"

"Do I hear sixty-five?" The auctioneer brandished the list, a slim portfolio with ragged corners. It would have been easy enough to mistake it as a businessman's files, or an old batch of letters, something to be shoved aside on a desk or tossed into a trash bin.

As a second bidder cried out, Victor stood, clutching the back of his chair. The place was furious with sound. Victor's body had started to betray him, his heart thudding in his temples and his breath coming in short, childish gasps. He was there again, at the camps, and the smell and the din of the place took his mind from him. Murmuring an apology to the denizens of the second row, he peered over at the exits. They were no longer guarded. The professor contemplated returning to his seat, completing the mission he was assigned—but he could not. Victor staggered out the door and into the streets.

The Jester

Marc Aubrion had always liked the idea of being wounded in action. He just thought it would be a tad more romantic, was all.

"Christ, Theo, did you have to hit my head so hard?" Aubrion fingered the knot on his forehead. "Shit," he hissed. "Mother of *Christ*, that stings."

"The boy left to get ice," said Mullier, with a halfhearted attempt to help Aubrion into a chair. The lightbulb Aubrion had tried to fix the other day, the one that still hangs on a string in the hollowed-out corpse of the FI headquarters, flickered.

"The Americans give out medals to *their* wounded. All I get is a bag of water."

"You can't nurse a wound with a medal." René Noël came downstairs with a stack of newspapers, his waistcoat speckled with ink. He tossed them on a table, whistling at Aubrion's wound. "Damn, Marc, who did you irritate this time?"

Aubrion's pulse pounded in his forehead. "Theo Mullier, apparently."

"I was pretending to be a Nazi," said Mullier. "At the auction."

"And you accuse *Spiegelman* of pretending too well?" said Aubrion.

"I assume it worked," said Noël.

"As far as we can tell." Aubrion put his feet up on a table, knocking over an empty inkwell. "The auction seemed to be going swimmingly after Mullier hauled me out of there. No one had any reason to suspect Victor."

"Good. I suppose we'll find out soon enough whether Victor won the list. Does the *Ahnenerbe* run background checks on people who win auction items?"

"They do, but Victor's background is airtight. As far as they know, he's a mediocre professor who did some fieldwork in Germany and Italy. Which, now that I think about it, is not far from the truth."

"When is Tarcovich having the books delivered?"

"You mean the pornography for *der kinder Nazis* or whatever we're calling it? Tonight." Aubrion tipped his chair back. "Do we award medals to the wounded?"

"How the devil should I know?" said Noël.

"Unlike me, you're in charge of something."

The Pyromaniac

It was then I ran into the basement with a bag of ice, my heart still thudding from my dash to the icehouse and back. I started to hand the bag to Marc Aubrion, holding it reverently, in both hands—but recoiled at the sight of his face. It was not his purple forehead that arrested me, or the blood-colored ring around his left eye; rather, it was the pain and exhaustion in Aubrion's eyes that shook me to my bones. I had been hurt, and I had been tired, but not Marc Aubrion. He was not allowed.

"Good Lord, Gamin," Aubrion said, laughing, "am I that close to the grave?"

"No, monsieur."

"You're a bad liar. It's a quality you'll have to shed if you want to stay in this business."

Saying nothing, I stared down at the holes in my shoes. I was crying because I was sad, and then because I was ashamed. Without looking at him, I handed Aubrion the ice.

Sighing, he held it up to his head. "You were right, René. Medals be damned."

"Is there anything else I can do for you, monsieur?" I asked.

"Not for now, Gamin."

"All right, monsieur."

"Buck up! Want to hear a joke? Eight men walk into a war..."

Aubrion's eyes shone. I felt the laughter take hold of me and shake the sadness free from my chest. For an instant, just the one, I could see the world as Marc Aubrion did. I could count the constellations in the ink dots on Noël's waistcoat.

The Dybbuk

Wolff followed Martin Victor from the auction house and through the streets. Though Victor had made eye contact with him shortly before leaving, Wolff had no reason to believe the professor had recognized him; Victor's audible gasps and sweating pallor seemed to indicate he was experiencing an episode of his illness, and the professor's eyes did not see the world as it was. Still, Wolff remained cautious. He stayed fifty meters from Victor whenever possible, guided by the heavy plod of the man's footsteps—which turned into splashes as it began to rain.

Though the *Gruppenführer* never would've admitted it aloud, nothing made sense. Why would Aubrion and Victor go through the trouble of slipping past the Gestapo to enter the auction, only for Victor to leave before buying anything? How had they gotten past the guards in the first place? Was there any logic to the timing of Victor's departure? And why would they stage Aubrion's arrest—a brilliant ruse, Wolff had to concede—if they weren't about to do something devious? The clear answer was that they had done something illegal, something so subtle it had snuck under Wolff's attention.

Wolff's boot slipped in a puddle. "Damn," he muttered, catching himself before he toppled. A vagrant on a curb snickered, then sneezed. The rain had brought out the worst in Enghien: the stench of disease, the refugee families huddled around their fires. These things were evidence of the Nazi Party's necessity, Wolff thought. The Nazis existed to cleanse the earth. The *Gruppenführer* hurried after Victor, his boots crusted in mud.

Wolff watched Victor pause at the entrance of the *Front de l'Indépendance* headquarters to give the password. Despite the FI's precautions, the Nazis had known the location of their base for nearly a year. The FI was smart to have hidden it in plain sight, another slender building among the toy shops and markets, that old meatpacking factory that had looked abandoned for years, but people always slipped; there were always mistakes. Though Manning had suggested razing the building, Wolff knew the FI would simply make another home elsewhere, that it was better to keep an eye on them until necessity demanded a confronta-tion. Now was such a time. August Wolff raised his arm.

"Move in," he said.

The *Gruppenführer* watched his men materialize from the fog. A group of them surrounded the squat brick building, kicking in the doors at the front and back.

"Against the walls! Against the walls!" the soldiers said, the last words so many people heard. They hurled the men and women of the FI against the stone walls, until the rooms were blanketed in screams.

The Pyromaniac

Aubrion managed to say "Wolff?" before a black-uniformed German grabbed him by the shoulders. Poor Aubrion was slammed into the wall for the second time that day, and his only consolation was that this time, Theo Mullier came with him. My head was pressed against a wall, so I could not see the fury written on Aubrion's face. But I heard it when he shouted: "What the hell are you doing?"

"Checking on my operation," said Wolff, approaching Marc Aubrion. He waved to a group of his men. "Search the base-ment. Round up anything suspicious. Send a battalion—"

"Jesus Christ."

At this voice, we all turned—me, Wolff, Aubrion and Victor and Mullier and Noël, the soldiers and their guns—to see Lada Tarcovich standing in the entrance. She was accompanied by a dozen women in painted faces and short skirts. Each woman held a wooden crate.

The *Gruppenführer* looked at Aubrion. "I gave you a chance," he said, genuinely distraught, "to enter into a business partner-ship. You have taken advantage of my kindness."

Wolff gestured at his soldiers. They surrounded Tarcovich and the prostitutes, ordering them to drop the boxes. As his soldiers pushed Tarcovich and her girls to the floor, Wolff pried open a box, the one Lada Tarcovich had been carrying.

"Books?" he said. "Tear them open."

Wolff's men ripped into the crates. I almost wept at how gleeful they looked. They gutted the boxes as if they were butchering pigs, spilling their contents across the floor. The *Gruppenführer* surveyed the carnage, his brow furrowing.

"The Wet Ones," he muttered, *"She Romances the Reich, A Big, Bad Love Story..."* Reddening, Wolff turned on Aubrion. "What the devil is this?"

Laughing, Tarcovich glanced up at him from the floor, where she'd laced her hands obligingly over her head. The floor muffled her voice. "If you don't know, *Gruppenführer*, it's no wonder you're so disagreeable."

YESTERDAY

The Scrivener

"SO," SAID ELIZA, leaning across the table, "you were caught."

Helene's lips twitched. "This surprises you?"

"I just didn't know." Eliza clasped her hands together, enraptured, breathing like she'd nearly drowned, like she was grateful for each breath of air that did not taste of water. When Aubrion used to tell his stories, Helene would look on that way, Gamin would sit marveling at each improbable twist.

"Of course we were caught." The old woman laughed, her eyes dancing. She reached across the table as though grasping for someone's hand. Using her walking stick to brace herself, Helene put her feet on the table. Her worn-out shoes had laugh lines on them, where the leather had met the streets one too many times. "Wolff was not stupid, was he? We were bound to be caught sooner or later. I'm surprised Aubrion didn't anticipate it, though Noël probably did."

"You weren't prepared for it?"

"*Prepared*? God, no. We weren't prepared for anything."

13 DAYS TO PRINT

DAWN

The Pyromaniac

WE HAD NOT concocted a story to tell the Gestapo if we were caught; after all, *Faux Soir* had come about in the first place because we'd *already* been caught. So, when August Wolff stormed the basement to interrogate us—*each* of us, mind you, separately—on the state of *La Libre Belgique*, we had to decide on our own stories. Fortunately, we all came to the same conclusion: to think like Marc Aubrion. That was how we each found ourselves tied to a chair in a different room of the FI headquarters, yelling some permutation of:

"Honest to God, monsieur, the dirty books are a distraction! To throw off the rest of the factory!" (Me.)

"It's a distraction. The rest of the factory thinks we're distributing pornography. To other rebels. To boost morale." (Theo Mullier.)

"Obviously a distraction. Why else would we order erotica? For David Spiegelman?" (Tarcovich.)

And: "We're interested in *Le Soir* only insomuch as it is the most popular collaborationist newspaper in the country. That is what we were doing on the chalkboards, you understand? Trying to devise a calculus for ensuring that *La Libre Belgique* consumers will turn to *Le Soir* after the success of this endeavor." (Victor.)

"How the devil should I know what's on the chalkboards? It's Aubrion's doing." (Noël.)

"Christ, Wolff, would you settle down? We are just trying to make sure the market turns to *Le Soir* after we're finished with *La Libre Belgique*. We're doing you a favor." (Aubrion.)

The only people who were not playing along were the prostitutes, who simply repeated "We know nothing," until the music of those words filled the warehouse.

After three hours of questioning, the *Gruppenführer* was satisfied. He ordered his men to untie us and set our workers free, and he called everyone into the main room.

"Ladies and gentlemen," he said, "my name is *Gruppenführer* August Wolff. Forgive me for this rough treatment. I am part of a new program in the Ministry of Perception Management that is aimed at building alliances with the underground. You have created an impressive operation here. I am giving you eleven days to decide whether you would like to begin working for the Reich—after which, I'm afraid, I will have to deal rather harshly with those of you who say 'no.' But those who say 'yes' will be rewarded with a stable income, a good job, and the knowledge that you will remain safe and comfortable in the hands of Germany. That is all."

With a businesslike nod, Wolff and his men filed out of the building. We watched them go, one by one, until the only evidence of their existence was a few overturned chairs.

While René Noël remained upstairs to calm the men and women of the FI—indeed, to see how many had not fled the base immediately after the raid—Aubrion and I and the others banished ourselves to the basement to figure out what the devil just happened.

"It makes sense," said Lada Tarcovich, sitting backward in a cracked chair.

Aubrion kept trying to sit, but every time he spoke, he stood up to pace. "What about this makes sense?" he said. His agitation disturbed me. I could not sit still, either.

"That Wolff would drag the workers into this mess," said Tarcovich.

"He is threatening us," Victor agreed. "Holding the others who work here hostage. If we slip up before *La Libre Belgique* is complete, he will kill us and those who work with us. That is what he's saying."

"But by betraying him," said Aubrion, "we've already condemned our brothers and sisters to death." He seemed to be realizing this fact only now. Aubrion put his hand on a discarded propaganda poster, a charcoal sketch of a mother carrying her child from a ruined building. Our brothers and sisters at the FI—the writers and artists and journalists and delivery boys—they may not have been famous, and history may have been careless with their names, but by God, they labored for us. My dear friend Aubrion picked up this poster, cradling it. "They will be killed for our sins," he said.

"Do we have any reason to think Wolff is telling the truth?" said Mullier. "He'll probably kill them regardless of what we do."

"Why would he lie?" asked Aubrion.

"Why wouldn't he?" Tarcovich shot back.

Mullier's fist came down on a table, frightening the typewriters. "He's a damn German!"

"Obviously," said Aubrion, "but we can't just—"

"All right, everyone." Noël came downstairs with his hands raised. His ink-splattered waistcoat was ripped at the bottom, and exhaustion shaded the skin below his eyes. "There is no use analyzing why Wolff does what he does. He wanted to check up on us, remind us who we're working for. We must remain focused. We can all agree on that, right? Well?" Everyone muttered an assent. Noël nodded. "Let's get back to work. Gamin? Coffees for everyone, please." I left to fetch the coffees, but hovered at the top step to eavesdrop. The director said, "Monsieur Victor, can we have an update on the distribution list?"

Victor muttered, "I was not successful."

"What the hell does that mean?" said Aubrion.

"I do not have the list."

"Martin, you had *one* task."

"And a great deal of money," said Lada.

Aubrion advanced on Victor. "Out of all of us, *you* had the easiest job—"

"Did I?" said the professor. "Then tell me something. Why wasn't I informed of your plan? Didn't you think I might want to know you were going to pretend to be captured by Nazis?"

"No need to snap," said Aubrion. "We thought it would be more realistic if we waited—"

"Who is 'we'?"

"What?"

"Who did you collude with?"

"Theo and I, and that's not what that means."

"You were part of this?" Victor demanded of Mullier.

Mullier grunted. "It made sense."

"I don't believe it." Victor rubbed his forehead. "I don't believe it. How on earth am I to trust either of you if you won't tell me your bloody plans?"

"You're the one who botched this operation," said Aubrion. "We were not the ones—"

Their voices faded as I dashed upstairs to fetch the coffees. One of our men had just returned from a coffeehouse with a pallid, sickly brown tumbler of the stuff. Upon my return to the basement, René Noël had his hand on Aubrion's shoulder.

"Marc," said Noël. It looked as though Aubrion might shake

him off, but he did not. The fury in my friend's eyes waned. "Let it go. Martin, you too. Perhaps your 'failure' was a blessing. Wolff would have caught us if you'd been successful."

Victor would not acknowledge that.

"We will find another way to get the list," Noël went on. "I have faith in our creativity. Speaking of such, where's Spiegelman?"

"He's working on a Maurice-George Olivier column for *Faux Soir*," said Aubrion, "and a bit for *La Libre Belgique du Peter Pan*—so we'll have something to show Wolff. He sent me a telex that he'll be in Brussels for most of the day."

Noël nodded. "Good, good. Tarcovich? The books?"

Tarcovich's cheeks and nose were flushed as though she'd been out in the cold. She unwrapped her blue scarf. "As you might have noticed, they've been delivered."

"Where were you all day yesterday?" Mullier grunted.

"I don't believe that's any of your business."

"Oh, I believe it is."

"Fine. You want to know?" Tarcovich threw down her scarf, like a gauntlet. "I was with Judge Andree Grandjean. She has agreed to help us raise funds for the Nazi school caper. There. Do I have your approval?"

"*With* her?" said Aubrion. "As in 'with' her?"

"We're not discussing this," said Tarcovich.

"You were *with* her!"

"Shut up, Marc."

"I thought you were *with* a different woman. What was her name? Titanic? She was strangely obsessed with ceramic."

I handed Tarcovich a mug of coffee, which she wielded rather irresponsibly. "Titania is fucking a *man* now, someone named Joseph Bucket or Becket, so I haven't seen her in ages."

"Joseph Beckers?" I said, passing a mug to Aubrion.

Tarcovich looked at me in surprise. "You know him?"

I nodded. "If he's the fellow with the huge mustache, the one who dresses smartly—"

"That does sound like him."

"Doesn't that sound like everyone?" asked Aubrion.

"Not you," said René Noël.

"What about him, Gamin?" asked Aubrion.

All attention was upon me. "Well, monsieur." I licked my lips, chapped from the cold. I was conscious of my every word. "The paperboys and me—and I—we all know Beckers. He's the one who makes sure all the newspapers get to where they need to be. Beckers is in charge of the postal service, you see, and you were just talking about a distribution list, if I heard right."

Aubrion's eyes caught fire. "The postal service?" he said, and my heart sang.

"That's him, monsieur."

"No, but that's splendid," whispered Aubrion, "far too splendid."

"If there's a distribution list, I'd wager ole Beckers got it on him," I said.

"Gamin has a point," said Victor, handling my urchin's name between a pinched thumb and forefinger. "Men like Joseph Beckers are required to carry classified information on them at all times. It's standard procedure for the Reich. Where he goes, the distribution list goes with him."

Aubrion snatched up a piece of chalk, scrawling *Joseph Beckers!* on the chalkboard, like the title of one of those shoddy plays that used to be popular in Brussels. Stepping back, Aubrion regarded the fellow's name, which sprinted wildly across the blackboard.

"A collaborationist runs the post?" said Mullier. "Isn't the postal service in our hands?"

The professor said, "Most of the postal workers are for the resistance, to be sure. Just not the fellow in charge."

And this was true. I knew the rumors, the whispers that would coalesce into facts and figures only after the war. Whenever the

Nazi High Command sent a letter ordering the imprisonment or execution of a Belgian citizen, it passed through the hands of a postal worker before landing on a bureaucrat's desk. But these men and women who worked at the post—and there were so many women, once the men began to disappear—they took it upon themselves to destroy the letters. Though this would not stave off the Germans forever, it would allow the condemned enough time to flee the country. The Germans later began shipping little fabric Stars of David to every town in Belgium; when the men and women at the post learned of the Stars' purpose, they took the Stars home and burned them.

Joseph Beckers may have been in charge of the post, but that meant nothing. Think of it. You know of the brave soldiers at the front, their bayonets held high and cheeks flushed with victory. But did you know of the quiet postal worker with her grim smile, the small acts of resistance that saved a country?

"You said your Titania is going with him?" Aubrion asked Tarcovich. "With this Joseph Beckers?"

"She is not *my* Titania. But yes."

"Fascinating," said Aubrion. "Is there going to be a wedding, do you think?"

13 DAYS TO PRINT
MID-AFTERNOON

The Smuggler

EVADING THE GERMAN patrols was an art, in those days, and Tarcovich knew all the places where the patrols did not venture. She'd trafficked books and supplies through every vein and artery in Brussels; she knew the abandoned farmhouses, the torn-up bridges. Tarcovich led Aubrion over one such bridge, a small footbridge that straddled a ravine. The Nazis believed the bridge to be structurally unsound and instructed their patrols to avoid it. "It *is* structurally unsound," Tarcovich said to Aubrion, "but thankfully, so are we."

"That's not the comfort you intended it to be," said Aubrion, placing one tentative foot on the bridge.

Below them, the ravine gagged on human detritus: ripped-up shirts and urine-stained trousers discarded by refugees. Lada held her breath. She heard Aubrion's heavy footsteps as he picked his way across the snow-dusted wood.

"What's it called again?" said Aubrion. "Your judge's organization?"

"The Society for the Prevention of Moral Degradation. And she is not my judge."

"Not your judge, not your Titania... You're not doing too well any longer, Lada. Are the glory days of your youth so far behind you?"

"Fuck off."

"Sounds horrible," said Aubrion. "This 'society,' I mean."

"Yes, well." Tarcovich stepped off the bridge, landing in a puddle. She swore at the mud on her boots. "Hopefully yours is a minority opinion."

"What's Grandjean's plan?"

"Christ, Marc, do you have to be so *loud* about it?"

"No one knows what we're talking about."

"Could we keep it that way, do you think?"

"All right, all right."

Aubrion sped up to walk beside Tarcovich. The road from the footbridge was unpaved, a dirt trail leading to the middle of town. Houses and shops bordered the road, grief-stricken in their bare wooden facades. People had stopped repainting their homes after the air raids; there was no point to it, and besides, where would they get the paint? Enghien sat naked in the cold, vulnerable to whatever the world had planned for it. As a light snow began to fall, mothers and their children emerged from the houses to cover their windows in wax paper. They worked and worked, and the snow performed a vanishing act in their hair.

Marc Aubrion was, as per his usual, underdressed for the weather, shivering in his rolled-up shirtsleeves and short trousers. He looked like a beggar to Tarcovich, a happy beggar who stole bread and whispered a thank-you to the sky. She wondered whether his childish fervor insulated him from the cold.

"What *is* the plan?" Aubrion stage-whispered.

Tarcovich rolled her eyes. "The plan is to make the fundraiser the event of the year—hell, the event of the century. We'll need ads in all the major newspapers."

"René can arrange that."

"And posters, all across the country."

"I'll have Gamin and his friends do it. What else? Do we have a location?"

"Apparently there was a building owned by the *Ahnenerbe*—"

Aubrion froze. "*No*. That was her?" He told Tarcovich about the old woman at the auction, the one Grandjean had sent to purchase the auction house. "It's brilliant. I am in awe of this Grandjean person. I don't think I've ever been in awe of anyone."

"Yourself."

"Oh, right."

"But of course, ads and posters will not be enough." Tarcovich kept walking in the direction of old Enghien, the part that had not been bombed out by the Americans and the Royal Air Force. The clouds were gray with unshed tears. They cast a shadow over the city, bathing Enghien's shopkeepers in false, shifting hues. "Inviting and cajoling can only get you so far. The FI's recruitment numbers have told that story clearly enough."

"What does she have in mind? My God, Lada, she sounds utterly fantastic. I'd love to meet her."

"Yes," Tarcovich said flatly, "she feels the same about you."

"Does she *really*?"

"It will not happen."

"Why not?"

"She wants nothing to do with the *Front de l'Indépendance*."

"Clearly *that's* not true."

A girl, no older than ten, walked up to Lada with her hand out and head down. Lada was accosted by the familiar animal smell, everything human stripped away—or perhaps the most human of smells, the body reduced to something primeval. Lada could not look away from the girl. The bones that slid beneath her skin told a story that would end in death, if the child was lucky.

"Sorry, I have nothing," said Tarcovich. There was a bit of strength around the girl's eyes, which reminded her of Andree Grandjean. As the child walked away, it occurred to Tarcovich that she hadn't the slightest idea where Andree had been born, what her parents were like, whether she had any siblings. Their hiding and secrets had left little room for the mundane.

Aubrion passed the child a coin with an air of secrecy and watched her disappear. "Where do they all come from?" he murmured.

"Who, the refugees?" asked Tarcovich.

"How do they end up here, of all places?"

"They end up everywhere, Marc."

"Do you ever wonder how much they make per day?" Aubrion looked around, perhaps searching for others—and there were others, there were always others. The air raids had left most of Enghien dessicated and raw, but this part of town looked almost ordinary. Only the papered-over windows, pocked streets, and refugees betrayed the truth. Aubrion said, "Is it more or less than the average laborer, do you think?"

"I'm guessing less. Look at the way she's dressed." Tarcovich ached to clothe the poor girl, to give her soup and a trade. Though she hadn't many regrets, Tarcovich was often reduced to tears over the girls she could not save, the stories that would be cut short.

After a brief pause, Lada continued, "Think about it, Marc. With her resources, Andree Grandjean would be a fool to join the FI."

"Why, what does she know that we don't?"

"How this is going to end."

Aubrion trudged to a halt. He was in front of Tarcovich, so she could not see his face, but she watched him put his head down and rub the back of his neck. In some sense, Lada believed, Aubrion wrote and acted and made art to extend his childhood. Denial was the magic spell that kept it whole. Death was a bedtime story to him. It had been that way even before *Faux Soir*, when the war had only just begun: he would not call it a war until the king's surrender, and he would not call it a surrender until blood ran in the streets. Tarcovich feared that the shock of their task—not the story, but the ending—would not reach him until moments before it was all over, when it was too late for him to grapple with it. She longed, improbably, to hold him.

"Anyway," said Tarcovich, coming up beside Aubrion. He lifted his head, the expression in his eyes unreadable. "Grandjean thinks we should have some important people there, at the fund-raiser, and that we should make it—not just desirable, really, but *vital* that they attend."

"How's that?"

"Theo Mullier."

"Oh, *yes*." Aubrion laughed. "If their reputations are shot to pieces—"

"—they'll want to be seen at a fund-raiser promoting the moral fiber of the Reich."

The pair stopped in front of a fabric shop. Wind carried the heavy scent of wool out the door and into the streets. Lada knew the seamstress: a girl who used to work in her brothel and had learned a trade and saved up for a shop. The plan was to ask the girl to sew textbook covers for the erotic novels.

"This is tremendous," said Aubrion. Then he added, as though he'd rehearsed the line: "Thank you, Lada."

Tarcovich waved a hand, batting away his gratitude. The plan *was* tremendous—a ridiculous word, one of Aubrion's favorites— and yet it looked small and wretched to her. Each tremendous task was another sin against Andree Grandjean. At Andree's invitation, Lada had made a home inside of her: a tiny, vulnerable place against the world. Only Lada knew the home would crumble on top of them as they slept. The hours they spent together were built of lies and false hopes. Lada despised herself for it.

"What's the matter?" said Aubrion.

"Nothing," said Lada. "We should go in. It will take the seamstresses a while, I think."

"Why," said Marc, "you don't think they get orders for two hundred Nazi book covers every day?"

Tarcovich was not sure whether he was joking. She and Aubrion had that in common.

13 DAYS TO PRINT
EARLY EVENING

The Professor

THE BASE ATE TOGETHER, an early dinner of stew and watered-down beer, and then Mullier joined Victor and the businessman Ferdinand Wellens in the basement of the FI headquarters. Wellens was pacing, smoothing out his trench coat after every fourth step, while Victor looked over a document with a pen between his teeth.

Noticing Mullier, Victor removed the pen and said, "Ah, good. Shall we get started?"

Mullier nodded, craning his neck to see what the professor was reading. It had long been clear to Victor that Mullier did not trust him. The professor's expedition to Auschwitz, his subsequent missions to camps and excavation sites and capitols and trenches (each of which was funded by a Nazi ministry, for they all believed he was doing research for the Reich)—all of that was considered evidence of Victor's loyalties to the resistance. He had ventured to Auschwitz on the FI's orders, on assignment for *La Libre Belgique du Peter Pan*: to find out where the trains were taking the Jews, the Roma, the homosexuals, the bodies. Everyone in the underground knew him after that. But the FI was too quick, Mullier often said, to trust a man who lied for a living.

"I believe I have made considerable progress on my sales pitch," said Wellens.

"Let's hear it," said Victor.

"Gentlemen of the Ministry, welcome to *Schule für die Erziehung von Kindern mit ewige Liebe.*" Wellens paused, clearly pleased with himself. "Our mission is to—"

"Don't stop like that," interrupted Mullier.

Victor adjusted his glasses, which kept slipping off his nose; one of the greatest inconveniences of war, he'd found, was the persistent lack of eyeglasses shops. "Mullier is right," said the professor. "If you pause after you say the name, they'll know you've only said it three times."

"Four now."

"Well, make it five, and stop *pausing.*"

Wellens cleared his throat. "Gentlemen of the Ministry, welcome to *Schule für die Erziehung von Kindern mit ewige Liebe.* Our mission is to enlighten a generation—"

"You can't do that, either." Mullier sat on a stool near a chalkboard, removing an ever-present apple from his pocket so his hands would have something to do. Victor understood the impulse. The saboteur shared Victor's fondness for odd sleeping habits, so they often encountered each other in the softest hours of night and morning, while the rest of the base slept. Victor had caught Mullier nearly weeping over the pain in his clubfoot; Mullier knew of Victor's affliction, having found him pale and shaking in the privacy of midnight. The professor believed there to be a silent understanding between them, a tacit agreement to ignore each other's vulnerabilities. Aubrion, devil take him, wasn't the only one who played games of make-believe.

"What is it this time?" groaned Wellens.

"You rushed into the next sentence, after you said the name of the school." Victor pointed at Wellens as though calling on a student. "Can't you deliver your pitch the way you're speaking to us? Does it have to be so contrived?"

"Fine, fine, I'll try it again, then." Wellens took a breath. "Gentlemen of the Ministry, welcome to *Schule für die Erziehung von Kindern*—what's the rest again?"

Victor jerked his head at Wellens. "Are you sure he's the man we want?"

"We don't have much of a choice," said Mullier. "He's got connections. And most businessmen don't like the FI."

"Why not?" asked Wellens.

"We are not," said Victor, eyeing Wellens with purpose, "a *profitable* enterprise."

12 DAYS TO PRINT
MORNING

The Jester

THE NEWSPAPER COULD hardly contain its excitement. *For sale!* it said to Marc Aubrion. The text of the column was shaky—it was clear the printer had produced this copy of *Le Soir* only minutes before running out of ink—but that only made it seem *more* desperate, *more* eager for Aubrion's attention. *Three pairs of boots, lightly worn. Fine, dark leather! Inquire at the address below. For sale!* the adjoining column said, shoving its neighbor aside in its eagerness to be heard. *A wool hat.* This was a scuffle for Aubrion's attention, and this hat would not be beaten. *One hole (very smaaaall*, it promised); the typesetting device had gotten stuck on the letter *A* halfway through the word *small*, so the word contained four *As* instead of one and looked as though it were screaming for help.

Disgusted, Aubrion cast the paper aside. He rubbed his eyes, resting his aching head on the desk between two typewriters. The devices were alive with the smell of ink and grease. Lifting his head, Aubrion ran his loving fingertips across the keys, misshapen with age. The *K* key was missing. He wondered where it had gone. Did someone pocket it? Was it on the floor somewhere, had they been kicking it around the *Front de l'Indépendance* headquarters since the day it fell? Aubrion poked the spidery grave where the letter had been.

He got up, absently grabbing a piece of chalk. Aubrion remembered when these "for sale" ads began appearing in *Le Soir*. It was a few weeks after the occupation.

"Have you seen these?" he'd asked René Noël.

Noël had been fixing something, his arms buried in a printing press. He'd rolled up his shirtsleeves, ink staining his arms up to his elbows. The director had fancied himself a surgeon with printing presses, for a while. Now the FI could hardly afford the repairs.

"What is it?" he'd asked.

Aubrion had held up a paper. "These ads in *Le Soir*."

"For shoes, coats—"

"Yeah."

"Of course I've seen them. Hand me a mallet."

Aubrion did so. "Have we been running them in *La Libre Belgique*, as well?"

"Obviously not."

"Why obviously?"

"My God, you really don't know, do you?" Noël had extracted his arms from the press and wiped his hands on his trousers. "They're not selling their clothes. The Nazis are sponsoring those ads. Look, it's simple. What do you do when you've conquered a country and killed ten percent of its population, but the other ninety percent needs clothes to get through the winter? You sell the clothes."

"The dead people's clothes?"

"Now you're getting it. The average reader sees that and thinks, 'Well, now, the people must be fairly content if they're putting up their things for sale. So cheap, too!' And then the average reader buys a hat from the Nazis, thinking they're actually tossing their pennies to Peter the Happy Citizen."

In the shadow of this memory, Aubrion looked down at his copy of *Le Soir*. *Three pairs of boots, lightly worn*, he read. He wrote *Peter the Happy Citizen* on a chalkboard, underlined it three times. That was his audience, the sort of man willing to be fooled by a Nazi ad. This man was going to buy a copy of *Faux Soir*—to laugh at it or not, to toss it in a trash bin or bring it to a pub. *Good writing is a conversation, and everything else is pretentious shit*; that's what Aubrion always said. But what conversation could he have with Peter the Happy Citizen? What should Aubrion say to make him realize that those were Nazi ads, that he'd been fooled, to make Peter angry and confused and hurt, but also to make him laugh?

"A fake ad!" Aubrion exclaimed as I crept down the stairs to the basement to see him pounding the chalkboard. I'd seen him get that excited before; it was frightening. Given my upbringing among the writers of the FI, I don't use analogies lightly—but Aubrion was a force of nature, a natural disaster. Leaping from his chair, tripping over himself, he reached for a scrap of paper and pen. The words were conspiring; they wanted to escape. Aubrion let them go:

For sale! Two dozen shirts, lightly worn. Belgian cotton! Bullet holes in each (but only if you look hard enough). Inquire at the address below, which is in no way affiliated with the Third Reich and which, in fact, denies all connection thereto, and frankly, resents any implications otherwise.

Aubrion realized he'd been holding his breath. He exhaled. Gripping the paper, Aubrion read his ad over and again, until the words became music, and the music lost meaning. Only then was he satisfied. "How about that, Peter?" he whispered.

The Smuggler

It was a skinny little thing, the book in Lada's hands, with a mantle of dust around the edges. She held it up so Andree could read the title.

"*She Romances the Reich?*" Andree Grandjean's face twisted. "And people read that?"

"I don't think people read *this*, actually." Tarcovich blew dust at Andree. "It was sitting on a shelf at the whorehouse."

"Did it belong to a—customer?"

Lada tried to ignore the way Andree stumbled over the word. "No, I smuggled it into the country a few years ago. You might be surprised to learn that erotic romances featuring an American woman and her queer English friend who end up fucking Hitler's toupee off his head are illegal in German-occupied territories." Lada tossed Andree the book. She missed, and the book landed on the floor. Grandjean picked it up. "You might also be surprised to learn that we're in a German-occupied territory."

"Careful, I might faint," said the judge, turning the book over in her hands. The cover featured Hitler's bare buttocks with a swastika tattooed on the left cheek. "I can't believe someone wrote this. Do you know who it was?"

"Oh, God, I wish."

"Are there many of these?"

"Erotic Hitler books? I have a whole collection. It's my favorite sort of protest."

Andree laughed. "I never thought of it as protest."

"How is this anything other than a—" here Lada Tarcovich lifted her middle finger "—to the Reich?"

"That is true, no doubt. I've never thought of protest as anything more than..."

"Men in the streets."

Andree turned over the book to find even more colorful illustrations on the back. "Does anyone wank off to it, do you think?"

"I've never heard you say *wank*."

"You've known me three days."

"In which you had a wealth of opportunity to say it."

"Well?" said Andree. "Do you think they do it?"

"Do what?"

Andree smacked Lada with the paperback, punctuating the slap with: *"Wank."*

"Of *course* not. That would be ridiculous."

With a guilty smile, Lada took the book from Andree and walked over to the judge's bookshelves. As Lada scanned the shelves, Andree Grandjean switched on a light. It was barely morning, and still dark: clouds, furious with rain, smothered the sun.

"What are you doing?" asked Grandjean.

Lada slid *She Romances the Reich* between a copy of *Legal Statutes* and its leathered friend *Tortes for the District Judge: Third Edition*. The two books glared at their new companion. Smiling, Lada stepped back—but as Grandjean laughed, Lada recalled the first time she left a book and then a shirt and then a painting at her previous lover's flat, the slow, quiet blending of lives. Time had permitted their two lives to pool and harden into one; time would never give her and Andree such a chance. It infuriated Lada. In her desperate wish to be with *someone*, to feel a woman's body against her own, she had wasted her years. Lada buried her face in Andree's neck.

"What is it?" Andree murmured. "Why are your eyes so sad?"

Though Andree had spoken quietly, the question felt sharp. "My eyes are sad?" said Tarcovich, laughing faintly. "Well—" Lada kissed her and broke away "—someone should have a talk with them about that."

"Lada—"

"Oh, I nearly forgot." Eager to distract Andree, Lada rummaged through the satchel she'd brought with her. She emerged with a sheet of paper. "This is the poster they're printing for the fund-raiser."

Andree Grandjean took it. The poster was a somber grayish-brown. Printed in polite, roundish letters were the words: *The Society for the Prevention of Moral Degradation has saved nearly eight thousand children and mothers since its humble beginning.* And then, on the next line, in larger letters: *WE NEED YOUR HELP TO SAVE MORE.* The last line simply read: *Join us on THE FIFTH OF NOVEMBER at 7pm,* followed by the address of the auction house-turned-fund-raiser venue. In a word, the poster was brilliant: pointed yet drab, evocative yet unspecific.

"I can't believe something so perfect came out of the FI," she said.

Tarcovich snorted. "We do have our moments. I'm sending some of my people over to the auction house you bought to start fixing it up for the event. Later today. This afternoon, probably."

"My God, I'd love to join. What do you have in mind?"

"I could tell you, but where's the fun in that?"

YESTERDAY

The Scrivener

HELENE GOT UP abruptly and left the room. She returned with a wrinkled newspaper, which she placed on the table. Eliza's breath shuddered in her throat. The paper was yellow, the color of sickness and ancient tombs. A sepia, bookish smell curled through the room. The top of the page read *Le Soir*.

Holding her breath, Eliza rested her hands on the table. They lay just above the newspaper. She hesitated as if frightened to hold a new lover's hand—terrified of what might come next, of what might not.

"Is that it?" whispered Eliza, even though it was a ridiculous question.

Helene nodded, her eyes smiling.

Eliza asked her, "How many copies survived?"

"I don't know."

"Many?"

"It could be." Helene licked her fingertips as though preparing to turn the page, but hesitated. "I read the fake ad later, the one Aubrion wrote. It frightened me, I confess. But I do not find Aubrion's mockery of death so terrible any longer. To take death seriously when it surrounded us—*that* would have been terrible. To meet it as an equal—*that* would have been profane. Laughter was the noblest, most honest answer to death we had."

Eliza reached out to touch the newspaper again, but once more, she could not. "Why are you showing it to me now?"

"The time is right," said Helene.

12 DAYS TO PRINT
EARLY MORNING

The Gastromancer

IT WAS LATE at night—early in the morning, however you wanted to think of it—and David Spiegelman was writing. The trappings of his quarters and his body felt like props from a play: hands, office, pen, pulse. Spiegelman spread a copy of *Le Soir* on his desk—sweat-stained, limp with misuse—the issue from last Wednesday. Newsies sold more copies on Wednesday than any other day, for Wednesday was the day Maurice-George Olivier came out with "Effective Strategy." Indeed, "Effective Strategy" sat in its usual spot on the first page, bulging across three columns. Spiegelman read:

There is no doubt in my mind, in anyone's mind, in the minds of any person across Belgium—indeed, across Europe, even in Russia—that the army of the Germans is reaching the apex of its movements, and that we will soon see, all of us, together, a greater, more momentous effort culminating in the most important victory of the war. The great warriors of Germany are now mounting—or have already mounted, depending on how you view the situation, whether from above or within—a campaign the likes of which has never been seen before now, and might never be seen again.

Most of it was made up, of course, but the people didn't know that. How could they? The Nazis had eliminated almost every newspaper in the country, executing the editors who didn't co-operate, burning their factories with the workers trapped inside. To amplify their propaganda, the Germans relied on collabora-tors like Olivier—who, not twenty-four hours after the Germans occupied Belgium, turned up on the doorstep of the newly-established Nazi headquarters in Brussels, offering his pen in exchange for asylum. That was all David Spiegelman knew of Maurice-George Olivier. Everything else was speculation: where he came from, who told him what to write, and, most impor-tantly, why he needed asylum in the first place.

Of course, there were only a few possibilities. Olivier was not Roma—his name made that clear enough—so he must have been a refugee from some other discarded group. Perhaps he too was a homosexual—or perhaps he was something worse, like a pedophile, as the rumors suggested. Wolff had made it clear that the Reich granted asylum to all manner of deviants whose skills were greater than their sins. They worked in isolation, hearing only rumors of one another.

As Spiegelman read, he willed himself to absorb Olivier's voice, to be swept away on the current of the man's adverbs. The ease with which Olivier came to him was terrifying, exhilarating.

*There is no doubt in my mind, in anyone's mind, in the minds of any person across Belgium—indeed, across Europe, even in Russia—*and here Olivier would pause, Spiegelman imagined, to flatten his damp strands of hair against his forehead—*that the army of the Germans is reaching the apex of its movements, and that we will soon see, all of us together, a greater, more momentous effort culminating in the most impor-tant victory of the war.* Olivier would stop to catch his breath, his small eyes darting. *The great warriors of Germany are now mount-ing—or have already mounted, depending on how you view the situation, whether from above or within, or even below it, looking up—*Spiegelman saw him, gesturing upward with a smile full of false modesty—*a campaign the likes of which has never been seen before now.*

He put his pen down, wiping the sweat from his hairline. His *gift*—that's what Mr. Thompkinson and August Wolff and Marc Aubrion called it. But it was not a gift, not at this moment. Spiegelman felt as though Maurice-George Olivier was living inside his body, making parasitic holes in his stomach, as though the *dybbuk* had slipped inside of him when he wasn't looking, that he would not leave until he'd drunk his fill of Spiegelman's voice.

It is no secret in Berlin, where an apparent calm veils a certain anxiety not bereft of a vague hope that operations in the East have entered—or are about to enter depending on the angle from which one views the situation— a new phase which is hardly different from the present phase, except with certain changes. One could say, without fear of being contradicted even by Moscow's propaganda, that, thanks to the Autumn campaign, the Winter campaign followed the Summer campaign. So the course of these three campaigns in order shows that the German general staff have not lost at any time control over the sequence of the seasons, an element whose importance should not be underestimated.

Spiegelman got up from his chair, teeth chattering in the warm room. He could not bring himself to look at his draft of *Effective Strategy*, to acknowledge this evidence of his identity. What sort of a man was he if he could *do* that? If he could put himself in the mind of a man like Olivier, didn't some of that creature's evil live in David Spiegelman?

But the work *had* to be good; his promises to Aubrion and to the FI demanded it. He had to take the hammer in his hands again and beat these words until they sang, until his calluses bled. And so David Spiegelman reread each word.

The Dybbuk

Spiegelman was in bed when August Wolff came to call. The *Gruppenführer* knocked on his door, and, hearing no reply, called out:

"Herr Spiegelman?" Wolff knocked again. "Spiegelman, are you in there?"

The *Gruppenführer's* heart stopped. Embarrassed, he added a touch of steel to his voice. "Spiegelman, this is *Gruppenführer* Wolff. Please open this door." Still, he could hear nothing behind the chipped wood. Though the suicide rate on this particular Nazi base was low, there *was* that fellow with the shotgun last month, and the older man before that, the one with the Jewish great-grandfather. But Spiegelman hadn't said anything about feeling depressed lately, had he? Then again, they never did.

Wolff put a shaking hand on the doorknob. He took a breath, fighting to pull himself together. Spiegelman was a subordinate—a Jew—a homosexual. And given his past, Wolff should have expected such cowardice from him. If he found the man with a bullet in his heart, Wolff's memo would read that night: *Took the coward's way out. Buried this evening. Will search for a replacement tomorrow.* It would never read: *Lost a brilliant mind today, a writer and an artist.* Or, heaven forbid: *Lost a friend.* Wolff would do as he was taught; he would report the events as they occurred. Fire, after all, was for burning words, not for writing them.

But as he entered David's room, Wolff did not smell decay on the room's breath. For that, he was relieved. The figure on the bed did not appear to be moving, though. The *Gruppenführer* put a hand on Spiegelman's back.

Gasping, Spiegelman sat up. His eyes were glass, like those in the taxidermy animals on the office walls of Wolff's colleagues. Spiegelman's hands curled around Wolff's arm. Shocked at the man's grip, Wolff tried to pull away.

"Get ahold of yourself." The dark metal vertebrae in Wolff's voice made Spiegelman feel as though he had done something unspeakable.

Spiegelman blinked a few times, then let Wolff go. Wolff tugged at his collar. Spiegelman's room was damp: warm and damp and crowded. The *Gruppenführer* turned, expecting to find a half-dozen men breathing in unison behind him; it felt like a crowded city street. Spiegelman mumbled something.

"What did you say?" the *Gruppenführer* asked.

"I cannot do this for you anymore."

"Spiegelman—"

"I can't *write* for you anymore."

"What is the alternative?"

"Kill me. Have me executed."

"Tell me which assignment you were working on." Wolff slowed his breathing, silently begging his pulse to follow. "I will take you off of it." He paused, then added: "I understand—and I've heard about the toll that some of this work can take on us. None of it is easy, I know. You can ask for relief, Spiegelman. I will not condemn you for that."

"Do you know how I feel when I finish one of your assignments?" Spiegelman let himself fall back into bed, closing his eyes. "I feel—"

"I know, it is tiring to—"

"I do not feel *tired*, Wolff. Don't you see? I feel pride. It has always been this way, ever since I was a boy. Throwing my voice like that, becoming a general or a housewife—it's a skill that I have cultivated. I am proud of it."

"And you should be." Wolff had lost track of the path this conversation was taking, and that unnerved him.

"Look at me." Spiegelman glanced down at his own body. Wolff shuffled his feet, guilty at seeing the man in bed. "I've become fat with my own pride. I finish a document, perfectly imitating some poor, doomed nobody—his handwriting, the spelling errors he was never even aware of—and I am *proud* of what I have done."

"Desk work can smooth out a man's edges, it's true, but you can't allow that to upset—"

"It makes me ill. This is what I've become? A glorified Nazi clerk who takes pride in his job but no responsibility for its consequences?"

Wolff's heart hardened. He seized Spiegelman by the collar, hauling him upright. "Listen to me," he said, with quiet menace. "I will be candid. You have been given an opportunity denied most of your kind—"

"What is my kind?"

"Must we revisit this?"

"Jews, queers—"

"You are not in charge here," Wolff snapped. Spiegelman flinched, shocked at Wolff's outburst. With uncomfortable heat in his cheeks, the *Gruppenführer* smoothed out his uniform. His fingers brushed his lapels. "Shit," he said, for he'd forgotten to pin on the buttons denoting his rank.

"*Gruppenführer*," Spiegelman murmured, "why won't you let me be? I've done my job. I am ready to go now."

"Listen. I am giving you a chance." Wolff hesitated, then decided the time was right. "I had initially planned to execute Monsieur Aubrion when the *La Libre Belgique* project was at its end. This is regrettable, of course, but that is how these things are done. I am, however, considering a different tack—asking him to join my staff, to work with you. You would no longer have to perform your duties alone."

Spiegelman's fists were rigid at his sides. "Aubrion and I would work together?"

"I understand that you do not believe me, Spiegelman, but I want to help you."

"Right. I see." Spiegelman controlled his breathing. He would not prove himself to be as pitiful as Wolff believed, as Aubrion must suspect. Improbable though it seemed, Wolff had given him something precious. Spiegelman could survive this war, and he could take Aubrion with him. "What would you have me do?"

"I will tell you in time. But you must hold on until then, do you understand?"

Wolff's tone dipped into melodrama—or perhaps Wolff's body was not tailored for such feeling, and any swell of emotion seemed unnatural. Even so, Spiegelman nodded, not quite sure what he had agreed to, not daring to imagine.

12 DAYS TO PRINT
LATE MORNING

The Pyromaniac

I AWOKE IN the basement corner, shivering. I searched for something with which to cover myself. Martin Victor had left a coat on the floor; I draped it across my shoulders before returning to my corner. All the while, I could hear Aubrion. He was everywhere: at a chalkboard, walking, mumbling, hammering at a typewriter. He spoke to himself. In his youth, I heard, Aubrion would spend his restless nights swapping jokes for drinks at alehouses across Brussels. The war—specifically, the curfew, which was instituted a week after we started on *Faux Soir*—brought that habit to an end. And so, from dark until morning, Aubrion was a prisoner in the *Front de l'Indépendance* headquarters. Between fits of sleep, I watched him.

I'm often struck by the temptation to apply modern diagnoses to Aubrion's intensity. Many years after the war, I was reading something—a novel, perhaps; I don't recall—and the words *manic depression* shook me. I have since discovered other such names, angular and long, to describe my Aubrion: *attention def-*

icit, depression, hyperactivity. But if I could return to the time of *Faux Soir* with the tools to heal him, to let him sleep, I do not know whether I *would.* Like everyone, like Aubrion himself, I was selfish with Marc's genius. I am selfish with its beauty, and the memory of it.

I dozed, and was awoken again by the sound of Aubrion's footsteps. "Are you all right, monsieur?" I asked from my corner.

Aubrion yelped. "Gamin! I did not see you there."

"I gathered, monsieur."

"I came up with something rather fun, I think. Do you know those short stories in *Le Soir*, those cautionary fables about sleeping with Americans and not participating in the weekly rations? That sort of thing? I think we're going to do a parody. I might write it, or I might ask Lada to do it." Aubrion pulled on his coat. I noted a new hole in the left elbow. "That other paper—whatever-the-devil-it's-called—I think it did something similar last year, but it was so terrible that it's like they never did it at all." He headed for the stairs.

"Are you going somewhere now, monsieur?" I asked.

"Out for food and coffee."

I stood, feeling hazy. "I could get it for you."

"No, no, I need to walk."

Shaking myself, I went to the washroom to splash water on my face. When I was small, my mother stood over me as I brushed my hair, tugging it playfully when I was naughty. After she died, I cut my hair off with a French army-issue knife I found on a road. I was teetering on the edge of that age when boys and girls are visually indistinguishable, and with short hair, I could pass myself off as a young lad. But I often let it grow into a wayward thicket before cutting it again—until Lada Tarcovich, shortly after meeting me, thrust a comb and a pair of scissors in my hands with the words, "Do something about it." And so, whenever I finished washing my face, I ran her comb through my hair. Whether I missed my long hair, or my mother's touch, or her hairbrush with the French writing on the handle, words I've since forgotten—I missed *something*, that I knew, and I contemplated revealing myself to the others. But the right words eluded me, as indistinct as those on my mother's hairbrush.

I admired Lada's sturdy wood comb. Had it come from a customer, I wondered? Had she smuggled it across enemy lines? It occurs to me that she might simply have purchased it at a neighborhood shop. But back then, it was an heirloom, contraband of unspeakable worth.

The Jester

Aubrion returned an hour later to find René Noël sitting alone among the typewriters. He had his boots propped up on the wall and a stack of papers in his lap. Noël licked his fingers, turned a page, wiped his hand on his inky apron.

"Where is everybody?" asked Aubrion.

Noël said "hmmm?" without glancing up.

"No one's here." Aubrion spread his arms. Typewriters and papers peered at him like gawking spectators.

"I know I'm not *that* important, really," said Noël, "but that was harsh, Marc."

"You know what I meant. *Hardly* no one's here."

"Anyone."

"Right, right, anyone. Hardly anyone is here."

"Well, what did you expect?" Noël tossed his paper onto a desk. "Being tied up and interrogated by the Gestapo tends to make people uncomfortable, doesn't it?"

"Where did they all go? There is nowhere to run."

"I am sure at least a few former members of the FI discovered that last night." The director's tone started lightly enough, but it soon darkened, and he covered his mouth with a fist. He would not look at Aubrion when he spoke. "I suppose you don't know yet. About a dozen of our brothers and sisters tried to flee early this morning. Half were shot. The other half will be." Noël's eyes finally reached Aubrion's. They had hardened like leaves that had been pressed into a book and then forgotten. "Their blood is not on our hands, Marc. The Germans would have found our base even if we had not made this deal with Wolff."

"Did I say anything about blood on our hands?"

"Our soldiers know the risks when they sign on. I do believe one of them made it out. Bernard, if I recall."

Aubrion massaged his forehead. "But if they just would have stayed here—"

"What would have happened? Wolff would have killed them in two weeks rather than tomorrow?"

"But how are we going to print *Faux Soir* without anyone to do the printing?"

"We had better hope Lada's friend Andree Grandjean comes through. We can use a portion of her money to pay Wellens to print for us."

Aubrion scoffed. "We're putting our faith in Ferdinand Wellens?"

"No, in Lada Tarcovich."

"I feel only marginally better."

"Then think about it this way." Noël put a hand on Aubrion's shoulder. "She's putting her faith in *you*."

12 DAYS TO PRINT
LATE AFTERNOON

The Pyromaniac

I STIFFENED AS Theo Mullier took up Aubrion's preferred spot at the chalkboard. "The plan," said Mullier, "is simple." He rubbed at his beard, uncomfortable at our attention. "It's to get a dignitary—"

"Who's the dignitary?" asked Aubrion, cross-legged on a table.

"Sylvain de Jong's son."

"What's the fellow's name? I can't recall."

"Sylvain de Jong."

"Oh. That's why."

"Of Minerva Automobiles?" asked Victor.

"Yes," said Mullier. "The plan is to let the whole country know he's an Allied sympathizer. That'll guarantee he shows up at the fund-raiser."

"*Is* he an Allied sympathizer?" asked Aubrion.

"I dunno." Mullier eased himself into a chair. "Probably not."

Though she was seated at the back of the basement, Lada

Tarcovich's laugh filled the space. "Then how are you going to do that?" she said.

"He's going to say it on air. Like I said, simple."

"In the head, perhaps."

Mullier's blunt fingers dug into his palms. I shrank from him. I don't know a great deal about Theo Mullier's life, in all honesty; he rarely spoke to anyone about it, least of all to me. I do know, however, that people had been calling him simple in the head since he was a boy—starting with his father, a big-handed butcher who'd chased the boy around his shop whenever he tripped and knocked something over. "Damn simple fool of a boy," he'd growl, and of course Theo never made it far on that foot.

"Look who I found," said René Noël, with strained cheer. Noël was not a man easily given to cheer under the best of circumstances, and his good-naturedness had corroded as the war drew on. We all glanced up as Noël led David Spiegelman, whose hollow eyes remained on the floor, down the stairs and into the basement.

"Just in time," said Aubrion.

Noël took a seat near the door. "What did I miss?" he asked.

"We were discussing a very simple plan," said Tarcovich.

Spiegelman nearly smiled. "There aren't enough of those in the world."

"That's not true," said Aubrion. "Hitler has one."

"*Marc,*" said Tarcovich—Noël—Spiegelman—perhaps me, too.

"We were all thinking it."

"We were *not*," said Tarcovich.

"Anyway." Aubrion wielded the word like a broom, sweeping his insensitivity away. He grabbed a piece of chalk. "Two updates. First, Joseph Beckers's stag party is in two days."

"Stag party?" said Tarcovich.

"I'm drawing up a plan to secure the *Le Soir* distribution list during the party," said Aubrion. "It should be fun, don't you think?"

"Joseph Beckers?" said Spiegelman. "Isn't he in charge of the postal service?"

"He's the one."

"How are you going to get him to hand over the list?"

Aubrion grinned, rocking back and forth on his heels. "Catastrophically."

"Where is the location of the party?" asked Victor.

"Remind me: what's the address of your whorehouse?" said Aubrion, nodding at Tarcovich.

"Beg pardon?" said Lada.

"Haven't you heard? Before Beckers slips on the perfumed handcuffs of marriage, his pals are taking him out for one last hurrah. A night of revelry, of untamed masculinity. You know how these things go, Lada." Aubrion's hands went to his hair, his shirt, restless with anticipation. "They've chosen, as their venue, the best whorehouse in the city. I have here an invitation that was mailed to Monsieur Beckers last night." He pulled a slip of paper from his pocket. "Oh, right, *that's* the address. I knew it, too. Twenty-Seven Rue de—"

"Hang on a moment." Lada held up a hand, as though Aubrion's scheme was a physical thing—a boulder, or an avalanche—that she sought to ward off. "Joseph Becker, that wretched man in charge of the post, is having his stag party at *my* whorehouse?"

"You really are a tad slow today, Lada," said Aubrion.

"Did his friends plan this...*this*?"

"Of course! That is to say, I'm sure *one* of them did, though it's unclear to me—to Beckers, too, I'm sure—which of them it was. But no matter. A jolly surprise, don't you think? Isn't that the sort of word he would use? *Jolly?*"

Tarcovich's hand went to her throat. "Oh, God."

"Everywhere Beckers goes, the list must go with him," said Aubrion. "That is his agreement with the Reich."

Victor added, "That is the procedure for any top-secret information. For the Germans, that is. It must travel with the official who can give clearance."

"Did you really make poor Spiegelman draw up invitations for this?" said Tarcovich.

"I did not 'make' him," said Aubrion.

"You made him."

"He didn't refuse."

"You're cruel, Marc."

With a nod at Victor, Aubrion said, "Your girls show the lads a good time. You snatch the list from Beckers's pocket. What is Beckers to do, admit he was cavorting with prostitutes?"

Tarcovich had gone pale. "It is brilliant."

"Second update." Aubrion smacked the tip of his chalk against the board. It occurred to me that it was a good thing we did not have neighbors. "The posters advertising our fund-raiser are going up today."

Mullier asked, "Who's in charge of that?"

"Gamin is taking care of it," said Aubrion, and I sat up straight at the sound of my name.

"I don't know…" Mullier hesitated.

"What don't you know?" said Aubrion.

"The whole fund-raiser business. It seems needlessly risky. The FI is trusting too many people with far too little to lose."

"You mean Andree?" said Tarcovich, handling the question like it might burn her fingers.

"The judge is part of it." Mullier looked at Tarcovich. "I'll do my bit to get the guests to the fund-raiser, but I don't like it."

"We know perfectly well what you don't like," said Tarcovich. Mullier did not reply. Consider where we were, *when* we were. Mullier may have put his hands and wit and soul to work for the resistance, but he was still a man of faith, a man of the times. I am not sure Mullier would have shed blood for Tarcovich or Spiegelman.

"Third update." Victor got up out of his chair. "We will be performing the Nazi school caper tomorrow afternoon. Any last-minute suggestions would be appreciated." He pushed up his spectacles. "Or prayers. We will gladly take those, too."

"All right, then." Aubrion wrote *School caper tomorrow* on a blackboard, the way one might put an appointment in a datebook. "Monsieur Spiegelman, what do you have for us?"

Spiegelman buttoned up his coat as he spoke, for the November air had infected the brick and concrete. "I've written about five pages of material for *La Libre Belgique*. You can look over the draft if you'd like, but I believe it's ready to be presented to Wolff. I have also written a parody of Maurice-George Olivier's 'Effective Strategy' for *Faux Soir*."

"Have you really?" Smiling, Aubrion dashed *Effective Strategy* and four exclamation marks across the chalkboard. "That's brilliant. It's similar but not *quite* like that feature the Dutch paper did a few months ago, so it's *just* unique enough to capture people's attention. I'm surprised I didn't think of it."

"I also have an idea," said Spiegelman, haltingly. "For another column."

"For *Faux Soir*?" asked Aubrion.

"Yes."

"What is it?"

"In my time with—the Reich—" These last two words spilled out of him together, coagulating among the typewriters. "—I've come to see the sorts of people they usually press into service. Whenever they occupy a city or a country, you see, they fill their ranks with whatever that place did not want. I don't believe that's something ordinary people know about, or even think about."

Tarcovich leaned back, crossing her arms. "What sorts of people?" she challenged.

"All sorts," he said with a helpless gesture.

"Lada, let him finish," said René Noël, waving her quiet.

"My idea is to write a column mocking the Nazi ranks," said Spiegelman, a tad too quickly, speaking in clumps and shards, "showing our readers that they're full of the most unwanted members of our society."

"And this would be a joke column?" said Aubrion.

"As I've conceived of it."

"You would want to write it?" asked Victor.

"With your permission."

"What," said Aubrion, "would be the punch line?"

"The punch line?"

"Yeah, you see, every joke has three components—"

Tarcovich rolled her eyes. "Oh, God, here we go."

"—the setup, the meat, and the punch line."

"Don't take it too hard, David," said Tarcovich. "He's been giving me this speech for the past four years."

"So, your setup is that the Nazis need people. The meat is that these people are often undesirable, at least according to the rest of us. But what's your punch line?"

Spiegelman shook his head. "I suppose I will have to do a bit more thinking."

"David, we appreciate having you on this project," said Noël. "We truly do. But—"

"—this column isn't going to work," said Aubrion.

Spiegelman cheek's flushed. "Why not?"

"As Marc said." Noël picked up a bit of cloth and idly erased one of the blackboards. Some diagrams, a childish doodle of a face, and words in French and German disappeared with a sweep of his hand. "There's no punch line."

"And there's a bigger problem," said Aubrion. "It's mean-spirited."

"Does that matter?" said Spiegelman. "We're at war."

"It matters *because* we are at war," said Tarcovich.

"But isn't this whole project mean-spirited?"

Aubrion shook his head furiously, stepping down from the table. "No, God no, that's not what *zwanze* is." He approached Spiegelman, and I thought my friend might hit him or shake him. But Aubrion stopped, perhaps half a meter from Spiegelman. I heard, and I can still hear, the lecture he wanted to give, the one Marc Aubrion had delivered before: "*Zwanze* is punching up," he always said. "You can't hit people who are already on their knees. That's what *they're* doing." And yet he did not speak those words to David Spiegelman. Something gentle stirred in his eyes. "Spiegelman," he said softly, "I appreciate what you're doing here. I really do."

"But it's not right for the paper," said Spiegelman.

I watched Aubrion falter. "You have done beautiful things," he said, but if Spiegelman had rapped on those words with his knuckles, he would have heard their hollowness.

Lada Tarcovich said, "We all admire your work, Spiegelman."

As Tarcovich continued to reassure him, and Noël did the same, I ran to fetch him a stale mug of coffee. When I returned, Spiegelman looked as though he were sinking lower into himself, down where no one would ever find him.

I did not understand what had hurt him so until much later—until recently, if I'm honest. At the time, I'd thought it was simply the pain of rejection. Not so. It was that David Spiegelman believed *his* brand of work—writing that mocked people like him, like August Wolff—that *this* would be the thing that exorcised his hands, that eased his discomfort at what he could do. He meant to use his column as a torch to melt the ice of his prison walls. Aubrion had rejected not only his work, you see, but his escape plan. If the FI would not allow him to write this column, then he had nothing left; that was how Spiegelman felt. He could not atone for the evil he had taken into his pen. All he had were August Wolff and his promises.

12 DAYS TO PRINT
EARLY EVENING

The Pyromaniac

WHILE THEO MULLIER was explaining how he planned to wreck the reputation of one Sylvain de Jong Jr., Aubrion jerked his head at the door, signaling that it was time for me to leave. And so I went upstairs to gather up a few bags of supplies, marveling at how empty the building was that day. I set out into the streets as a clock tower struck noon, the lonely pang of bells cutting through the afternoon fog.

After two years by Marc Aubrion's side, I was an expert in getting people's attention. I marched past the Flemming Workhouse. One of the shifts was just getting out for their midday meal. They saw me, the lot of them, kids with accents flavored by every country the Germans had taken. When they called out to me—"Gamin, where are you going in such a hurry? What are those things you have, Gamin?"—I ignored them. Keeping my head high, I marched onward, away from the workhouse and toward the center of town. Naturally, the kids were curious; not even the smoke in their lungs and pipes in their mouths could diminish that. "C'mon, let's tail him," said one, and that was all it took. They set off after me. I marched in time with their footsteps.

My next stop was the Enghien School for Boys. I'd always kept away from it, hearing stories about what happened there in the dark, so I didn't know any of the lads who called it home. They'd heard tales of *me*, though, and shouted after me as I walked past, a Pied Piper with carpetbags and a ragged, noisy train of work-weary boys. "Gamin, where are you going?" I heard. "What's in the bags?" I did not look at them, kept up my march. High voices whispering and muddy footsteps behind me were the only indication of my success.

This went on until my train grew restless. Each stop was punctuated by groans and angry fists in the air from those who drifted away. After my last stop—perhaps my thirtieth, or my fortieth; I'd lost track some time ago—I took my followers into an alley. Only then did I drop my bags and turn around.

I gasped, for close to a hundred children stood behind me. They were mostly boys, as I'd expected, but a group of girls—eyes defiant—huddled off to the side, as well. Though I kept my expression neutral, my heart tingled with a curious longing. The girls mimicked the boys' posture: the half slouch of the career vagrant, at home anywhere and nowhere. Their hands sat loose in their empty pockets. These girls looked settled into themselves, wearing their bruises like badges. Was this true, I wondered, or was I spinning tales? Were they as comfortable with themselves as they appeared? When I first started masquerading as a boy, a thousand small cracks in the breastplate of my disguise—a pronoun here, a "good lad!" there—had left me desperate to tell Aubrion who I was. By God, I was drowning and kicking in the lie. As time passed, however, and our confidence deepened, I felt the lie less frequently, often not at all. I built my home out of the trappings of boyhood. I had thought it impossible to inhabit this new world as a girl, but perhaps it was simply that I had not *wanted* to.

I faced the crowd of kids, blowing smoke from their pipes, tossing around secondhand marbles or jacks, eating a candy bar they found in a dead soldier's backpack, pulling their caps down over their faces, chewing on bits of straw—all of them quiet, waiting for me to speak. So, I did.

"Marc Aubrion has a job for us. It's more of a game, really."

I cannot remember whether I actually felt that way or whether I repackaged my feelings for the others. I do remember that it had been so long since I'd said that word, the word *game*, that it tasted of a lie. There had been games before the war; there hadn't been any since.

My associates were skeptical. "What sort of a game?" asked a boy near the front. His high voice bounced off the alley walls. He was around my age, I think, no older than twelve.

I pulled a fund-raiser poster out of my bag, holding it up. "See this poster? The game is to put up loads of these things all over the place, anywhere you can get to. You get one point for every poster you put up. Two points if you put it up in a fancy neighborhood."

"Which neighborhoods is the fancy ones?" asked a different boy.

"Any ones where they'd kick out the likes of us. But be quick about it. No mucking around, or you'll be—" I fished around for the word "—disqualified."

"What's that mean?"

"It means you'll be kicked out, you dummy."

"What's the winner get?" called a tall girl.

"A reward." I hadn't quite worked that part out. "Something big, from Marc Aubrion."

"But you promised us something big if we helped with the other thing," said the first boy who'd spoken. "The bomb thing."

"Yeah, and have you helped yet?" I said. "Eh, you ass?"

The boy studied the holes in his shoes.

"That's what I thought. Any other damn fool questions?"

Everyone shook their heads.

"Good." I planted my feet far apart and put my fists on my hips: René Noël's posture. "I have two bags up here, filled with posters. Each of you lot gets no more than ten at a time. When you're done with your ten, you can come back to get more. But no wasting 'em, you get me? Marc Aubrion won't like that."

"Will we get to meet him?" asked a kid in a cap three sizes too big. "When we're done?"

"Marc Aubrion? He's got things to do, you know. He's not one for lazing around, not like the lot of you. Now make two lines before I change my mind about letting you play. One in front of each bag."

To my surprise, they listened—but I suppose that was to be expected. All they did, these children of the workhouses and boarding schools, was stand in lines from waking to sleep. They surged forward, a mass of oversized shirts and sticky fingers and wooden pipes.

"There's paste up here, too," I added. "But don't take more than what you need."

I watched as they reached inside the bags, grabbing no more than ten posters each, stopping only to make a polite request for paste. No one cut the line, or tried to cheat, or grabbed more than their share. Some of them even thanked me before they skipped off. Once or twice, a too-eager kid tripped and fell against someone else, usually someone larger. But no punches were thrown; the kid murmured an apology, and his apology was accepted.

Though rain threatened to interrupt our activities, my associates were undaunted. I kept an eye on the bags, trying not to gnaw on my fingernails as the supply of posters dwindled. I need not have worried: in the end, each kid got his or her fair share of posters, and there were more than enough to go around.

When the last boy ran off with his ten, I peered into the bags. A small stack of posters remained in each.

Sighing, I closed up my bags and took a seat under an awning some shopkeeper had set up in the alley. It would be at least an hour, I knew, before one of my associates returned for more. I spent most of that time marveling at how smoothly everything had gone. To this day, I remain convinced that I was once commander-in-chief of the most civilized army in Europe.

11 DAYS TO PRINT
NOT QUITE MORNING

The Jester

THE 3:00-A.M. PATROL marched overhead, escorting a tank through the streets. The ceiling lightbulbs jerked on their strings like dying legs at the drop of the hangman's rope. Aubrion did not notice. He was stacking ale bottles on the basement floor.

"Mullier wouldn't let me listen to the whole thing," Aubrion was telling Tarcovich, "but my God, Lada, my God! He persuaded de Jong to say, *while he was recording,* that he loves Winston Churchill more than life itself." Laughter threatened to shake Aubrion apart. "Isn't that extraordinary?"

"That can't be the exact quote," Lada said through a smile. He and Lada were sitting side-by-side on the basement floor.

"I have the recording upstairs."

"You do not."

"But can you hardly believe it?" Aubrion clutched at his glass of ale, contorting his wrist to keep from spilling it on the basement floor. Angular and clumsy on the best of days, Aubrion became an acrobat with ale in his hand. "It's artful. Mullier says it'll air this morning. I knew there was a reason we kept him around." Aubrion took a long drink of his ale, or rather what was left of it.

"You are not particularly good at sharing," said Tarcovich.

"*You* are not particularly good at asking."

"Please?"

With a sigh, Aubrion passed her the glass. She finished off its contents.

"Marc?"

"Hmmm?"

"What are we doing?"

"Getting drunk."

"No, we are definitely not doing that."

"Yes, we are."

"We have to work tomorrow. Today. What time is it?"

"Work be damned."

Through an agreeable haze, Tarcovich looked around at the chalkboards that lined the walls. Someone had drawn a caricature of Hitler on one of them, adjacent to a diagram showing the layout of tomorrow's pamphlets. The Allies had started dropping propaganda leaflets on both sides, strafing the countryside alongside bullets and bombs: the pamphlets shone bright with tales of bravery and dirty pictures for our lads, and lies and misdirections for theirs. FI artists were responsible for many of the leaflets. It was some of Aubrion's favorite work.

"Remember when the war started," Tarcovich mumbled, "and the king signed that—"

"The declaration of neutrality!"

"We were at the whorehouse together. Do you remember? In the attic." Tarcovich closed her eyes, remembering Aubrion with two bottles of good beer and no war, not yet. "My God, that was ages ago."

"The whorehouse has an attic?" said Aubrion.

Tarcovich's eyes snapped open. "So, you don't remember."

"Of course I do. We were thinking of getting out." Aubrion threw an arm over his face. Tarcovich had watched him do that a thousand times, a gesture of finality, exhaustion. She was bound to this man by her knowledge of his mannerisms and habits; they were inexorably tied, those two, imprisoned by a connection neither had named. He was funny; he cared for her in ways that surprised even himself. She told him when to get a haircut; she smacked him on the head when he said something he did not mean. "Well," Aubrion went on, "I suppose that's not true. We were *talking* about getting out. I don't think either of us is truly so wise. There was going to be a pamphlet, or something, that we were planning to write."

"What happened to that idea?" asked Tarcovich.

"What happens to any of them?"

"True." Tarcovich lay back, looking up at the concrete ceiling. "How many papers do you think we'll sell?" she said, somewhat lazily. "Before the Gestapo realizes the country is laughing at them and goes after the names on the paper."

Aubrion stretched out on the floor. "We're not using our real names, are we?" He rolled over onto his side, propping himself up on his elbow.

"I've never known you not to use your real name."

"There was that time in Brussels—"

"Not even then."

"Damn. Am I really so vain?"

"Yes. So, how many, do you think?"

"I dunno." Aubrion pushed his hair out of his eyes. When he was a boy, his mother took him to a barber twice a month. His eyes drifted to a crack in the concrete floor. "I thought Noël patched that."

"Patched what?"

Aubrion pointed at the crack. "It looks rather like a smile, I think." He did this often, seeing things in the world that weren't there, or making them up. It drove Noël mad: Aubrion's ten-

dency to point out hidden pictures, seeing the world as a madman's canvas. Tarcovich never told the others how she loved him
for it. "Or a frown, if you look at it the other way."

"Fine." Tarcovich got up, collecting Aubrion's glass. She
switched off the recording radio, which had been wheezing
old Polish songs into the dank air. "You don't feel like having
this conversation. I understand."

"What conversation?" As Tarcovich started toward the stairs,
Aubrion twisted around on the floor. "Wait, Lada, what conversation are you talking about?"

"I was asking about *Faux Soir*," Lada said over her shoulder.

"What about it?"

"How many copies—"

"I don't know."

"See, you don't feel like it." Tarcovich paused at the foot of the
staircase, turning slowly to face Aubrion. She felt claustrophobic,
like they were locked in a room without a light or a map, privy
only to shadows on the wall. "Listen here," said Tarcovich, and
her eyes had no mercy for Aubrion, "before this is all over—
and it's going to be over far quicker than you think—you need
to come to terms with everything."

"Everything?" said Aubrion. "Lada, do you believe I'm doing
this, any of this, because I think we're going to be successful?"

"If you don't think we're going to be successful—"

"No, no." Aubrion massaged his forehead. "That's not what
I meant."

"What did you mean?"

"That our success or failure doesn't matter to me."

"Then what does?"

"My God, Lada, you see them, too. The sad man who lost his
wife last winter, the one who lines up at the butcher shop every
Friday to get his meat rations. The women who get excited because the coats at the general shop are half-off, coats someone
stole from the back of some dead refugee. The man at the cof-

feehouse downtown who takes his cup alone, and you *know* it's the grandest part of his day..."

Tarcovich glanced away. "What of it?"

"They have fallen into a routine. The routine of subjugation."

"Oh, God, Marc, don't start."

"I'm *serious*."

"I know you are."

"But listen. Even if we sell one copy, even if the man at the butcher shop reads it, nods along, and tosses it away, I'll be happy. *He'll* be happy, for a second. We will have broken the routine. Don't you see? We can show him that there's something else, that his life is not just the Reich and meat on Fridays. Does that mean anything to you?"

"Of course it does."

"But?"

"But that is not my point." Lada Tarcovich looked down at the floor, then back up at Aubrion. Her eyes were rimmed in red. "Listen here. My mother once told me a story of my grandmother, who was executed by the Russians in Lithuania. Grandmother knew she would be shot five minutes before it happened. That was how quickly she was sentenced, they were all sentenced, in those days. And my mother, bless her, she always wondered how Grandmother passed those last five minutes. Did she suddenly believe in God? Did she wish she'd—I don't know—tried that recipe she'd been putting off? What did she think, or feel, before she could never think or feel again?" Tarcovich took Aubrion's hands. His touch came to her in an echo. "This is your last five minutes, Marc. I only wish you could see that."

Aubrion said nothing. Tarcovich was asking something of him, he knew; but that was the limit of his understanding. Aubrion felt her hands leave him, and it was as though he'd missed something, that the train had pulled out of the station without him, that he'd skipped a few pages in the middle of the book.

"She might not have felt anything out of the ordinary," he said, finally. "Your grandmother, before she died. She might have been thinking of the weather, if it was a nice day."

"I suppose she might have," said Tarcovich, her expression softening.

The Smuggler

They sat together for a time, until Tarcovich asked, "Have you thought about writing obituaries?"

"I know we aren't going to make it, Lada," said Aubrion, "but don't you think that's a tad premature?"

"For *Faux Soir*, you dolt."

"Oh. You mean satirical obituaries? How interesting," said Aubrion, and Tarcovich adored his unwitting smile. "So-and-so of Enghien, a loyal man of the town, died this afternoon following a long, heroic battle with his wife's chocolate mousse—"

Tarcovich laughed.

"—which had rendered him incapable of walking without erupting in a series of wheezing gasps his friends often mistook for French."

Tarcovich countered: "So-and-so of Brussels, an immigrant from the Mongol lands, died last night in a German air raid. The enterprising Germans, who had intended to bomb Allied territories, missed their target, and as a result, poor so-and-so died laughing."

Aubrion leaned against the wall to bear the weight of his own laughter, then stopped suddenly. "I cannot write that."

"Why ever not?"

"Far too many people have died. I cannot poke fun at death, especially not when these people—" he gestured around him, at the imaginary schoolchildren, the butcher, a lamplighter being questioned by a pair of Nazis, their script now routine "—will be reading it. It is too much. Spiegelman could do it—"

Tarcovich was incredulous. "*Spiegelman*, whose family died, whose *people* are dying?"

"I cannot, Lada. That's all I have to say about the matter."

She did not have the strength to press him. Tarcovich let her mind go free. The churches outside, surly and familiar beneath the clouds, chimed needfully. She'd usually cover her ears against the din, but suddenly the bells reminded her too much of Andree Grandjean. Those bells had chimed to awaken them the first time they'd laid together, so now the bells tasted of Andree, smelled of her, of awaking to each other's lips—nonsense. Lada had heard those bells a thousand times, of course, having lived in Enghien since childhood. But she'd never before associated them with a person, a face. The bells belonged to Andree now, as did everything else in the world.

After a time, Tarcovich said, "You know what, Marc? It really does."

"It does what?" said Aubrion.

Tarcovich nodded at the crack in the floor. "Look like a smile."

11 DAYS TO PRINT
MORNING

The Pyromaniac

SOMEONE NUDGED ME AWAKE. I rolled over, instructing them to do something obscene and anatomically impossible. They responded by applying their boot—gently, but persuasively—to my backside.

"What d'you want?" I snapped, rubbing the exhaustion from my eyes.

Aubrion and Victor were standing over me. The latter held chalk and a slate; the former held a bundle of blue-and-white cloth. Aubrion's hair stood up in apoplectic protest; Victor's glasses sat, partially capsized, on his twice-broken nose.

"What's going on?" I asked.

Aubrion threw the cloth at me. I held it up, realizing with dread that it was a pair of trousers and a shirt: one of those ridiculous little sailor uniforms that were popular until people realized they were dressing their children like men who rarely bathed and often died of syphilis. Making my disgust clear, I fingered the oversized lapels, the white stripe on the navy trousers, the starched shirt and cartoon buttons.

"You should put it on now," said Victor, "so you will be comfortable in it this afternoon."

"What's happening this afternoon?"

Aubrion smiled apologetically. "We've decided it would be a good idea to have a model student in our educational program, *Schule für die Whatever-the-Devil*. To show the Germans how effective and jolly good and all-around wonderful it is."

I held up the sailor outfit again. When I was very young, long before the Germans came to Toulouse, I had a fascination with the mythology of the Norse. One story in particular captured my attention, a tale in which the mighty Thor is forced to masquerade as a giant's bride. Even now, the memory of my father reading this story to me, raising his voice to a strained falsetto and then down to a cavernous grumble, is agonizingly clear, as though it happened yesterday and could happen again tomorrow. I thought of the story then, sitting on the floor of the FI basement with my lap covered in stiff white-and-blue fabric, and I felt, for all the world, like a god of thunder about to put on a wedding dress.

"It has *ribbons*," I said.

Victor sniffed. "Wearing a uniform is perfectly respectable. Many schoolchildren wear something similar, and have for centuries."

"With respect, monsieur, many schoolchildren eat paste, as well."

I bathed out of a tub Tarcovich set up in the basement. For reasons that were obvious only to me, I insisted on privacy. My morning ablutions rarely involved anything more than a cursory wash-up; soldiers of the resistance did not *bathe*. The thought of soaking in a tub like a swollen *hausfrau* felt like a wretched humiliation. But my body sank low into the warm water. I scrubbed myself until I was raw-red and smelled of lye. I had not taken a bath since Toulouse. I had forgotten it was even possible in this world.

When I finally extracted myself from the water, I put on that damned uniform. I then turned to look at myself in the mirror on the wall of the FI's water closet; someone got drunk one night and threw a bottle at it, so a thin crack split the glass with a frown of disapproval. Mute with shock, I studied myself—for I looked nothing like me. I looked like a lie, an artist's representation of what my life might have been if not for the war. I rubbed my cheek, newly liberated from a smudge of dirt. For weeks, I'd assumed my neck and face were latticed in bruises, but the water had revealed the truth: it was filth that had sunk its teeth into my flesh. So too had the bath exposed my pallor, that I was in dire need of more food, chronically dehydrated— and yet my body somehow looked more complete than it had before, a filled-in version of who I had been before the war. All that was missing was my long hair. I pulled at the stubborn weeds on my scalp. I cannot say I longed for the blond tresses that would return me to who I was before Toulouse; that is not quite right. Instead of longing, or wondering, I felt unfinished: crouched between the Helene of *then* and the Gamin of *now*.

Aubrion called down the stairs into the basement. "Gamin, are you still down there?"

"Yes." I cleared my throat and said, loudly this time: "Yes, monsieur. You can come down now."

Aubrion and Tarcovich appeared at the foot of the stairs. For a time, they said nothing. Then Aubrion's head tilted, and he emitted: "Oh."

"Oh?" I said.

"You look—"

"He looks precious," said Tarcovich.

"You should have something." Aubrion handed me some day-old pastries wrapped in newspaper. Though none of us had our fill of food, my belly rarely ached in the days of *Faux Soir*. Tarcovich fetched me hot chocolate, Noël left me little sandwiches of butter and cured meat, and my dear Aubrion had his pastries, always pastries, an endless and mysterious supply.

"Now what, monsieur?" I asked with my mouth full.

"Now, we make you respectable."

"All right, ladies and gents," said René Noël. "Everyone knows their parts?"

Victor, Spiegelman, Tarcovich, Aubrion and Wellens nodded; Mullier didn't nod, but he also didn't *not* nod, so everyone interpreted this as assent. Though the basement was frigid with early morning air, I could feel my shirt and coat growing heavy with perspiration.

The professor instructed me to stand before a chalkboard. I'd heard him up with the moon, passing another night without sleep. Like me—like most of us, really—Victor had nowhere else to go. He had sat alone in the basement, ill and shivering with his memories. As Noël reiterated the day's plan, I watched Victor concentrate on breathing.

"Spiegelman?" said Noël.

"I'm playing an instructor."

"Tarcovich?"

"Also an instructor."

"Wellens?"

"The director." (*Direct-tah.*)

"Victor?"

The professor took a breath, pausing half a second too long, so everyone turned to look at him. He manufactured a smile. "Associate director," he said.

Noël peered at him with his owl's eyes. "Are you quite in one piece, Victor?"

"A bit tired, is all."

"We shall have to pour some coffee into you. Aubrion, who are you playing?"

"Playing?"

"In the school caper, Marc. Christ Almighty, pay attention."

"Oh, right, yes. An instructor. Right?"

"*Yes.* Thank you. Mullier?"

"Aide."

"Gamin?"

I shifted in my uniform. "A student."

"Good." Noël rubbed his hands together. "Now, the books—the, um, the pornography—they've been covered so that they look like textbooks, but try not to open them too widely."

"Why not?" Ferdinand Wellens asked through his beard.

Tarcovich smirked. "Some of them are illustrated."

"Remember," said Noël, "our goal is to get the Ministry of Education to commit as much paper and ink as they can spare, so please, whatever you do, stress the fact that these young, impressionable youths need materials to learn to read and write and be productive *robotniks* of the Reich. Everyone clear?"

"So, Gamin," said Aubrion, "when the lads from the Ministry ask what you've learned in your time as our pupil, what will you say?"

My brief time in primary school seemed a thousand kilometers away. I searched my memory for what I'd learned there. "Sums?"

"No," said Martin Victor, "you tell them that you've learned obedience to the *Führer.*"

"That's Hitler, right?"

"God help us," muttered Tarcovich, getting up to straighten my lapels.

"Yes, but you should only ever refer to him as the *Führer,*" said Victor.

"Walk for us," said Tarcovich. "So we can fix your posture."

Feeling immensely foolish, I walked five steps, turned around, and walked five more.

"How was that?" I asked.

"Terrible," said Tarcovich.

Aubrion said, "I thought it was fine."

"Of course *you* did." Tarcovich placed one hand on my back and one on my chest. Then, with strength I did not know she had, she *pushed* me up and back so my bones cracked and my spine threatened to go on strike. "That's better, isn't it? Now walk again."

I started to walk. Before I could attempt my third step, Tarcovich stopped me.

"No, no, it's still wrong. Pretend you have steel in your spine."

"Begging your pardon, madame, but that sounds uncomfortable."

"Yes, walk like you're uncomfortable," said Aubrion. "I always get the feeling Nazis are uncomfortable."

I marched around the room like a flagpole, until Tarcovich stopped me thus: "I think that's good enough. Show us your Nazi salute."

I threw up my arm in the familiar way. Spiegelman flinched.

"Keep walking," said Tarcovich. "March a little."

"What is your favorite book?" asked Victor.

"I don't read much, monsieur."

"Incorrect. It is *Der Pimpf.*"

Aubrion laugh-snorted. "*Der* what?"

"Mention your heritage." Spiegelman talked as if he didn't want to be heard. "Do it often. If you run out of things to say, tell them your family has a rich Aryan lineage."

Tarcovich put a hand on her chest. "'I'm a blond, blue-eyed son of the Reich, with the waters of the Rhine flowing through my veins. I await the day I can thrust my flag into the moist soil of the Fatherland.' That sort of thing, you see?"

"And use the words *stock* and *breeding* a lot," said Aubrion.

"Right." René Noël untied his apron. "Let's go make fools of ourselves, shall we?"

We gathered in a storeroom behind a senile old coffeehouse to sell Nazi Germany a school that did not exist. The tiny space had a drooping ceiling, pregnant with mold, and drafty brick walls that let in a smell of sulfur. It was there that the men from the Ministry came to call.

"I am Isaak Jund." Aubrion stifled a laugh as Jund—a fit man with full gray hair that belied his unlined face—shook his hand. Only I knew what was so amusing: Jund looked like a caricature from a parody of a male potency pill ad that our comics had drawn last week.

"Good to meet you, Jund," said Aubrion.

Jund gave a swift nod. "These are my associates, Herr Royer—" Royer held out his hand; the fellow was bald, with a square jaw and a thick blond beard. "And this is Herr Hoch." Of the three, Hoch had the least impressive hairline, a defect that was offset by visible muscles and striking blue eyes.

The three men took seats around a low, straining table. They watched us as we prepared for the meeting; Tarcovich placed the crate of "textbooks" near the table, Aubrion wheeled a chalkboard to the front of the room, and the others stood back with their hands clasped, trying to look stately, or at least like they hadn't spent the past few days hiding a crate of pornography in their print-house.

Ferdinand Wellens—who Noël and Victor had persuaded to dress conservatively for the occasion, which meant an olive suit and bow tie—marched up to the blackboard. He shifted around for a bit, sweating around his collar. And then he began his pitch, and we were off.

"Good afternoon, gentlemen of the Ministry. I am Ferdinand Wellens, a humble businessman." Aubrion smiled, for Wellens said the word *humble* like it was in another language. "At the very beginning of this great war, I recognized the nobility of the Nazi purpose. As such, I wasted no time in pledging my support for the Reich, promising I would spare nothing—not even my life—so that the Reich could march across the earth. The system of education I propose to you today, my own *Schule für die Erziehung von Kindern mit ewige Liebe*—" Wellens said it a tad too quickly, but his eyes filled with triumph that he'd managed to say it *at all* "—is a product of that devotion."

I craned my neck to see the Germans' faces. They were, however, unreadable.

"Gentlemen, our mission is public enlightenment." Wellens wrote *ENLIGHTENMENT* on the board—in pudgy capital letters—then grinned at us like a ham-handed Siddhartha. "Through the application of our curriculum, which combines lessons on obedience and strength, we will forge the minds of the youth in the furnace of our classrooms. The Nazi aim—"

"All right, all right." Jund put up a hand. His wedding band caught the light. Aubrion wondered what sort of woman would marry a fellow from the Ministry of Education. A failed schoolteacher, perhaps: a woman named Gertrude with an overbite and thick legs. "We've heard quite enough."

Wellens recoiled. "You have?"

"We're busy men." Royer stood, as did his colleagues. "The Reich is growing and changing. Every time a church or a coffeehouse closes up shop, someone wants to start a school in the ashes. We have six appointments today—thirty-three of them this week."

"What my colleague is saying," added Hoch, "is that we'd appreciate it if you would get to the point."

Jund smiled. "What is it you need from us?"

Wellens blushed all the way down his neck. "Uh—um—we need—"

"We have a need for supplies, gentlemen," Victor spoke up. "Paper and ink is expensive in times such as these."

"How much of it?" said Royer.

"About two hundred thousand sheets of paper," said Aubrion.

"Two hundred *thousand*," said Hoch.

"Correct. And two hundred barrels of ink."

"Are you quite sure you need so much?"

"Think about how much paper and ink the average student could go through in a day."

"We have ambitious plans for our school, sir," said Victor.

To our surprise, Wellens added: "And reason to believe they are justified." He held up a thick folder. "We have put together a curriculum that spans fifteen weeks of educational material. It is poised to become one of the best in the nation. Our materials include—"

"Would you do us the honor of letting us observe one of your lessons?" asked Royer.

Victor blinked. "I don't see why not." He flipped through the (largely empty) file to buy time while he fished around for a topic about which he knew *something*. It had to be suitably innocuous, acceptably patriotic. "All right," he said. "Gentlemen, the lesson we have scheduled for this afternoon deals with the mathematics of—"

"Surely you have a lesson on the *völkisch* ideology?" said Royer.

I watched Victor's face turn red, then purple. "I beg your pardon?"

"The *völkisch*—"

"Oh, yes."

"You do?"

"We do, of course."

Ignoring Wellens, who was making eye contact with the exit, Victor dropped the file on a table and approached the chalkboard. He picked up a piece of chalk, seeming unsure what to do with it.

"The *völkisch* ideology," Victor said in a tone I had never heard from him, dignified and commanding, "teaches us two things."

Sitting cross-legged before the chalkboard, I began copying Victor's lecture. I wrote *felkish: 2 things* in round, deliberate letters: a bastardization of Marc Aubrion's handwriting.

"The first thing it teaches us is that our society is old." On the blackboard behind him, Victor wrote *1) Society = old.* "Very old.

Rooted in a tradition that comes from thousands of years of noble history. The second thing it teaches us is that our society represents the proper order of things." *2) Society = proper order.* "Anything less than our society is chaos. Anything more is decadence. We are at an equilibrium unmatched through the ages. Any questions?"

I raised my hand, as Wellens had instructed me to do: "They might ask him to teach, and no matter what he is teaching," the businessman had said, "you should ask this question. Even if he is lecturing on animal husbandry, it will be appropriate, I assure you."

Victor called on me. For a second, but only a second, I struggled to recall the word Wellens had taught me with his over-enunciated vigor. "What about ethnocentrism?" I asked Victor.

"Excellent question," said the professor. I heard Royer and the others mumbling with appreciation. Faint lines appeared around Wellens's eyes and mouth. "We believe that our race is superior to all others because we have *evidence* to suggest that this is true. This is a common misperception—that our views are simple racism. Not so. A good Aryan would never accept anything without evidence—" Victor wrote *EVIDENCE* on the board and underlined it three times. His chalk rained snowy powder. "And we have evidence in abundance."

"What sort of evidence?"

"Another excellent question. We have much evidence, to be sure, but the main bits of evidence are fourfold. In the days of the Holy Roman Empire—"

And so Victor went on: four pieces of evidence, three reasons for each, two historical roots of our public consciousness, three vignettes, five reasons Hitler owed everything to the *völkisch* ideology—an ideology, I remind you, about which Martin Victor knew *nothing*. The lecture leaped from the head of our professor, Athena-like and impeccably outlined. It was the grandest, most boring magic trick I had ever seen. When Victor had gone on in this way for about ninety minutes, Hoch held up a manicured hand.

"Thank you, Professor." He smiled. "Your knowledge is limitless. We are impressed."

"May we see a blueprint of the schoolhouse you plan to build?" asked Jund.

Of course, we had no such blueprints, as we had no plans to build a schoolhouse. But Ferdinand Wellens had prepared for the possibility that the Germans would ask. On cue, I got to my feet.

"Es zittern die morschen Knochen, der Welt vor dem großen Krieg." I sang the anthem of the Hitler Youth, which I still carry with me now, words forged in memory and time. *"The rotten bones are trembling, of the World before the great War. We have smashed this terror. For us a great victory!"* The men from the Ministry grinned like boars on the hunt. *"Wir haben den Schrecken gebrochen, für uns war's ein großer Sieg!"*

When I was done, I took a seat, the rafters still trembling with my high voice. Royer turned to Jund and nodded. Wellens turned to Victor and did the same.

"How splendid," said Royer.

"I'm interested, if you don't mind, in speaking to this young man here." Jund smiled at me. "What's your name, boy?"

I felt Aubrion's hand tighten around my shoulder. For all our preparations, we'd neglected to come up with a name for my character. "Hermann Sommer," I said, quickly thinking of street names.

Royer gestured at the others. "How do you find your instructors, young Sommer?"

"They're grand, Herr Hoch." Out of the corner of my eye, I saw Tarcovich put a hand on her chest. I straightened my posture.

"What have they taught you?"

"Obedience to the Führer."

The three men nodded to each other.

"What else?" asked Royer.

"Um—well—a great many patriotic songs."

Jund sensed my hesitation and pressed me. "Such as?"

"The, um—the one about our good stock and breeding."

Tarcovich snorted. Hoch turned to look at her, his blue eyes running up and down her body. Her jaw clenched.

"Are you an instructor, *fräulein*?" Hoch asked Tarcovich.

"I am, Herr Hoch."

"Do you like it? Teaching the young?"

"It is an honor."

Hoch stepped closer to her. "Do you wish to have children of your own someday?"

"Perhaps."

Folding his hands to obscure his wedding band, Hoch said, "Are you married, *fräulein*?"

"Not yet, Herr Hoch." Tarcovich smiled without humor. "I haven't found the right man, I suppose. And my excitement at finding a husband is matched only by my excitement at serving the Reich."

Aubrion drowned a laugh in a cough.

"Well, I believe we've seen enough." Jund walked over to the box of textbooks, which was flanked by Spiegelman and Mullier. He absently picked up a book. The room felt tighter as everyone—save the three Aryan specimens not privy to the textbooks' contents—held their breath. "You seem poised to do well, I think."

"I concur," said Hoch.

Royer nodded.

Jund turned over the book. The cloth cover, a simple tweed that demurred, in cautious lettering, *Die Fibel (A Primer)*, slipped. I heard Aubrion stifle a gasp as Jund was momentarily exposed to a blushing corner of *A Big, Bad Love Story*.

"How many textbooks do you have here?" said Jund.

Victor wiped the sweat from his eyes. "A few hundred."

"They're of your own design?" asked Royer.

"Indeed, sir."

"Excellent." Jund turned the book over again.

"But, sir," said Victor, panic creeping into his voice, "these are preliminary versions. They're not *quite* ready to pass muster, I think."

Chuckling, Jund said, "I'm sure you are being unnecessarily modest." He opened the book, and his expression changed immediately: to that of a man confronted with more nudity than he'd bargained for that day. Jund turned to Victor and choked out, "What is this?"

Victor held up a hand before Wellens could say anything. "Give it here."

Jund passed the book to Victor, who opened it. Though, to my knowledge, Martin Victor never received any theater training, you never would have guessed in that moment. His face contorted in shock and fury. Trembling, he dropped the book into my hands.

"Are you responsible for this?" said the professor.

"No, Herr Professor."

"Then who is, lad? Am I? Are our friends from the Ministry?"

I hung my head. "My apologies, Herr Professor."

"What do you have to say for yourself, lad?"

"I take full responsibility."

"For?"

"Putting those dirty pictures in our schoolbooks."

"Don't be too hard on the boy, Victor." Royer rested a heavy hand on my shoulder. "The boy is young. This is the natural order of things."

"I think we have seen enough, haven't we?" said Jund, glancing between Hoch and Royer. "Congratulations to you all." Jund shook hands with Spiegelman, Wellens, Aubrion. "I shall report to the Ministry immediately. Anything you need—starting with the paper and ink you requested—will be yours."

"It has been our pleasure." Wellens bowed.

Jund put on his fedora. "Be good, lad."

"I promise," I said, properly abashed. But as they turned to leave, I began to grin beneath the lie.

10 DAYS TO PRINT
MID-MORNING

The Gastromancer

SOME DAYS AGO, Aubrion had given Spiegelman a pocket watch. This was no small gift. I was not the only pickpocket in Enghien at the time; every week, the Nazis ransacked our homes and our schools, searching for metal to melt down for bullets and tanks. There were hardly any watches left, no wedding rings, few eyeglasses; people whittled spoons and forks out of discarded wood. Spiegelman kept the pocket watch close beside him as he worked, though it reminded him of his warring desires: to use his words in service to *Faux Soir*, or to August Wolff; to help realize Aubrion's mad, beautiful dream, or to help grant Aubrion immunity under Wolff's command.

Spiegelman positioned the pocket watch atop a stack of books. He'd just finished "Effective Strategy," garnishing his parody of the *Le Soir* column with a paragraph on German defense strategies. Only a month ago, Spiegelman had remarked to August Wolff: "Elastic defense, hedgehog defense...it's all the people hear about, all the papers ever talk about! What does it even mean? Do people care to know that—" Spiegelman waved his hands "—High Commander Rolfing created a network of strong points to advance in depth and break the momentum of the Allied offensive?"

Wolff's face had wrinkled up in an approximation of a smile. "That was very good." Despising himself for it, Spiegelman had blushed at the *Gruppenführer*'s praise. His grandmother had warned that the *dybbuk*'s purpose would become his own, that he would inhabit the body and soul of his host; each day proved her story. "You are right, of course—the people do not care about such details."

Spiegelman had said, "Then why is it in all our news? Our propaganda?"

"It is good to expose the people to information they don't understand. They'll believe that the German army is using the most advanced techniques to wage war—which, of course, means we must be winning."

The pocket watch slipped, tilting onto its side. Spiegelman wrote: *The tactics of hedgehog-retreat and*—Spiegelman fished around for an equally ridiculous animal—*porcupine resistance have been succeeded by elastic defense. The success of this should not be put into relief; beyond the fact that it brings the most striking rebuttal to the misrepresentation that the Reich lacks rubber, it also demonstrates in the least penetrating manner how little intellectually evolved is the idea that Stalin and his generals have of modern warfare. Up till now, they have not been able to oppose elastic defense, except through attack without truce or respite.*

"What else, what else?" he muttered, rifling through his copy of *Le Soir*. Words skipped past him; he was a train passenger watching their gentle blur through the window. *That* was it: he still needed to write on the Eastern Front. People always expected to see something on the Soviets: nothing substantial, just a reminder of the Russian Bear's existence. Spiegelman turned over his paper, the color of fresh buttercream, unpocked by faulty presses.

German Communique, Spiegelman wrote at the top. *On the Eastern Front, despite notable changes, the situation remains unchanged.* Spiegelman closed his eyes, willing himself into the body of an overstuffed general weighed down by medals and wine. *In trapezium-shaped Krementchoug-Odessa-Dnipropetrovsk-Mélitopol triangle, the enemy's attempts at penetration have been crowned with success everywhere, except in the places on the front where our soldiers have impeded the Soviet advance by the clever maneuver of surrendering en masse. In the structure of a colossal elastic defense, all towns have been evacuated by night and on tiptoe.* Spiegelman nodded. It would have to do.

The Smuggler

Anyone who happened to walk the streets of downtown Enghien that day would've seen what appeared to be—what *were*—twenty-five whores carrying Nazi tapestries and statues of Hitler out of an auction house. It had been Mullier's suggestion; though they were purportedly raising money for a German organization, the saboteur believed the Nazi trimmings would make guests feel threatened and uncomfortable. Aubrion had agreed: "That's the thing about Nazis. Strip off the uniform, and they're everyone's best friend." As Lada's girls cleaned and prepared for the fund-raiser, Tarcovich supervised, flanked by Andree Grandjean.

"I plan to have everything cleared out by the end of the day," said Tarcovich. "They should be finished well before the fund-raiser begins."

Grandjean eyed the heavy wood furniture surrounding them. Now that they'd started clearing away the remains of the *Ahnenerbe*'s presence, it was clear that the building was in poor shape. Years of misuse had left the ceilings cracked and the floorboards groaning.

"Do you think that's possible?" asked the judge. "It seems ambitious."

"That never stopped you, did it?" Lada kissed her and rested her head on Andree's shoulders, breathing in the wonder of her, the way Lada seemed to *fit* right there, right against her cheek, like she was molded for it.

"Hey, lovebirds!"

Tarcovich broke away. A group of her girls were laughing at her, making rude gestures with their fingers and tongues.

"Lazy bitch." One grinned. "Aren't you going to give us a hand?"

"I've given you lot a *job*," said Lada Tarcovich.

They laughed again, carrying an old wooden table out the door. Tarcovich smiled. It was a rare thing to hear them laugh. These girls were young, most of them just children—too young to be working at all, let alone in this trade. Though she rarely let on, it tortured Lada Tarcovich to use them this way. "I'm giving them some money, a home," she'd say to Marc Aubrion, "but what are the costs of such things?" He'd try to assure her that she was doing the best she could, but these girls and their stories followed Tarcovich to bed each night.

The air swelled with the clamor of church bells. Tarcovich cursed.

"What?" said Andree Grandjean. "What is it?"

"Oh, nothing. I don't have much time here," said Tarcovich.

"Why not?"

"The stag party is this evening. I'd managed to forget."

"What stag party?"

"It's all part of some fool plan Marc Aubrion dreamed up."

Putting a hand to her aching forehead, Lada turned away from Andree. She couldn't imagine how many hours she would not spend with this woman because she was off planning some manic caper for this suicide operation. Part of her—a very large part of her, she could not deny—ached to end it all entirely. She could cut ties with the FI, smuggle herself and Grandjean out of the country. It would not be much of a life—and that was assuming they made it across the border—but it would be a life, and she could wake up in this woman's bed.

Grandjean leaned forward to murmur into her hair: "What's the matter?"

"I do not want to go," said Lada. She smiled, kissed Andree's cheek. "What time is it? I wasn't listening."

"It's half past nine," said Grandjean. "On the thirty-first of October. In the year of our Lord nineteen hundred and forty-three."

"Who the devil has a November wedding?"

Grandjean laughed, then regarded the walls—which were white, now that they'd cleared away all the evidence of German conquest—and the polished oak floors. "The place is clearing up nicely. How did you find so much help in such a short time?"

Tarcovich snorted. "I've discovered something remarkable. When given a choice between catering to the whims of sweaty old men and carrying around *paintings* of sweaty old men, people tend to choose the latter."

Grandjean shook her head. "I don't understand."

"What don't you understand?"

"Are these women—"

Tarcovich folded her arms across her chest. "Are these women what?"

Glancing around, Andree lowered her voice. "Prostitutes?"

"What are you whispering for? Are you afraid they'll find out?"

"Well, are they?"

"Prostitutes?" Tarcovich said, louder than she'd ever said it, three sharp syllables that both affirmed her identity and fled from it. "Yes, of course they are."

"You couldn't get someone else?"

"Someone else?" Tarcovich mocked, childish. She reveled in the hurt in Andree's eyes, then despised herself. "Who else?"

"I don't know."

"Whores and escorts. Like it or not, it's what we've got to work with. Anything more is too expensive. Anything less is too dangerous."

"I suppose." Grandjean drifted away from Lada.

"What's the matter with you? Andree, wait." Lada caught Grandjean's arm, searching her face. In a heartbeat, Andree had become an empty book again, pages without words, just as she'd been when Lada first met her. Tarcovich spoke quickly, willing her to come back. "Andree, listen. These are good girls, you must believe that. They're reliable. They're not going to steal anything. What more could we want for this job?"

Andree took a breath. "You didn't ask me."

"Ask you what? You are not FI. It's none of your concern."

"But Lada," Andree hissed, "I don't agree with it."

"Prostitution?"

"Yes." Andree licked her lips. "Prostitution." She said it the way tightrope walkers take their first step.

"Well, neither do I."

"Then why are you doing this? Any of this?"

"Do you agree with everything that's written up in the law?"

"No, but—"

"Oh, allow me to guess. But this is different, isn't it?"

"It *is*."

"Why? Because you get to work with your clothes on?"

"I have to leave." Grandjean ripped her coat off the back of a chair. She put her arm through the wrong sleeve twice, three times. Her face was twisted up by something—anger? fear?—that Lada could not discern. "There is somewhere I have to be."

"You don't work today."

"I work every day, Lada." Grandjean's voice crumpled with tears. "As do you, I'm sure."

Tarcovich wanted to go to her, felt her fingers twitch with the impulse to hold Grandjean's hand—already a reflex, already like breathing. Instead, she let her go, trembling under the weight of all that had been said. Perhaps this quarrel would cut their bonds. That was how it always happened in the stories; the couple fought, exchanging forbidden angers like wedding vows—and that was it. These storybook quarrels were magic, freeing the lovers of hard choices and compromise and disappointment. Lada prayed it would be so.

The girls watched Lada stand there for a long while. They came and went, laughing in rooms far away, while Tarcovich stood without moving in the cold quiet of the old auction house.

YESTERDAY

The Scrivener

THE OLD WOMAN had been swaying to the rhythm of her story. But here she sat upright, the ancient leatherwork of her voice smoothing into uniform grains.

"You already know something of Professor Victor," said Helene, "or you would not have found me. But you do not know all."

Something in the tenor of Helene's words alarmed Eliza. "I know he was sick—"

"That is not the whole story."

"I know his journals survived to carry the legacy of *Faux Soir*."

The old woman's laugh was as dark as the sky in this new world, where the streetlights outshone the stars. "The *legacy*."

"What else would you call it?"

"I hope you are not writing such nonsense in that notebook."

Eliza took a breath. "Did Victor do something to hurt Aubrion and the others?"

"He did," said Helene simply.

"Are you sure?"

"Are you surprised?"

"I guess I—"

"Don't be. Every man and woman alive in those days did something hurtful. Oh, don't look like that. We speak of the war in such grand terms now—good, evil, *legacies*." Eliza blushed at Helene's ridicule. "But to us, each day was just a day. I had a ball and paddle that I played with, sometimes. Other times, I loaded rifles for the men."

"What did Victor do?" asked Eliza.

"Before I go on, you should know the truth of it. I learned some of his story from a diary I found after it was all over. Aubrion told me the rest. This is what I know."

3 YEARS BEFORE
FAUX SOIR

The Professor's Witness

THE CLAMOR OF the train no longer disturbs Victor. He can even sleep now, if he wishes. This is the fourth day of his travels, the fourth night he will make a pillow of his coat to lie upon the seat. The engine's fury lends him an awful privacy, so he rarely hears the other passengers' voices. He feels truly apart from this world.

A young couple is traveling in the car adjacent to Victor's. Their child's cries are so much worse than the train engine. She is quiet for hours, and then he hears her sobs again. Victor knows the child is a girl because he has heard her parents begging her *please, Dottie, please, sleep*. Victor has come to feel as though the child is pursuing him to Poland, through the country and into Katowice. Sometimes he wakes, certain her cries have roused him. But he hears nothing but the train.

There has been no time to write to Sofia. Victor's every hour is occupied by what he must do. The matter is clear enough, but it grows clearer when expressed in ink. The professor writes in his notebook:

The FI has received reports from the Comité de Défense des Juifs *that the Germans are pressing Jews into some unholy service. We have heard similar reports about other sorts of downtrodden—Roma, homosexuals, loose women, orphans. Once captured, the prisoners are forced onto trains bound for southwestern Poland. I've heard they only take healthy ones, sturdy young men and women with strong backs, which suggests the Germans engage them in some manner of hard labor. They are building something, perhaps. The men of the FI have taken to whispering about super-weapons. Though the concept of the thing tilts precariously toward the absurd, it is not too far beyond the realm of possibility, not in these strange times.*

My task is a simple one. I am to find out where the trains are going, so that the armies of Europe may know where to direct their aeroplanes. If I have it in my power to do so, I am also to find out what the Germans are building. It shall take no more than a week, of this I am certain. As God is my witness, there will be more than enough time to write to Sofia.

Katowice is a forgettable city. The matronly shops and homes squat beneath electric cables that are strung like fat cobwebs. A faint smell of something sweet, unpleasantly so, clings to everything. Where there are trees, the brush has faded to an underachieving gray. Victor's inn is situated behind a clump of such trees.

The professor arrives at the inn unmolested. His papers pass through the hands of Nazi officials without incident; the FI is a large and clumsy organization, by Victor's estimation, but it is somehow adept at what it does. Other passengers on the train to Katowice were less fortunate. The couple from before, crying Dottie's parents, had shown their papers at the border. His were in order; hers were not. Victor writes in his notebook: *Lord protect her. As in the days of Solomon, the fair ones suffer most.*

He takes his lunch at a bistro three blocks from the train station. As he returns to the inn, Victor's skin feels too tight, his hands and feet pinpricked with fear. Of course, the professor had known, prior to coming here, that the Germans had occupied Katowice. But he had not known the profound, oppressive silence that comes with it. Victor walks alongside other men and women and children in the chapped and fallible streets, and the silence is unbearable, but also thin and crackling as though it aches to burst forward in a spectacular display. The professor examines the faces that pass him. They are ordinary faces, some ugly, some fine. The same lot populates every city on this earth, regardless of how conventional or how foreign their customs. But the sounds of life—the meaningless chatter, the gossip, the pleasure, the bickering—have fled these streets for somewhere safer. These people do not speak.

It has long been a quality of mine that I am not given to fear, Victor writes, back at the inn. *This is not boasting but a statement of fact. Sofia used to say it takes a certain measure of fearlessness to stand between scientists and philosophers with one's fist raised, and that is precisely what I have done. But by God, I am fearful of what the occupation has brought to this city.*

Victor sits on his bed and remembers the day the swastika came to Belgium. Like his countrymen, he had sheltered in his home until the fighting was done and the countryside trampled, until the men shouted through the windows that they could come out, that they would not be shot. Sofia had remarked on their thick accents, their poor grammar. His Sofia did not go out, but Victor did. They'd needed bread and other things. Victor remembers walking to the bakery and avoiding his neighbors' eyes, as though he had brought shame on them and could only pray they might forgive him. But without the benefit of his neighbors' confirmation, he grew paranoid that the occupation never happened, that it was something devised by his feeble mind, that he was the only one who knew of it. Victor's eyes lifted, he remembers, and he looked at them, his brothers and sisters in Christ. He looked for some flickering candle of recognition, a sign that this truly did happen, that it was not simply his imagination. And he found it. He finds it. He finds it in their footsteps, quiet and relenting.

I do not know where to begin. I sit alone in my room, where there is no desk, only a bed and a trunk and a thin carpet. The FI gave me what they had, which was not much. I am traveling with merely enough money for food and simple lodging. My notebook is in my lap. I've started a letter to Sofia, given it up. My notebook is filling like the belly of Jonah's whale. I hesitate to write it all down, for fear of making it true. But writing it will make no difference. The laws of nature are extant regardless of whether men capture them in ink. Gravity binds us to the earth; Newton did not make it true. God created the Heavens; the prophets did not make it true.

I shall begin in the bistro, where I met four men from the Service du Travail Obligatoire. *It seemed risky to me, four Frenchmen traveling together in the city. But it appeared to me, after I watched them for a time, that they needed each other for what they were about to do. I saw it in their posture, the way they addressed me by name but murmured among themselves.*

"Tell me," I said. "Where are the labor camps?"

The men stared into their glasses. I'd bought a round of ale. It seemed the Christian thing to do.

"There are no labor camps," said the oldest of the men. I made a note of his name, but it is smudged, and I cannot read it now.

"None? Then where are the Jews?"

Another man spoke. He sounded as though he were talking in his sleep. "They are being killed, sent to gas chambers." None of the Frenchmen would look at me. They had eyes for someone else, someone who was not with us. "Their bodies are being burned, not far from here. Our children ask about the smell."

"Gas chambers?" It was all I could say. The concept was self-

explanatory, but the idea—the very notion—that someone would think of such a thing and then put it into practice—it was unfathomable to me. It is unfathomable to me. "How long?" I whispered.

"A long time," said the first man, the older one. His fist was curled on the table. "We thought you knew—that the resistance knew. Why has no one come for them?"

I could not answer the man's question. In truth, I do not know why we haven't come for them, why we haven't heard their cries. After I left the bistro, the existence of these camps—not labor camps, death camps— seemed obvious to me. The German purpose is the creation of a "perfect" race. This is, of course, a farce, but the only way to perpetuate the farce is by cleansing, by moving away from imperfection. Labor camps would have delayed the inevitable. Labor camps would have been inefficient.

It has been two weeks since I've heard from Sofia. Has her illness passed? Is her sister looking after her? Forgive me—although this is not a journal in which to deposit private notions and conversations, it helps me to write things out, to see them and turn them over. I have been thinking about Sofia and whether she is well. Sofia told me, before I departed, that it was not the illness that plagued her; rather, it was the shallowness of feeling one heartbeat where there had been two. I wonder what she would have looked like. We had planned to name her Eliza.

The name of the camp has followed me, will not leave me in peace. It chased me back to the inn; it hung in the air like the scent of death on an undertaker's gloves; it formed on the colorless lips of every child, woman, and man I saw—Auschwitz, they said, Auschwitz. I've sent a letter to the FI asking whether I am to travel there, but I have packed already.

There is nothing new in this world; there are only new ways of looking at it. Victor and his body sit outside Auschwitz. He has never thought to separate them before, Victor and his body, but they have been cleaved apart by some boundless force, by the shock. There are only new ways of looking, Victor says to someone, *Université Catholique de Louvain*, the new field of sociology, class of 1920 maybe, though it was so long ago. Everything on this earth, Victor says to someone, has been witnessed by God, and because this is so, God has accepted everything in it—or He does not exist, but this is impossible. Sofia has often listened—so patiently and so skeptically!—to this very lecture. And if He has seen things, then Victor has an academic and spiritual obligation to accept and understand this new world. Does that make sense, everyone? Any questions? God has witnessed the striped children, and the naked trees, and the concrete rooms from which they must be carried out. God has accepted the bars of soap unused and stale on the shelves, and the barbed wire, and the starved bones, and the little ones, and the old ones, and the smells. *Humans are not new, and human behaviors are not new*—Victor explained it all in his research proposal, six pages, typed, formatted, edited by Sofia as she sipped tea over her swelling belly—*but we have hitherto failed to examine ourselves through the lens of science*: *If we can delve into ourselves and discover the forces at work*, Victor wrote, *the pushes and pulls that beget conflict or love, we can begin to water the parched soil of our humanity.*

That is Victor's belief. He has written justifications of sociology before, he shall do it again, he shall probably write them on his own grave. The professor—*profess, declare publicly, profiteri*—does what he does because it is a sacred thing. That was too unscientific for the research proposal, but that did not stop him from explaining it during his dissertation defense, from believing it, from holding it like a prayer in his heart. *How can one read about our history, Sofia, about the noble Egyptians, the wars between the Persians and the Greeks, how can one look at the pottery and the stonework, how can one sing the epics, how can one read the bawdy jokes graffitied on the ancient walls, how can one do any of these things without being moved to study human life?*

We are strange and beautiful specimens; that was Victor's belief. It stood beside him like a steadfast companion. It took turns holding his notebook, witnessing his agony and peace. *I've lost my friend. I cannot find him now.*

10 DAYS TO PRINT
AFTERNOON

The Professor

JUND, ROYER AND Hoch from the Ministry of Education greeted Victor across the street from the Nazi headquarters with a handshake and a bundle of documents. The professor signed them unread. Smiling, Jund handed him an envelope.

"It contains a key to a warehouse just east of here," he said. "The paper and ink for your school will be delivered there in two days' time."

Tucking the envelope into his tweed coat, Victor proceeded to the office of August Wolff. He had a shuffling, oversized walk, of which he felt quite self-conscious, and when he wore a hat—as he did on this day—he pulled it low on his face, so as to cover his eyes. The professor crossed a street, and a cart shot around a corner and nearly bowled him over. Wiping an indignant spot of mud from his coat, he carried on to the Nazi headquarters.

"Professor." August Wolff greeted Victor in the foyer. His footsteps were so quiet he might have been walking on velvet rather than brick. Armed guards paced nearby. "Thank you for meeting me here."

"Of course, *Gruppenführer.*"

Wolff tucked an envelope in Victor's hand. It matched Jund's almost exactly. Aubrion might have wondered about how the Reich ordered their stationery.

"The five thousand francs I promised you," said Wolff, "for *La Libre Belgique.*"

"We will use it well, I assure you."

"I've no doubt of that. Now, is there anything else?"

"Yes, actually." Victor took a third envelope from his coat, noting with surprise that Wolff did not flinch as the professor reached into his pocket. The envelope was made of coarser stuff than the Reich's. "*Gruppenführer,* if you wouldn't mind—" Shaking his head, Victor thrust the envelope in Wolff's hands. "Read it, please."

Wolff nodded. His eyes were Aryan steel—but Victor did not believe in the "Aryan" race, the false mythology that the Germans had conjured. It defied everything the professor had labored over; it was a knife in the back of honesty and truth. Victor looked away as the *Gruppenführer* said, "At your service, Professor."

The Dybbuk

August Wolff marveled at the professor's handwriting. The curls were delicate, unafraid to bow when the situation demanded it of them. But other lines, the cross of the *T* and the backbone of the *I*, were resolute and firm. It was several minutes before the *Gruppenführer* paid any attention to the content of the letter, partially because of his admiration, but largely because he already knew what it would say. Victor's letter read:

> *My dear sir:*
> *It has come to my attention that at the end of the enterprise in which my colleagues and I are presently engaged, some of us—that is to say all of us who will remain alive, by your good graces—will*

be in desperate need of asylum. It is likely no secret to you that my colleagues are involved in all manner of activities of which you are not aware. That is to be expected. I mean to assist you with this problem. I agree, on my word as a Catholic, to provide you with information about these activities in exchange for a promise. You must promise that I, Professor Martin Victor, will be granted a position as a researcher for the Reich for the duration of the war. To be specific, my requests are twofold: that you will provide some means for me to leave Belgium after the completion of this project (including swift transportation and personnel to carry my possessions across the border), and that you will provide some means for me to remain employed with a decent living while the war continues. I realize you have no reason to believe that I am being truthful. But you seem as though you are a good judge of character.

I remain, sir, your servant,

Prof. Martin Victor

Since the beginning of the war, the Gestapo had been aware of Victor's exploits; it was said that top-ranking officials, on their first day of work, received a copy of *Mein Kampf*, instructions on budget-making, and Professor Martin Victor's file. His record was extraordinary. It seemed implausible that a man of his loyalty and reputation would offer himself to the Nazis. But rumors began to spread, tales of Victor's illness. War did odd things to the best of men. Wolff had seen it before: giants turned small, men reduced to shivering children.

Wolff fed a sheet of paper to his typewriter. *Professor Victor*, he typed. *I have read your letter with great interest.* A corner of Victor's paper had begun to curl, as though the words were recoiling from each other—*desperate need of asylum and occupation*—whimpering words for the man who once ventured to Auschwitz not with a rifle or a tank but with a notebook. If the war could cripple a man such as this—if the war could turn Professor Victor, Wolff could hardly hope to make it out alive. *I accept your proposal*, he typed.

The Professor

Victor paused at a street corner to gather himself. He felt the need to do that more frequently these days, like there were fragments of him scattered everywhere and he was constantly searching for a mislaid piece. Wolff would accept his proposal, Victor knew. The man was, of course, obsessed with information; he would not refuse the promise of intelligence. But if the FI got word that there was a leak inside the base, Aubrion might suspect Victor, and all would be lost. At university, many of Victor's colleagues believed that a man could not be both pious and cunning, but Victor had crossed himself and outwitted them all. Here, too, he would do the same. Though the guilt of it pained him, the logical move—the *cunning* move—was to divert the others' attention. The professor would make them believe that someone *else* had leaked information to August Wolff. And the victim was obvious. Victor pulled his hat over his eyes, as though to shield his face from God. But there was no need, was there? God kept men like Victor in His hands, and He had no love for men like David Spiegelman.

10 DAYS TO PRINT
LATE MORNING

The Pyromaniac

A FIRE STARTED that morning in a barn just outside town. The local paper would report that a stable-boy kicked over a lantern near a pile of hay. Though no one in town knew what had actually started it, the Germans didn't want anyone to believe *they* were responsible, and so they waved it all away with a harmless tale. I watched the smoke from a thousand meters off, counting the plumes as they hitched a ride on the wind.

I do not spend too much time these days thinking about my motivations for starting fires. "Motivations lead too easily to justifications." That is what Aubrion taught me. Because I was a child at the time of *Faux Soir*, a time when I was setting one or two fires a month, the motivations and justifications come too easily to me: I did not know any better; I made sure no one was hurt; I craved emotional release—and so on. But to allow myself to accept these justifications as truth is to absolve myself of my transgressions. I *did* know better; a child of ten or twelve years, while not emotionally complex, is not emotionally dumb, either. I did *not* make sure no one was hurt, for I destroyed property and livelihoods. I did *not* crave emotional release; the FI gave me a family, and a home, and a safe place to hide that which frightened me.

I bring this up because the fire, the one I started in a barn north of Enghien, shook me. At the time, I did not know why. I'd started many fires by then, and this one was no different from the others. But I felt hollow, used-up.

When I was small, I used to go wandering in the field near my parents' house, picking up bits of treasure that I'd bring to my father for inspection.

"What's this? What about that one?"

"That is a bullet, from a battle that happened here many years ago during the Great War."

"A bullet from a *gun*?"

"A rifle, and an evil one, at that. Do you see how the middle of the bullet has been hollowed out? It is lighter than a normal bullet, but so much more terrible."

Perhaps the fire shook me because I remembered that bullet, and I remembered what I did with it after my father explained what it was: I cast it into a river, where no one could find it.

Shortly after I returned to my newsstand, a courier delivered a message to me. He was one of the scabby-kneed lads who'd gone to work for the FI after he lost his parents, who probably ran notes for the Germans too on his off-days. "It's from Madame Tarcovich," he said, and I gave him a coin to get rid of the nosey lout. I unrolled the little slip of paper, which informed me: *We're going to see Pauline.*

Only thrice in my time with the FI did I receive such a note. The first note took me to a farmhouse, where the farmer's wife had hidden a crate of Austrian hammers and nails (precious commodities in those days, when everything was so tightly regulated); Tarcovich and I loaded the crate into a rusty Nash-

Kelvinator and smuggled it to a resistance base. The second note took me to a warehouse packed to the roof with banned novels, some of which I loaded into a cart that Tarcovich and I drove to a safe house. And so, this third message inspired a thrill of anticipation and fear that chased me down the street, where I met Tarcovich in front of an abandoned cobbler shop. There, she repeated her message. "We're going to see Pauline."

I have forgotten Pauline's last name. I am not sure whether I knew it in the first place. Though Pauline served as Tarcovich's accomplice on countless smuggling jobs, I only ever met her those three times, when Tarcovich needed me to play-act as her child. "The patrols are less likely to look twice at a mother with a child," Tarcovich explained. "Besides, you'll calm poor Pauline's heart. She's such a nervous thing." While we walked to the post office, Tarcovich told me Pauline's story.

Pauline is a minor figure in the tale of *Faux Soir*, which is exactly why I wish to spend a moment with her. On Pauline's seventh birthday, her mother promised the girl she'd grow up to do tremendous things in this world. With a shudder, Pauline replied: "God, I hope not." When rumors of invasion flooded our town with the first spring rain, she took a job at the postal service outpost in Enghien. If the Germans did march into Belgium, Pauline wanted them to find her behind a dull, harmless, and thoroughly nonpartisan desk. After the Nazis invaded, they did indeed allow Pauline to keep her appointment at the post office.

A year into the occupation, Tarcovich received a telex at the whorehouse. She never found out how the woman on the other end—halting voice, broken sobs—discovered Lada's identity or how to contact her. The woman introduced herself as Pauline and begged Tarcovich to come quickly. Tarcovich put on a respectable dress, tucked a pistol into her purse, and walked to the postal service outpost.

When she arrived, a thin woman with a vulture neck and

dowdy brown hair led her to the mailroom. There, bolts of yellow cloth lay stacked up to the ceiling, like the body bags that littered the towns near the front. Tarcovich snorted. "Is this a joke," she'd said, "or are you mad?" Wordless, Pauline unrolled one of the bolts to spread it across the floor.

The cloth was about the size of a large blanket, perhaps four meters by two meters. Someone had sewn—with a sewing machine, judging by the look of the stitches, and here Tarcovich stopped breathing—someone had sewn yellow Stars of David into the fabric. It must have been an industrial sewing machine, operated by a factory worker with a keen eye, for the stiches were clean and precise. Each star was labeled *JUDE*. Tarcovich felt her knees buckle. It was the math, the math that did her in: There must have been ten dozen bolts of fabric, and there were twelve post offices in Enghien, and there were five hundred and eighty-nine municipalities in Belgium, and Belgium was one country, one out of many. The stars were perforated, ready to be cut out. Pauline pointed at a box stamped with the German eagle and swastika. Tarcovich looked inside. Scissors grinned at her from under a modest layer of cloth. "That was it," said Tarcovich. "It was the scissors that did it." That was when she knew this was going to be a long war.

Pauline wept softly. "I sorted their mail, their orders." The woman was as young as Tarcovich, not very old at all, but she looked much older, matronly even, with ugly chipped nails that she'd chewed raw. "I knew what the letters must have said. They had that horrid...*thing* on them, the swastika. But I didn't open them. I never read them. It was out of my hands if I never read them, wasn't it? But *this*."

"I will take them," said Tarcovich.

She left just long enough to borrow a van; one of Lada's girls had a brother who worked as a trash collector and who was off duty that day. After loading the cloth into the van, Tarcovich drove shaky and breathless to the whorehouse. Numb with terror, she brought the fabric up to her attic, one painful bolt at a time, certain she would be caught, that she'd feel the eye of a gun against her throat. Still trembling, Tarcovich sent Marc Aubrion a telex.

When he arrived, Aubrion laughed at the stacks of fabric. "I know things are bad, Lada, but you're not about to take up quilting, are you?"

Tarcovich unrolled a bolt of fabric. The life drained from Aubrion's face. She watched him perform the same calculations she had done at the postal office: adding it all up, multiplying the figures. This was not just murder. Murder would have been painless. This was premeditated, industrialized, mass produced. This fabric came from an assembly line.

"I couldn't just leave it there." Tarcovich sank onto her bed, her shoulders heaving—but no tears, no strength for tears. "The poor woman at the post office was in a state."

Aubrion said, "Yes, you bloody well *could* have just left it there."

"There's no telling what she would have done with it."

"What are you going to do with it?"

"I told her I have a plan."

"Do you?"

"Of course not."

Pacing, Aubrion studied the yellow cloth. "Shit, Lada."

"I know," she said.

"This is—"

"It is."

"But do you know *how* bad this is?"

"Oh, I know exactly how bad this is," said Tarcovich, for the Stars of David posed a unique challenge. She'd smuggled all manner of things before: books, eyeglasses, building supplies, sanitary belts, even parmesan and mozzarella, things she'd taken out of the city in carts, or into the city in motorcars, sometimes both in one day. But she could not simply take the fabric out of the city, where it would be put to the same purpose elsewhere. Even smuggling it out of the country would not help. The fabric had to be hidden or destroyed.

"Did they send scissors too?" asked Aubrion.

"Yes."

"Those bastards."

"That's too kind."

"I don't suppose we could just—I don't know, really—cut up the fabric and leave it somewhere?"

"They'll find out," said Tarcovich, and Aubrion knew it to be true.

"Well, don't expect me to help you with this." Aubrion backed away from the fabric as though he might catch some terrible illness from it. "This is your mess, pal. I'm just an innocent bystander."

"Is that so? And how many of your 'messes' has *this* innocent bystander been forced to clean up?"

Aubrion relented, as she'd known he would. Tarcovich told me they talked and quarreled and planned all night, until the two of them fell asleep in a pile of Nazi ingenuity.

It was just after dawn when Tarcovich awoke. Some noise from downstairs had disturbed her. She stretched, working out a knot in her back. But *then*— Tarcovich cast off the muddle of sleep, nearly stepping on poor Aubrion. Ignoring his questions, she ran out into the church bells and spring rain, alive with a marvelous, stupid idea.

I clung fast to her words as she relayed this tall tale. When we neared the post office, I said, "Please, madame, but what did you do?"

"Have you ever attended a church service around here?" said Tarcovich, her smile enchanted by what I did not know.

"A service? No, madame," I said, puzzled. "I'm not one for church, really."

"Well, if you had, you would have noticed the tables."

"The tables?"

"Indeed. It's a peculiar thing. Under all those candles and statues and what-have-you, each one is decorated with a lovely yellow table runner." My heart skipped. I quickened my pace to keep up with Lada, to walk alongside her in this valley of death. Her act of mercy could seem small to you, now that we know the numbers and the magnitude of it all, but it felt infinite then. It blanketed my whole world. "I can't explain it," she said, laughing. "They seem to be all the rage."

Pauline saw us through the front window. Her nervous jerk of the head indicated we should use the rear entrance. I followed Tarcovich to the back. As she'd predicted, Pauline's breathing slowed a tad when she noticed me.

"Oh, sweet child," said Pauline. "I wish my daughter was still your age. Grown up with suitors already. What's your name, dear?"

"They call me Gamin, madame."

"Did you pass along the package?" said Tarcovich.

That look of wretched discomfort returned to Pauline's eyes. "The man at comet twelve took the package." She wrung her hands. "Comet four was neutralized this morning, so you'll not stop there."

"How long do we have?"

"He says you have until half past three before he destroys it."

"Then we should be on our way."

As I watched Pauline, I realized I both pitied and respected this woman. Our code words and army euphemisms hung off her like a dress three sizes too large. I have no doubt she prayed each night for a quiet job, a tidy house. But here is what you must understand: when confronted with the naked treachery men could do, Pauline sighed, pursed her lips, and rolled up her sleeves. That is why I have spent this moment with her, you see. Neither Churchill nor Roosevelt stopped the Germans from distributing their Star of David badges to Belgium's Jews. Pauline did that: Pauline, who worked at a post office in the city, who wished her daughter was young again, who chewed her nails when she was anxious. No one heard her prayers, and thank God for that. She did tremendous things in this world.

Tarcovich and I proceeded to comet twelve, our code name for a farmhouse east of the FI base. The "man at comet twelve," a farmer with a nervous tic and two anemic sheep, told us he'd passed along the package to comet three. Tarcovich and I took a cab to a schoolhouse. From the schoolhouse, we drove to a miller's shop, and from there, we walked to a pub. The barmaid—"the woman at comet sixteen"—instructed us to wait in her cellar. While we stood there breathing in the smell of cheap ale and our nervous sweat, I marveled at this network that Tarcovich had cultivated. It must have taken years to find them all, to feed them the information they needed to do their jobs, to keep them from knowing so much they could compromise the other comets' identities. And the risk, by God: each "comet" on our trail risked capture, execution, torture, their families ripped apart and sent to the camps. Men of action had always been my heroes. I just never knew who the men of action really were.

The barmaid emerged with a slim packet. Tarcovich took it from her with a nod of thanks.

"Don't thank me, dear," said the barmaid. "I don't know what it is you got in there, but promise me you'll use it to kick them right in the balls."

Tarcovich clutched the packet, the photographs of Hitler for *Faux Soir*, to her heart. "I give you my word."

10 DAYS TO PRINT
LATE AFTERNOON

The Pyromaniac

I FOUND AUBRION pacing and mumbling in front of a blackboard at the FI base, pausing now and again to scratch out a note. His entire face seemed hazy and still, like a summer night.

Noël came up behind him. "Marc, are you quite all right?"

Aubrion turned. It took a moment for his eyes to focus. "René," he said, mostly to remind himself who he was talking to. "Oh, I'm fine. Absolutely fine. Just working."

Noël put up his hands. "All right." He turned his attention to the blackboard, but quickly looked back to Aubrion when confronted by the chaos of words and arrows.

"I will need to coordinate with Lada and Victor," said Aubrion, "and perhaps Spiegelman, as soon as possible."

"No one has seen Spiegelman since last night."

"He's probably at the Nazi headquarters."

"Actually not," said Spiegelman, and Aubrion and Noël looked up to find him coming downstairs with a mild smile. Victor trailed in behind him.

"Oh, Spiegelman," Noël said strangely. He had the queasy

appearance of a man who'd found himself suddenly forced to make a speech without notes.

Spiegelman took a sheet of paper from his attaché case and placed it on a table, behind a typewriter René Noël had been trying to fix, its insides open and exposed for surgery. All of us were gathered around in the basement, standing apart from each other—silent and tired from our labors. David Spiegelman picked up the paper he'd just put down, regarded it, handed it to Marc Aubrion. I noted how Spiegelman's shoulders seized up, how he dug his fingernails into his palms.

"It's the 'Effective Strategy' column from *Le Soir,*" Spiegelman said, for want of something to say, "or rather my version of it."

Martin Victor stepped forward, his arms folded across his chest. After a moment, he nodded, though I saw no indication that he'd read the paper.

"Are we going to use it?" Tarcovich asked, though I got the sense she was asking something else.

"Why wouldn't we?" said Aubrion.

"All right, then." René Noël took the paper from Aubrion's hands, turning to Spiegelman with a tight-lipped smile. I had a feeling that I was missing something, that a decision had been reached without my knowledge or consent. I believed Aubrion felt the same. "Thank you for your contribution, Monsieur Spiegelman. It's most appreciated. I must speak to Aubrion about something confidential."

Spiegelman, who'd quickly learned during his time with the Nazis to detect when he'd been dismissed, took his leave of us. No one spoke in his absence. The pause grew longer and more bizarre.

"Why the devil are you lot acting so strangely?" said Aubrion. "What's going on?"

Noël placed a hand on Aubrion's shoulder. "Spiegelman has fulfilled his role here."

"Of course he has. Why are you acting as though he betrayed us?"

"I received word from our colleagues in France," said Victor, "that information has been leaving the base."

Aubrion shook his head. "What are you talking about? What sort of information?"

"Information related to our troop movements."

"There has been a leak," said Noël, heavily. "The details aren't important."

I saw a convulsion go through Aubrion's body, as though he were wracked with fever. "I'd say the details *are* bloody important," snapped Aubrion.

"We've come to a consensus." Victor had the air of a reluctant executioner. "Spiegelman served a useful purpose, but he is a security risk we cannot continue to allow."

Aubrion cried, "When did *we* come to a consensus? You believe Spiegelman is a mole? That makes no sense at all, don't you see? He would not risk his life to join up with us and then toss his loyalty so casually aside—"

"We talked about it earlier, once I found out about the leak." Noël shrugged, rubbing at his beard. His eyes were more red than white; the vicious hue had spread like a disease. "He seems the likely culprit, Marc. In truth, I have been uncomfortable with his presence since Wolff's raid, as have the rest of us. It was good to have him, and you made the right decision in bringing him here. But his time has come."

"Spiegelman is one of us," said Aubrion. "He's a vital part of what we've set out to do."

Noël shook his head, and Aubrion knew there was no convincing him. "Would you do it, Marc?" the director asked. "Would you tell him?"

"When?" said Aubrion. As a very small child, I carried a blanket that I would rub when sad or afraid, until the edges went smooth with my worry. Aubrion's words took on the texture of that cloth. "Tonight?"

"Tonight," said Noël.

10 DAYS TO PRINT
EVENING

The Smuggler

THE SOUND OF the stag party reached the whorehouse before the sight of them: the laughter and backslaps of overcompensatory masculinity. Tarcovich looked out the front window. Joseph Beckers was in the back of the group, flanked by a half dozen of his mates on either side. Through a crack in the window, Tarcovich could hear one of them managing to work six euphemisms for male genitalia into a single sentence. Beckers laughed harder than the rest of them; his laugh had a stale and violent quality to it.

As the stag party approached the whorehouse, their unbuttoned collars and bloodshot eyes came into focus. They looked well fed, as few did those days. And they were clods, the lot of them, shoving each other, making rude gestures. The illustrious Beckers, head of the Office of the Post, gestured for one of his mates to knock on the door.

Tarcovich turned to her girls, who were assembled in the foyer. "Remember what I told you. Their cups must be kept full." The young women nodded. Tarcovich had often watched soldiers from the FI ready themselves for battle; her girls applied lipstick and adjusted their bodices with the same blank-eyed determination. "From the sounds of it, they are drunk already. But that is no reason to clutch your bottles too tightly. Hortense, you know what you must do?"

"Yes, madame," said Hortense, a girl with thin hair. Though Lada never let customers with heavy fists through the front door, a few slipped past her guard, and it was Hortense who taught the other girls how to cover their bruises with makeup. "I must take Joseph Beckers into the fourth room."

With a smile, Tarcovich pressed Hortense's hand. "You'll do well."

When the knock finally came, Tarcovich motioned for Hortense to open the door. Laughter and the smell of cheap drink erupted in the foyer. Lada's girls began taking the men's arms, putting glasses in their hands. "Who's the lucky gentleman?" Hortense called over the din. She'd gotten into character splendidly, tossing her hair and letting her corset slip just a tad. The lads shoved Beckers forward.

"I'm the lucky one!" he said. "Did you hear that, boys?" Hortense pulled him toward the staircase. The other girls did the same, leading the men into plush, red rooms.

When the foyer had emptied, Lada sat and drank in the quiet. Someone was giggling in the room above. Smiling at the absurdity of it—*zwanze*, as Aubrion would have remarked—Lada took a watch from her pocket. It would be fifteen minutes before she went upstairs, she decided, rubbing at a scratch on the watch face. That should be long enough.

Tarcovich knew she should probably feel nervous; if she did not secure the list of newsstands, shops, and the like that sold *Le Soir*, the whole scheme was lost. "It is important, vitally important," Aubrion had reminded her before she left, "that we disrupt all the channels they use to distribute *Le Soir* so that Peter the Happy Citizen can buy *Faux Soir* instead. Nothing has ever been more important, Lada, I swear it. The real *Le Soir* cannot hit newsstands at the same time as *Faux Soir*. If Peter and his mates see *both* newspapers on display, they will think the Germans are subjecting them to some kind of loyalty test, and they'll be too spooked to buy *Faux Soir*." Tarcovich had rolled her eyes at his insistence—but he was right, and should she fail, even Aubrion would have a devil of a time coming up with another scheme to secure a distribution list. Despite the weight of her task, Tarcovich was not nervous. A frigid calm had inhabited her limbs, as though she were falling in slow motion and there wasn't much she could do about it.

Tarcovich checked her watch again. A little over fifteen minutes had gone. She stood, her back cracking, and retrieved the flashlight she'd stashed behind a sofa. Clutching it tightly, Tarcovich exited the whorehouse.

She darted around to the back of the building. The wind carried unholy sounds from the open windows above. Trying not to listen, Tarcovich knelt in a patch of flowers behind the whorehouse. She felt around in the damp soil until her fingers brushed a metal handle. With a grunt, Lada tugged.

A trapdoor groaned open, raining dirt and beetles. Tarcovich brushed off her dress and mounted a ladder at the mouth of the door. When she was halfway down, she pulled the door shut.

It had been Aubrion's idea to turn the sewage system beneath the whorehouse into a tunnel. He'd first mentioned it shortly before the invasion. Tarcovich had scoffed, for this was the stuff of penny dreadfuls; "the escape tunnel," Aubrion had called it. But a year later, the Nazis arrested a prostitute who'd smuggled a bag of flour into Brussels, later depositing her mangled body in the middle of town. Aubrion and Tarcovich hired some lads from the FI to dig the tunnel, paying them in food and old francs. Three rooms in the whorehouse had a trapdoor hidden beneath a carpet. If needed, Tarcovich could disappear in seconds.

At the bottom of the ladder, Tarcovich switched on the flashlight. The tunnel wound through the underbelly of the building. Here and there, ladders stuttered up the walls. When she reached the fourth ladder, Tarcovich threw aside the flashlight and climbed up.

She pulled open the trapdoor at the top. The heavy door swung downward, hammering into Lada's elbow. But she did not cry out; she kept her mouth closed until tears stung her eyes.

When the pain subsided, Lada became aware of a wet grunting in the room above. Nausea curdled her stomach. Her ears started to ring, as they often did when she was overwhelmed with feeling—but she pushed it aside, she pushed it all aside, willing herself to concentrate. Lada probed the rug that covered the mouth of the trapdoor. With some effort, she recalled the layout of the room: the rug was located behind the bed, adjacent to a dresser, so Beckers was unlikely to see her. Holding her breath, Tarcovich gathered the dusty fabric in her hands and slid the rug aside.

Lada climbed into the room before she could think about it a moment longer. Her pulse pounded in her injured arm. As she'd thought, Beckers's view was blocked by the headboard of the bed. She could not see him (or Hortense), so Beckers could not see her. Lada crouched low, trying to think. The horrible sound of this man—Joseph Beckers, head of the Postal Service, a collaborationist brute—threatened to take her. Tarcovich would not let it. She scanned the room.

Beckers's clothes lay in a pile just out of reach. The list of locations at which *Le Soir* was distributed would be in a small ledger, Lada guessed—and there it was, sitting atop Joseph Beckers's trousers: a bashful little book with a leather strap tied around its waist. Lada exhaled sharply. One of the most important bits of intelligence in the country was lying in a man's undergarments. *Good show, Beckers*, Lada thought.

She closed her eyes, gathering herself—just for a moment,

a heartbeat—and then she *lunged* for the book and for Beckers's wallet. Clutching them to her chest, Lada scrambled back through the trapdoor. As she pulled the carpet over the opening, she realized, with some dismay, that she would have to tell Aubrion she'd used his insufferable "escape tunnel" after all.

When Beckers and his mates passed out from drink, Tarcovich directed her girls to deposit them on the lawn. She waited by the window for them to wake. They did so loudly, protesting their headaches and stomach cramps.

"That *bitch*," he said, wobbling to his feet. "That bitch stole my bloody things."

"I'll kill her," said a second. He advanced on the whorehouse with his fists raised. Tarcovich watched him trip a little—not even a real stumble, but a half-committed lurch, like a precocious toddler. "I had fifty francs, by God. I'll kill that whore."

"Hang your fifty francs," said Beckers. "Have you any idea what the bloody Germans would do to me if they learned I was here?"

Hortense appeared at Tarcovich's side. "The wallet was a nice touch," she murmured. "They will never guess the ledger was your real aim."

"This was a shoddy idea for a stag party, now, wasn't it?" said Gert. "Who the bloody hell thought of this in the first place?"

Beckers tilted his head. "I assumed it was you."

"Me?"

"Took us down to Madame B's house for Otto's stag party, you did, so why—"

"I'm married, mate."

"But you came!"

"Coming and planning are two different things. And in any case—"

"Hang on a tick," said Beckers. "Who the hell sent those invitations?"

Tarcovich grinned, wishing she could capture this moment for David Spiegelman. The men looked at each other. Suspicion lent their features more complexity than they deserved, Tarcovich thought. One could almost be fooled into thinking they'd half a brain. But they didn't, of course, which is why the lot of them—Beckers and his dear, loyal mates—spent half the night arguing over why they were there at all.

10 DAYS TO PRINT
NIGHT

The Jester

TO REACH THE Nazi headquarters from the FI base, Spiegelman always took a shortcut through a nameless cemetery at
the border of the city. The place was far enough from Enghien
that the Germans never patrolled it, and so it became a popular
spot for midnight trysts and quiet walks, and for Nazi deserters
to contemplate their options. Aubrion had heard stories: young
lovers, on the verge of consummating their union, being interrupted by the sound of a bullet, or stumbling across a body in
a uniform on their way back into the city. That night, with his
head bowed, Aubrion tailed Spiegelman from the FI base until
they were surrounded by graves.

"*Spiegelman,*" he stage-whispered.

David Spiegelman whirled, his hand flying to the pistol in
his pocket.

"It's only me." Aubrion stepped out into the open, his hands
raised. "Marc Aubrion."

"You followed me?"

Aubrion stepped closer, tripping on a headstone. He could barely make out Spiegelman's face. From that distance, the city lights were nothing more than smallish bright dots, a careless constellation.

"I am not going to harm you, I promise," said Aubrion. "I've just come to talk."

"Talk about what?"

Marc Aubrion sighed, breathing in the ancient musk of the cemetery. He longed to be anywhere else. Though he did not know how to express it, Marc Aubrion felt an admiration—halfway to a kinship—for Spiegelman. Spiegelman had few instincts for comedy, and his penchant for good timing was accidental at best, but by God, the man could write. His work was a magic trick, without the pulleys and wires: *real* magic, the kind children unlearned as they aged. Aubrion felt pain—physical, immediate pain—at the thought of cutting off Spiegelman's access to a stage upon which to work. Given the opportunity to tell Spiegelman what he felt, the writer Marc Aubrion summarized his feelings thus:

"I don't like this, Spiegelman."

"Don't like what?" Spiegelman asked quietly, though Aubrion got the feeling he knew.

"Being here."

"But why are you here?"

"We are getting closer to our goal, and the risks are greater." These words tasted like ash. Aubrion took a breath and forced them out of his chest. "We can't have you around any longer, not given your ties to the Nazis."

Spiegelman's body went still. "May I continue to contribute?"

"I am sure Wolff will want you to assist with *La Libre Belgique*—"

"But can I write for you, Monsieur Aubrion? For *Faux Soir*?"

Aubrion paused. The voice that came out of him was not his own. "It wasn't my decision. I'm sorry."

Spiegelman took hold of Aubrion's arm with shocking

strength. "Please, Aubrion. You know they are not just words, to me. It is not just work, to me. Don't you?"

"I do."

"Don't you?"

"I do, Spiegelman. I have my—" Aubrion gestured, helpless. "It's just as I—" He shook his head. "You know I do."

"Then how could you do this?" The sentence took a different road halfway through. Spiegelman's voice shattered. "If you know what it means, how could you do this to me?"

He knew how he sounded, he knew he was pathetic, shrill, almost mad. For a heartbeat, Spiegelman could not let go of Aubrion's arm. If he did, Aubrion would leave this graveyard to walk into his own; he would write things without Spiegelman beside him; the world would turn and Spiegelman and Aubrion would be left behind. But Spiegelman remembered Wolff's promises. Exhaling, he allowed the *dybbuk* to shift inside him. Spiegelman released his grip.

Aubrion said nothing, for he knew what this meant for Spiegelman. He feared no monsters, no demons, but *obscurity*—Marc Aubrion could not bear the thought of that. Obscurity was not ugly, like sorrow or pain; it was blank. It was a piece of paper that had been folded up and cast away before someone had written on it. Spiegelman had lived behind others' voices and pens all his life, so he must have understood it; he must have longed to be seen, as Aubrion did. And if Aubrion denied him the *Faux Soir* caper, if he sent Spiegelman away, then David Spiegelman would disappear. But if Aubrion resisted Noël and the others, if he refused to send Spiegelman away, then Aubrion himself might be cast out. He could not allow that. This was too important, too thrilling an adventure, to surrender. And so Aubrion shook his head again, powerless to say what he felt.

"I am sorry," he whispered.

Spiegelman's voice had journeyed somewhere far, too far for him to follow. He walked through the cemetery with the heavy footfalls of a man who belonged there.

9 DAYS TO PRINT
MORNING

The Pyromaniac

SINCE THE DAY PRIOR, I had been fighting an ugly pain rolling through my stomach. This was nothing extraordinary, mind you. We were eating secondhand food, left to fester on dirty countertops or picked clean by ungodly fingers. Hardly a week passed without someone complaining of a bad stomach. A month into my service with the FI, one of our linotypists died after eating a bit of rancid meat; the man had escaped execution, had managed to run away from a *firing squad*, but was done in by a herring. We had accepted food poisoning into our ranks like a clumsy yet deadly rifleman.

But by nightfall, the pain was no longer just an irritation: it had grown into a beast I could not ignore. The beast kept me awake most of the night, tearing at my insides until my skin burned white-hot with its bile. I lifted up my shirt to look at my stomach, certain I would see something moving beneath the skin. Twice, I got up to wake Aubrion or Noël, who were both asleep upstairs—but I could not bring myself to disturb them over something as banal as this, not when they needed so badly to rest. I reminded myself, perhaps halfheartedly, that I was a soldier of the resistance, that I would not be felled by spoiled cabbage.

I lay there with my eyes fixed on the basement window. I remember it was snowing that night. I could see the stars, and then the gentle wash of blue that wiped them away. I think I must have dozed. When I awoke, a bird was singing its morning eulogy for October. I stood up to use the washroom.

It's hardly necessary for me to describe what I saw there. There isn't a woman alive who does not know how this story ends. I had a few older friends back in Toulouse—girls who laughed heartily and played marbles with me, whose faces I had forgotten already—so I should have known not to fear this thing, what I later knew as my period. But I was so far removed from the trappings of an ordinary girl's life that it never occurred to me. I thought only that I was dying.

I stumbled out of the washroom. My vision pulsed with each beat of my heart. Lada Tarcovich had arrived since I roused myself from my cot; I don't know how long I must have been in the washroom. She sat reading a newspaper, sipping her coffee.

"I was wondering who'd been in there all bloody day," she said, eyes on her paper. "I tried the door ages ago."

When I didn't respond, Tarcovich glanced up. I can't imagine how I looked at that moment. My only clue is that Lada Tarcovich, who had seen and done things unimaginable for most, dropped her coffee mug.

I opened my mouth to say something, though I haven't the foggiest idea what that could be. Fortunately for all involved, Tarcovich never gave me the chance. She picked up her mug, folded her paper, and got to her feet.

"Not a word," she said. "Anything that comes out of you— well, anything *more*, I suppose—will only make it worse. Here, take this." Tarcovich pulled something out of her purse. It looked like a thick washcloth with fabric strings. "Go back into the washroom. You will know what to do with it."

In some divine act of mercy, she was right. When I was done, Tarcovich beckoned for me to follow her upstairs. My shellshocked legs carried me out of the basement and onto the streets. Tarcovich hailed a cab and gave the driver the address of her whorehouse. We rode in silence. I don't believe I speculated on the purpose of our journey. Every part of my brain was devoted to a strange, all-consuming mix of gratitude and terror.

When we arrived, Tarcovich marched me upstairs to her private room. I'd heard much about it from Aubrion—the stolen treasures, riches from across the world—so I could not stop myself from gawking at it, not even then. Tarcovich put a halt to *that* by ordering me into a stiff wooden chair. I sat. She did not.

Tarcovich planted her fists on her hips. "Well?"

I'd lost all powers of speech and thought. I could only parrot her: "Well?"

"What do you have to say for yourself?"

"Thank you?"

"That's a fine start," she said, laughing.

Finally, I sputtered, "You know about me. You've *known* about me."

"Of course I have. What do you take me for?"

"But the others—they don't—they never—"

"They're men. You can hardly expect them to *notice* things."

"But madame, you've known this whole time?"

Tarcovich shrugged. "For a long while now, yes."

I stared down at my shoes, blinking away tears. I do not know why I cried. Perhaps it was the thief's release at finally being caught, the odd relief of the handcuffs. Or maybe I was grateful to be seen for what I was—what I am—after burying the truth under so many layers of character and time. Do not mistake me: I loved my identity as Aubrion's errand boy, a soldier of the resistance. It was not a role I played, or a story I made up;

that was a piece of my soul. But even a half-truth is a lie, in the end. God help me, I was a terrible liar.

Noticing my tears, Tarcovich knelt by the chair. "Come now," she whispered. Her hand was on the small of my back. "Worse things have happened, I promise you that. And I won't give you away, not if you don't want me to."

"I know you won't," I managed to say.

"Then is it really as bad as all that?"

"I don't know."

"Let me say this," she whispered, "from one con artist to another—it was a damn good ruse. Not many others would have noticed, not even other women."

"Thank you, madame." There was nothing false about my gratitude.

"What's the matter, then?"

"I don't know."

"It's all right." She pulled me into her arms. "You don't have to know."

There is a wretched brand of crying that I hope you'll never endure, when you weep so hard and so long that your body turns on you. Fed up with your own nonsense, you fall into a sort of sleep. That is what became of me. I wept until there was nothing left in my body, using up every bit of feeling I owned until I was a raw, withered husk. Then I dozed in Lada's stolen chair. When I came to, she was sitting on the floor beside me.

I remember that I kept still and looked at her without speaking, grateful that there was nowhere to go and nothing to do. This was me and Lada Tarcovich, this woman who'd slept in my home, who'd fought beside me, who knew me for who I was. I wanted to trap this moment with her in a firefly jar. I said to myself that I would preserve this quiet no-man's-land with Lada, that I would keep the memory for all my days—and I have. Only when I was confident that the memory was burned in me did I speak.

"Will it happen every day now?" I asked her. "For the rest of my life?"

Tarcovich smiled. "Don't you think I'd be even more disagreeable than I am already? No, we are cursed only once a month."

"For how long each time?"

"Perhaps a week, perhaps less. You'll find out soon enough, won't you?"

"Is there any way to make it stop?"

"It stops on its own, when you're old."

"And, if you please, madame, where do you get…something like *that*, what you gave me, when there's a war on? I've never seen one anywhere, not even Thomas's shop on Third."

"From America, of course."

"America?"

"That was actually how I got my start—it was books and sanitary belts." She paused before going on. "When we first started batting around the word *Nazi*, in the beginning, I knew bad business was on the way. Marc thought they were too stupid—*unoriginal*, he said—to last long. But I told him otherwise. That's their strength, I told him. The Nazis are unoriginal enough to last forever. In any case, I smuggled books and sanitary belts into Belgium. Grew quite the stockpile, actually. When a shiny black boot comes to town, it always steps on words and women first." Tarcovich paused, no longer looking at me. "I planned to sell them. But I kept some, and I gave the rest away."

Without knowing what I was doing, I let my head fall on Tarcovich's shoulder. She did not seem to mind. We were both women, I understood, who had been compelled to make decisions and sacrifices we otherwise might not have. The intimacy of our shared circumstances was not lost on me, even then.

"How did you know, madame?" I said, after a time.

"You're too smart to be a lad." She tweaked my nose. "What's your real name, then?"

I thought about it, distressed nearly to tears, but it proved impossible to remember in the abstract. I had to conjure up my mother's voice, pulling it from my sleeve in a noxious sleight-of-hand, *Helene, pick up these marbles, I nearly slipped and fell to my bloody death!*

Tarcovich misread my pause: "You don't have to say, if you don't want to tell me."

"Helene," Gamin said—for it was not *Helene* who said it, not the *Helene* who had been named by my parents. The name *Helene* stood over me, gawky and too close. I felt nothing for it, not hatred, not love.

"Like Helen of Troy," said Tarcovich.

"The face that launched a thousand ships," I said, something my father said.

"You poor thing." I looked at her, shocked at the sorrow in her eyes. "Except you'll lead them all in the end, you'll see. That is the difference. Troy will not fall this time, not if I have anything to do with it."

"Yes, madame," I said, for I knew not what else to say.

The Dybbuk

Many Nazi bases, the Enghien base included, contained libraries of books the *Führer* had deemed objectionable, so that Nazi officers could study them and learn the topography of the perverse mind. After much negotiation, Wolff had received permission for David Spiegelman to roam the library unsupervised. It was there Wolff found him, brushing his fingers across an unlabeled shelf.

"Are you looking for something specific?" asked Wolff.

Spiegelman reeled. *"Gruppenführer,"* he stammered. "Not really, if I'm honest. I needed a bit of peace, was all." Wolff nodded, keeping his face neutral. *"Gruppenführer,* may I ask a question?"

"By all means."

Though the library was empty, Spiegelman leaned in close. "Does the Reich—on the base—"

"Please, speak freely."

"Could you put me in communication with a spiritual advisor, do you think?"

Wolff frowned. He'd expected Spiegelman to ask whether he could leave the Reich, perhaps, or take a male lover, but *this* seemed out of character. "You mean a priest?"

"Something like that, yes."

"A Catholic priest?"

"Any manner of priest would be fine."

"Have you lost your faith?" The question, despite what Spiegelman might think, was not meant to probe his loyalties. Wolff was genuinely curious.

To Wolff's surprise, Spiegelman smiled. "I'm a Jew."

"Help me understand you." Wolff massaged his aching temples. "Are you seeking some kind of guidance? Would you like to make a confession?"

"I'm not sure." Spiegelman glanced down, kneading his hands. In the otherworldly brightness of the library, his face was all pockets and shadows. He'd aged rapidly since Wolff met him—not in the way of young men who do things they've never experienced, but in the way of old men who are about to die. "I think so. Yes, I would."

"You should get some rest." Wolff started out of the library, beckoning for Spiegelman to follow. With a lingering glance at the books, Spiegelman came along. The *Gruppenführer* feared for Spiegelman's health; he'd never before spoken of confessions, or of religion. "I'm taking you off the *La Libre Belgique* project for a few days. Take that time to recuperate."

Spiegelman got in front of Wolff, holding out his palms to the *Gruppenführer*. "Please don't. That would be hell for me."

"I've given you an order."

"I *need* the work, don't you understand? My hands must be kept busy."

"Get ahold of yourself, man," snapped Wolff.

Muttering an apology, Spiegelman stepped out of the *Gruppenführer*'s way. He'd chewed his nails down to the skin. Wolff had only ever seen prisoners do that, prisoners and deserters and madmen. The *Gruppenführer* believed there to be a touch of madness in all homosexuals—something must have happened to them, after all, to produce such urges—but he'd hoped Spiegelman was different. A man of his talents should not spare a moment's breath for madness. The Reich needed him too much.

The *Gruppenführer* straightened his tunic, reassured by the weight of the patches denoting his rank. "I've given you an order, Herr Spiegelman. Get some rest. I will summon you in two days."

"Yes, *Gruppenführer*," Spiegelman said.

"And remain in your quarters. I don't think it's appropriate for you to be in here."

"But I am permitted to—"

"I have given you an order, Herr Spiegelman."

"Yes, *Gruppenführer*."

Wolff paused a moment, the way he'd seen torturers pause in the midst of a beating. "What was the order?" he said. "Repeat it, please."

Spiegelman monotoned like a reluctant pupil: "To remain in my quarters."

"And?"

"And to rest."

"Very good, Herr Spiegelman."

Wolff left the library, closing the door on the smell of dust.

9 DAYS TO PRINT
LATE MORNING

The Pyromaniac

VICTOR, WHO LOOKED like he'd wrapped the wounds of his sleepless night in liquor and coffee, joined me and René Noël in the basement. Noël lay beneath a printing press so that only his ink-splattered legs were visible; the machine had swallowed up the rest of him. I crouched nearby, passing the director tools at his request.

"How did he get the printing press down here in the first place?" Victor asked me.

"Beats me, monsieur."

Victor squatted by the machine. "Noël? Could you spare a minute?"

"I'll be right with you." Noël's voice rang hollow from the guts of the press.

The printing press had rusted out completely, its iron arms and cogs reduced to ghosts of what they were. We'd had an increasingly difficult time tracking down materials to maintain the FI presses. It was easy to convince the higher-ups we needed more guns, more bullets—but another wrench, or a can of oil, or (God forbid) some paper and ink to feed it with? Over the past year, Victor had started writing to the FI commanders to ask for money instead of materials, ostensibly "for the purpose of weapons and ammunition to defend ourselves in situations of attack." The money, of course, went straight to the wrench in Noël's hand and the screws in the printing press. But it was never enough.

"All right, then." René Noël slid out from under the press, tossing aside the wrench. "What can I do for you, Professor?"

"I wanted to speak with you about printing. Now that the school caper is done with, we have the material we need to print *Faux Soir.* We remain, of course, limited by what we will actually be able to *distribute* on the eleventh, before the Gestapo figures out what we are doing and puts a stop—"

"There is no sense worrying over that yet."

"I agree. But we *do* need to worry over our plans for printing. What is our capacity here?"

Noël rested a hand on the battered press. "Not enough for fifty thousand copies, heaven help us. We could print perhaps two hundred copies in a twenty-four-hour period—and I don't think we'll have much more than a day. For God's sake, we haven't even finished writing yet. We haven't finished figuring out our distribution *methods* yet, how we're going to distract the Gestapo, how we're going to get the paper out into the streets. And even two hundred copies would tax our presses and personnel to their limits." With a self-conscious glance upward, René Noël lowered his voice. "We've lost so many, since Wolff knocked on our door. What do you have in mind, Martin? Anything?" I was taken aback by the desperation in Noël's voice. Even in our bleakest hour, I'd never heard him speak that way.

"I have a plan." The professor put on his glasses, rifled through his pockets for a bit of chalk. "It's a bit risky, perhaps, but I do believe it will work."

★ ★ ★

Ferdinand Wellens, (accidentally) renowned businessman and architect of the *Faux Soir* school caper, was having a bit of a tantrum.

"No one does, or ever will, understand my plight." He paced his office, throwing back his cape with every fourth step. "*No one, I say.*"

"Perhaps if you'd explain..." said René Noël.

"But it's so simple."

"Then surely it won't take you very long."

"All right, if you insist. People are fleeing the country, or the city. God knows why."

"Indeed," Victor said dryly.

"And printing is not the sturdy profession it once was. People work on assembly lines now. Assembly lines! As if we need any more automobiles with their smell and their noise."

"They are noisy," Noël agreed.

"Soon, I predict, I will no longer have the manpower necessary to operate this factory." Wellens stamped his foot at the word *this*. "What am I to do then, I ask you? And that is not the half of it, I tell you. I am losing resources, too. The Nazis have contracts with so-and-so and that other fellow, and the FI— well, you have your own factories... The point is I have nothing to print and no one to print it. How am I to eat, I ask you?"

"A problem indeed." Victor's eyes went to Wellens's paunch, and then pointedly (indeed, the word must have been invented for Victor's expression)—his eyes went, *pointedly*, to René Noël. Noël returned his glance with a nod.

"We are very sorry," said the director.

"As it happens..." Noël started. "On second thought, no. This would not interest you."

Wellens stood up straight. "What is it?"

"It would not interest him, would it, Victor?"

"No, Noël, I think not."

"What?" Wellens looked back and forth between the two as though he were watching a game of tennis. "What is it?"

Sighing, Noël said, "We have a project."

"The FI?" asked Wellens.

"Indeed." Victor closed the door to Wellens's office, drowning the noises of the print factory. "We aim to produce a fake newspaper designed to look, at first glance, like *Le Soir*."

"It's meant to be a satire," said Noël. "We are poking fun— of *Le Soir*, obviously, but the Germans, as well." Noël had been play-acting at a commander's detached confidence to keep Wellens's attention, but he could not keep it up when speaking of *Faux Soir*. "Think of it, Monsieur Wellens. What do the people have to laugh at?"

"And you want to use *my* factory for this satire?" said Wellens, halfway between shocked and offended. "What about manpower?"

"We would bring over some of our workers to assist," said Victor.

Wellens rubbed his beard. "How many copies are you thinking?"

"That, we cannot say." Victor held out his hands, palms up. "We are still raising money. It could be as few as two hundred copies—"

"—but it could be as many as fifty thousand," said Noël, who tried, in that instant, to breathe life into the skeletons of his words with all the conviction he had.

"Fifty thousand." Wellens paced, tossed his cape over his shoulder. He tapped his foot, fixing the two of them with a bright glare. "This could be dangerous, yes?"

"It is dangerous," said Noël.

Nodding, Wellens paced the room a second time. He stopped, turning in the direction of his factory floor. His voice took on a quality that Noël and Victor had not heard from the businessman, the sincerity of a man with wild, beautiful dreams: "But it could be *something*, couldn't it?"

"It could be," said Noël.

Wellens looked at Victor and Noël in turn. "My factory is yours."

9 DAYS TO PRINT
MID-AFTERNOON

The Saboteur

I SAT AND watched Theo Mullier finish two things in turn: first, an apple, and second, the lives of half the famous people in Belgium. The former he accomplished with damp gusto; the latter he'd accomplished already—it was only a matter of taking stock of his success. Though I never learned the extent of Mullier's work, I knew he'd spent the past days sabotaging the reputations of men and women across the country: planting scandal, architecting intrigue. To redeem themselves in the eyes of the Reich and their countrymen, these patriotic Belgians would have little choice but to attend our fund-raiser supporting the Society for the Prevention of Moral Degradation.

From my perch on a broken-backed press, I strained to see the list in his lap. The artist Paul Matthys made an appearance, as did Sylvain de Jong of Minerva Automobiles, their names written in tight, chunky letters. Gnawing absently at his apple core, Mullier circled the people whose reputations he'd compromised, underlining those who were still at large.

I accidentally kicked the leg of the press, startling Mullier, and I can still call to mind the anger that flickered in his eyes. While I didn't understand it at the time, I know now that this anger was not intended for me: it was for those who had done wrong in the world, who were protected by their reputation and good standing, those who Mullier had not yet unmasked for the sinners they were. Mullier had come of age during the First Great War and had grown old during the Second. He was, in a word, jaded. The saboteur had no time for the boy who never grew up, who lent his name to *La Libre Belgique du Peter Pan*. This was a world for hypocrites and those who exposed them. Everyone else fell through the cracks.

In the days of *Faux Soir*, Theo Mullier frightened me. Unlike my dear Aubrion, Mullier did his work with a grim precision that made it all—our mortality, *Le Soir*, the FI, the war—so much more tangible than I wanted it to be. Though the others worried about having the manpower necessary to print *Faux Soir*, I believe Mullier was glad Wolff's presence had inspired the less committed among us to flee. In his mind, only the most steadfast, the most loyal workers remained. And Mullier was old; that scared me, too, if I'm honest. He was old in the manner of a cathedral. I used to wonder whether he awoke one day to find himself in that state. I did not know the answer to *that* until much later, when I became old myself and young lads began to stare at me in wonder.

There came a commotion from upstairs as Martin Victor and René Noël returned from their meeting with Wellens. The base was quiet in those days, and any noise—any comings and goings—shook the body of our operation in a fevered tremor.

Mullier pushed his chair back to stretch out his leg. He hurt, I'm certain. But after a time, pain like that turns to white noise, like the sound of the drainpipe in the wall. Mullier's head turned.

"You staring at me?" he said, squinting in my direction.

"No, monsieur." I lowered my head, only to peek at him a

second later. Mullier had his eyes closed, his thick printer's hands kneading the muscles in his leg. As I peered at him with my head down, he opened his eyes and held up his list. He studied it with the eye of a soldier, a baker—someone whose hands and head were kept occupied by dirty, meticulous things. This was business to him, and Mullier did his job with an almost religious sense of duty. I did not see in Mullier any of Aubrion's sense of fun, his childishness. I suppose that, more than anything, was what frightened me: the notion that someone could take what we were doing so seriously.

The Smuggler

Lada Tarcovich smiled as Aubrion studied the outside of the auction house-turned-fund-raiser-hall, waving at her girls. Gone was the building with its broken back, its hanging shutters and tilted columns. In its place sat a stiff little structure, attractive yet honest: a perfect location for a fund-raiser supporting the Society for the Prevention of Moral Degradation.

"Not bad, is it?" said Lada.

"I'll say." Aubrion shook his head. "Can I see the inside?"

"By all means."

Inside, Lada Tarcovich's girls were decorating. It did not have to be a palace, obviously, but the rooms needed to look clean and modern, a place where would-be donors could feel at home. Already, the girls had populated each room with tables and chairs, mirrors and paintings, the odd planter or light fixture where it seemed necessary. They were finishing up now, their excited chatter following Tarcovich as she gave Aubrion a tour.

"Where did you get most of it?" he asked.

"Most of what?"

"I don't know, the *stuff*. The furniture, the watercolors—"

"Well, to start with, I borrowed a good deal of furniture from the whorehouse."

Aubrion laughed. "So, our desperate powdered heads will be sitting in the same spot where a thousand Enghien country-boys lost their virginities?"

"I wouldn't say a *thousand*—"

"It's perfect, Lada."

"It's a miracle, really, that I was able to put this together at all, with René's budget."

"René never funds *my* projects."

"When was the last time you finished one?"

Aubrion and Tarcovich wandered through the halls, one of which still smelled of mold. Tarcovich stopped a young woman carrying a feather duster.

"Give that hallway another scrub, would you?" said Tarcovich.

The girl protested: "We scrubbed it twice already."

"Thrice it is, if you please. We'll not be thwarted by a bit of mold."

"I saw a group gathered in front of one of our posters for the fund-raiser," said Aubrion. "Upper-class sorts, mostly."

"Gamin did well, the little bugger." Tarcovich adjusted a framed watercolor she'd snatched from the waiting room of the whorehouse. "Between the posters and Mullier's...*efforts,* we should have a fine turnout. Should this be here, or somewhere closer to the front?"

"I think it's fine there. You don't want the placement of things to seem too intentional."

"But it is intentional."

"Exactly. Is Grandjean coming?"

Giving the painting a final look, Tarcovich hurried into the great room, which used to be the main floor of the auction house. She pretended not to hear Aubrion. He was rarely attuned to others' feelings and goings-on, so she'd assumed he would not ask after Grandjean. She had hoped he would not ask.

"Lada?" he persisted. "Is Grandjean joining us tomorrow?"

"I'm not sure. We had a bit of a falling-out." Lada fixed her eyes on the floor—spotless, she realized with pride. Her girls had done well, Grandjean's reservations be damned.

"Over what?"

"Some nonsense. She did not want me using my girls to fix up the place."

Aubrion scoffed. "Why the devil not?"

"She's against prostitution."

"So are your girls, I'm sure."

"That's what I tried to tell her. Andree has lived a rather charmed, sheltered life, Marc." For all her talk of justice, Andree Grandjean's life was defined and demarcated by rules. Tarcovich made up the rules as she went along. Their differences might spell their end, if *Faux Soir* did not spell Lada's. Tarcovich added, "And she only just discovered herself, as it were."

"What's that?"

Lada gave Aubrion a meaningful look.

"Oh," he said.

"Oh indeed. So, it's a problem, you see."

Aubrion thought. When he spoke, his voice was uncharacteristically soft. "Do you—"

"Yes, I do." The words were out and in the world before Lada could cage them. They surprised her, even though she'd felt their gentle presence days before.

"Does she—"

"I can't say." Lada Tarcovich shook herself. "In any case, Marc, there's nothing I can do. The rest is up to her."

"Have you tried writing stories again?"

Closing her eyes, Tarcovich breathed in through her nose and out through her mouth. "This is not a discussion I am in the mood to have right now."

"I was just asking. You might feel better, don't you think?"

"I don't know."

"You could write something for *Faux Soir*—"

"I will," said Tarcovich, unblinking, "when you write a damn obituary, Marc Aubrion."

Aubrion closed his mouth, a first for all involved.

"Come." Tarcovich put a hand on his shoulder. He shied away. "Let's see the rest of the place. All right?"

"All right."

"Cheer up. We only have twelve more hours to prepare, and tomorrow is our one chance to cheat these people out of everything they own. This is your favorite part, isn't it?"

8 DAYS TO PRINT
EVENING

The Dybbuk

MANNING KNOCKED AND entered Wolff's office, his impeccable posture at odds with his stained suit. The bureaucrat's fastidiousness had been slipping of late. There were whispers about the Germans' performance on the front, the *Führer's* manic rages, the strange pills and opioids his doctors prescribed him. Wolff did not concern himself with such things—was it because he no longer cared to, or was he above these sordid rumors?—but the rumors had taken a toll on morale. Even staunch Manning looked shaken.

"*Gruppenführer*," said Manning, "we've received word that a fund-raiser of some sort is taking place in the city today, for the Society for the Prevention of Moral Degradation."

"I've not heard of it."

"That's the trouble, *Gruppenführer*. It's not a registered organization."

"How interesting." The *Gruppenführer* jotted down a note. Perhaps Martin Victor would know something of this fundraiser. "Where is it to take place?"

"That's another odd thing. At the *Ahnenerbe's* old place, that building we were about to tear down."

"Didn't an old woman buy the building?"

"Elise van der Waal. She is no one important, just a townsperson whose husband died fifteen years ago. We have no evidence she's for the Allies, but we have no evidence she's against them, either."

"Who said anything about the Allies, Herr Manning?"

Manning sighed. "No one, *Gruppenführer*. It's just disconcerting, is all."

"As always, we will avoid jumping to conclusions." Wolff set a folder atop his first note so Manning would not see his handwriting. "It's probably nothing. I'm sure we have a simple case of an old woman whose house was vandalized by some youths and who decided to do something about it." To appease Manning, he said, "But I will send someone to inspect."

The Jester

The guests milled about in front of the former auction house, smelling of wine and cologne and dwindling self-respect. The atmosphere was rather strange: somewhere between a wedding and a funeral. The guests who'd come of their own volition chatted excitedly, while the guests who'd come because Mullier ruined their reputations engaged in the somber calculus of reputations and charitable giving.

Holding baskets of brochures, Aubrion and Victor watched the guests from half a block away. "Baskets, it must be baskets," Aubrion had said earlier, "not folders or anything else. Baskets are upstanding, unthreatening. What was her name, from the fable? Gretel? No, *Goldilocks*. Goldilocks carried a basket." Tarcovich had replied: "Yes, and Goldilocks was nearly eaten—by a wolf, I might add."

Victor took a leaflet from his basket. "I suppose these will have to do."

Aubrion looked them over, stifling a laugh. "They are rather good, aren't they?"

They *were* rather good. The cover said *Society for the Prevention of Moral Degradation* in small, modest letters. Under the name sat a photograph of a plain woman lifting her arms in prayer. Aubrion and Noël had spent hours choosing the perfect photograph— "She looks too strict, she's not friendly enough, he's a man and it has to be a woman, she looks like she's rather unconventional in bed, he's *probably* a man"—before settling on the woman with the face of someone's neighbor.

When opened up, the leaflet was divided in two. On the left side, four short paragraphs enumerated threats to the morals of Belgium: "You may not realize it, but the dangers are all around us! Even things that seem benign could be traps for the faithless. Did you know, for example, that eating sweets can put you on the road to immorality? Pastries can make you lose your connection to the bitter realities of the world and drive you away from good Belgian ethics." Below them, the leaflet reassured: "All of your donations are used to educate people on the dangers and sources of immorality." On the right side of the leaflet, Marc Aubrion had pasted a photograph of a dove in flight. "Why a dove?" René Noël had asked. "What man can argue with a dove?" Aubrion had replied.

"Shall we go inside?" Aubrion nudged Victor, who rankled at the treatment. "It's nearly time, and Lada is waiting."

The Pyromaniac

The collaborationists and sympathizers from Mullier's lists entered in a scatterbrained line. Lada Tarcovich greeted them all. I stood in the great room with Lada's girls, dressed in Biblical whites and blues. Though I had seen little evidence of God since leaving Toulouse, I offered a whisper of thanks that I did not have to wear the sailor's uniform again.

"Good afternoon, madame, monsieur." Tarcovich nodded at the guests. I recognized some of them from the papers: cartoonists, politicians, manufacturers who'd sold themselves to the Reich. "Lovely to see you, Monsieur Matthys." Tarcovich's smile was painted on. "Please, make yourself at home. There are refreshments inside. Good to see you, madame—"

We formed something of an assembly line, Tarcovich and me and her girls in their prim dresses. Upon their arrival, the guests received, in turn, a greeting from Tarcovich, one of Aubrion's brochures from me, and a glass of champagne from one of Lada's girls. When they had run the gauntlet of our welcome, the guests were free to mingle. Remembering to smile—"obediently, not mischievously," Aubrion had cautioned—I handed a leaflet to a well-dressed older man. Though I can't recall his face, I remember his hands: spotted, manicured, the hands of a man who'd eaten too much and worked too little.

"And what's your name, young man?" asked his wife.

"Gene, madame."

The man's thick eyebrows came together. "Are you an orphan, Gene?"

I fought the urge to close my eyes and disappear from this place. "Yes, monsieur."

"What do you do to keep from straying to sin, lad? With no parents, it must be difficult."

It *was* difficult—to be civil. Hands like *his* did not clutch the guns that came to Toulouse, but they signed the orders, the death warrants. He might as well have killed my parents.

"Yes, monsieur," I said, thinking back to the leaflet. I tried a disguise, the way Aubrion would, perking up like the good lad I was. "I avoid meats and things made in factories by the Allies, monsieur. And also unsavory company."

The couple nodded, the woman patting me on the head. "Good lad."

One of Lada's girls smirked at me.

The last time Marc Aubrion was onstage, it was to half-drunkenly heckle the playwright who'd written that Henrik Ibsen parody. Now, leaping to the stage at the fund-raiser, Aubrion asked me to offer a prayer that no one like *him* was in the audience. With an actor's grin, Aubrion held up a hand for silence. He was dressed in a suit Lada had procured for him, a navy jacket and a well-meaning hat with a sharp brim. She had also made Aubrion shave at the last minute. I'd barely recognized him on our way to the event.

"Good evening, ladies and gentlemen." Aubrion smiled in what he probably hoped was an approximation of piety. It looked, to me, more like narcolepsy. "My name is Marcus Aubrey, chairman of this organization. Thank you for attending the first annual fund-raiser for the Society for the Prevention of Moral Degradation." Aubrion stopped to allow for polite applause. "Our organization was founded last year by an old widow, a dear, dear woman named Heloise." Aubrion, who was making this up on the spot and enjoying himself more than he should, bowed his head. The audience murmured, touched by his display of affection for the old woman. "Heloise recognized the need for societies such as this when she lost her husband to a ring of artists. From then on, she vowed to dedicate her life to halting the spread of moral corruption.

"This evening, we will treat you all to a dinner, food of the finest sort, for which you may choose to donate whatever you think this society is worth. If you believe we are worth two francs, then we will accept your two francs with gratitude. If you think we are worth two thousand francs, then we will be humbled and flattered by this gesture." Putting his hands together as if in prayer, Aubrion finished: "Thank you all, again, for coming." Aubrion bowed and left the stage, nodding at Tarcovich as she took his place.

"Thank you, Monsieur Aubrey," she said. "Ladies and gentlemen, while our lad Gene comes around with the donation box—" on cue, I ran to grab the donation box from Victor and Mullier "—I would like to give you the opportunity to ask questions about what this organization has done to keep Belgium safe. I see a hand up in the back—yes, madame?"

"I'd like to ask, if I may." Aubrion craned his neck to see who was talking: a middle-aged woman with a severe part down the middle of her head that lined up perfectly with the gap between her front teeth. "What has your society done to help get rid of—" the woman paused, blushing "—prostitutes?"

"Prostitutes are indeed a blight," said Lada Tarcovich. Aubrion covered his face in his hands, choking down laugher. "Currently, our program focuses on their rehabilitation. We have already taken a dozen former prostitutes and gainfully employed them as—" Aubrion watched Tarcovich's eyes fall on her girls "—domestic servants."

The guests applauded and murmured their approval. This was a respectable position, but nothing *too* respectable: just good enough for a former prostitute, a girl led astray by her betters.

As Lada continued to take questions, I started passing around the donation box. I was surprised at how many people donated, and how much. Wads of francs—the old francs, too, none of the new stuff—went into the box without a second thought. "Thank you, madame," I said. "Your donations are appreciated and will be put to good use." Sylvain de Jong looked slightly green as he donated what must have been a year of savings. "Thank you, Monsieur de Jong."

Mullier wandered among the crowd like a ghost. He registered the faces of his victims with slight nods, his lips barely moving to form their names. After a time, I saw Mullier take the list from a pocket to study it.

I caught Professor Victor staring at Mullier. The professor joined him by a planter Tarcovich had stolen from a former customer. I crept closer to listen.

"What do you think?" said Victor.

"We will raise at least forty thousand, is my guess, if we can keep this up." Mullier looked up at the stage, where Aubrion had rejoined Tarcovich. "We should bring out Lada's girls. Have them sob, talk of how the program has changed them, the like."

Victor nodded. "Matthys brought a piece. He's offered to auction it off, with all proceeds going to the society."

"Good. What is it? A painting?"

"Oil on canvas."

Mullier scratched at his beard. "Perfect. We can—"

"Hang on." Victor was looking behind Mullier, adjusting his spectacles with trembling hands. Mullier turned to follow the professor's gaze—but he was shorter, and the guests were moving about, so he could not see anything of note. "Did we invite anyone who might have reason to arrive in a uniform?"

At these words, I turned and tasted iron. In my shock, I'd bitten my tongue. My eyes went to Aubrion, and I ran to him, keeping my body between his and the Germans' guns.

The Smuggler

Like most smugglers, Tarcovich did not care much for surprises, let alone surprises that came in pairs: the first surprise, in this instance, being the men in Gestapo uniforms who stepped into the room with guns clutched to their chests, and the second being Judge Andree Grandjean, who was only a few steps behind them. Her heart pounding, Tarcovich watched Andree scan the room. Had she led the Nazis to them, was that it? Clearly not, though, for her eyes were too wide, too frightened. Tarcovich reddened, for she never should have doubted.

Across the stage, Marc Aubrion rambled on about a school

the society built. Though she'd lost track of the discussion entirely, Tarcovich interrupted him:

"That is true, Monsieur Aubrey."

At the sound of Lada's voice, Grandjean looked up to the stage. Tarcovich shook her head questioningly, risking a glance at the Germans. To Lada's surprise, the Nazis were ignoring her and Aubrion, instead making their way through the guests. Were the *Nazis* guests, perhaps? Was this one of Aubrion's tricks? Andree Grandjean gestured, frantically, for Tarcovich to join her offstage. Tarcovich cleared her throat for Aubrion's attention, intending to excuse herself for a few minutes. The Nazis never gave her that chance.

The Dybbuk

Manning entered Wolff's office without knocking. "*Gruppenführer,*" he panted, "Himmler has instructed me to ask whether you sent someone to that fund-raiser, the one for the moral society in—"

"I sent out three good men, with backup at the ready. All Gestapo, of course." Wolff spread his hands. His office was never in disarray—he was an officer of the Reich—but an open window had scattered papers across his desk and floor. The *Gruppenführer* felt self-conscious about the mess. He had been in the process of typing up a memo: *Operation proceeding on schedule. No danger of turncoats, as far as I can see.* "Why do you ask?"

"*Three?* Oh, God."

Wolff sat back, surprised. "Herr Manning, I must reprimand you for your language."

"There is a warrant for the arrest of someone who is there."

"At the fund-raiser? Why does that concern us?"

"This person is associated with the *La Libre Belgique* project."

"*Shit.*" Wolff rose from his chair, took a step toward the door—but there was nowhere to go, no one to contact. Once the German machine put an order in motion, it became an act of God. Only a devil or a miracle could stop it, and the Germans had seen to it that they were the only devils in Europe, the only miracle-workers. Wolff made a fist, furious at himself for losing control, at Aubrion for being careless, at Himmler, at Spiegelman, at everyone. Manning's predator-eyes saw everything.

"I apologize," said Wolff, trying to slow his breathing. "Of course, there is nothing we can do. We must allow this to play out. If we step in, we risk compromising the secrecy of the project. The FI command would take notice."

"But I worry—"

"There is no *point*, Manning," Wolff snapped. "Himmler will understand that, too."

Manning nodded. "I suppose, *Gruppenführer*."

Wolff sighed, forcing himself to uncurl his fist. "What is the warrant for?"

"Civil disobedience. A year-old offense."

"No way out, then." Wolff rubbed the bridge of his nose.

"Absolutely not, *Gruppenführer*. It'll be a camp, or execution."

Manning looked Wolff in the eye, though his expression was as unreadable as it had been earlier. Perhaps he blamed Wolff for this person's fate. To hell with him, Wolff decided, and to Himmler, and to the rest of them; their whims and desires were none of his concern. He did not live to please them, but for his rank and country.

"Who is the warrant for?" asked Wolff, softly. He licked his lips. "Not Marc Aubrion?"

"Oh, no, *Gruppenführer*."

"Good. The others are expendable."

YESTERDAY

The Scrivener

THE OLD WOMAN SAT, breathing the ancient quiet of the room. Eliza barely moved. Dust motes floated in the air between them. The lightbulb in the ceiling swayed on its string, turning the dust into galaxies.

"Tell me," whispered Eliza. "Who was it? Who was the warrant for?"

Helene rubbed her eyes. Here was the danger of remembering. Remembering was glorious, for it granted Helene permission to see her friends once more—but remembering was also treacherous, for she had to let them die again. She felt her muscles tense as though preparing to receive a blow. It was Helene's duty to remember, and by God, she was a soldier of the resistance, and she would do her duty. She owed it to Marc Aubrion and Lada Tarcovich and all the rest. They had written their story—had helped Helene write her own story; it was her duty to tell it.

"This is what happened," said the old woman.

8 DAYS TO PRINT NIGHT

The Pyromaniac

I REMEMBER SHOUTING, though I couldn't tell you what I said. My feelings left me before I had words to contain them; only the feelings remain. The men, all three of them, were on Theo Mullier in a heartbeat. Two pinned him to a wall while the third snapped handcuffs around his wrists. All the while, Mullier stayed quiet, his mouth pressed into a grim dash beneath his beard. Victor stood watching, aghast. Around me, the guests yelled their shock and fear.

"In the name of the *Führer*, Theo Mullier, you are under arrest for civil disobedience." The man shouted as he tightened Mullier's handcuffs. I knew a little German from my days on the streets, enough to understand. "You will come quietly or be executed."

Mullier elected to do the former. He remained quiet as the men in their uniforms, with their guns and sharp eyes, walked him out the door. The guests parted to let them through. I saw them marveling at Theo Mullier, gasping and muttering and wondering what horrible thing he'd done. Still, Mullier kept his mouth closed, his eyes open and straight ahead forever. It would not do to sabotage his own capture.

I watched Victor bound up to the stage, grabbing Aubrion by the elbow. "We did not discuss this part of the plan," said the professor, hissing through his teeth. "When were you planning to tell me? An hour from now? A day from now?"

Aubrion's eyes were haunted. "This is not part of the plan, Martin," he said.

The Smuggler

Lada jumped down from the stage and into the crowd to grab Andree Grandjean's hand. She pulled her into an adjoining room, shutting the door behind them.

"When did you find out?" Lada demanded.

"Just thirty minutes ago." Grandjean's rough tunic and trousers were rumpled, stained with sweat. "I saw the warrant. A colleague had it on his desk. I came here straightaway to warn you." Grandjean's eyes searched Tarcovich's face, begging for mercy or forgiveness or something neither of them could articulate. "Lada, I'm sorry I—"

Tarcovich put a finger on her lips, and—she couldn't stand it anymore, *couldn't*—Tarcovich pulled Grandjean into her arms. The two of them stood motionless, as though the embrace had stopped their hearts. Then they wept together. It was a good, honest sort of sobbing, and Tarcovich felt content, for she fit *there*, right there, and she knew she couldn't leave Grandjean again.

After some time, Lada broke away. "It's a good thing we had a row," she said, "or you never would have gone back to the courthouse or seen the warrant."

"What does it matter? I was too late anyway."

"But you might not have been. In another life, you weren't."

Andree smiled, lifting a gentle hand to Lada's face. "You're a fool."

The Gastromancer

David Spiegelman tasted fear in the night's sweat. Fear was the order of things, in those days, especially in the dark, but this evening felt worse than most. Spiegelman put his head down to avoid the eyes of the children congregating on the sidewalks, their hands over small grease fires—and yet there was no avoiding it: the terror bloomed on their faces until the night was fragrant with it. Spiegelman's hands shook in his pockets.

Though he was long past due at the Nazi headquarters, Spiegelman could not quite work up the will to go back. And so he walked the length of the town, circling the patrol units that walked the night. The hair on the back of his neck prickled and itched, as did his feet and palms. Spiegelman tried to recall whether there was a raid scheduled for that night; the Germans always informed Spiegelman when they planned to round up the strays and Jews and queers ("a courtesy," Wolff had called it, "to a friend of the Reich"). But he hadn't heard anything about arrests, not in a while. When the night patrols began shouting for people to go indoors, Spiegelman walked back to the Nazi headquarters. Fear lingered on his tongue.

He arrived as a car was pulling up. It was a Mercedes, a Gestapo car. Two men jumped out, yelling for Spiegelman to stay back, hauling someone out of the car. The prisoner stumbled, his right leg buckling under him. Spiegelman heard the shorter man order the prisoner to stand upright.

His body went numb. It was like those stories Spiegelman used to read as a child, those fairy tales that started innocently but ended with the protagonist's death, but he couldn't keep reading, even though he wanted to, and Spiegelman clutched his stomach as though he might be ill. The Germans had caught Theo Mullier; he could not be anyone else. The soldiers and their prisoner disappeared into the building.

Spiegelman collapsed against a shop wall on the sidewalk

across the street. His thoughts went from door to door, knocking. Two things became eminently clear: he needed to see Aubrion, and he needed to see Wolff. Though the horror of this thing was obvious, the advantages were equally so. Here was a path that led Spiegelman back to the FI and out of the Nazis' arms; here was a question and an answer. The FI would try to mount a rescue, Aubrion would insist on it, and Spiegelman would be the one to assist, Spiegelman alone could help them. They could not deny him that. David Spiegelman had found work for his pen again.

7 DAYS TO PRINT
JUST BEFORE DAWN

The Pyromaniac

WE WERE HOME, sitting around the FI basement, all of us except Marc Aubrion. "He should not be out by himself," said René Noël. "Not after this." Tarcovich and Grandjean brought him to the base shortly after sundown. I'm not sure where they found him. All our regulars—the few folks who had remained to work at the typewriters and machines—they had gone home for the evening, so we left Aubrion alone upstairs, sitting among the remains of their work. Aubrion finally came to the basement when the sun rose, casting the sky in a fever blush. He didn't say anything. He just threw away an apple core he'd found under someone's chair.

Lada Tarcovich lay with her head in Andree's lap, and I sat next to them, listening to the basement's moans. That pipe in the wall rattled, louder than usual, sending obscene echoes out into the streets. Every once in a while, the pipe sent us the voices of those on the floor above, our colleagues muttering their way to work. I heard another sound, faint but higher than the others: Marc Aubrion was humming. He sometimes hummed—and I use the word *hum* rather liberally, for friends of mine have tortured cats with less jarring results—when he was preoccupied or upset, a habit I'm not sure he ever realized he had.

"I know we are all rather shaken," said René Noël. The sentence ended in a faint question mark, as though he were asking our permission to be rather shaken, too. Aubrion sat by Noël's feet, twirling a bit of chalk, and I stood up and hovered near them both, just to be close. "But in this line of work, losses are inevitable. Would Theo want us to dwell on his capture?"

"Since we're being pragmatic," said Victor, "I will pose a question. What if he talks?"

Lada snorted. "He hardly talked to *us*. Do you really think he'll talk to the Nazis?"

"The Nazis have techniques that you and I—"

"Couldn't possibly imagine? Mullier will not talk," said Lada, and Andree squeezed her hand. "That much should be obvious, to any of us."

"I agree," said Noël.

"What I don't understand," said Lada, "is that we were promised immunity. Wolff was to protect us, was he not?"

Victor shook his head, his hands kneading each other in his lap. "Our immunity is to be granted after we complete the project. That was the agreement."

Aubrion jumped to his feet. "We can't leave him there."

"Oh, God," said Tarcovich, her eyes like stars. "Marc, my love."

"Marc, don't," said Noël.

But Victor took the bait: "What do you propose?"

Aubrion pounded a desk. If it had been anyone other than Aubrion, the gesture would have seemed performative. "We have resources, don't we? Money? Some guns? We can get more if we need them. René, you must know what we have."

"Marc, I—"

"It doesn't have to be much of a plan, just *something*. But we can't leave him there. Mullier is—"

"Mullier is dead," said Victor, the way a baker might announce the day's bread.

"Fuck you." The muscles in Aubrion's hands and neck stood rigid. I recoiled from him, this man I called my friend. But in my peripheral vision, I saw Tarcovich standing firm. She was the only one among us who knew him as well as I did, so her calm reassured me.

"Marc, you know it pains me as much as it does you," said Victor.

"It doesn't sound like it pains you at all."

Andree sat up. "Have you ever seen the inside of a German prison, Monsieur Aubrion? Or the outside, for that matter? I am guessing he's at Fort Breendonk. It is impenetrable. We could have an entire army at our disposal, and still our hands would be tied."

"*Our* disposal?" said Aubrion, in ugly tones. "Is it *we* and *our* now, Judge Grandjean?"

It was Lada's turn to sit up. "Stand down, Marc. She is with us."

"She is not with us." Victor made a chopping motion with his right hand, as though he were cutting Grandjean from the body of our operation. "Madame Grandjean, you know nothing of what we're trying to accomplish here, am I correct?"

"Yes—that is, no—but I'm here to help Lada."

"Then you are not with us. We cannot risk a security breach."

"Calm yourself." René Noël put a hand on Victor's shoulder. "Judge Grandjean, we appreciate what you've done to aid the FI. You are welcome here as our guest. But at the moment, there are matters we need to discuss—"

"Say no more." Andree smiled at Lada, then kissed her on the mouth. They lingered, reaching for each other's warmth, for Lada did not want Andree to go. Then Andree squeezed Lada's hands, a silent promise she would return. "Gentlemen, if you need me, Lada knows where to find me." With a nod, the judge took her leave of us.

Noël spoke, bringing us back to life. "All right, then. Let's take stock of the situation. How much did we make from the fund-raiser?"

"About forty-nine thousand," said Victor.

"Forty-nine *thousand* francs?" sputtered Aubrion. "The old francs? That's remarkable."

Noël ticked off this first item on his fingers, then turned to write *1) fund-raiser success* on a chalkboard. Though our director sounded calm, Tarcovich noticed he kept wiping his palms on his apron. "Second, we need to begin taking distribution a bit more seriously. How are we going to get *Faux Soir* onto the streets? How are we going to disrupt the normal distribution channels for *Le Soir*?"

Victor stepped in front of René Noël. "If *Le Soir* makes it onto the streets on the morning of the eleventh, before people have a chance to buy *Faux Soir*, it will all have been for nothing."

"I never knew a Catholic to be so dramatic," said Tarcovich.

"I'm not dramatic, I'm pragmatic."

Tarcovich snorted. "Anyone who thinks the two are mutually exclusive has never been in front of a Nazi death squad."

"He is right, though," said Noël. "We can't ignore the logistics any longer. Any thoughts?"

"Gamin is in the process of procuring bombs for one of our distractions," said Aubrion.

I felt a rush of panic at not having accomplished this task.

"Of course, but we'll need to be prepared—" Noël glanced down at me, lowering his voice "—in case something happens."

"Nothing will happen," said Aubrion.

"Monsieur Noël?"

We looked up at this unfamiliar voice calling down into the

basement. One of our typesetters, a stout man whose name Tarcovich could never remember, but who reminded her of a bricklayer she once knew, came downstairs. He waved for René Noël's attention.

"What is it, Hans?" said Noël.

Hans said something that I missed completely.

"He's here?" said Tarcovich.

"Yes, madame," said the fellow.

"Who is here?" asked Aubrion.

Noël sighed, wiping his hands on his apron. "Spiegelman. David Spiegelman is here. I'll escort him in."

The Gastromancer

Their eyes followed him into the basement, until Spiegelman's legs nearly buckled under the weight of their attention. They were all standing around as though he'd never left them: Victor pale and sweating, oversized in his chair, Tarcovich and René Noël, and Aubrion—blessed, foolish Aubrion—his hair standing on end, grinning at Spiegelman like he'd just stumbled upon a secret passageway that they alone knew about.

"You might find this question tedious," said René Noël, "but why should we trust you?"

Spiegelman replied, "I saw them escorting Theo Mullier into the Nazi headquarters. The Germans are transferring him from Enghien to Antwerp, to Fort Breendonk."

"*Fuck,*" said Marc Aubrion.

"Christ Almighty." Victor made the sign of the cross.

"Just as Andree guessed," whispered Tarcovich.

Even I had heard stories of the place. At the time, I had thought they were greatly exaggerated—tales of prisoners who were thrown into pits with half-starved animals, or who were forced to stand naked in moats of icy mud until they froze— but I later learned the stories were true. We spend our entire childhoods waiting for monsters, but when they find us at last, we are incredulous, unbelieving that such horror exists. Fort Breendonk did not seem real, and yet it was.

Tarcovich folded her arms across her chest. "Listen. Let's say we trust you. I *do* trust you, only because I do not think you're stupid enough to come here without a very, very good reason. Even if we trust you—"

"I've come here because I want to help you rescue Mullier," said Spiegelman, and his face twisted into something Aubrion could never have described, not with all the words he kept inside him. "I understand that I pose a risk to your operation—but think of what I offer. I have connections to the Germans, resources that we can use to save him. Please, give me that chance."

"What do you have in mind?" said Aubrion.

"I am going to put a stop to this before it goes too far," said René Noël. "Be sensible, you lot. Aubrion, we need to be working on distribution and content. Victor, we must be ready for tomorrow, and after tomorrow, we must be ready for the next day. We have a week to accomplish our goals, seven bloody days. If we had twice that time, we'd still need a miracle. As it stands, all we have is our focus and God's hand, but if we *lose* focus…" Noël paused, suddenly out of breath. He rubbed at his beard, inky fingernails scraping his hollow cheeks. Behind his eyeglasses, our director's eyes sparkled. He made several attempts to speak again before he managed: "I felt for Mullier the same as any of you did." Noël's voice weighed more than any of us could carry. "I still do—of course I still do."

"So we are to do nothing," said Aubrion; the word *nothing* entered Spiegelman's chest and lodged there, bland and indifferent.

"We cannot afford to lose momentum when we are so close," said Noël. "His life and ours will have meant nothing if we are diverted."

"I am sorry to have disrupted your work." Spiegelman picked up a sheet of paper and folded it, pressing his nails into the creases. *Nothing* was still living inside of him, crafting a home near the *dybbuk*'s, spreading its talons beneath his skin. He wanted desperately to keep talking, though he did not know what to say—but as long as he spoke, he did not have to return to the German base, to Wolff, to his desk and his liar's pen. As long as he spoke, Spiegelman could remain among the books and the posters and the beauty. "I needed to come here," he said, truthfully. "I had to offer my services to you one more time. I could not have lived with myself otherwise."

7 DAYS TO PRINT

AFTERNOON

The Pyromaniac

I WAS WALKING back to the *Front de l'Indépendance* headquarters after stealing a bit of lunch when I spied Marc Aubrion in one of his usual spots. I watched him from a distance.

"Excuse me, monsieur?" Aubrion was saying, tapping a man's shoulder. The fellow, who'd been leaning against the wall of a church, turned around, aghast at having been touched. But then his spectacles turned on Aubrion's disguise, his tailored suit and trousers, and he nodded in greeting. "May I trouble you a moment?"

The man said, "Of course."

"Where can a fellow buy a copy of *Le Soir* these days? I have been abroad, and I'm afraid I've lost track of the kiosks."

"Down the street, make a left, then another left." The man squirmed as he spoke. A banker, Aubrion guessed. He was not accustomed to being so useful. Aubrion noted the banker's perspiring neck, his unimpressive hairline. A banker with an overweight wife and four children. Possibly Flemish.

"Thank you, monsieur." Aubrion tipped his fedora. "Good day."

Shortly, Aubrion had a copy of the paper tucked under his arm. He found a spot under a tree and unfolded it. *November 5, —43*, it informed him. Aubrion skimmed the headlines, avoiding the walls of text beneath as if they were seats on a grimy train. In moments, Aubrion learned of a *Decisive German Victory!* but also that the *Reich Calls on Heroic Citizens to Ration Meat Wisely*, that there would be an *Opera in Brussels* that evening, and that *Monsieur Edward Danners 1886-1943* died the previous day after a career as a butcher. *Le Soir* was a boring but capable host, never giving away too much, never leaving its patrons with any excuse not to return.

Aubrion folded the paper, settling in under the tree. Coal from the factories down the road, which the Germans were running at twice their normal capacities, had blanketed the tree in ash. Aubrion ran his hand across the trunk. His fingers smelled of fire. I watched him rubbing his fingers together, perhaps imagining he'd touched the back of some ancient beast and come away stained by its scales. Wind shook the ash free of the leaves above, depositing the gray flakes onto the face of *Le Soir.* Aubrion leaned against the tree trunk, thinking.

I approached, waving vigorously to get his attention.

"Ah, Gamin!" he said, finally. Aubrion patted the ground next to him. "Come, sit by me. I am very busy."

"Doing what, monsieur?" I sat, raising a cloud of ash as I sat.

"Nothing in particular."

"I see."

"I came here to escape my thoughts of Mullier and *Faux Soir.*"

"But you're reading *Le Soir*, monsieur."

"I did not say I succeeded." Aubrion smiled at me. The ash had turned his hair a powdery gray. I cannot think back on this day without despising myself. I was a fool for not relishing the sight of my friend with gray hair, a sight I would never see again. "I am not a stupid fellow." Aubrion rubbed at his cheek absently. "I know the potential costs—" he stumbled over the words, which were not his own "—of breaking Theo out of Fort Breendonk. We could—" Aubrion caught sight of something behind me. "Do you see that woman with her children, over there?" I tried to follow his gaze. A woman with thick braids led her three children past a fish market. "I see her every day. Where do you think she goes?"

"To market, monsieur?"

"Every day?"

"Her children might eat a lot."

"And she always wears the same dress. *Is* it the same dress, do you think? Or did she buy four of the *same* dress?"

"I can't say, monsieur."

Aubrion grew quiet as the woman faded from view. An ellipsis took form between us. Then he said: "You know, Gamin, we could lose a great deal."

"If your plan with *Faux Soir* doesn't go well?" I was proud I knew to say *well* instead of *good*.

"Have you ever really sat down and *read* one of these?" Aubrion made an obscene gesture with his thumb and forefinger, then flicked his copy of *Le Soir*. It scooted over a few inches, indignant at this treatment. "It's horrible. I don't know how any of these people put their names on it. I'd rather lick mud off of Wolff's boot. I could not even make it through an entire paper without almost falling asleep. It's *embarrassing*."

"It is terrible, monsieur, I must—"

"They deserve better than this."

"Who, monsieur?"

He would not reply. Each word sounded so unlike the others, as though a different musical note accompanied his every thought. Aubrion balled his hands into fists. "But I risk depriving them, if things do not go as planned."

Here, Aubrion folded up *Le Soir* and held it under his nose as though he were a sommelier inspecting a bitter wine. I waited to see whether he would speak again. He did not. I took advantage of Aubrion's infrequent moments of silent contemplation to persuade him to play little games with me. When he remained quiet, I jumped up.

"What's the matter, Gamin?" he said.

Blocking the sun with my hand, I pretended to scan the horizon. "I spy a ship."

Aubrion got into character immediately. He was always a one-eyed pirate in our games, with foul breath and a nasty grin. Squinting one eye, Aubrion began to fold *Le Soir* into a sword. "Aye, a ship!" he cried. "Bearin' black sails?"

"Aye aye!"

"Run out the guns, First Mate."

"Aye aye, Captain."

"Bring us hard to starboard."

"We have them in range of the long nines."

"Steady, man. You are to fire when ready." With a look of comic horror, Aubrion froze. "Hang on a tick. *We* have black sails. We're pirates! You're about to fire on our own ship, First Mate, don't do it, *don't*—"

Our laughing bodies tumbled and crashed under the tree, where the world was made of ash and seawater.

I used to play games of make-believe with my older sister, who indulged my elaborate quests for hours. Indeed, our games were so long and intricate that I remember them more vividly than my childhood home, or my parents' faces; our made-up experiences are inseparable from my real ones. For all his love of disguises, dear Aubrion was never able to carry on that long. And perhaps it was partially my fault, for it is harder to disappear into a game when reality breathes ever nearer. Still, we always laughed at the end.

Aubrion was talking about *Faux Soir* again. I had lost track of the conversation. When that happened, I always resorted to the same question. "What are you going to do, monsieur?"

"Everything, Gamin. Everything."

★ ★ ★

Although I longed to sit with Aubrion a while longer, I had
a mission to complete. On the eleventh of November, a fleet
of vans bearing the insipid but considerable weight of *Le Soir*
would leave the print factories on their usual route—unless, of
course, I put a stop to that. Though I did not necessarily need
to *destroy* the vans, that seemed the easiest way to ensure they
would be out of commission long enough for us to distribute
Faux Soir. There was no harm in being thorough.

And so I left Aubrion there and walked to the Flemming
Workhouse. The boys were waiting for me. One of them, a kid
with a mangled hand, passed me a stuffed pipe. I inhaled the
smoke, stamping down my urge to cough.

"So, what's the job?" the kid wanted to know.

"Remember that business we talked about before?" I took
another drag on the pipe, inhaling too forcefully. As the boys
cackled at me, I doubled over in a fit of sputtering coughs. After
this had gone on a minute or two too long for my dignity, I
held my breath and forced a lopsided grin. "With the bombs?"

"Wait a tick." A smaller boy stood on tiptoe. "What bombs?"

"He needs bombs," said another. "Loads of them."

"Marc Aubrion needs bombs," I amended. "He's planning
something big. He'll need about a dozen of 'em."

"How're we supposed to make a dozen bombs?" the smaller
boy piped up.

"I got the stuff we need." Though I was not being completely truthful, I did know where to get it. I figured that was
close enough.

A boy in a cap with no brim came up to me and took the pipe
from my hands. "And what're we gonna *do* with these bombs,
once we made 'em?" He stuffed the pipe stem in his mouth.

"That," I said, "is the easy part."

7 DAYS TO PRINT
MID-AFTERNOON

The Professor

VICTOR SLIPPED OUT of the FI base and hurried to the Nazi headquarters in the wan, snowy quiet. Two little girls were building a snowman just outside. Their shrieks of delight made a strange contrast with the swastika flags; the world felt unbalanced. The professor had loved the snow as a boy, but he despised it now. Snow muffled the world, turning benign sights and sounds into phantasms. He jumped as a man came up beside him.

The professor brushed off his tweed coat, hoping, perhaps, to extinguish the smell of drink. In his boyhood days, Victor's father used to say, "The Lord never begrudged a man a bit of the bottle." Victor learned that well; Victor learned *everything* well. He had quit the bottle at his wife Sofia's insistence; he'd taken it up again the day she died. Victor still felt Sofia's admonishing eyes every time he took a sip from the thing, which he did, at least three times, while August Wolff led him deeper into the Nazi headquarters.

"I was intrigued by your letter," said Wolff, when they arrived at his office.

Victor tucked the flask into his coat pocket, opposing his pistol. Wolff's soldiers had confiscated the weapon when he entered the Nazi headquarters, but Wolff insisted they return it.

"What did you find intriguing?" asked Victor.

"That a man of your loyalties would write it in the first place."

The two men sat. Wolff nodded at the decanter of sherry on his desk, which Victor politely declined.

"That sounds more like disapproval than intrigue, in my view," said the professor, for although he hadn't the right to be haughty, Victor could not stop himself.

"You must admit that it's rather strange, isn't it? Your record is nothing short of impressive. Why would you tarnish it?"

"Though I am an academic, I'm also a practical man, *Gruppenführer*. Things change. Times change."

"Men change."

"Indeed." Victor glanced at his watch. "*Gruppenführer*, I must ask that this conversation be short. I have a meeting in thirty minutes, on the other side of town."

Wolff nodded. "What was Mullier doing at the fund-raiser?"

Victor weighed his response, a chemist pausing before tipping a beaker. It would be unwise to give Wolff *everything*, he reasoned. "We needed a way to quickly raise the funds necessary to complete our operation," said the professor. "With all due respect, *Gruppenführer*, the five thousand francs you gave us were not enough to execute something of this scale."

"Ingenious. Aubrion's design?"

"Naturally." Victor paused. Though it was probably unwise to ask, he felt he could not avoid it. "He is in Fort Breendonk, isn't he?"

"Herr Mullier? We had him transferred yesterday."

"God save him."

Wolff poured himself a glass of sherry. His wristwatch was

too loose, Victor noted. Aubrion might have wondered whether it meant anything.

"What else can you tell me?" asked Wolff.

"Do you know of a Judge Grandjean?"

"Andree Grandjean?"

"The same. She is sympathetic to the Allies."

"We have long suspected her, but we never had any evidence." The *Gruppenführer* drained his glass. "Do you?"

"Grandjean agreed to help us raise funds for our project," Victor replied.

"A shame. She has a good record."

"But she's taken on no political cases."

"As I said, we had our suspicions."

"Andree Grandjean has become quite close to the FI. She is with Lada Tarcovich now."

Wolff's head tilted. "*With* her?"

The professor reddened. "I thought that information might be useful to you."

"It is. Thank you, Professor. Anything more to report?"

Victor shook his head. The more he handed over, the less he had to work with; the way things stood, Wolff did not know the entirety of Aubrion's plans, and Aubrion did not know Victor was feeding information to Wolff. Only Victor held the whole story.

"Not at this time," Victor said. "But I trust we will meet again."

"Surely. I won't keep you any longer." Wolff stood, lifting his glass of sherry. "Are you sure I can't interest you in a bit of something before you go? You are a guest here."

"I am quite sure, *Gruppenführer*," said Martin Victor, "but you are a gracious host." He took August Wolff's hand in his own, surprising them both with the strength of his grip.

7 DAYS TO PRINT
EVENING

The Jester

THE TYPEWRITERS HAD gone to sleep for the evening, taking their needful melodies to bed with them. Aubrion hated the silence. Silence reminded him of everything that was frightening in the world: night and death and audiences that didn't applaud. At the beginning, when the war was still new, people would gather around the graves of the freshly dead and sing songs or recite poems, or just watch with their raw eyes; after we lost Theo Mullier, Aubrion looked like one of those men, the ones who stood in the back and did not say anything. He took careful steps through the basement and stopped at a printing press. René Noël lay asleep at its feet.

"*René.*" Aubrion shook the fellow, whose eyes spasmed open. "Wake up."

"I have already done that," muttered Noël, rubbing his eyes. "For the love of God, what are you about, Marc? Christ, you smell. Where have you been?"

Aubrion spoke softly, so as not to disturb the quiet. "Have you heard Gamin call this place his home? He does it, you know. He sleeps here. This *basement*. I did not realize I do it too, not until recently." At the sound of my name, I stirred from my cot under Aubrion's favorite blackboard. I kept still so they would not know I was listening.

Noël sighed, infinitely weary. The night passed, lonely and strange, and the two men did not look at each other. I thought Aubrion might have left the room, so I opened my eyes a tad. He was still sitting there, his head against the wall. Behind the concrete, a drainpipe wept.

"Do you know," said René Noël, "the identity of our last Peter Pan?"

"*La Libre Belgique du Peter Pan*? The editor-in-chief of *La Libre Belgique*?"

"Theo Mullier."

Quiet Theo, Theo with his half smile and his monosyllabic abuse, his apples—it was inconceivable to Aubrion, and it is still inconceivable to me, that Theo could have orchestrated, at least for some duration, the writing of the greatest underground paper of our time.

"I never liked him, not really," said Aubrion. "But I loved him."

Noël nodded. "I know you did."

Aubrion whispered something, joining hands with Noël in the silence. They were ships in a grand ocean, these two men. Time alone has made them extraordinary. They were small ships, and only the brightest lighthouses could find them.

YESTERDAY

The Scrivener

AFTER SPEAKING THESE WORDS, Helene went quiet. Dread clung shivering to the air. Eliza felt like she was standing in an empty art gallery, dank and timeless after closing. She kept her eyes on her notebook to give the old woman the illusion of privacy. This was no simple history lesson to Helene, Eliza knew. This was a memory, a nightmare, a confession, a hallucination.

"I don't know exactly what happened to Theo Mullier during his time at Fort Breendonk," said Helene finally, startling Eliza. "But I have tried to piece it together, based on what I've read of the place. Do you know it?"

"Fort Breendonk?" asked Eliza.

"It still stands."

"Have you been there?"

"I have seen it, yes. As far as I know, this is what happened."

6 DAYS TO PRINT

The Saboteur

ON THE ROAD to Fort Breendonk, a whisper interrupted the choir of jangling chains. "What are those things?" someone asked. "Those obelisks?" One of the soldiers in leather coats—the pale man walking alongside the line of prisoners—tugged on the manacles with a "Quiet, you," and that was the end of that. Theo Mullier lifted his head—probably the first time he had done so since the Gestapo shoved him out of the car with orders to walk on, to walk until they said he should stop. It was Mullier and four other men; I tried for years, but I was never able to uncover their identities. They were chained together at the wrists and ankles. Their chains sang as they walked.

Ahead, just beyond the wire fences surrounding the fort, a gang of obelisks stood with their wooden backs to the sky. The prisoners were half a kilometer away from Fort Breendonk, and the distance must have given Mullier a clear view of the whole thing. As I told you, I once went to the fortress, with a tour guide and a walking stick and a dozen or so children with cameras. It was an old, historic-looking structure at first glance.

The sky there, in Flanders, is perpetually mute-gray, and the buildings themselves are gray, and the grass is gray with coal-streaked frost; and so the fortress does not feel like it is *there*, but somewhere else, sometime else, living in the 1800s when they still built such things and were proud of them. That was what Mullier must have seen. But as he and the others drew closer, the grass-painted domes, black-gray walls, watchtowers dotted with men and their guns, the barbed-wire fences—the historic, painted quality of the place became viscerally immediate. Only the obelisks did not belong.

At the mouth of the fortress, where the lips of the barbed wire parted, Mullier might have felt the others slow. Grumbling in German, the men in their uniforms and trench coats would have pulled on Mullier's chains. He would've walked faster, along with the others.

I cannot know the content of Mullier's thoughts. Was he thinking about his youth, people he loved and would never see again? Friends from his childhood? Aubrion and the resistance? I don't know what people think about on the way to their deaths. David Spiegelman told me years ago that his parents thought *only* of death—theirs, anyone's—in the days leading up to their own. He believed the Germans killed his parents twice: first their souls, then their bodies. Was it the same for Theo Mullier, I wonder? Was he alive when he went into Fort Breendonk to die?

The men in trench coats ordered Mullier and the others to stop. They murmured among themselves for a minute. Mullier might have watched; he saw everything. Then one guard stepped forward with his pistol drawn, a shorter, curly-haired man. He unshackled Mullier from the others, tucked a key into his coat, and snapped handcuffs around Mullier's wrists.

"You will report to the business room." That's what they said to prisoners, in those days. "You will not fall behind. You will not speak. If you do either of those things, you will be shot without delay." Many prisoners did not speak German. Mullier probably surmised that would get them killed before the week was out. Someone would order them to do something, and they'd do something else, and they would be shot without delay. To Mullier, the guard said: "You will report to the business room. You, too, will not speak. You will not resist. If you do either of those things, you will be shot without delay."

The guard tugged on Theo Mullier's handcuffs, leading him down a brick road and into the main administrative building: the wide, concrete forehead of Fort Breendonk.

One of the things that has surprised me most since the days of *Faux Soir* is how the caricature of the Nazi has taken root in our consciousness. I have no doubt you are thinking about this picture now, as I tell you about Theo Mullier: the trench coats, the hooded faces, the Nazi's use of the words "you *will* do this" rather than "you must," to indicate that the object of these orders no longer has any choices—all of this is familiar. It's in our stories. And it is familiar because it is true. What is *not* in our stories, and what Mullier must have noticed as the German led him into the large building at the center of the fort, are the faces of these men. Mullier must have noticed that the men in their leather coats, the men with lightning bolts on their lapels, did not have Gestapo faces. There were no twisted noses to be found, no distended brows, no pockmarks or scars. They had ordinary faces, the faces of neighbors. That man over there could have been a shopkeeper, if not for his uniform. That woman could have been a file clerk.

A scream penetrated the hallway. Mullier tried to look out a window, to see into the courtyard, solemn with obelisks, but he was stopped by the guard's hold on his handcuffs. Thinking better of it, the guard *pulled*—"You'd like to see, then?" he snickered—turning Mullier toward the window.

Two Germans stood before a thin fellow with a beard. They had lashed the man to one of those strange obelisks. Mullier realized, with a start, that he recognized the man: he was the prisoner who'd spoken, the one who'd whispered a question as they approached the fort. "What are those things?" the man had asked. "Those obelisks?" The Nazis leveled their rifles at him, and the prisoner got his answer.

When I visited years ago, the keepers of Fort Breendonk had left the business room more or less how it looked in the days of *Faux Soir*. The room lay behind four or five barred gates, through a series of cellar-like corridors. Inside, a portrait of Heinrich Himmler oversaw everything: the swastika flag spread out across a long table, the naked wooden chairs, concrete floors, concrete walls. Below dim, reddish bulbs, the men and women of the Gestapo entered and exited the room. They were dependable-looking people. They did not speak to Mullier; they never spoke to anyone. In lieu of their voices, all he heard was the slamming of doors, the prison cells he'd passed on the way into the room.

The man from the Gestapo, the one who'd led Mullier into the business room, flagged down a passing clerk. He stopped, producing a clipboard. Although I can't know the precise nature of their conversation, I imagine it went something like this.

"Name?" the clerk said in German.

Mullier said nothing.

The curly-haired fellow from the Gestapo nudged him. "He's talking to you."

Mullier licked his chapped lips. "Theo Mullier."

The clerk made a note. He paused, tapping his chin with a pen. "*Nullier* or *Mullier*?"

"With an *M*."

"*Mullier*," he said, exaggerating each dip and twist of Theo's name. "Is he new, or a transfer?" the clerk asked the man in the trench coat.

"Transfer from headquarters in Brussels."

"Crime?"

"Just put down 'political.'"

"But there is so much room on this page. See? They expect details."

"I can give you a full list later."

"Fine, fine." The clerk scribbled away. Mullier's bad foot had gone numb from standing so long. "Did he have any possessions on him at the time of his capture?"

"Two false identification cards, a wallet, not much else of consequence."

"And the name of the commander who signed off on his capture?"

"August Wolff."

"Wolff?" Mullier gasped. "That son of a bitch—"

Pain erupted across Mullier's face. He doubled over, tasting iron. When his vision cleared, he saw the curly-haired soldier wiping blood off the butt of his pistol.

Taking obvious care not to look at Mullier, the clerk said, "I'll just require a signature, right here," and handed his clipboard to the soldier.

"Is that all?" the soldier asked.

"That is all." The clerk took the clipboard with a nod. "Good day, sir."

Under Father Himmler's supervision, the curly-haired man led Mullier out of the business room. The trade was brisk, and he had no time to waste on pleasantries.

Mullier had suffered worse blows in his day, far worse than the taste of the soldier's pistol. Such things were unavoidable in our line of work. But this blow had been different, for it contained in its character the flavor of what was to come. Think of it: when a man punched Mullier on the street (which happened, more than once), he could punch back, for Mullier was free. Not so in Fort Breendonk. There, this blow communicated to Mullier—as it did to all prisoners, for they all got a first blow sometime, and there was no getting around that—that torture and death were no longer vague concepts: rather, they were tactile inevitabilities. The Germans could punch him in the face; they were *permitted* to punch him in the face. They would do with him what they pleased.

In a windowless vault just beyond the business room, someone had hung a chain with a curved iron hook at one end. The curly-haired soldier affixed the hook to the handcuffs behind Mullier's back and exited. Shortly, another man joined Theo Mullier. The gray uniform of the SS clung to his short, stocky body. A horsewhip swung from his belt.

"Good day, Monsieur Mullier. You may call me 'Lieutenant,' if you'd like." Lieutenant spoke French with the sunken vowels of a Berliner. He sounded like a good-natured fellow, like he usually offered to buy the first round at a pub. "You're an intelligent chap, so I've no doubt you know why you're here. But I am told I must explain anyway. I am going to ask you some questions about your involvement in the FI. Some will seem quite strange, or even boring, but here we are. You must do your best to answer them regardless. Do you understand my instructions as I have given them to you?"

Mullier nodded.

Lieutenant's mouth crinkled into a frown. His eyes seemed misplaced, too close together and too deep. "I will need you to say 'yes' or 'no,' please."

"Yes," grunted Mullier.

"Thank you. Now, who were your accomplices at the FI?"

Mullier kept his eyes on the floor. I know this because all prisoners kept their eyes on the floor, unwilling to look up, believing that as long as they looked down, it would not come, it would not happen. A crack split one of the concrete tiles. Aubrion would have said it looked like something. Aubrion would have had a sarcastic remark and fake names for Lieutenant. Mullier had his silence, and that was all.

"You were based in Brussels, yes? Who was your director?"

The gap-toothed crack smiled up at Mullier. That was what

it looked like: a smile, to match the crack in the floor of the FI basement. Lieutenant stepped on the crack as he walked behind Mullier. Something *clicked*, and then the chain raised Mullier three feet off the floor. The muscles and joints in his shoulders caught fire. Mullier hung like that for a few seconds, and his entire world folded up and crumpled into his shoulders. He gasped, sweating, spitting wordless curses. Just as the pain reached such heights that it no longer existed, when it became its own anesthetic, Mullier's shoulders *wrenched* from their sockets. He cried out, falling, caught by his own dislocated arms, which were knotted up behind him like frayed rope. Torture, I learned on my tour of Fort Breendonk, is from the Latin *torquere*: to twist.

5 DAYS TO PRINT
EARLY HOURS OF MORNING

The Smuggler

LADA TARCOVICH SLIPPED past a Nazi soldier on patrol, his face illuminated by the tip of his cigarette. She took quiet, deliberate steps, keeping her breathing slow. But he did not notice her, or perhaps he did not care. Most Germans stationed on the bridges and walkways in downtown Enghien were young boys. It was still dark out, not quite dawn, so Lada could not see their faces, but she felt sure she'd recognize a few of them from her trade.

But the patrols had thinned with the snow, so the road to Andree's building was mostly deserted. Lada paused on a hill overlooking the town center. With the sun crouched behind the miniature buildings, the gentle rivers, the bony trees holding fast to the snow, the wooden homes—it was a postcard, a fairy-tale city. The snow kissed Lada's face and neck with corpse's lips. They were a month from Christmas, Lada realized. The lights would go up soon; not even the Germans could put a stop to that. How had she spent her last Christmas? The memory floated just out of reach. It had rained, she could remember that. People were singing something outside. Outside where? There might have been a small dinner, but maybe not. Lada's pulse quickened. She felt suddenly that she *must* buy ornaments and wrapping paper, that she must light a candle and sing carols and all the other silly, stupid things she'd never done before, she must go wassailing like the song instructed, whatever that meant, whatever it entailed. Lada looked up at a tree, memorizing the snow's gentle handprints on the branches. She must do it now; she must do *everything* now.

Lada forced herself to stop this nonsense, to keep walking until she reached Andree's door. She had wanted to come here yesterday, but yesterday had been a day for mourning, with no room for love. Once there, she knocked.

Andree Grandjean opened it, falling into Lada's arms. "I am so sorry about Monsieur Mullier," she whispered into her hair.

Lada nodded, taking Andree's hand. She fell into her eyes, too dark and serious and bright. "I need very much to sit with you."

"We can do that."

"And drink."

"We can do that, too."

"And make filthy jokes. And possibly have sex."

Andree smiled as she led Lada inside. "We can do one of those, but not the other."

Tarcovich looked at her quizzically. Andree was paler than usual, she noticed—and, indeed, the judge put a sickly hand on her stomach.

"Oh, Christ," Lada groaned. "It's your time?"

"Sorry."

"Not as sorry as I am. I'll brew some tea."

Lada drew bathwater while Andree fiddled with the teapot. When the bathwater cooled and Lada's skin grew wrinkled, she climbed out of the tub, wrapped a towel around her body, and returned to Andree. They sat with the teapot between them, sipping from chipped mugs. Sleet pattered against the window, but it was somehow warm anyway. They did not say anything for a while. Lada enjoyed that, not having to say anything. Both of her lives, as a smuggler and as a whore, were so loud. Silence felt easy here, like something that had always been.

"This is terrible," said Lada, lifting her cup. "What is it?"

"I am not sure." Andree Grandjean stared into the brownish stuff. "A woman sold it to me at some outlandish price. I thought it would be good."

"You bought it without sampling it first?"

"Never again, I promise you."

Lada poured more water into her cup, to drown out the flavor. "It tastes like a twig."

"Then don't drink it."

"A muddy twig."

"Is anyone forcing you to drink it?"

"That a dog shat on."

The two looked at each other, then laughed, longer and harder than they had any right to. Lada almost spilled her tea. She put her cup on the table, still laughing. But then the laughter lost its way and became tears. Sobbing, Lada Tarcovich fell into Andree's lap. She cried at her feet like a child.

"What is it?" Andree murmured. "What's the matter, my love?"

"It's nothing."

"You are a liar."

"Theo is gone." Lada wiped her nose with the back of her hand. Andree's eyes were red, and Lada was sure her eyes were red, too. They stung. "And I have an idea for a story."

"For *Faux Soir*?" Andree touched Lada's hand. "You said you could not write a story."

"I lied," said Tarcovich, but even *that* was not the whole truth. Lada herself might suffer the same fate as Mullier; she herself would be caught and killed and Andree may never know why she disappeared. But even this small admission felt like clean air. So Lada said it once more. "I lied."

5 DAYS TO PRINT
EARLY MORNING

The Pyromaniac

WHILE THE OTHERS mourned Mullier, *somebody* had to do their job. I knew, as we all did, that time was running out. We had five days until *Faux Soir* was to be released, until Wolff expected *La Libre Belgique*. And so I set out to do two things: to build bombs, and figure out where to hide them.

"Your job is an important one, Gamin," Aubrion had said to me, days before. We were in the basement, as per our custom, and a drainpipe rattled in the wall behind us. I remember the sound, a throaty hissing. "Listen closely. Every afternoon, at four o'clock, all the printers and linotypists in Brussels end their shifts. They've been hard at work, printing copies of *Le Soir* for Peter the Happy Citizen. They're desperate to get home to the wife and kids. Do you follow?"

"Sure, monsieur."

"They get off work, but elsewhere, a different sort of work is just starting."

"The vans."

"Precisely! Vans line up at the factories to collect the day's copies."

"Then the vans drop off the papers, monsieur. I know this bit. They take them to the newsstands and such."

"Right, that's how it is. Here's what we need to do. We need to delay the distribution of *Le Soir*, of the real thing, long enough to push out our copies of *Faux Soir*."

"Naturally, monsieur."

"Naturally, naturally. I knew I could count on you, Gamin." Aubrion grinned, mussing my hair. "The way René and I see it, there are two ways we can do it—or at least two points when it can be done. We can delay their distribution *before* the vans leave, or we can do it *as* the vans are leaving. But once the vans have reached their destinations, the game is up."

I nodded. "Do you have a plan for delaying the vans as they're leaving, monsieur?"

"It's going to depend on Spiegelman, but yes, I do. And *you*, Gamin—you are my plan for delaying the vans *before* they leave. You are to sabotage them in any way you can. Make it so that they cannot depart. You don't have to—say, blow them up—"

"Blow them up, monsieur?"

Aubrion looked at me as though trying to discern whether it was fear or hope in my eyes. It was a bit of both: I hungered to turn the Nazi uniforms from black to red, but I feared losing myself in the flames. "I'll have to see what kind of authorization I can get from René." Aubrion made a face at the word *authorization.* "But whatever you do, those vans must not leave, and you must not get caught."

Making bombs was easy. The tricky part was making bombs without tipping off the police or the Germans. You see, whenever the Nazis invaded a country, one of their first moves was to register things. Anything that could be used to make weapons— raw metals, scrap metals, assembly lines, screwdrivers, nuts and bolts—and anything that could be used to tell people that you'd made weapons—printing presses, radios—received a serial number and an entry in a logbook. If a copper or a man from the Gestapo or a Nazi guard stationed in town encountered something without a serial number, they destroyed it. The system was simple.

The problem for me, then, was that everything I needed to construct bombs had been assigned a registration number. And if the Germans caught wind that someone in Enghien was buying up pipes, charcoal, matches, and the like, there would be trouble in a black uniform. With that in mind, I devised a plan. All I needed were my workhouse boys, a construction site, someone's grandmother, and twenty-four hours.

The Gastromancer

David Spiegelman received Wolff's summons like a man resigned to his death sentence, or to a bad meal at a relative's house. This was something to be endured, not worth trying to avoid. Spiegelman stood before Wolff's desk with no memory of walking there.

"Please sit down," said August Wolff.

"I'd prefer to stand." Spiegelman knew that if he sat down, he might weep. His knees were weak, so standing up required effort, which steadied him.

"As you prefer. I've invited you here—" Wolff's eyes moved up and down Spiegelman's body, a parody of Spiegelman's desires. "Please, Herr Spiegelman. I cannot speak to you this way."

"Why not?"

"Only my inferiors stand up when they speak to me."

Spiegelman lifted his chin, suddenly aware of his paunch and narrow shoulders. "Am I not your inferior?" He did not know what game he was playing here, but he was giddy with the recklessness of it.

"You are my advisor." The *Gruppenführer* tried to adopt what he clearly believed was a friendly expression. To Spiegelman, it looked pained. "Correct?"

"Am I free to leave this place whenever I choose?"

"Spiegelman, you know I do not make decisions about—"

"Order me to sit down." Spiegelman spoke these words like a dare.

Wolff's mouth clamped shut. A pair of men laughed at a joke as they passed outside the office. The laughter floated into the room like an ill-mannered ghost.

"I beg your pardon?" said Wolff.

"Order me to sit down," replied David Spiegelman.

Wolff pulled on his shirt to straighten it. The *Gruppenführer* might have been a handsome man in his youth, but his deeds had sculpted his face into narrow, tired lines. "I order you," he said, "to take a seat."

Flushed with a triumph he could not name, David Spiegelman sat across from August Wolff. "As you command, *Gruppenführer*."

Wolff took a sip of water. "Herr Spiegelman, your temporary leave from the *La Libre Belgique* project is no longer temporary. Given the circumstances, it is not a good idea for you to continue."

"Which circumstances?"

"The circumstances under which—"

"Are you saying you don't trust me?"

August Wolff leaned back. "Do you trust yourself?"

"More than I trust you."

The *Gruppenführer* adopted a surprisingly petty tone. "I have never done anything more or less than what I've had to do. I've been lenient—"

"*Lenient?*" The sharpness of the *T* hit Wolff like a slap. "Wolff, my family was murdered because they were—"

"They were executed."

"Is that where you'll quibble with me? Over terminology?"

"I don't have time to entertain this discussion. I do not know how or why, but you have gotten involved in Marc Aubrion's affairs. I am not sure whether this involvement is logistical or emotional, or something more perverse, but I can only turn a blind eye for so long. Do you understand me?"

Spiegelman would not acknowledge the question.

"We had an agreement," said Wolff. "I promised that if you kept quiet and did your duty, I would try to grant Monsieur Aubrion immunity at the end of this endeavor."

"I never—"

"You never did what?" The *Gruppenführer* dared Spiegelman to say that he never got involved, that he had never entertained thoughts of betrayal. Of course, Spiegelman could not muster such a lie. "I have another meeting to attend." Wolff got up and straightened his shirt again. The bars denoting his rank and medals clattered against each other. He showed Spiegelman to the door. "Good day, Herr Spiegelman."

"Does this mean you will not grant Aubrion immunity?"

"That is a decision I will make at a later time."

Wolff ushered him out and closed the door before Spiegelman could muster a protest. He stood, white-knuckled, in the hallway, listening as the wind blew past the tapestries.

The Jester

Spiegelman turned. Aubrion, who was flanked by Martin Victor, gave a halfhearted wave. It seemed the two had been waiting in the hallway. "Fancy meeting so many close friends today," said Aubrion, but the quip felt weak.

He and Victor moved past Spiegelman to enter Wolff's office, closed the door, and sat. "How goes it, Wolff?"

Wolff's posture was stiff. "Good day, Monsieur Aubrion, Professor Victor."

Aubrion passed Wolff a folder. "The latest." He could hardly look at the man, this creature—not while Theo, the brilliant bastard, was being tortured and shot while the *Gruppenführer* drank sherry. Wolff's manners did not make him any less of a murderer, of that Aubrion was certain. The *Gruppenführer*'s swastika armband had slipped down toward his elbow. Mourners wore armbands: people who had lost those they loved. Aubrion wondered what Wolff had lost.

"We have four additional pages for *La Libre Belgique*," said Victor.

Wolff withdrew Aubrion's documents from the folder. "Give me a summary." He started to look them over.

"One of them questions the motivations of Roosevelt and Churchill," said Aubrion, "while another questions their morals. We've invented all manner of depravity for those two."

"We say none of it outright, but by the end of the paper," said Victor, "our readers will be assured that Roosevelt is a greedy, immodest—"

"—parasitic, irreligious—"

"—beastly Satanist."

"And that Churchill is a homosexual."

Nodding, Wolff returned the folder to Aubrion. "Be careful not to exaggerate too much. Black propaganda is a subtle art, remember that."

"Have you seen photographs of Churchill?" said Aubrion. "The only greater fantasy than a man wanting to sleep with him is a woman wanting to sleep with him."

"What of the other two pages?" Wolff asked Victor.

"Two columns focus on the war," said Victor. "Essentially, we pick apart every tactic the Allies have ever come up with."

"Throw a few jabs at the Soviets, for good measure," added Aubrion.

"I see." Wolff paused, and Aubrion filled that pause with all manner of conspiracy theories. Despite his looks, the *Gruppenführer* was no idiot. He must have known Spiegelman had lent his pen to a scheme unrelated to *La Libre Belgique*. If Wolff interrogated the situation, Aubrion was not sure how he might defend himself. But Wolff said, "Well, that is all for now, I think. I would like to see one more draft before we print."

Aubrion was too stunned to speak, so Victor spoke for both of them: "Of course."

"Professor, may I have a word with you in private?" said Wolff.

Victor glanced at Aubrion, his expression unreadable. "Absolutely, *Gruppenführer*."

Ever the showman, Marc Aubrion took that as his cue to exit.

The Dybbuk

"Professor," said Wolff, "I will not mince words. I need to know whether David Spiegelman is attempting to defect." Wolff's mouth was dry. The room tasted of sulfur and heavy furniture.

"Could I trouble you for a glass of water, *Gruppenführer*?" Victor's eyes wandered to Wolff's naked bookshelves, decanters, framed certificates.

Wolff poured him a glass. "You look pale."

Victor drained the glass, then set it on the table a tad too roughly. "I am feeling poorly."

"Please, take your time." Wolff had heard tales of how this disease manifested, how the voices outside an office might churn and turn from laughter to cries, murmured chatter to screams.

Victor took a moment to gather himself. "As I was saying… Was I saying something? Yes, David Spiegelman has tried to throw in his lot with Aubrion."

"I see," said Wolff, keeping every muscle in his body still. "What has he done for you?"

"Not a great deal." Martin Victor massaged the bridge of his nose. The angle of his shoulders spoke eloquently of his pain. Though Wolff himself had never toured Auschwitz, he felt as though he were seeing a list of German atrocities written on Victor's skin. They were *not* atrocities, of course, but necessities. Wolff would repeat it and make it so. "My interactions with him have been limited, but here's my understanding of the situation. Once he learned Theo Mullier had been captured, he grew concerned for his own safety. He offered to help break Mullier out of Fort Breendonk."

"I fail to see how that makes any sense at all," said Wolff.

"All I can do is report what I've seen."

A wave of something like hope churned Wolff's stomach. "So it would be safe to say that David Spiegelman's loyalty still lies with the Reich?"

Victor took off his spectacles to wipe them on his shirt. "My belief has always been that David Spiegelman's loyalty lies with himself. That is all I am prepared to say about that."

Wolff fiddled with a pen to keep his hands busy. *Idle hands build weapons for the enemy*, his instructors had said. *Idle hands, sinful heart*, his mother had said. But that had been before the war, before Auschwitz, when men like Victor would live a lifetime without seeing a corpse. What had he done for fun as a young man? How had he kept himself occupied? Did he go for walks back then? Did he ever stop for a drink at a pub? It frightened him, how little he could remember. It was as though his life were split into two volumes, the first of which was kept locked away in a cabinet he could not reach.

"Thank you for telling me this," said Wolff. "Forgive me for asking, but—"

"Where does *my* loyalty lie?" Victor smiled thinly.

"Well, yes. To be blunt."

"It lies with my work, *Gruppenführer*. We have that in common, you and I."

The Jester

Aubrion cornered David Spiegelman two blocks from the Nazi headquarters. "Spiegelman!" he called. "Wait, Spiegelman—David!"

Spiegelman turned listlessly. "Hello, Monsieur Aubrion," he said, his hands loose in his pockets.

"You look like shit."

"You do not look much better."

Aubrion clapped Spiegelman on the shoulder, steering him toward an alley and away from Nazi ears. "Listen. I know neither of us do very well with this sort of thing."

"What sort of thing?"

"Exactly."

"Monsieur Aubrion—"

"Please call me Marc. My father, devil take him, was Monsieur Aubrion."

The two stopped in an alley. Aubrion shivered. He was not wearing a coat, and he kept his sleeves rolled up. The cold felt like someone's nails raking lines across his bare arms.

Spiegelman seemed unaffected by the cold. He said, "I have no idea what you're talking about."

Aubrion, who once halted an FI sting operation to buy a toy train for a boy in the streets, waved his hand in what he believed to be the direction of Fort Breendonk. "Losing," he said. A breeze folded the wintery air around them, carrying with it the smell of fresh cold. It might snow soon, Aubrion realized. He adored the snow. Snow was the color of clean paper.

"We have not *quite* lost the war yet, have we?" said Spiegelman.

"Not losing versus winning." Aubrion became very agitated. "You see, this is precisely why homonyms are so very dangerous. If I could obliterate them all, I would."

"Not losing versus winning?" Spiegelman prompted, gently.

"No! Losing, as in—" Aubrion could not draw the word through his lips. So, he repeated: "Loss."

"I see your meaning," said Spiegelman. "Monsieur Aubrion—"

"Marc."

"Marc, I appreciate what you have to say." Spiegelman turned his head to the sky. It was gray-green, the color of the *Schutz-staffel* uniform, and Spiegelman's eyes glistened. "I did not know him. Mullier, I mean. But I am grieving him, as you are. More than that, I suppose—I am grieving the loss of *Faux Soir.* The loss of something I will never see to the end." He looked down, embarrassed. "I don't know. Perhaps this is foolishness. I'm sorry."

Aubrion picked his mind's pockets for the right words. He found them, bent and crumpled, in a corner he never visited. "How would you like to do something really and truly crazy?"

Chuckling, Spiegelman wiped his eyes with his fists. "Are you not doing that already?"

"No, but *us.*"

Spiegelman looked at him. "What about Noël?"

"I will take care of René. I must warn you, though, it is *truly* crazy."

"The *zwanze* sort of crazy?"

Aubrion grinned. "Far beyond *zwanze,* but just as beautiful. Something that will probably never work, and that would make René put me in a straitjacket if he learned of it."

"He doesn't know?"

"Christ, no. Walk with me. Does Wolff permit it?"

"Permit me to leave the base? He knows I have nowhere to run."

"Excellent." Aubrion set off; he heard Spiegelman hurry to keep up with his long, frantic strides. "We need to make sure the vans that carry *Le Soir* each day never make it to their destination on the eleventh."

"I thought Gamin was taking care of that."

"We should have another plan ready, in case he fails."

"Which is where I come in?"

"Which is where you come in." Aubrion smiled at the eagerness in Spiegelman's voice. He needed this as much as Aubrion did, that was obvious. He hungered after it, too. "What is the greatest distraction you can think of?"

Spiegelman laughed bitterly. "Aside from the one that would land me in prison?"

"No, no, think bigger. What would cause the greatest possible disruption to *this*?" Aubrion gestured at downtown Enghien: the children, the shopkeepers wary and eager with their sparse goods, the beggars, the Nazi patrols, the buildings with their weathered bodies. "To all of this?"

"It would have to be catastrophic. Like a volcano."

"Name something more plausible."

"I don't know. An air raid, I suppose."

Aubrion's eyes glowed with unspeakable colors.

5 DAYS TO PRINT
LATE AFTERNOON

The Pyromaniac

I USED TO love playing near construction sites as a child, smelling the reek of tar and dodging falling planks and the shouts of workmen. As the Nazis moved through Europe, these workmen disappeared; it is difficult, I suppose, to build something out of rubble and used mortar shells. So, when I needed access to a construction site for my plan—what better place to find pipes and charcoal for constructing bombs?—I turned to the only resource I had: the businessman Ferdinand Wellens. I cornered him in one of our printing rooms.

"What can I do for you, lad?" said Wellens. "Is something amiss?"

"Not at all, monsieur. I was wondering…"

"Yes, yes, wonder away!"

"What sorts of businesses are you involved in? I'd like nothing more, monsieur, than to be a businessman someday."

As I'd predicted, Wellens puffed out his chest. "I'm involved in just about everything you could name, boy—printing, meat-packing, automobile parts, oat harvesting—"

"Construction?"

Wellens thought about that. "Why, yes, now that you mention it, I do have a few construction sites. Obviously the war did a number on me in that area. Bad business, that. But yes, I do have a few sites left. There's the site in Flanders, the site in Enghien—"

"You have a site right here in Enghien, monsieur?"

"Two kilometers north of here, in fact. I was contracted to build a church, I think."

After another hour of small talk, two workhouse boys and I set off to Ferdinand Wellens's construction site.

Wellens had vastly oversold it, I soon found. The "construction site" was really just a tar pit, the skeleton of a building, some half-empty cloth bags, and three metal beams left to freeze in the wind. When the boys and I got there, the workers were eating pastries. They threw their crumbs into a congress of malnourished pigeons.

I motioned my lads behind a tree. "All right, now. Here's what you'll do. You two are going to find yourselves a bit of fun around here until the sun goes down."

Leon, a tiny afterthought of a boy with a knocked-out tooth and a hat he claimed to have stolen from some baron, said: "We have to stay here until after dark?"

"That's the deal."

"We'll be whipped for sure when we get back," said Nicolas, the other boy.

"But there's money in it, *and* it's for Marc Aubrion." I shoved Nicolas.

"All right, all right. Christ, Gamin."

"Christ has got nothing to do with it," I said, echoing what Aubrion always said. "So, when the sun goes down, you scurry right back here and lift two things. You hear me?"

"We aren't deafs, now, are we?" grumbled Leon.

"You might as well be deafs. *Two* things." I made sure to repeat myself, the way René Noël did. "One, you'll grab at least a dozen metal pipes."

Leon was twisting his cap in his hands.

I slapped at it. "Stop that."

He snatched it away. "Sorry, Gamin. I'm nervous, is all."

"Nothing to be nervous over. Nervous fingers is the only thing that should make you nervous here." I cringed at my incorrect verb. It was easy to slip around these boys. "All right, two—you'll grab a bag of charcoal. Hear me?"

"Pipes and charcoal," said Nicolas.

"Anything else?" asked Leon.

This seemed harmless enough, the business of stealing things. Neither Leon nor Nicolas—nor any of the other boys I knew— were strangers to theft. It was what we *did*, you understand. But I could not let them know how dangerous, how different, this operation was. We weren't stealing bread or tankers of gin this time. We were stealing things the Nazis cared about, and there could be repercussions beyond anything these boys had ever known. I had been muttering to myself all morning, "I am a soldier of the FI," but I had barely a glimmer of what that meant. I'd seen men at our base weeping on their knees. What could make a grown-up cry? I did not wish to know.

"Don't let them see you, hear me?" I said, because that was the most I could say.

My next task, as I mentioned, was to find a grandmother. I sat on a bench, waiting. A potential target lined up to buy bread at a stall on the Rue de Grady. Though I had only faint memories of my own grandmother, this woman reminded me of her.

"Please, madame," I said to her. The woman had wrapped herself in blankets and scarves. Only her eyes were visible. "I am so cold. Do you have any matches?"

She ignored me. The bread line was hardly moving; she took half a step forward, following the trail of hungry hands and tired eyes that led to the baker's stall. Men in dark uniforms paced around the line. Fights often broke out when the bakers ran out of bread, and the guns were around to keep those fights from turning into riots. I stayed sharp, ready to dart if the soldiers noticed me.

I tried a different tack. "Please, madame. My grandmother was so gentle, like you."

That did not work, either. As a matter of fact, she seemed to resent the comparison. With an indignant sniff, she took another step forward in line. I tried once more.

"The other woman I tried, *she* did not give me any matches. But I knew, madame, as soon as I saw your face, that you were far too kind to leave my sister and me in the cold."

The change was immediate. "Oh, you poor boy." Hand on her chest, the woman bent to touch my cheeks and forehead. "People don't want to be heroes, Gamin," was what Aubrion always said. "They just want to be a bigger hero than their neighbor." My bigger hero patted at her dress. "Your cheeks are ice, you poor boy." She stuffed a matchbook into my hand. "Take this and warm yourself. Do you need money for bread?"

I said I did not, and went about my business. My business, in this case, involved finding another old woman at the other side of town. Bright patches dotted her clothes; that is all I can remember of her. She stood outside a butcher shop, squinting against the wind.

"Madame." I kept my head down, my eyes down. "Please, madame, I am so cold—"

My pockets were soon weighed down by matchbooks, wrapped in scraps of cloth to keep them dry. This was, you must realize, a problem. I was as an opium addict with vials of powder, a drunk with bottles rattling around in a cart. As I walked on, I ached to stop and strike a match—not only because it was cold, which it was, but because I longed to see the flame, to brush my fingers across the strands of red.

"Good madame, sweet madame," I pled. The woman was peering through the boarded-up windows of a trinket shop. "Please help me and my—"

As the woman turned, I realized my mistake. The good madame, sweet madame was, in fact, the first grandmother I'd spoken to that day.

"What game are you playing at, boy?" she said. I was about to jog off, thinking she'd leave me alone—but I had not yet learned that our fear of tyranny makes us loyal to it. "Police!" the woman called. "Police, he is a pickpocket!"

There were no police any longer: only Germans, who came after me with their rifles. "*Dieser Junge!* That boy!" the Nazis said. They were not firing, not yet, but they were running in my direction, so I took off down the street, the matchbooks in my pockets slapping my thighs.

I turned a corner, weaving through carts and horses and shopkeepers and children. The buildings in Anderlecht have not changed in seventy years; they are lean and narrow now, as they were then. They cast a slender, blue shadow on me and the Nazis and the ice-slicked street. The Germans wore fine black boots that made music as they gave chase, while I wore a pair of shoes I took off a dead refugee, two sizes too large, and full of holes. I slipped as I ran; the Germans did not—and every time I slipped, my pursuers grew closer.

After a few minutes, the cold air started to burn my chest, and my head swam. I had not eaten much that day, I'd not had much water, and I was still on my period. I came across a building of brick and stone, broader and pointier than the others. With a tense glance behind me, I began to climb the building. I heard the Nazis engage in a few seconds of discussion—"*Sollten wir? Ja?*"—before a couple tried to follow me up. But, just as I had calculated, their equipment was too heavy, their clothing too much. They were no match for the agility of the half-starved.

I crouched atop the building, my arms shaking. Pieces of conversation, chopped up by the wind, came to me; the Germans considered finding another way to the roof, but I wasn't worth the effort. When the Nazis departed, and were unlikely to return, I stuck my shivering body over the side of the building and climbed down. I paused halfway to the bottom, concerned my descent might cause someone to raise the alarm. Nothing. I suppose the people of the city had seen odder things than a boy sliding down a drainpipe.

It was too soon to return to the center of town, but too cold to remain outside. And so I began to walk, feeling rather purposeless. In doing so, I happened upon a building, even slenderer than its neighbors, with two powder-blue doors and a boarded-up gate. I stood on tiptoe to peer between the boards. Though I could not tell what the building had been before, it was clearly abandoned now. Taking care that no one saw me, I squeezed through the boards and into the inky unknown. I paused to listen for footsteps outside. I heard none.

YESTERDAY

The Scrivener

THE OLD WOMAN watched Eliza smile, an expression that came so easily to those who knew Marc Aubrion. It wasn't an ordinary smile, but rather a slow appreciation for something she could not *quite* comprehend. "A building with blue doors?" said Eliza. "Is it *this* building? The one we're sitting in?"

Helene leaned back in her chair. "It might be."

"*Might* be?"

"The mind of an old woman is a fickle thing. I may have forgotten the particulars."

"Helene." Eliza laughed, realizing the old woman was toying with her. The table separating them seemed to disappear, like there was no distance between them at all, like they were one body and one person. Helene felt a warmth for Eliza she'd hitherto reserved for Aubrion. She was passing the girl something delicate, piece by piece. Eliza held out her careful, willing palms, ready to build anew.

5 DAYS TO PRINT
LATE AFTERNOON

The Pyromaniac

I EXPECTED, through the years, that the terrible things I saw and did would stay with me—and they did. But even as other memories died, one parasite remained, swollen and vulgar, inside my body. It started in that abandoned building—*this* building—the one with two blue doors.

The room had been painted in faces and eyes. They were everywhere, those faces, and I can see them now, just as I saw them then: hundreds of faces papering the walls, carpeting the floor, draped across tables and desks, sticking to my shoes. I lunged for the door. In doing so, I dropped my match, which expelled an irritated puff of smoke and went out.

"Shit," I whispered. The room tasted of sawdust and iodine, and the darkness filled my mouth and lungs like sewer water. Panicking, I fumbled for another match. I was terrified I would drop my matches, that I would lose them to the darkness. After three or four tries, I had light again.

This time, I was prepared for the sight. I collected myself, repeating something René Noël had told me before the days of *Faux Soir*: "When you most want to close your eyes—that is when you should keep them open." And so I forced myself to look at the faces. They were simply photographs. I had stumbled into an old photography lab.

Holding the match aloft, I explored my surroundings. The room looked almost exactly as it does now: narrow, with angular bends and points. Half a dozen tables lay scattered about the perimeter. Each was laden with small vials, pans, sheets of paper, cracked bottles.

My match went out, stinging my hand. I cursed and lit another.

As I approached the largest desk at the back of the room, I gagged on the smell of rotting eggs. Most of the vials on the desk contained a silver powder. I picked up a bottle, sniffing its contents. Perhaps, I realized, Aubrion could make use of something here.

I turned to examine the room. Bullet holes dotted the wall behind me. About half the tables had been overturned, some photographs torn to shreds. Something illegal had happened here, that much was clear. But the Germans' work was done, and they were unlikely to return.

Careful to keep my match away from the floor, I picked up a photograph of an older woman. She had smile lines and flowers in her hair. My mother had tried to teach me what different flowers were called, when I was a child. I had not paid attention; I could not remember their names.

The Germans would not search for me all night; their search would die with the sun. So I waited for my flame to go out. I sat and made up names in the dark.

5 DAYS TO PRINT
EARLY EVENING

The Jester

"AH, THERE HE IS," said Noël, and Aubrion heard the director come downstairs and into the basement, saw him touch Spiegelman's shoulder, a tacit indication that he was welcome in their home. Aubrion was surprised, for he had expected to spar with the director over Spiegelman's sudden appearance. Noël tried to glance over Aubrion's shoulder, failed, and tried again with Spiegelman. A piece of blotting paper sat between them. "What on earth are you two doing?"

"I thought I would get started on this now that Spiegelman is here," replied Aubrion.

"But what is *this*?" said Noël.

The paper was alive with Aubrion's fierce lettering, his arrows craning their necks at Spiegelman's diagrams and tired, timid script. Noël stepped away as though he feared the paper might reach out and seize him by the throat.

"It's our distraction," said Aubrion. "René, I need you to make me a promise."

"He wants you to promise not to put him in a straitjacket." Spiegelman almost smiled.

Wellens, who'd moved a chair under our remaining lightbulb to read some dull finance paper, laughed. "Some of the best ideas have come from men in straitjackets, I daresay!"

Noël rolled his eyes. "All right, I promise." He fished a wrench out of his apron pocket and tossed it on the floor. "At least for the time being."

"To stop the vans carrying *Le Soir* from getting where they need to go," said Aubrion, "Monsieur Spiegelman and I are going to make the Royal Air Force bomb the city."

Aubrion had expected a variety of reactions to this idea, including anger, disbelief, incredulousness, even laughter. Silence, however, was not among these options. The others lapsed into the loudest quiet Aubrion had ever heard. Victor chose that moment to come downstairs and step in the silence as though it were mud.

"What did Aubrion do now?" the professor asked.

"He is going to make the RAF bomb Belgium," said Tarcovich. With a wicked smile at Aubrion, she lit a cigarette.

"Oh, Christ keep us," moaned Victor.

"What did Wolff want?" asked Noël.

Victor rubbed his forehead. "Nothing in particular. Just to double-check the information Aubrion gave him. What in God's name is this business about the RAF?"

"I have two words for anyone here who doubts it can be done." Aubrion paused, as he always did before a punch line. "Bomber Harris."

"Who is that," said Tarcovich, "and what comic book did he crawl out of?"

"Bomber Arthur Harris." Wellens put his paper down. "Commander-in-Chief of the Royal Air Force." He said it rather like he was introducing the man at a party.

"Christ Almighty." Noël put his hands on the back of a chair to steady himself. "I suppose it *can* be done."

"Can someone enlighten those of us who have no bloody clue what's going on here?" demanded Tarcovich.

Aubrion started thus: "Everyone hates Bomber Harris, because Bomber Harris is the foremost and perhaps *only* advocate for area bombing."

"Area bombing?" asked Tarcovich.

"The practice of bombing a target *area*, such as a city or a town," said Victor, assuming a lecturer's posture, "instead of a specific target, such as a building or a military unit."

Tarcovich blew out a furious cloud of smoke. "He's the arsehole responsible for the *blitzkrieg*? The reason Londoners have to step through a pile of bodies to get a pat of butter?"

"Assuming there's still a full pat of butter left somewhere in London," Victor said softly, "that's correct."

"Do you know him, Wellens?" asked Noël.

Wellens went uncharacteristically quiet. "I've had dealings with him."

"I still don't understand why 'Bomber Harris' is the reason this is going to work," said Tarcovich.

"The Allies are desperate." Aubrion twirled a piece of chalk. "This war has completely changed the way armies work. Think about it. If General Eisenhower is sitting in his rotting trousers on some godforsaken island in the Orient, and he needs to make a decision that might change the course of the war, does he have time to radio Monsieur Roosevelt and ask for permission? Christ, no. He's got to make his decision *now*. Armies and army commanders think for themselves now, do you understand? And Bomber Harris is no different. Churchill hates his guts, but there's nothing old Churchy can do. He's got to let Harris do what Harris does, which largely involves bombing the bloody hell out of anything he wants to." Aubrion stabbed the blackboard with his chalk. "He is destructive, unpredictable—"

"Religious," Victor added.

"Very religious. Listen to this." Aubrion nodded at Spiegelman, who retrieved a file that had been tucked under the blotting paper. "This is a statement Harris delivered a few years ago."

"'The Nazis entered this war,'" read Spiegelman, "'under the rather childish delusion that they were going to bomb everyone else, and nobody was going to bomb them. At Rotterdam, London, Warsaw and half a hundred other places, they put their rather naive theory into operation. They sowed the wind, and now they are going to reap the whirlwind.'"

Tarcovich whistled. "Now *that's* a male ego."

"Last month," said Aubrion, "Churchill issued a statement to the German people—this is incredible, actually—apologizing for all the women and children who'd died and all the homes that had been destroyed in Harris's area raids. He wanted to emphasize that this damage was unintentional but unavoidable. And Bomber Harris? What did he do?" Aubrion laughed. "That glorious son of a bitch issued a counter-statement that said... Spiegelman?"

Spiegelman read: "'The aim of the Combined Bomber Offensive should be unambiguously stated as the destruction of German cities, the killing of German workers, and the disruption of civilized life throughout Germany.'"

"The disruption of civilized life!" Aubrion repeated, shaking his head.

"So, he's odd, and he's religious," said Tarcovich, cataloging these traits on her fingers, "and he's unpredictable, and people don't like him. If not for the religion bit, you and he could make great friends, Marc."

"Don't you see?" said Aubrion. "Add this all together, and what do you get? Someone who is *emotional.* What does that mean for us?"

"It means he can be goaded," said Spiegelman, almost to himself.

"Let me be clear on this," said Noël, steadying himself on a chair. "You are going to goad Commander Arthur Harris into bombing Belgium."

"Just the city," said Aubrion, "but yes."

"On the eleventh of November, before four o'clock, when the vans leave."

"Yes."

"To stop the vans from distributing *Le Soir*."

Aubrion rocked back on his heels, a content smile spreading across his face. "Now you've got it. Was that really so difficult, René?"

"And yet the raid can't be *that* destructive," said Victor, folding his arms across his chest, "or people will shelter in their homes all day, and then who will buy *Faux Soir*?"

"Right," said Spiegelman. "We will goad him, but we must not infuriate him."

Victor regarded Spiegelman, looking down at him like an overdue library book. The professor was at least two feet taller. "Who put you on this project?" he said.

"Come off it, Martin," snapped Aubrion. "David is here, when he would be far safer with the Germans. That is proof enough of his loyalty."

"Wait, wait." Noël rubbed his hands across his face and beard, perhaps wiping himself clean of this madness. "There is a logistical problem here that I feel is being overlooked."

Lada snorted. "Just one?"

"Why on earth would Harris read a communique from the likes of us?"

"He wouldn't," said Aubrion.

Spiegelman broke in. "But he would read a communique from Winston Churchill."

The Gastromancer

As Noël and Tarcovich busied themselves with a batch of *Faux Soir* proofs, Aubrion invited Spiegelman on a walk through northern Enghien to look for an open pub. Though Aubrion hadn't said anything of the kind, Spiegelman suspected he felt guilty for cutting him out of the *Faux Soir* endeavor. His invitation was an attempt at an apology—though rather lopsided, perhaps, like a crooked painting.

"I'll buy you a drink," said Aubrion, holding open the door for Spiegelman. "The beer around here is mostly water, and the water tastes like beer—"

"I don't care much for alcohol, if I'm honest." Spiegelman shoved his cold hands into his coat pockets, wishing desperately for a pair of gloves.

"Well, that explains a great deal. A religious concern?"

"A not-looking-like-a-fool concern."

Aubrion threw his head back and laughed, with careless abandon. "Everyone looks like a fool, David. Some of us have simply learned not to care about it. Coffee?"

"Gladly. Thank you, Aubrion—that is, Marc."

"Think nothing of it."

The two hurried down the street, walking quickly to warm up. It was a brittle afternoon, with a crisp snap to the air. Not many people were out, mostly women with small children. The labor camps had taken most of the men, and the nighttime raids had scraped the rest of them off the streets. Aubrion and Spiegelman crossed a street to avoid a pile of rubble. The Nazi boot had trodden softly on Enghien compared to London or Warsaw. Spiegelman had visited both cities on assignments with Wolff. When he was walking through Poland, he knew to expect the potholes that the tanks had ripped into the streets, or the wounded homes, the wreckage, the refugees. But Enghien was different. Spiegelman had never grown accustomed to finding a shattered window in a perfect wooden building, or a rusty ball of cloth on a street corner.

"Nearly there," said Aubrion.

This was an odd thing for Spiegelman, this small friendship with Marc Aubrion. It seemed fragile: trapped inside the cocoon of something greater. Spiegelman felt eminently conscious of his body and speech: if he moved the wrong way, if his finger twitched or his voice cracked or he laughed a second too long, this delicate thing might break in his hands.

"Are you from Enghien originally?" asked Spiegelman, for wasn't that the sort of thing one asked a friend?

"We should turn here." Aubrion pointed down a tree-lined street. Though many of the trees had withered away to skeletons, a few clung stubbornly to their red and gold. "There's a good coffeehouse a block away."

"I didn't know there were any good coffeehouses left."

"Well, the war has diluted the definition of 'good.' Now it's nearly as watered-down as the beer. But the coffee is cheap, and the barman has no love for the Germans.

"No, I'm not from Enghien originally. From Brussels, land of sodium carbonate. Did you know that? Sodium carbonate was invented—invented? Is that the right word for it? I don't know. In any case, it was *happened upon* in Brussels."

"I can't say I knew that," said Spiegelman. "Did you like living in Brussels?"

"Possibly."

"Possibly?"

"I don't know."

"Whether you liked it?"

"The war has made me nostalgic for many things I did not like at the time."

"Such as?"

"Farfalle."

"The pasta?" Spiegelman laughed.

"I never thought of farfalle a day in my life before the Germans, and now I can't be rid of it. What an astounding creation it is! Henry Ford could not have designed a superior vehicle for pesto. Ravioli is clumsy, penne is impolite, tagliatelle is inconvenient, tortellini is too ambitious—but farfalle, blessed farfalle, the quiet casualty of this horrid war. Turn left."

"What?"

"*Left.*"

The coffeehouse was a slight building tucked onto a street corner. Aubrion led Spiegelman inside and ordered for them. As Spiegelman sat, he was accosted by a sudden inspiration.

"Is there any paper around?" Spiegelman asked Aubrion as he placed their coffees on a table.

"For what?"

"For writing. I have an idea for the—you know." Spiegelman mouthed *Churchill.*

"Oh. Oh, Christ. Do you have a pen?"

"I always have a pen. I simply need paper."

"A napkin?" Aubrion offered.

Spiegelman took it and began to write:

MY DEAR COMMANDER HARRIS,

For a long time I have watched with admiration your efforts to defend and conquer in the name of Great Britain and for the relief of suffering across our sacred lands. I believe I have made clear my profound gratitude to you, Commander Harris, for your sacrifice and vigilance in the face of the constant death and splendid horrors of war.

Spiegelman showed the napkin to Aubrion. "I have read some of his writing, particularly his letters, but perhaps not enough," said Spiegelman. The napkin was rough-hewn cloth, embroidered with the image of a teacup. The teacup now appeared to be leaking ink. "I'm just trying to gauge how far off the mark I am."

Aubrion squinted. "*Conquer* is wrong. The Nazis are conquerors, the Allies are saviors. That is the crux of Churchill's rhetoric. Try something alliterative."

"How about *defend and destroy*?" said Spiegelman.

"Perfect. I do like *splendid horrors*. It could bloody well be the name of his biography."

Spiegelman nodded. "I'll keep at it."

I trust then you will understand the nature of my communication with you to-day, Spiegelman wrote, *and that this communication is intended in the best of spirits, that you understand our aims are aligned, our goodwill paramount in these times of historic distress. Commander Harris, I have heard intelligence from our men in London, intelligence of a ghastly sort, that President Roosevelt, a fine man and a soldier of spirit and suffering by any estimation, means to conduct a campaign over the skies of Enghien on the eleventh of this month. This he intends to do without consulting either of us, and I have reason to believe that these things the intelligence-men say are in fact truthful, for they would not lie, and have not the opportunity for misdirection. Upon learning this news, I was anxious to express it to you, Commander Harris.*

Having exhausted his napkin's available real estate, Spiegelman stole another from an adjacent table. He reread what he'd written. To his gratification, Spiegelman felt his lips move with the cadence of Churchill's speech: the over-enunciation, the pauses, the audible punctuation. Churchill had a lisp, as a boy. His parents believed he'd never speak to their satisfaction. He'd labored over words, won them over. They became his fondest companions. Churchill wrote like a glutton, swallowing whole paragraphs where sentences could have sufficed, taking fistfuls of adjectives and packing them into fat phrases. Spiegelman, reading, ate them alive.

Churchill's script had proven difficult to copy. He did not write with the lofty curls and swoops of the nobility. "A lot of people don't know it," Aubrion told Spiegelman, "but Churchill was born a commoner." In his writing, he waffled visibly between pride in his station and shame at his origins. Churchill's handwriting looked, all at once, unpracticed and refined, artistic and rote. Each period skirted away from the end of its sentence, as though Churchill were leaving room for extra words to slip inside. His paragraphs tended to climb up toward the left side of the page, running from him as he wrote.

> *My second purpose in addressing you today,* Spiegelman con-tinued, *is to enjoin you not to act on this information. I must re-peat, Commander Harris, lest my intentions and the correct course of action to you remain unclear, that you must not act on this in-formation. We should allow President Roosevelt's men and the Americans to enjoy what promises to be a great and gallant victory above the cathedrals of Belgium. I believe this to be important for the war efforts, and for our continued relations with the Ameri-cans now and evermore.*
>
> *I must conclude this letter, Commander Harris, by affirming my gratitude for your works and my knowledge of the comfort your men provide the English people.*
> *WINSTON S. CHURCHILL*

"How is this?" asked Spiegelman.

Aubrion's cheeks flushed as he read. "This is splendid," he whispered.

"Is there anything I should add?" asked Spiegelman. "Any-thing I should take out? I was uncertain about the wording of that last paragraph."

"At the closing of the letter, when he concludes with his name—it should be entirely in capital letters. He always ends his correspondences that way." Aubrion failed to stifle a laugh. "Self-important bastard."

The Jester

When Spiegelman and Aubrion returned to the FI base, Spiegel-man greeted Noël by offering him four napkins. Quite alarmed, Noël brushed off his chest and shoulders.

"What is it?" said Noël. "Is something on me?"

"No, no, René, those are from Churchill," replied Aubrion. Noël recoiled. "Spiegelman, I did not take you for a fan of Churchill. How the devil did you get ahold of his napkins?"

"Oh," said Spiegelman, "I think you misunderstand. This was all I had for paper. We were at a coffeehouse, and I wanted to get started on the Bomber Harris project."

"You've started already?" Noël looked over the napkins, smiling a little. "'We should allow President Roosevelt's men and the Americans to enjoy what promises to be a great and gallant victory above the cathedrals of Belgium.'"

"God, it'll *infuriate* him," said Aubrion. "Have you seen photographs of this fellow? The man's like a walrus stuffed in a suit, the sort of man who becomes furious at things."

"I can confirm that," said Wellens. "In the four meetings I had with him when I was a businessman, I saw him blow his top during each and every one."

Spiegelman hardly heard the last of Wellens's sentence. He was fixated, instead, on how Wellens had referred to his career in the past tense. It was odd: though Spiegelman had long since traded his pragmatic loyalty to the Reich for his foolish loyalty to Aubrion, to the resistance and to *Faux Soir*, this was the first time he truly acknowledged that his career, too, was over. Gone was the literary ventriloquist who'd pledged his services to Nazi Germany. David Spiegelman would be a footnote in this war, if he was anything at all. He thought he should feel something at this realization, but he did not. If Spiegelman peered inside himself long enough, he might find, in the dredges of his heart, something akin to relief—but that was all. In salvation, there was no triumph: only exhaustion.

Tarcovich came downstairs, pausing when she reached the bottom step. "Spiegelman?" she said, with a curious squint. "Why do those napkins have Churchill's handwriting on them?"

He and Aubrion quickly explained. When they were done,

Tarcovich held up a hand. "I have a question. Are we trying to cause a tiny little air raid, or the Third Great War?"

"I'm afraid we're not close enough to causing either." Aubrion put down the napkins. "This is brilliant work, but it is not enough to make a seasoned commander bomb a country."

"We need a feud," said Tarcovich.

"What's that?" inquired Aubrion.

"A feud could be dangerous"—this from Martin Victor, who was sitting backward in a chair, shivering as though he had the flu.

Tarcovich shrugged. "If danger will keep *Le Soir* off the streets—"

"But danger might keep *everyone* off the streets."

"A feud between whom?" said Aubrion.

"Churchill and Roosevelt." Spiegelman got up so quickly he became light-headed. He wrote BOMBER HARRIS on a chalkboard. The handwriting was half Winston Churchill's and half his own. "Look here. Churchill is pressuring Bomber Harris not to strafe Belgium." Spiegelman wrote CHURCHILL to the left of HARRIS, drawing an arrow between them. "Roosevelt is going on about what an enormous victory this is going to be for the Americans. Is that not his word of choice? 'Enormous?' Everything is enormous in this war."

"*That* is not true," Tarcovich said with a smile.

Aubrion snorted.

"And so Harris is caught in the middle." On the blackboard, ROOSEVELT took up residence to the right of CHURCHILL. Spiegelman drew an arrow connecting ROOSEVELT to HARRIS. "He feels pressure from both sides."

"A feud between Churchill and Roosevelt?" said Victor. "I do not see it."

Spiegelman said, "That is because there is no feud between Churchill and Roosevelt—but Harris *manufactures* one in his head."

"We manufacture one in his head," marveled Aubrion.

"It is *that* feud that is dangerous." Spiegelman gestured with the chalk for emphasis. "And it is *that* feud that causes Harris to bomb Belgium."

"Monsieur Spiegelman," said Noël, whose eyes had not left the board, "our resources are at your disposal." The director glanced around the room. "By the way, where is Gamin?"

"Still out gathering bomb-making supplies," said Aubrion.

Noël looked up, as if he could see the paling sky through the ceiling. "The patrols..."

"Don't start in earnest for another hour," said Aubrion. "He will be fine, I'm sure."

"Monsieur Noël?" An aide had come down the stairs, a younger woman they'd hired last month. She had a timid, forgettable face. "A visitor is here for Madame Tarcovich. She knew the password."

"How did she know the password?" said Victor. "That is top secret information."

"Who is it?" asked Lada.

"She says her name is Grandjean, madame, and that it's urgent. Something to do with 'your girls,' she said. If you would like, I can take a note—"

Tarcovich ran past the aide, up the stairs, and into the evening-clad streets.

5 DAYS TO PRINT
NIGHTFALL

The Pyromaniac

WHEN THE SKY purpled and the sun went down, I left the blue-doored building. About a hundred paces from the construction site, I became aware of an odd sound: a high bleat that reminded me of the sheep my uncle kept before the Nazis came. I shook my head, wondering if it was my imagination. But the sound persisted, growing louder as I drew nearer.

The workers had left for the day, so the construction site lay in eerie solitude. It had stopped raining, stopped snowing. The night dried its eyes on the stars. Every so often, the wind picked up in just the right way and whistled through a metal pipe, tunelessly, the way Aubrion did, the way my father used to do, Beethoven fluttering like a newlywed's heart as my mother and I gasped with laughter. I darted under a wooden beam, searching for Nicolas and Leon.

To my left, I heard something *snap*, and the bleating started up again. I lit one of my matches. And there, crouched in the dark, was Nicolas, holding up his hand against the light. He cried out when he saw me, scurrying back into the shadows.

"Nicolas," I hissed. "What is the matter with you?"

"Leave me be. I done nothing, nothing."

"Nicolas, it's me."

"Leave me *be*."

"Did you get the charcoal?" I crept near him, trying to move slowly so I would not scare him. But he kept retreating into the dark, beyond the reaches of my match's light. "Where's Leon?"

I stepped on something. I remember thinking that I should not look down, that I should leave whatever it was to lie there untouched. But, fighting to keep the match still, I looked down to see what I'd stepped on. Beneath the thin sole of my boot were the remains of Leon's hat, crusted in red and brown.

I'd never held such a fine cap. An animal piece of me wanted to brush off the blood and muck and try it on. Indeed, my hands went to my head as though they'd conspired against my dignity— but then I saw Nicolas's eyes in the dark, and I flung the cap away. My duty here was clear: I was to calm him, assure him. I was a man of the FI; Nicolas was my wounded soldier. And though he was not quite my friend, familiarity and time had given us a closeness that I did not share with many others. I did not want him to hurt. I tried to fashion my words into sentences, reaching for bits of René Noël, fragments of Martin Victor. "Please," I whispered. "Please, please, please, please—" I am not certain what I was pleading for, but Nicolas seemed to understand, for he did not inch away from me. Moving slowly, the way I used to move around wounded animals on my uncle's farm, I crouched near him.

Nicolas's eyes swiveled in his head, their whites enormous. "I'm so sorry, Gamin, I—"

I searched the ground by Nicolas's shivering body. "Do you have the charcoal?" Completing the mission: this was the first order of business for a soldier of the FI. We had manuals on this topic; I'd never read them, but I'd seen them.

Nicolas was rocking back and forth. "I couldn't go back for him."

"Do the Nazis have him?"

He looked past me, into the ruined body of the construction site.

"Nicolas," I said, "this is important. If the Nazis have him, they can get him to talk."

The boy licked his lips, opening and closing his hands as if trying to hold on to his words. After a minute or two, Nicolas made this revelation: "I don't think he's alive any longer."

I grabbed him, his arm a frigid pole in my hand, and hauled him to his feet. "Come now. We're going."

"*No*, leave me *be*—"

"We're going, Nicolas."

"Where?"

"Someplace safe."

He said he did not believe me and, in all honesty, I did not believe me, either. I hauled him and our bag of supplies across the construction site, carrying him over planks and beams and discarded, broken tools. We slid down a muddy hill, at which point Nicolas decided he was capable of walking on his own, and trailed behind me, wiping his nose on his sleeve. Twice, I questioned him about what went on back there. Nicolas never answered me, not really. I think I remember hearing him murmur something about "those big men," but that could be the editorializing of time.

I felt that he must hate me. Didn't all soldiers hate their commanders, though? I thought Aubrion had told me as much. After some time, I tried to apologize to Nicolas; for what, I do not know. But then I realized that I was doing all the talking, so I stopped. And so we passed the hours of our journey back to downtown Enghien.

About a kilometer from the construction site, two roads crossed suddenly and continued into town. I shushed Nicolas and he stopped sniffling. We were passing into territory rigorously guarded by the Germans. Every time we stopped to catch our breath, I could hear the whispers of their boots, or catch the smell of their cigarette smoke on the wind. By the grace of God, I recalled the location of the blue-doored building. Nicolas and I sheltered here, in this room, that night.

By the wavering light of a cracked lantern, Nicolas paced the photographer's ruins, making restless footprints on the faces. I used a stick to draw shapes on the floor. I tried on narratives and excuses like used clothing, reminding myself that Leon was an orphan, that he fell in the name of duty, that this war probably would have taken him even if I *hadn't* come along with my mission, that he would have suffered more if he'd stayed alive. But I could not keep it up for long. While Nicolas napped, I shed tears for Leon, for the boy with the fine cap. I wept because he was my soldier and he died, because I felt relieved that it was Leon and not Aubrion or Tarcovich or anyone else, because I felt guilty. I wept for the pleasure of weeping.

When Nicolas stirred, I pulled myself together and handed him a book of matches. "The mission isn't over just because it hurts," I told him. "We have a job to do."

The Smuggler

Andree was looking away when Lada found her: standing by the door to the FI base, a trickle of snowflakes going into hiding among her curls. Her silhouette was achingly familiar against the dim. The stars were few; Lada didn't know the mechanics of it, but something about the lights from the howitzers and fighter planes blotted them out. Victor had told her about it in tedious detail. The stars could not outshine the deep, unsettling glow of battle. War had taken everything but the snow.

Though she could not see Andree's face, Lada could not rid herself of the feeling that she had, in that instant, lost her, too, that Andree had looked off into the world and would never look at back at her again. Lada Tarcovich reached out and touched Andree's wrist, lightly enough to be mistaken for a breeze. Andree turned, her eyes grieving.

"Lada..." the judge said. She managed, somehow, to enunciate the ellipsis. "The book you put on my shelf. You wrote the password in it."

"What were you doing going through my books?"

"What were *you* doing leaving passwords about?"

"I always write in my books."

Grandjean smiled. "As do I."

"I have a copy of *The Hobbit*. You can hardly read it for all the writing."

"It is the same for me and Tolstoy."

Lada nodded, though she was desperate to know what game this was. "Andree, you did not come to the FI base to talk about Tolstoy. What is this business about my girls?"

"They were caught, somewhere out in the country. Two of them." Grandjean sounded as though she was talking in her sleep. "With falsified documents."

"Caught by whom?"—but it was a ridiculous question, Lada knew.

"A German patrol."

"Christ."

"What were they *doing* out there?"

"Trying to see their parents. Their mother has taken ill." Lada turned, her fists connecting with a wall. She heard the hollow tremble of plywood but felt nothing. "Fucking Christ. What am I to do?"

"It was in my district."

Lada turned, waiting for Andree to clarify. But the judge would say no more.

"What do you mean?" asked Tarcovich.

"The arrest, Lada. It happened in my district."

Grandjean was telling her something important, Lada knew, for Lada could see her lips moving, and she wanted to kiss them, because that would be easier than understanding their movements and sounds. The sharp little fragments of whatever Grandjean was saying—they kept falling through Lada's hands, cutting her palms.

"That means," Tarcovich realized, "they will be tried at your court."

"Yes." The word barely escaped Andree Grandjean's lips.

"But this is wonderful news." Lada seized Andree's shoulders. "They are as good as freed, aren't they? When is their trial? I'll wait at the courthouse to bring them home."

"Lada, I can't let them free."

Lada let go of Andree. "Why? You are their judge, aren't you?"

"If I let them go, the Germans will know something is amiss."

"But you've let dozens of political prisoners—"

"I never let them go free." Andree's eyes were as wide as the earth. "I had them transferred to different courts, in different districts, so I would not have to be the one who sent them to the noose. But they all hanged anyway."

The snow and the look in Andree's eyes had turned Lada's blood to ice. "Andree—"

"Lada, *think*. If I let them go free, the Gestapo will have me investigated, possibly arrested. Another judge tried that last month in Antwerp. They sent him to Fort Breendonk."

"So let them go, and then join me underground."

Andree's eyes returned to the stars. She would not speak for ages. In that time, Lada began, quietly, to weep. It was a wretched thing, what Lada said to this woman she loved: if Andree joined her underground, she would share Lada's fate. As Lada cried, Andree said: "I can get them a lesser sentence—"

"A *lesser* sentence." Tarcovich laughed without smiling. "Tell me, Andree. What do you consider a lesser sentence?"

"Perhaps two years—"

"Two years? Two *hours* is time enough for a girl to be raped and beaten in prison."

"Lada, those girls—those young women—they have to…"

"You're sentencing them to prison, and you do not even know their names?"

"I hear many cases, sometimes five or six a day. *Many* of them are prostitutes." Andree shook her head, a twitchy, unfamiliar motion. Her curls were wild and rebellious in the snow. "Do you understand what you are asking of me? If I let them go free, I sentence *myself* to die. Is that what you want? Are their lives worth more than mine?"

"*Is* your life worth more than theirs?" said Tarcovich.

"I didn't say that."

"You didn't have to. Andree…" Tarcovich held out her hands: praying, begging. "My God, my God, how did this happen?" She did not know what *this* was, and yet *this* felt like everything. Lada loved her, this impossible woman who drew sharp lines around everything, who spoke of her duties and morals as though they were all so clear. But Lada could not understand the choice Andree was making right now, the choices they were making together. When people wrote about the war, they painted it in black and white; it was something Tarcovich and Aubrion discussed often. But the colors ran together every day, and each one was harder to see than the last.

Grandjean was looking away again. "If I save these girls and fall to a German bullet, then what good am I to the resistance?"

"The *resistance*. Listen to yourself. If you don't know their names, then what good are you to the resistance?"

Tarcovich laughed, a wretched laugh. It was funny; it was absurd; this woman who spoke so loftily of her ideals meant to resist the Germans on *their* terms, not her own. She may as well have put on a *zwanze* performance with Marc Aubrion, for all the good it would do. And this was the thing that divided them, this is what tore them asunder—one of Aubrion's favorite phrases, borrowed from many an unwilling church sermon— Grandjean refused to leave the Nazis' world behind to make her own. Her story and *their* story were still intertwined. Tarcovich saw it now, clearer and more persistent than the remaining stars.

"I can't," said Lada. "I won't do this."

"You won't do what?" said Grandjean, but she knew. She held out her hands, silently pleading with Lada to stay.

"Their names are Lotte and Clara." Lada turned her back on Andree. "And mine was Lada Tarcovich."

The Gastromancer

With Noël's permission, Spiegelman had excavated notes and letters, communiques and telegrams, speeches and photographs of the most delicate sort, all from the FI's archives, and all from Franklin Roosevelt. And now, after hours of research, Roosevelt was everywhere. He lounged across the typewriters, quoting Dante here, Cicero there, but remaining, at all times, impeccably amicable: his sentences brief, easy to grasp. Roosevelt sat in the chair closest to Spiegelman, and the chair farthest away; his handwriting was nearly impossible to read, but one got the sense that, whatever it said, it was as winning and charming as anything.

Aubrion walked in, stepping on a letter young Roosevelt wrote to his mother. He stooped to pick it up. "'Dear Mommers and Poppers'?"

"Mommerr and Popperr," Spiegelman corrected him without looking up from his work. "With two *R*s."

Aubrion held the note between his thumb and forefinger. "A bit disturbing, isn't it?"

"Hmm."

"I'm surprised his parents are still alive."

"Look at the year, Marc."

"Oh." Aubrion tossed it away. The note fluttered to the floor like an affable bird. "Are you almost done?"

"I believe so." Spiegelman sat back to look over his labors. He'd never before worked with so many materials. It was no secret that the Reich had impressive archives. But even their records shriveled in comparison to the offerings of the *Front de l'Indépendance*. In a way, Spiegelman found the information overwhelming. His job was usually to reconstruct a voice from a whisper; now, he felt as though he was reconstructing shouts from an echo.

"But are you sure," Aubrion said, sitting in a pile of Roosevelt's pedestrian adjectives, "you really *know* the man?"

Spiegelman sat back with a tight-lipped smile. "I must thank Monsieur Noël for allowing me access to all this."

"You should thank Monsieur Mullier for gathering most of it." Aubrion seemed to tremble, just for a moment. "How are you holding up?"

"I am fine. And you?"

"Never better," Aubrion said, viciously.

Spiegelman passed Aubrion his latest work. "Shall we look it over? I think it would be best to get the first set of letters out tonight."

"You read it aloud." Aubrion handed it back to Spiegelman. "I am going to close my eyes for a bit."

"You're sure you are all right? We could review this later, if you—"

"Shut up. I'm listening to Roosevelt."

"'My dear Mr. Prime Minister,'" Spiegelman read. "'Regarding the Belgian campaign: on behalf of all Americans, I must express my appreciation for your willingness to stand aside. All intelligence suggests it will be a victory for the ages, and I am certain it will make abundantly clear to the world that all of our intentions are deliberate and correct.'"

As he read, Spiegelman adopted a slight American accent, falling into the radio announcer's cadence of Roosevelt's speech. It was sufficiently odd that Aubrion had to open his eyes to make sure this was still, in fact, David Spiegelman who was reading. The voice did not suit him. Spiegelman had a high, uncertain manner of speaking, declarations that belonged in parentheses. He began his sentences as though he were surprised at having thought of them; he ended his sentences as though he'd never intended to speak in the first place. It was singular. Aubrion could not help but wonder, as Spiegelman continued, what this man's life would have been if he'd been born with the voice of Franklin Roosevelt. Perhaps he would not have been able to inhabit so many others.

Spiegelman continued: "'I am told you have already communicated this state of affairs to Commander Harris. I know he understands the necessity of an American triumph in Europe. It is important, in the days to come, to keep our good men close. Commander Harris is among the best.'" David Spiegelman permitted himself a smile. Nothing would infuriate Harris more, he knew, than the idea of Franklin Roosevelt paying him a compliment. Harris would interpret his compliment as pity, and his fist would curl more tightly around the joystick of his bomber.

"'Europe is bleak, Mr. Churchill. The dark quiet of our final days might be upon us, if we do not act. We must be swift. We must be, when the situation calls for it, merciless, for only in our mercilessness will we achieve mercy.'" While mostly plainspoken, Roosevelt sometimes opted for the dramatic. Spiegelman was not sure, though, whether it was *too* dramatic. The man was never quite poetic, after all. "'The Belgian campaign might be the final chapter of our old tale, or it might be the first chapter of our new one. It falls on our individual efforts and our collective efforts and our local efforts and our international efforts.

Let us give thanks for good men, Mr. Churchill. We will need them in the days to come.

"'Very sincerely yours, Franklin D. Roosevelt.'" Spiegelman set the paper aside, raising his arms over his head in a stretch. "Does it need anything?" he asked Aubrion.

"To be on Bomber Harris's desk." Aubrion kissed his thumb and forefinger like a food critic after a grand meal. "That last bit—*that* is the part that's going to buy us an air raid."

Aubrion gestured for Spiegelman to follow him upstairs to the telex, where they sent Spiegelman's documents with a message: *Dear Commander Harris: Please find below two letters that I trust will be of interest to your office. I hope you will not hesitate, now or at any moment to come, to communicate your thoughts and considerations with me and those close to me. Yours most sincerely, Winston S. Churchill.*

When that was done, Aubrion found a bottle somewhere and poured two glasses. Though he did not drink, Spiegelman accepted his without comment.

"A toast," declared Aubrion.

Spiegelman snorted. "To what?"

As though it were obvious, Aubrion waved his glass at the contents of the basement. Spiegelman breathed it in: the letters, the posters, the notebooks, the pamphlets, the chalkboard drawings. This was a war room, he realized. This was a place of death and new beginnings. It was no wonder Wolff referred to *La Libre Belgique* as a propaganda bomb. David Spiegelman was an arms dealer, the only arms dealer in Europe who couldn't load a gun.

"To this," said Aubrion, "the Third Great War."

"No." Spiegelman lifted his glass. "To the First Small War, fought by great men."

The Dybbuk

Wolff laid each page to rest near its fellows, a parade of lies and misdirections. In all, Aubrion had given him five pages of material for *La Libre Belgique*. That was more than he'd expected, enough to build a propaganda bomb for the ages. Wolff arranged the material on his desk. *La Libre Belgique d'August Wolff* would go to Himmler and Goebbels in two days. If all went well, it would go to a print factory in three.

The *Gruppenführer* reviewed what he had. Now that these words were in his possession, his vision for the paper was clear. First, he'd have a title page, with the date and the editors and all the rest, the name of the paper printed in crooked, plaque-colored letters. Below the title would sit the first article: *Vos heures sont comptées*... Wolff thought it a tad dramatic, but Aubrion had insisted the Belgians were fond of such theatrics. *Your days are numbered*... A citizen would see that, would see the drawing of a skull in a Nazi helmet half-sunken into the earth—and the citizen would prepare himself for a column thrashing the Germans, counting the steps to their defeat. Not so. The column—a collaboration with Spiegelman—detailed the moral transgressions Allied soldiers had committed on their march through Europe.

"We have it all," Aubrion had explained to the *Gruppenführer*. "Beatings, rapes...just enough to be believable. By its end, you will be convinced your days *are* numbered, if you happen to associate with the morally bankrupt—the Allies, that is."

On the second page, after the citizen's appetite for Allied depravity had been suitably whetted: three articles from the war's victims. Spiegelman had written these. A homeless mother of four, an old man and a young girl who lost her innocence to the Allies—their voices harmonized in a triptych of articles. The layout of this section was of particular importance. Aubrion believed, and Wolff agreed, that the articles should be arranged in three columns, with the mother's on the left, the old man's on the right, and the girl's in the middle. No one could read all three at the same time, obviously, but—and here was Aubrion's genius—as the happy citizen read either the mother's column or the old man's, they would catch glimpses of the sweet girl's story out of the corner of their eye. Bits of phrasing, snatches of language would assail them as they read, coloring their experience of the other two stories. Wolff reread the three articles. The keenness of the voices always impressed him. If he had not known Spiegelman, the *Gruppenführer* would've believed he had interviewed these people.

The thought of Spiegelman drew August Wolff away from his desk to the hallway. He stopped a passing clerk.

"Send for David Spiegelman as soon as possible," said Wolff.

"He left this morning, *Gruppenführer.*"

"Left?" Wolff tried to quash his alarm. "Did he say where he was going?"

"For a walk, *Gruppenführer.*"

The clerk could not comment further. Wolff did not know exactly what he feared—that Spiegelman had put a pistol to his head? That he had thrown in his lot with the FI? The *Gruppenführer* shook himself, for a German commander did not worry over his men this way; it was improper. He returned to his work.

On the page opposing the victims' columns, the *Gruppenführer* envisioned a sprawling display: a full-page article, written by an American turncoat, on why he threw down his arms. The loyalty of the Americans was said to be almost disgusting, so this would come as a shock to many. Professor Victor, who'd studied the psychology and sociology of the Americans, collaborated with Aubrion and Spiegelman on that one. It contained a number of phrases of which Wolff was especially fond, including "the illness of the many-faced Allied beast" and (Aubrion's favorite) "whoring for the illusion of liberty."

The two remaining pages were devoted to miscellany. Aubrion had written a couple of advertisements, a column on patriotism, a communique from the Eastern front, an opinion piece on the political upheaval that might result from an Allied win. Spiegelman's contributions were similar, as were Victor's. Tarcovich had overseen a piece on women who'd turned to prostitution during the war. It was all fine work: convincing and true, in the way of tall tales.

And yet the *Gruppenführer* was not content. He knew, of course, that most everyone involved in the project would die upon its completion. Despite what he'd suggested to Spiegelman, that he might commission Aubrion to work alongside his staff, Wolff knew that would not be so. Aubrion would die with the others. That was the plan. In some ways, that was the *strength* of the plan. But as Wolff's breath stirred the pages of Aubrion's art, he did not feel strong—he felt impossibly weak. Although Wolff often referred to Aubrion as a fool, he knew—in a part of him that he kept boarded-up—that Aubrion was no fool. Indeed, to call Marc Aubrion a *genius* would have been to reveal the limitations of the word. Aubrion was not a fool, and he would not die quietly. Wolff could no longer pretend that the mad, brilliant little creature was not up to something.

A stack of arrest warrants lay under the *Gruppenführer*'s right arm. A pen sat nearby. He did not reach for either. Instead, August Wolff sat back to reread Aubrion's work, folding the pages like a friendly old paperback.

4 DAYS TO PRINT
EARLY MORNING

The Jester

AUBRION WAS GREETED, at the first sliver of morning, by the irate squawking of the telex on the floor above. He yelped, got up, nearly tripped over the notebook he'd been using as a pillow, and roused Spiegelman, disturbing the Roosevelt materials under the fellow's head.

"What is it?" said Spiegelman. "Is it from Harris?"

"Who else but an angry Harris would be contacting us at this hour?"

They ran upstairs, and Aubrion ripped the tape from the mouth of the telex. His shoulders slumped as he read.

"Is he not angry enough?" asked Spiegelman.

"It's from one of our suppliers. A shipment of flour is in. We don't even *use* flour." Aubrion tossed the tape aside, disgusted with the entire institution of flour.

Spiegelman rubbed at his face and eyes. He looked—as Aubrion imagined they both did—like he needed another twelve hours of sleep. "Did Gamin return last night?" he asked.

"Not yet. But I have faith in him. If he has not returned by noon, I'll go look for him."

"I should get back to the base before I'm missed. Wolff will have a fit."

As Spiegelman gathered his things to take his leave of the place, Aubrion put a hand on his arm. "If you go back there, it will be one of the dumbest things you've ever done."

René Noël, who managed never to look bleary-eyed even at that hour, entered and smiled a greeting at the two. "Good morning, Marc. You're starting your charm early today, I see. What Monsieur Aubrion means to say, Spiegelman, is that Wolff is no idiot. He has almost certainly caught on to what you're doing."

"Has he?" Spiegelman's lips twisted. "I do not even know what I'm doing, so if *he* knows, I do wish he'd tell me."

"He knows your allegiance, is what I'm saying. You could very well find a warrant waiting for you upon your return."

"I understand, Noël."

"And yet?"

"And yet he's going to go back anyway," said Aubrion, his irritation tinged with admiration. Most men did not have time for those who did stupid things; Aubrion did not have time for those who *didn't*. "Look at him. He has the face of a fellow who has already made so many poor decisions."

"You, Marc Aubrion, are uniquely qualified to recognize such a face," Spiegelman retorted.

Aubrion tilted his head, glanced at Noël, returned his gaze to Spiegelman. "Was that a joke? Did David Spiegelman make a joke?"

Noël threw his head back and laughed, harder than he had in ages.

"I do not think Wolff will arrest me," said Spiegelman, blushing to his collar. "Eventually—but he needs me, for now. And besides, if I do not go back, he will know for certain that I've joined up with you lot, and that something is amiss. If I return to him, I will buy you some time, as it were."

"You are right, of course," said Noël, his head bowed.

"It's still a stupid decision." Aubrion's goading was simply reflexive, and Spiegelman knew it. Aubrion touched Spiegelman's arm as though ensuring that he was still there, that he had not yet left them. "What does Wolff need you for?" he said quietly. He could not keep Spiegelman from leaving, nor would he try— not really. But he had to keep up appearances.

"He has his—what the devil does he call it?—his propaganda bomb." Aubrion made a face. "*La Libre Belgique* is finished, as far as Wolff is concerned. It's due to print in two days."

"No, no," said Spiegelman. "That was not what I meant. Wolff needs me in another way. I believe he's come to rely on me, in certain respects."

Noël started tying on his apron, filthy from yesterday's work. "I don't understand."

"I pity him, you know." Spiegelman shook his head. "I think the poor bastard's lonely."

The Pyromaniac

We labored over our matches and pipes in the blue-doored building. The sun assisted us through the boarded-up walls. After much effort, we had assembled a small arsenal: twelve pipe bombs between the two of us. After a time, Nicolas fell asleep, and I sat listening to him dream. As a child, I dreamed avidly, carrying out grand adventures before daybreak. But Nicolas did not sound as though sleep had taken him to enchanted forests or faraway lands, but rather back to the construction site, to Leon and those men. He whimpered and twitched for most of the night. I longed for a blanket or coat to cover him, but we had nothing.

I inspected the pipe bombs as Nicolas slept. The handiwork was sound, for the most part. One of the FI's best soldiers, a young woman whose name is now gone, had taught me how to make bombs, and I taught Nicolas. A couple of the ones Nicolas had put together—the first two he'd made—needed a bit of tweaking. I popped open the tops, adjusted a wire, refilled the charcoal. It was quick work. Soon, I'd examined all the bombs for imperfections. While the work wasn't perfect, it was better than what many Allied soldiers could have produced. I placed the bombs in a dry sack for safekeeping. When I realized I would not be sleeping that night, I made it my goal to construct three more bombs. Working quickly, I put together four more of the things before the sun rose.

Nicolas awoke to find me with a knife in my fist. I'd discovered a shard of glass somewhere among the photographer's supplies. Doing my best to stay quiet, I'd sharpened it to a point and wrapped a cord of leather around the duller half. If the Germans did discover us, I would not give myself up without spilling blood. Nicolas's eyes fell on the knife, and he paled.

"It's all right, it's all right," I said. "I'm standing guard, is all."

Nicolas leapt up. "Christ, Gamin, I've got to get back to the workhouse before—"

"You aren't going anywhere," I said, lifting the sack. "Think we made these for our health, do you? We have to actually *put* them someplace now."

"Gamin, I can't. I'm glad to have done something for Marc Aubrion and all, but there'll be a lashing for me if I don't get back."

"There'll be a lashing for everyone if we don't do our jobs." But his face told a story that Nicolas could not: the lad had done all he could, had paid for it with the blood of a friend. If I pushed him any further, he would fall, and I would fall with him. "All right, go on with you." He thanked me and followed me out of the blue-doored building.

4 DAYS TO PRINT
EARLY AFTERNOON

The Dybbuk

WOLFF HAD NOT read this way since boyhood. He read for hours. He read like idle summers with Dumas; he read for the pleasure of adverbs, his eyes skipping through dashes and semicolons, falling into grassy comma fields. He read *La Libre Belgique d'August Wolff* until he'd committed it to memory, then sat in mourning. The paper would never be new to him again. Wolff might laugh at it—he might admire it—but the melody was no longer mysterious. The ink of Aubrion's prose bled onto his skin.

Ashamed at himself, Wolff pushed aside *La Libre Belgique*. This was madness. His loyalties did not lie with these little men and their newspaper. For all their pretenses, Aubrion and Spiegelman were confined to the realm of small ideas. They did not grasp the completeness of the Nazi cause. Aubrion and Spiegelman did not aspire to perfection, as Wolff did.

But the Nazis would never produce something as perfect as *La Libre Belgique*. Wolff knew this to be true, as clearly as he knew his own name. They were missing *something*. Aubrion had it in his pockets, and he'd take it with him to the next world.

Wolff rubbed his forehead, trying to ease his headache. He was exhausted. That was all. This was foolishness, and he was exhausted, and there was nothing more to it than that. The *Gruppenführer* turned to examine his arrest warrants. Naturally, the Germans did not *need* warrants to do as they wanted; the warrants were meant to confer legitimacy, to show that they were not barbarians, but civilized organizers who got things done and left a paper trail while doing it.

He filled out the warrant without reading it. Arrest warrants were simple; they had to be, since the Germans issued so many of them. On a line separating two chunks of text—*Haftbefehl* to the left of the line and *de Kommandatur 2477, Enghien* to the right—the *Gruppenführer* wrote *David Spiegelman*. Then he lifted his pen, his cheeks flushing at his childish letters. On the line below the first, he wrote the date, gripping the pen tightly— *November 6*, he wrote—and then a pause to breathe before the year, *1943*.

Exhaling, the *Gruppenführer* dropped his pen. Droplets of ink kissed the page. Before he could think about it any further, Wolff snatched up his pen to sign on the bottommost line, forming the letters of his name in one jerky, suicidal motion. Then it was done, all of it, save the stamp. No document could be processed unless it bore the eagle-and-swastika seal of the Reich. Wolff took the stamp from his desk drawer.

He hovered over the paper, stamp in hand. Wolff did not have any reason to believe Spiegelman was a traitor—but he had no reason to believe he was *not*. After all, he'd offered to help save Theo Mullier from Fort Breendonk; Martin Victor had said as much. Of course, Spiegelman might try to claim that Wolff had no evidence, only suspicion. But that was enough; the suspicion was enough.

Wolff was an honorable man, the sort of man who gave people chances. But Spiegelman was a Jew, a homosexual. He'd been corrupted long ago: his death was an inevitability that had nothing to do with August Wolff. And if Wolff stamped the warrant, Spiegelman *would* die. He would be arrested before the day's end, executed in a fortnight. The *Gruppenführer* could speed that process along, if he wanted, saving Spiegelman a night in Fort Breendonk. It would be mercy, really. August Wolff was a merciful man. He gave people chances, when he could. Wolff summoned David Spiegelman.

The stamp was still on Wolff's desk when Spiegelman came in, but the warrant was not. Wolff had placed it in his top drawer, easily accessible if he needed it, yet out of Spiegelman's sight. The *Gruppenführer* kept his hands below the desk, like a gunslinger with a hidden pistol.

"I am told you left the base yesterday around seven in the morning." August Wolff checked his wristwatch. "Is that correct?"

Spiegelman took a seat without asking for permission. Wolff stiffened. Though Spiegelman was not a man of rank, and did not have to ask before sitting in Wolff's presence, he had always asked before. The space between them sparked with change.

"You seem to know where I am," said Spiegelman, "far better than I do."

"I asked you a question, Herr Spiegelman."

"Yes, I was out."

"I truly hope, for your sake, you are not taking cues from Marc Aubrion."

"Because he is disposable?" said Spiegelman.

"He is."

"And I am not?"

The *Gruppenführer* shook himself. This was not how he'd envisioned this conversation playing out. "As you know, Herr Spiegelman, I am not one to treat my colleagues like children. I never questioned you, never asked about your whereabouts.

You will agree that I have been reasonable. But in light of recent events, I feel I must ask you. Where have you been?"

The Gastromancer

"It is nothing as sinister as you hope, *Gruppenführer*," replied Spiegelman. "I have been with the FI. I know you took me off the project, but Aubrion requested that I look over some materials. I thought Aubrion might find it suspicious if I refused to comply."

Spiegelman was almost disconcerted at how easily the lie came to him. He put his hands on his thighs: an easy, open posture. Though he was warm, and his clothes felt too tight around his midsection, he was not sweating the way he usually did around Wolff. Perhaps he *was* taking a cue from Marc Aubrion, as the *Gruppenführer* had suggested—or perhaps the *dybbuk*'s spirit was bleeding from his hands, leaving behind the residue of his lies.

Wolff was nodding slowly. "But why did you remain overnight?"

"It was late. I was tired, and uninterested in getting shot."

"What did you work on, with Marc Aubrion?"

"The final draft of *La Libre Belgique*." Spiegelman prayed Wolff would not press him for details. He had not even glanced at the final draft of *La Libre Belgique*.

"I trust you know that I have ways of verifying your story."

"I am smart, for a Jew."

The *Gruppenführer* did not take the bait. "Herr Spiegelman, you are confined to the base for three days' time. That is today, tomorrow, and the day after. You may move about the base as you please, but if you step outside, even for an instant, I will issue a warrant for your arrest. Is that clear?"

Although he had expected this sentence, Spiegelman felt Wolff's words like a death blow. This was it, then. This was the end for him. *Faux Soir* would be released into the world, would have its moment onstage, and would pass—and Spiegelman would see none of it. In fewer than twenty-four hours, Aubrion and Tarcovich and the others would venture to Ferdinand Wellens's factory to oversee the printing of *Faux Soir*: fifty thousand copies of a newspaper that should not have existed. People would buy it, and they'd laugh, and Spiegelman would miss it all. And then Aubrion and the rest would be captured and killed. They'd be lined up in front of a wall to be shot, if they were lucky. Their story would be scattered across the world like ashes. But not David Spiegelman—David Spiegelman would live.

"And our agreement?" he ventured, even though he knew the answer. "Will you spare Marc Aubrion?"

"I will not," said the *Gruppenführer*, and the whole world and everyone in it went still.

Spiegelman lifted his eyes to Wolff's face. He was not an old man, the *Gruppenführer*, and yet his skin was lined and pocked, like a new road that had already seen too much use. "Why didn't you shoot me," Spiegelman asked, for if this was his end, he could ask what he pleased, "that day in my grandmother's house?"

Wolff sat back, his eyes wide. "I saved your life," he said, as though this was obvious.

"Is that what you believe?" said David Spiegelman. In the tales, the *dybbuk* never left a man's body until its task was done. But David's grandmother had never told him what happened if the *dybbuk* was slain, if it was even possible. Spiegelman got to his feet, so that Wolff had to look up to see his face. "Far be it from me to give you advice, *Gruppenführer*, but you should have saved your own."

The *Gruppenführer* started to reply, but he could not finish the task. Spiegelman drank greedily of Wolff's silence. When he'd had his fill, he turned his back on August Wolff.

The Professor

Martin Victor found a table at the back of the coffeehouse. He sat, waving over the lazy fellow behind the counter. The professor ordered a coffee, poured a dash of cheap gin into it. As his lips and hands began to tingle with the stuff, Victor took out a paper and pen.

My dear sir, he wrote, deliberately avoiding Wolff's name, *I am writing to you because I am embroiled in a conflict which I feel we must discuss. Please do me the honor of allowing me to make my case. I am, as I have repeated to you, a man of my word.*

Victor reread the sentence, taking a sip of coffee. He *was* a man of his word, and yet the phrase was so misused by other men that it sounded empty. The professor scratched it out. It was not like Martin Victor to start writing something without an objective in mind, and yet here he was, allowing his pen to take him where it willed.

"Damn," he said, for he'd managed to choose the only pen at the FI headquarters that was nearly out of ink. Victor shook the pen. A bit of ink dribbled onto the table. Cursing, Victor cleaned off the nib with his thumb. After several aborted attempts, he was writing again.

I must admit I have not been as forthright in our exchanges as I should have been. These are dishonorable times. We have both had experiences we would rather forget. As I learned in Auschwitz, the struggle to survive makes vultures of us all.

This, too, was true. Still, Victor thought, it seemed disingenuous to blame these times for what he'd become, for his inability to remain loyal to the FI or to Wolff or to himself. The war had not changed everyone; Marc Aubrion was the same bastard as he'd always been. If anything, he had flourished. The professor struck out the line about dishonorable times.

What matters most, I suppose, is that I resolve, here and now, to give you any and all information you might need to indict Marc Aubrion and his colleagues. If you cannot accept my apology, please accept my assistance. Victor nodded. It was brief, to the point. And if it could be phrased so succinctly, there must be some truth to it. This was the right path, *his* path—giving himself over to the Reich entirely. The Allies had done nothing to end the war, after all. It went on, and nothing changed: nothing, except men like him.

Let me begin with the most important information: things are not what they appear to be.

4 DAYS TO PRINT
EVENING

The Gastromancer

HE WAS CARRYING Churchill around in his head, and bless
the fellow, he was starting to get heavy. Replaying one of the
man's letters, David Spiegelman retreated into his office and
locked the door. He never did that, really: lock the door. It was
a meaningless gesture, like the time Spiegelman hung a pinup
poster above his dressing table. If the Germans wanted to get
in, they would get in, and a bit of metal would delay them only
an extra second. But Spiegelman needed an extra barrier between himself and the Germans, and people did foolish things
for all manner of reasons—so he bolted his door. In his head,
Churchill was still going on about the price of freedom. Spiegelman let him.

David Spiegelman sat on the floor and took stock of what he
had. He had the best telecommunications equipment in all of
Europe at his disposal, and yet communicating with Marc Aubrion or anyone associated with the FI was out of the question.
The German Command monitored all communications in and

out of the base. If Spiegelman tried to get a message to Aubrion via courier, telex, smuggler or carrier pigeon, he would be shot. In addition to communications equipment he couldn't use, Spiegelman was also blessed with archives he couldn't access. If he requested access to the Nazi Hall of Records to get more Roosevelt and Churchill material and continue the Bomber Harris caper, Wolff would know something was amiss. He also had the pocketwatch Aubrion gave him; though Aubrion himself might have devised some ingenious way to use the watch to communicate with Bomber Harris, Spiegelman was not so creative. Spiegelman glanced at his mattress, behind which he'd carved a hole in the wall to stash a pistol. He considered grabbing the pistol and stepping into the hallway, firing at everything that breathed until the inevitable returned him to his family. But Spiegelman knew himself. He'd probably shoot the ceiling, hyperventilate, faint, and then wake up at Fort Breendonk.

More out of habit than anything, Spiegelman dragged himself to his desk. It was mid-afternoon, and most were taking their lunch. Laughter and muted conversations floated past his door. He picked up a pen, a green Parker Duofold, the kind he'd favored as a boy. Without thinking, David Spiegelman began to write. *We live in a terrible epoch of the human story,* he wrote, Churchill wrote, *but we believe there is a broad and sure justice running through its theme.* Spiegelman studied the elegant lines, the gentle rounds of the letters. He felt his heart quicken. There was indeed, he realized, a way for him to shoot his way out of the Nazi headquarters without landing in Fort Breendonk.

Spiegelman would not even need a pistol.

The Jester

Aubrion had never done well with silence. Silence was a blank canvas his mind could paint with horrid things. It was also boring; after all, he had no one to irritate. He drew idly on a blackboard, stepping in Roosevelt and Churchill's documents. After Spiegelman left for the Nazi headquarters, Noël ran out to pick up the shipment of flour no one was going to use, Wellens went to prepare his factory for printing, Victor decided to brood elsewhere, and no one had seen Tarcovich in a while. Only Aubrion had nowhere to go. He considered running out to search for me, but he trusted me to complete the mission without him. So he languished, and in the silence, he began to feel Mullier's death. It sat on Aubrion's chest, weighing down his body.

The basement was quiet; no footsteps above. People were not coming in to make things anymore. The FI—*this* part of the FI, Aubrion's home—they created such wonders: the posters, the books, the leaflets. They spun art out of nothing. People who could have picked up guns instead picked up pens, and they drew pictures, and they wrote words. That was what had drawn Aubrion to the FI in the first place. The Allied cause was noble and good, of course, and the German cause was not, and that mattered, too, but, really—the FI made beautiful things. The Nazis did not.

Aubrion rested his back against the frostbitten brick with his eyes squeezed shut. It was there Lada Tarcovich found him.

"How long have you been down here?" she asked, but Aubrion rolled into a fetal position. Tarcovich knelt by him. "Marc? You can't stay down there forever."

"I can." His voice was muffled by his arm, which he'd thrown across his face halfway into Lada's sentence. "I am ignoring you."

"And how is that going?"

Aubrion tried to burrow into his own arm.

"Please get up," said Lada. "Here, I'll help you."

He felt Tarcovich put her arms around his waist. Aubrion let her help him sit up.

They did not look at each other for a while; they just left each other in peace. Tarcovich started crumpling up copies of Churchill's speeches and tossing them across the room. It was a careless act, something Lada never would have done before. But it would all burn soon anyway.

"Lada?" said Aubrion.

"Hmm?"

"Do you remember that play I wrote two years ago?"

"*Tried* to write. You've never finished a play, my dear."

"It was a one-act about how Hitler is secretly a woman who could never have children. There was a line about his 'barren breasts.'"

"Oh, Christ," said Tarcovich.

"You do know it, then."

"Unfortunately."

"I had quite a plan for it, you know. It was going to be a leaflet. We were going to drop it on the doorsteps of every house in Belgium."

"*We* were?"

"But René didn't share my vision. In the end, he never let it print."

"It occurs to me I've never told René how much he deserves a medal. Marc—"

"Don't say 'Marc' right now. 'Marc' always kills my plans."

"I know he does."

As they conversed, a radio crackled on a table. The radio was always on, listening for troop movements, for cities with strange names. Soldiers watched over the radio like it was a wounded friend gasping through the dawn. Lada walked over to shut off the newscaster's bleary German. Our workers preferred the German radio stations, since they were more likely to spell out the truth of our losses than the resistance stations. Even back then, I knew this was a point of contention for Noël, who disagreed with our friends at the information office on the demarcation between *news* and *propaganda*.

Lada watched Aubrion lace and unlace his fingers. His nails were chipped, his hands stained black with his craft.

"You know," said Aubrion, "I had a plan for a column. It would run in *La Libre Belgique*. I was going to do it on the day the Americans joined in the war—this was back before they'd joined, you see. I envisioned two pages, the second and third in the newspaper, so the reader had to turn the first page to see the whole thing. On the left side, we'd list the names of every Belgian who died since the invasion—René could get that from his pal in Flanders, the one with the toupee—and the right side would simply be the date and time that the Americans entered the war. Or perhaps we'd count down the days with tally marks, like on a prison wall. But I'm thinking about it now. We don't have enough people to do it." Aubrion seemed to gaze past the ceiling and into the empty rooms above. He did not notice, but Tarcovich started at this raw vulnerability. "We have lost nearly everyone who worked here."

"Of course we have." Tarcovich lit a cigarette. "August Wolff threatened to kill them. Anyone with any brains would have left after that. And those who didn't leave immediately..." Shrugging, Tarcovich puffed on her cigarette. "They heard what happened to Theo. You can hardly blame them."

Aubrion grew silent again. It was the habit that annoyed Lada most, he knew. When he was done speaking, he was done with it, and nothing could exorcise a word or feeling from him. But then Aubrion held his hands out to her like a beggar.

"Listen here." A hoarseness had entered Aubrion's voice. It was not the hoarseness that comes of speaking too much, but of whispering. Marc Aubrion had whispered for too long. He ached to raise his voice, to test it against the length and breadth of the sky. "There was a time when I had never seen a body before—never a dead body, not once. Do you ever think about that? It's so strange now. I passed my whole life without seeing a body. Now I can scarcely pass three days without it." He paused. "Why does it take buttons so long to decompose? Does anyone know the answer?"

Tarcovich studied him. "Are you angry about the Americans? Because time will judge the Americans for when they entered the war. And it hardly matters now. You know the Germans won't last."

"You don't know that."

"Just yesterday you called them *bouffons*. Wasn't that the word you used?"

"If *bouffons* never won anything, our political history would be a great deal nicer." Aubrion's voice dropped to a whisper. "Lada, I don't know. I only wish I knew what to do."

"Stay here." Tarcovich got up. "I will be back shortly."

She went upstairs. Aubrion shut his eyes and allowed time to pass, luxuriating in the nothingness of it: no plans, no running. After a time, Tarcovich returned, carrying a small, leather-bound notebook.

"What is it?" Aubrion asked.

"What's it look like?" said Lada.

"A notebook."

"Nicely done, Marc." Lada flipped through the book. Her touch was light on its cool, virgin pages. Specks of dirt peppered the spine. She brushed them away. "I have had it for ages. I've been meaning to use it for my stories."

"Your dirty stories?"

"No, for *real* stories—things I wanted to write but never did. Every now and again, I take the notebook from wherever I stashed it last, I pick up a pen—you know. But I never do anything more than that. I only hold it." Tarcovich rested the book in her lap. "Remember what I told you before? That you should write fake obituaries for *Faux Soir*?"

Aubrion shrugged in a way that suggested he did, but wished he did not.

"You wanted to know what to do." Lada held the notebook close. "I am telling you."

He seemed to consider this. Then: "What will *you* do?"

"I have this," said Tarcovich, who folded her hands across the notebook. It was a skinny thing, the leather bony and pocked. The book's pages were few. She might, if she worked at it, fill them up before her days' end.

"Really, Lada," said Aubrion, "you never listen to a bloody thing I say. I called the Germans idiots, not *bouffons*."

Despite herself, Tarcovich had to ask, "Is there a difference?"

"Of course there is! What a question. Here's the trouble, though." Aubrion's smile passed through Lada's body, through the walls, out into the night where the stars made promises they would forget by morning. "Only the *bouffons* know what it is."

4 DAYS TO PRINT NIGHT

The Pyromaniac

WHILE NICOLAS MADE his way back to the workhouse, I returned to the *Front de l'Indépendance* base. The guard was at the door, like always, and I gave him the password so he'd let me in. But the inside of the place was a corpse. The typewriters had been abandoned, some chairs overturned. A stack of posters lay near our assistant director's desk, as though he would be back in an instant to review them, like he'd just stepped out for a bite. One of our workmen had left his wrench and screwdriver on a desk, his empty tool belt at its feet. I thought for a moment that it was a Sunday; perhaps I'd lost track of time. But I knew that could not be so: it was Wolff's raid that had left my home barren. A breeze carried the smell of rain inside, stirring papers on the floor; Aubrion once told me there's a word for the smell of rain, *petrichor*, and I marveled at the wonder of that every time I remembered it.

I found Aubrion and Tarcovich in the basement. They were seated on opposite sides of the room, at work with paper and pen. I cleared my throat for their attention.

"Gamin!" Smiling, Aubrion got up to embrace me. He smelled of chalk and of him, but his smile did not reach his eyes. "Are you all right? I had begun to worry."

Tarcovich wagged a finger at me. "It's about time you showed up, young *man*." At this last word, her smile broadened.

Aubrion offered me a seat, which I took gratefully. As he questioned me about the day's events, Tarcovich fetched me a glass of water and a sandwich. I spoke, businesslike and monotone, between mouthfuls.

"I can't believe our good fortune." Aubrion made a note, tapping his fingers on a desk. "This building sounds as though it will be perfect for our photographs. Where did you say it was?"

I swallowed a bite of sandwich. "Up north, monsieur."

"Go on, Gamin. What about the bombs?" Aubrion was gripping the arms of his chair. "You did find a place to stash them, didn't you?"

"Oh, go easy on him, Marc." Tarcovich glanced between me and Aubrion. "It is not the end of the world if you couldn't find somewhere, Gamin."

"I *did* find somewhere, madame." I eyed the rest of my sandwich. Another bite remained, but I was no longer hungry. I put it aside, wiped my hands on my trousers. "I dropped them in a dumpster outside the *Le Soir* print factories. My mate Nicolas says they only empty the things every other week, if that. He used to be a garbage boy."

Aubrion leaned back in his chair. "It's bloody brilliant."

"And this lad Nicolas?" said Tarcovich. "He is safe, isn't he?"

"He's fine, madame. I saw him off to the workhouse all right." It was not a lie—Nicolas was fine, he had returned to the workhouse—but I said nothing of Leon. I remember that those words, *He's fine, madame,* were flavored with sulfur and iron. I can taste them now. I will taste them until I die.

"Excellent, excellent," said Aubrion. "René will be pleased.

Actually, René will be pessimistic and boring, but I'll be pleased on his behalf."

"Hang on a tick." Tarcovich tapped her chin with a pen. "Didn't you mention another lad? One who came with you to Wellens's construction site?"

My words caught in my throat. I had a feeling that I'd done something bad, or that I'd found out something I was not supposed to know. I made another attempt to speak but tasted the salt of my tears.

"Oh, no, you poor thing." Tarcovich lunged forward to catch me as I fell out of my chair. I collapsed into her arms, sobbing. Even now, I recall the fresh smell of her sweater and scarf when I am sad or lonely. Her arms became my world. "Hush now. Hush." I still could not tell her what became of Leon. When I accepted my position among the men and women of the FI, I accepted everything that accompanied it: the life of a soldier, and the death. I don't know for certain that Leon died, of course; I did not see a body. But I never tried to find out, and for that, I carry unnamable guilt.

Aubrion got up, aware that he was supposed to do something, unaware of what it was. He had come to think of me as a colleague, you see. I did the same work everyone else did, took the same risks. He'd never seen me cry—not because I was hiding it, you understand, but because I didn't do it. "They made the Marquis de Lafayette a commander at age thirteen," Aubrion used to joke, "and *he* probably had syphilis. You'll be running the show in half a year." And suddenly I was neither a colleague nor a friend; we were fighting together, in a *war*. Aubrion watched me wipe my tears with my fists. He was doing this—all of this— to a child. Later that night, when they thought I was asleep, he confessed these feelings to Lada Tarcovich. "We are all just children, Marc," she said, surprising me—surprising him, too.

"You poor thing," Lada was still saying, an incantation meant to keep me whole. But this business with Leon had turned death from a prankster into a reality. I had seen people die from afar— I had seen my own parents trampled to death—and I had seen bodies in the streets. I sang the same ballads as the other soldiers, "The Fair Lad's Last Stand," "Belgium Shall Rise," "Mighty Brussels Again," the same foolish words and yet it all meant something different now. I was *not* whole. The reality of death had shattered me into fragments.

I believe that is why I chose this moment to tell Marc Aubrion who I was. It was not a choice so much as it was an attempt to put myself back together. I needed a map, you see, to show me the way back to myself, to find meaning and worth in a world that suddenly meant nothing. I needed a map, and a mapmaker cannot tell lies.

"Monsieur?" I said. "I have something to tell you."

Lada released me from her embrace. As I faltered, she nodded me on.

"What is it, Gamin?" Aubrion knelt by me on the floor, his wide eyes meeting mine. "Tell me."

"I'm not—well—there's something you think I am, but I'm not."

Aubrion nodded gravely. "Before you go on, let me say this. Socialism has acquired a bad reputation through an unfortunate series of circumstances *entirely* beyond the control of anyone affiliated with the movement itself, and possibly even orchestrated by an uninspired but determined cadre of political professionals who don't care a wretched *lick* about anything but their own pocketbooks—"

"Oh, my God," said Lada, "she's not a bloody socialist, she's a girl!"

At this revelation, Aubrion looked at me, at Lada, back at me, and then heavenward, saying: "Are you sure?"

"I'm afraid so, monsieur." I knew Aubrion, with his trunk full of disguises and false mustaches and wigs, would not ask *why* I did it. If Tarcovich understood the pragmatic motivations for my identity, Aubrion understood the fanciful. But I felt compelled to tell him the reason anyway. "It was easier this way, when I was coming here from Toulouse. With all of the bad men around, you know. I heard things from my mother, before—before. It wasn't a lie, not really. I've felt comfortable this way, monsieur. And I wanted to tell you, I did, but after a time—"

"You knew about this?" Aubrion asked Tarcovich.

"Wouldn't you be more surprised if I *didn't* know?"

"I suppose it does seem like something you would know." He said to me, "Why have you told me this now?"

I told the truth. I was drawing my map, and the lines were clean and sure. "It felt like it was a good time to say it, monsieur."

My dear Aubrion seemed to accept that. "Well," he said, "I can't argue with your dramatic timing." His attention drifted toward one of the blackboards.

Tarcovich stepped between Aubrion and his next scheme. "Aren't you going to ask what she's called?" she said.

It is not enough to say that Aubrion merely smiled at me, for while that is accurate, it is not true. Aubrion smiled at me, yes, but like he *knew* me, all of me—the parts that hurt, the bits that faltered, the things that were laughable or strange, the patches that tried valiantly to cover the scars. If that is what it means to *smile*, so be it, but I will never see another smile as long as I am alive.

"Why would I do that?" said Aubrion. "I know exactly who Gamin is."

3 DAYS TO PRINT
FIRST LIGHT OF MORNING

The Gastromancer

THE ALLIES HAD gotten into a row on Spiegelman's desk. Franklin Roosevelt had started it.

Dear Commander Harris, the president had written. It had taken Spiegelman two tries to get the handwriting right. He'd written so much Churchill over the past day that he felt as if the man had seized his pen and refused to give it back. *I am certain you have received word of the impending American press into Belgium that shall begin within a week's time. My dear friend the prime minister has conveyed to me his understanding of the tactical and spiritual significance of such an assault. He conveyed to me, too, your comprehension of the necessity that this be an American undertaking. I will be the first to speak to the extraordinary military accomplishments of the English.* Spiegelman crossed out "extraordinary" and wrote "extra-ordinary" next to it. For reasons that were his alone, Roosevelt both pronounced and wrote the word that way. *America,* he continued, *has yet to achieve a victory on this scale in the skies of Europe. It is necessary, it is important, it is vital that this change immediately.*

The reason I am writing to you is that I would like to personally give my thanks for your understanding. A man of your talents does not sit idly as his countrymen or his allies work to achieve that to which he has devoted his life. Spiegelman tapped his pen against the desk. That sentence was important, he knew. Bomber Harris would either read it and resolve *not* to sit idly by, or resolve to *ensure* he sat idly by—to spite the Americans. *I am aware of the depths of your commitment, Commander Harris. These next days will be difficult for you.* Spiegelman paused, then struck out the sentence. He thought the better of it, writing: *These days will be difficult for you, I trust.* The two extra words, though brief, added a wealth of condescension to which even a bureaucrat-general like August Wolff could only aspire. *I can only hope any frustration is swallowed by the sense of duty that has distinguished you from your peers.*
—*Franklin Roosevelt.*

Spiegelman reread the letter, freezing in terror each time he heard a footstep outside his door. If the Germans caught him at work, the game was up—not simply for him, but for Aubrion, Tarcovich, Noël, everyone. Though he did not know whether he would have the time or presence of mind to follow through, Spiegelman planned to burn the offending letters if the Germans were to come through his door. Pleased, Spiegelman set aside Roosevelt's note and began a second one. It would be brief, to the extent that Winston Churchill was capable of brevity.

MY DEAR PRESIDENT,
I have been informed of your communication with Commander Arthur Harris. I am, and I will forever be, thankful to the Lord our God for the bond of friendship you and I have forged in the flames of this bloodiest of wars.

Spiegelman shook himself, dizzy with prepositional phrases. He crossed out *flames* to replace it with *fires.*

Ours is a bond of deep and mutual respect. We are aware of the delicate nature of war and the artful touch one requires in dealing, diplomatically, with one's own people and with those on the other side. That is precisely why

Spiegelman dropped his pen, certain he heard someone fiddling with the door handle. But, no, it must have been the wind, or his imagination. He stared at his paper for a moment, trying to figure out what he'd planned to say. And then he finished:

I am writing to you to-day. My dear Roosevelt, I must humbly suggest, with the greatest admiration for you and for our shared work, that you send to me all communications intended for the men in my military and diplomatic ranks so that I may forward them to their proper place. I have long believed that if we are to muddle through these apocalyptic days and if we are to emerge unscathed in the fields of revelation, we must be aware of all that transpires within our ranks. It is in this spirit I humbly make my request.
WINSTON S. CHURCHILL

Spiegelman drummed his fingers, thinking. Most of the base went to sleep by midnight. He could probably access the communications room around two in the morning, with minimal risk of detection, and send the letters to Bomber Harris. Though they'd tried to develop the technology, the Germans did not have any means of automatically recording telex communications that left their bases; it had to be done manually. The greatest risk was that Bomber Harris might respond, and that the telex operators would awake to find his message. "The odds are very low," Aubrion had said when Spiegelman brought up that concern the day prior. "I don't believe he's ever responded to a communication from Churchill or Roosevelt, since the beginning of the war. The man is impressively antisocial."

The letters rested uneasily on Spiegelman's desk. Though his options were few, they seemed vast: send the letters, risk detection, and invite death in two days' time, or burn the letters and die chained to this desk. Spiegelman stood, putting his hands on the wall like a prisoner clutching the bars of his cell. His time there was limited regardless of what happened with *Faux Soir.* Someday soon, Wolff would tire of him, or he would tire of Wolff, and then it would be Fort Breendonk or bedsheets knotted up into a noose. Spiegelman removed his pistol from the nook behind his bed. He'd held it twice, maybe three times, in as many years. His eyes on the ceiling (the victims, the ones who stood before the firing squads, they always kept their eyes on the sky), Spiegelman pressed its cold lips to his temple.

He'd only ever kissed one man in all his days: a boy, back when he was young. It had been in the schoolyard, and Mr. Thompkinson had watched from the window. That boy grew tall and lean. He had married a rabbi's daughter.

Spiegelman threw down the pistol. He had never chosen the easy stories; he had always read the most difficult books first, even as a child. And so David Spiegelman would send the letters. Any other story ended too easily. He owed it to Tarcovich, to Noël, to the others who'd taken him in—and he owed it to Aubrion, who'd never hesitated to raise his voice.

David Spiegelman would send the letters, and his words would run free from this place.

3 DAYS TO PRINT
AFTERNOON

The Jester

HEARING A CLAMOR on the floor above, Aubrion glanced up from his pad of paper; he'd habitually tear off corners of his paper as he worked, so the pad was frayed at the edges, Aubrion's desk littered in flecks of white. Red-faced and huffing, Noël came downstairs. He was holding something, maybe an envelope, and a photograph, too. Noël did not notice Aubrion. The photograph seemed to demand everything of him: his posture and attention served only the cheap blotting paper.

Aubrion knew, intellectually, that he should excuse himself and permit Noël some privacy. Of course, he did not.

"René?" said Aubrion, startling the director.

Noël clutched his chest. "Marc. You've been sitting there."

"How charitable of you to notice."

"Right."

"What's that?"

"This? Nothing important." Awash in his lie, Noël held the photograph and looked at it. The director usually moved with such strict economy, conserving his energy for where it was most needed. But he was chaotic now, all limbs and heavy breathing. Aubrion feared he might burst a blood vessel. "Do you remember Margaux?"

"Your wife?"

"You met her a few years ago. Did I ever tell you how I convinced her to go to America?"

"I don't think so."

"She took the girls, you know. I asked her to. I knew they weren't safe here."

Without waiting for Aubrion to answer, Noël walked over and handed him the photograph. Aubrion did indeed recognize Margaux: a plain woman, large-shouldered, with a patrician forehead and aristocratic nose, like someone had fashioned her out of two different characters. In the photo, Margaux's hands were on two young girls' shoulders—Noël's daughters, Aubrion recalled. The girls had Margaux's eyes and Noël's smile.

"Lara and Bette." Noël tapped the photograph. His eyeglasses, which he wore more often these days, slipped to the tip of his nose. "Margaux sent this to me. She meant to shame me, I'm sure. Make me feel guilty for staying behind, insisting they go to America without me. I haven't the slightest idea how she knew where to find me. But that was my Margaux. She works as a seamstress now, in a place called the Bronx."

Aubrion leaned over the photograph. He noticed a rip in the sleeve of Margaux's dress, which she'd attempted to repair with coarse string and uneven stitching. If she was a seamstress, she was a poor one. It surprised Aubrion that she'd spend money on a photograph.

But then it was clear to him that she had taken this photograph specifically for her husband, to taunt him and beg him and slap him all at once. Though her eyes had frozen over, she was still wearing her wedding band. And her daughters, those poor girls: they smiled to obey an order, and nothing more. An otherworldly fire spread through Aubrion's gut. The poor girls had their father's thin lips. They would look like him when they grew up; they would smile at their lovers and friends with Noël's sardonic lips; they would frown in that uncompromising manner; they would *grow up*. They would speak a different language than their father. They probably did already. A muscle tightened in Noël's jaw—and then he cried out their names, the names of his daughters. Aubrion looked away, frightened at the man's tears.

Noël could not speak, for a moment—could not move. Then he said, "I told her I was having an affair."

"What?" said Aubrion.

"That's how I convinced Margaux to leave. It's the only way I could do it. I tried, but she wouldn't leave."

"Are you?"

"Am I what?"

"Having an affair."

"Marc, when the bloody hell have I had time to carry on an affair?" And then the photograph had fluttered to the floor, another snowflake to be trodden upon by pedestrians and German boots. Noël erased a chalkboard. "Where is Wellens?"

"Sorry?"

"I need to speak to Wellens," Noël snapped. "We have things to do, matters to prepare. This is my *duty*, and I do not sit idle, do I? Have I ever?" The director ran a hand through his beard. He was staring at the broken printing press, Aubrion noted, as though it were the locus of all his troubles. He went quiet. "Please, Marc. Where is Wellens?"

Aubrion put his hand on Noël's shoulder. The director stiffened, but he did not move away. Marc Aubrion thought of Noël as the personification of the *Front de l'Indépendance*, and in many ways, he was. He was stoic, impenetrable, unflappable, a tad ridiculous. He wore that horrid uniform with the oversized trousers, by God, because it was *proper*. But Noël was a man, too, a man who loved dark beer, who was given to loud political discussions over strong liquor, who'd married young and had two girls and then given them up, trading them in for that wretched uniform. Aubrion saw in him a strength he'd never before noticed.

"Wellens is at the factory, getting everything ready for tomorrow," Aubrion said quietly.

"And do we know," asked Noël, "what became of Spiegelman?"

"Spiegelman will not be coming back." Victor descended the stairs to the basement, looking distracted. "I've been out gathering intelligence. Wolff has caught on to Spiegelman's involvement and has banned him from leaving the Nazi headquarters."

Aubrion's chest tightened. He and Noël fell quiet. Their eyes went to the stairs, as though they expected Spiegelman to come join them, laughing at their gullibility, at his finest prank. Of course, that did not happen.

"Is there any way—" Aubrion began.

"No, Marc." Noël shook his head. "If we try to slip him a message, we will put him in even greater danger."

Aubrion could not argue. He felt suddenly off-balance, like those cases he'd heard about, the ones where people woke up feeling out of sorts and died of a heart attack before the day was out. Though it made little sense to him now, he'd expected to see Spiegelman once more before they printed *Faux Soir*, to celebrate with him properly. But it would not be. It was like he'd missed the end of a great play, one he'd never get the chance to see again.

The Professor

Martin Victor took his leave of the FI base and walked to his flat. There, he took a checklist from his pocket to tack it to the wall of his study. "Three sets of clothing," he read, ticking things off on his fingers, "trunk, encyclopedias, coat and hat." He was allowed to take as much as he could fit in a cart; that was what Wolff had said. The clothing was already folded and tucked into an attaché case. The trunk contained Victor's most important books and papers, and he'd packed it days ago. All he needed was to rummage for his encyclopedias.

He licked the tip of his pen, then crossed off *three sets of clothing*. Victor dropped the pen before he could do the same for *trunk*. His hands grew more unsteady each day, and he could no longer rely on them. Not for the first time that week, Victor contemplated taking a pistol to his head. If a man could not trust his own hands, what was left for him? The professor had betrayed his colleagues, himself, even August Wolff—but to take his own life would be to betray his work, his faith, his wife's memory. He did not know how to do such a thing.

<u>YESTERDAY</u>

The Scrivener

HELENE BLEW ON her hands to warm them, though the room was no colder than it had been previously. "It was close to the end, you know," she said. "I knew that, even then. It rained all night, and Marc Aubrion was writing. I cradled an empty mug, the cocoa gathering in clots at the bottom, watching him from my seat atop a printing press. Once every hour, he'd look up, confused, as though he could not figure out why he didn't hear the scratch of his pen. Then his eyes would turn to the basement window. He'd give the rain a reproachful nod, continue with his work. This went on for ages."

The old woman paused. "I could not explain how—and I still cannot—but I knew I would survive *Faux Soir*. It was not just the optimism of youth, or the ignorance of someone who hadn't seen death. It was a good deal more than that. This was a war for great men, and I was too small. Aubrion, in my eyes, was the greatest."

2 DAYS TO PRINT
MORNING

The Dybbuk

NOVEMBER 9, —43, WOLFF TYPED. *Conducted raid of book-shop, The Spool, in eastern Brussels. Purged nearly two hundred pieces of objectionable and pornographic material. Two executions. Nine arrests. David Spiegelman remains under temporary confinement.* La Libre Belgique *is on schedule.*

The Jester

The rain decided it'd had enough of Enghien, startling Aubrion into wakefulness. He stretched, working the knots out of his legs on the way to the washroom. As he stooped to wash his face, Aubrion blinked at his reflection in the cracked mirror. With his manic curls and wide, dark-rimmed eyes, he looked like a tragic character from a play he once saw, something about Greek gods. He'd walked out of the second act and made up a scathing review about the ending. Shivering, Aubrion pulled his sleeves over his hands and returned to the basement.

Tarcovich had taken his place by the broken printing press, her hair wet from a bath or the rain. She'd draped her blue scarf around a simple tunic and trousers. Aubrion waved, and she handed him a mug of coffee.

He wrinkled up his nose at it. "What's this?"

"Drink it," said Tarcovich, her hands wrapped around a matching cup.

"Are you poisoning me?"

"Yes."

"Finally." Aubrion drank. "Christ, that's good. This isn't German."

"I'd been saving up, since all this began—you know, since the war. Just in case. Waste not, want not, and all that." Tarcovich sniffled, though her eyes were dry. "But this morning I looked out the window, and it was..." She waved at the ceiling, her eyes bright. "You saw it. I wondered what the devil I was saving all that money for. And so." Shrugging, Tarcovich drank her coffee. "Only one coffeehouse in Enghien still makes coffee worth drinking."

"The Easterner?"

"Easterner's been closed for six months, Marc."

Aubrion set his coffee aside. "George's place?"

Tarcovich nodded.

"Fuck," said Aubrion.

"I think he got out."

"He had three kids."

"Two kids. Two girls."

"Where did they go?"

"I couldn't tell you."

Aubrion stared into his cup. "I got drunk with him the night the war came to Belgium."

"I remember. René spent all night trying to find you. He told me he'd never work with you again." Tarcovich put down her mug, looking over Aubrion's frayed pages of writing. "Are these them? Your obituaries?"

As Aubrion started to respond, Noël and Victor came downstairs, talking in low tones. They stopped when they reached the bottom step.

"Good morning, all," said Noël. His beard was a tad overgrown, which made his eyes look unnaturally small. "We just received a telex from Monsieur Wellens. He's nearly ready for us. We should lay everything out for printing."

"Anything from our pal Harris yet?" asked Aubrion.

Noël shook his head. "Sorry, Marc."

"There is a problem," said Victor. "We have several unprocessed photographs, and Wellens doesn't have the equipment we need to deal with them."

"I knew he wouldn't," said Aubrion. "But Gamin does."

The Pyromaniac

We piled into the Nash-Kelvinator, sitting on top of each other like used books at an estate sale. I sat in front so I could direct Noël to the blue-doored building.

As he and I took care of the business of driving, Aubrion told everyone about old Dr. Borremans. "Born in Flanders in 1895, died in Brussels in 1943," he read from his notepad, which was helpfully labeled *Faux Soir Obituaries*, "Dr. Miet Borremans was renowned in his community for popularizing the traditionally German idea of eugenics. This paper wishes to acknowledge that many of Dr. Borremans's friends and patients were skeptical of the principle upon first learning of its importance to the Reich. Always a visionary, Dr. Borremans conducted a thorough study of the idea and published his findings in leading scientific journals. His fifteen-year marriage to Eugenia Claet of the Claet family, an old Belgian lineage with which our readers will undoubtedly be familiar, produced an accomplished daughter with a bad ear and a strapping young son with polio."

I laughed, as did everyone else. Noël almost missed a turn onto the main road. "Oh, no, make a left *here*, monsieur," I directed.

Grinning, Aubrion read from the second page of his torn-up pad of paper. "Born in Ghent in 1864, died in Enghien in 1943, Madame Edith Van den Berg was, in addition to a loving mother and wife, a noted patriot. She was often seen, as her neighbors will attest, participating in parades, rallies, and discussions on the politics and moral strength of Mother Belgium. Last year, at the age of seventy-eight, she organized a debate between a German political thinker named Gunter and a Belgian dissenter whose name shall not tarnish this reputable paper. Though she was born in Belgium and lived here all her life, and though the debate lasted a mere six minutes, Madame Van den Berg, a woman of conscience, did not hesitate to award a victory to the German."

Again, the car shook with our laughter. In truth, I understood only a fragment of the obituaries, and I could not have articulated why they were so funny. But it was good to hear the others laugh.

"These are actually splendid, Marc," said Noël.

Aubrion shuffled the pages. "Could you make *some* effort to sound less surprised?"

"I am never surprised at the quality of your work."

"Then what are you?"

Tarcovich leaned over as though she were about to tell Aubrion a tremendous secret. "He is surprised," she whispered.

"How many of these obituaries did you write?" asked Victor.

"Seven." Aubrion thumbed through the paper. "No, eight."

"They are a bit…" Victor shrugged, pulling off his glasses with unsteady hands. "They are irreverent. I read a piece on satire by a fellow named Stevens, who argues that the *meaning* of a satirical piece should be buried beneath layers and layers of genuine comedy."

"Layers and layers," repeated Aubrion, flatly.

"It's very transparent satire, is what I am saying. The satire leaves little to—"

"Oh, shut up, Martin."

"The piece is funny," said Tarcovich. "It's *zwanze*. I vote to leave it in."

"Lada has spoken," said Noël.

We pulled up to the blue-doored building: an unassuming structure, three stories of disinterested lines and arches. Since Nicolas and I had sheltered there, someone had graffitied the words OUI, NON, and MÈRE on the wood, a Freudian couplet in moss-colored paint.

"Park a block or two away," said Victor.

Noël did so. We got out and walked toward the building in pairs, for the whole group of us would have aroused suspicion. Victor accompanied Noël, Aubrion walked with Tarcovich, and I followed closely behind.

"I do not know," said Tarcovich, nodding at his rolled-up sleeves, "how you aren't cold."

Aubrion looked up at the sky; it was ashen, like the face of a man who'd just been shot. "Is it cold out here?"

Tarcovich ran her fingers across his arm, speckled with goose pimples. He shuddered at her touch. Aubrion could not recall the last time a woman had touched him, and though he thought of Tarcovich as a sister, her touch made him wonder at things that would not be—that *couldn't* be, not anymore. Droplets of rain began to fall. Aubrion quickened his pace.

"You could roll down your sleeves, you know," said Tarcovich. "Or wear a coat. Do you own a coat?"

Aubrion said nothing. They walked on, for a time, and then he asked her: "Do you know the cemetery at the border of the city?"

"The one where they bury the political prisoners? Of course. Young lovers go there after curfew all the time." Tarcovich smiled. "You can hear them until well after dawn. The families who live in the tenements on Eighth—the parents tell their children it's just the wind."

Aubrion tucked the fake obituaries under his arm. He was grasping, I think, for a feeling or something else. The Germans would not bury Theo Mullier in that cemetery, the one for political prisoners. More likely, he would be tossed in a pit outside Fort Breendonk—he already *had* been, to be sure. But the spirit of him was in that cemetery, pieces of who he was, things he did. The spirit of him was in this city, in Aubrion's work, in everything. "These obituaries," Aubrion said, still grasping, but he was out of time. "I was at it all night, you know. And all day."

"I know." Tarcovich turned up her collar against the rain.

They ducked into the blue-doored building and waited for the others to follow. A band of light, which had escaped through a hole in the blue door, illuminated Aubrion's face. When everyone was inside, Aubrion threw a bundle of papers onto a table.

"These," he said, "are undeveloped photos for the paper, including the Hitler photographs Lada so kindly procured for us. From what Gamin tells us, there's enough chemicals here to develop that lot."

"I can set to work on that," said Victor. "I shall need to see what we have here."

As Victor proceeded, Aubrion righted a table and placed the Hitler photographs atop it.

"I have an idea for what I want it to look like." Aubrion slapped one of the photographs. In it, Hitler stood with his arms outstretched, his mouth wide. Though the exposure was terrible, and you could only see half of his face, the likeness was unmistakable. "I want this one on the bottom left-hand corner, framed with three lines of text. Something about how our pal the *Führer* meant to deliver a speech in Berlin, something about patriotism and the progress of the war—only he got his papers mixed up, you see. He had a copy of a speech Churchill gave last week, and he delivered that instead."

Noël cleared his throat. "I don't like it."

"Why not?"

"We cannot equate Churchill with Hitler," said Noël, "regardless of how little you care for either of them."

"Not even in jest," said Tarcovich. "And look at the photograph. You can't see his face."

"Sure, you can," said Aubrion.

"Only part of it."

"Enough to know who it is."

Tarcovich said, "The point of the photograph—you said so yourself—is to show them he's not immortal. But look at his face. The lighting, the exposure…it's too dramatic. He looks too powerful."

"All right, all right, so we'll toss this one out." Aubrion passed the offending photograph to me. "Shred it, Gamin."

"Yes, monsieur," I said, but I intended to keep it, and I still have it.

"What about this one?" Tarcovich picked out a second photograph.

It was a tad grainier than the others, and smaller. Hitler's sepia body and torso blended and faded into black. He was oddly proportioned: his torso took up most of the frame, and his head seemed smaller than it should have been. Squinting, Aubrion held the picture up to the light. The gray and black grains, cheap-looking as they were, articulated the fury on Hitler's lips, the passion in his eyes. Even so, the *Führer* appeared to have been caught off guard, for his hands were perched weakly on his chest, like he'd received a bad scare, or had heartburn.

"I like this one," Aubrion said.

"But what is the story?" asked Noël.

"It's easy." Tarcovich took a cigarette from her purse, then, perhaps remembering where we were, put it back. She walked the perimeter of the abandoned laboratory, stooping every now and again to pick up a photograph. Aubrion and Noël and I watched her. After several minutes of this exercise, she said "ah!" and emerged with a picture she'd found tucked beneath a lamp. "Here we are." Tarcovich passed it to Aubrion.

He blew the dust off it. The photograph depicted a flying fortress, one of those fat-bellied bombers with the pug noses. It cleaved through a patch of clouds, the gaudy American star barely visible on its backside. The bomber was flanked by three of its compatriots.

"We put this photo on the top left-hand corner of the front page." To illustrate, Lada took it from Aubrion's hands. "We put the Hitler photo in the bottom right." She placed the two photographs on a table, adjacent to each other.

"But *Le Soir* only ever has a single photograph on the first page," said Aubrion. "Our readers will know immediately that we're playing some sort of game."

"Which is exactly what we *want*, isn't it?"

Noël leaned over the desk, studying them. I stood on my toes to see, too. I don't believe I had ever noticed the crow's feet near the director's eyes.

"So, the two photographs?" said Noël.

"Neither of you see it yet, do you?" Tarcovich's smile was wicked. "What are the two things the people out there are afraid of?"

Victor lumbered over to join us, wiping his hands on a cloth. "Hitler is one, obviously."

"Air raids," said Aubrion. "That bloody siren."

"Precisely," said Tarcovich. "The best thing we can do is to set these two figures against each other—the bomber and the arsehole—by showing *Hitler* being afraid of the flying fortresses. And so, we put the first photograph, the one of the bombers, *here* with some caption, perhaps 'in the middle of action.' We put the second photograph *there*—"

"We could splice them together, to make it look like they are parts of the same photograph," said Aubrion.

Victor grunted. "That would take at least a week."

"We don't need to," said Tarcovich, smacking Aubrion on the back of the head. I laughed—*giggled*, really. I have searched endlessly for a word to describe my excitement, my pure joy, at watching these people at their craft. "We'll write a note saying our typesetter made an error, that the two separate photos should be one. Our photographers were on the scene at the precise moment when Hitler caught sight of the Americans flying above Germany. Gave the poor *Fuhrer* such a fright."

"Do we want to inspire that kind of sympathy for Hitler?" asked Victor.

"That will not happen," said Tarcovich.

"And to make sure it will not happen," said Aubrion, grinning madly, "we'll caption the photograph."

In the dramatic pause that followed, Noël sighed and asked: "What's the caption, Marc?"

"I am so glad you asked, René. Allow me to tell you a story about Kaiser Wilhelm II."

"Oh, God," said Tarcovich. "Here we go." But she was smiling. I saw it.

Aubrion continued: "If you recall, at the start of the First Great War, we all blamed Germany for the blood and the suffering and all that."

"Because it was Germany that started the blood and the suffering and all that." Victor folded his arms across his chest. "I know you were a babe in your mother's arms at the time, Marc, but others of us were not."

"But Germany did not—and does not—believe it caused all that. Have you seen their textbooks?" Aubrion tapped the picture of Hitler. "They teach their children that Germany's hand was forced. It's all propaganda, of course. And the propaganda began long ago, after the first major battle of the Great War, up in Flanders."

"I know this one," said Tarcovich. "Wilhelm arrived after the battle to see the carnage."

Aubrion nodded eagerly. "He was silent for a moment, bowed his head in meditation. His advisors waited by his side. Then, overtaken by feelings that we poor mortals can only imagine, the Kaiser looked up to the sky and cried out—"

"Ich habe das nicht gewollt!" I supplied, for I'd learned this tale in school.

"Stellar, Gamin." Aubrion winked at me. "'I did not want that.' At least one of ole Wilhelm's advisors had the presence of mind to bring a notebook on the trip—or so I guess, because those words were plastered across every propaganda poster and leaflet the Germans produced until the end of the war. Proof of the Kaiser's innocence. Spoken evidence of the Reich's moral purity." Aubrion rolled up his fake obituaries and pointed them at Victor, like a duelist's sword. "If you are concerned someone might feel sympathy for Hitler, here is your answer. We caption the second photograph with something like 'here the *Fuhrer* catches sight of the American planes and borrows the Kaiser's words—*I did not want that.*' Yes, yes, of *course* Hitler is innocent. As innocent as the Kaiser."

Noël clapped Aubrion on the shoulder. He started to say something, but he was overcome. Aubrion smiled at him, and we got to work on the business of making a paper.

LAST DAY TO PRINT
MORNING

The Gastromancer

EVERY MORNING, a team of intelligence officers wrote a nine-page document outlining the state of the war. It was always nine pages, never eight or ten, which perplexed Spiegelman; it was such a gawky number. A clerk usually slipped the leaflet under his door, and Spiegelman ignored it. He did not wish to know the state of the war, nor did he trust the intelligence officers to report it as it was. Today, though, he flipped through it eagerly, looking for any indication that the Royal Air Force was preparing to bomb Enghien. His search proved less than fruitful. Apparently, the Italians had bombed the Vatican; the Red Army had taken Kiev from someone; and the Allies had seized Castiglione. Frustrated, Spiegelman tossed the leaflet to the floor.

The Smuggler

Church bells rose above the moaning wind, admonishing Lada Tarcovich. She made a rude gesture in their direction. Despite her fury at Andree Grandjean, Lada needed to see her again, and she was a fool for it. When she closed her eyes, she was tormented by the grim finality that awaited her—but more than that, by the idea that her story would fade to black and Andree would never know what had become of her. Even the most obvious stories have endings; Aubrion used to say that. "What begins with once upon a time, Gamin, must end in happily ever after, or the audience will demand their money back." If their story had indeed ended, then Lada and Andree needed to put that ending on paper for all to see. Two years into the war, Aubrion wrote on a blackboard in the basement: "An ellipsis is a poor substitute for a period, and don't let anyone tell you otherwise..." An ellipsis would not do, not any longer, not *this* close to the end of *Faux Soir*.

Besides, Lada couldn't have Andree thinking she was so insecure that she'd leave a relationship—even a relationship that was two weeks old and somewhat lopsided—without saying goodbye.

It was past eight now, so Andree Grandjean was just beginning to hear the day's cases. Lada flicked away her cigarette. The sky stirred, a light rain dusting her coat and gloves. Turning up her collar against the cold, Tarcovich looked up and down the road. Her favorite pastry shop was open today, one of the few left in the city. Lada toyed with the idea of getting a croissant. But she would have to stand in a line, and she was not sure she had the patience for that. And so Lada started down the road to downtown Enghien.

It was a rather long walk to Andree's courthouse during the afternoon, but twice that in the morning. Though the city was a ghost of what it'd been before the war, it greeted each day as loudly as ever. The city yowled at Lada Tarcovich, the way starved cats yowled at empty bowls. People offered her things from their carts: bread (some of it fresh, most of it stale), meats, chipped plates, blankets. Every night, shopkeepers sent their workers—often small children—out to the roads around Enghien. There, they gathered the discarded things that refugees traveling out of Belgium decided they could live without—usually toys, bars of soap, that sort of thing. Those who were not caught returned with cheap goods, sold for half their worth. As Lada walked, street vendors waved old wooden animals and ugly mirrors at her. Everyone had necklaces and bracelets that no longer shone.

Tarcovich stopped near an alley to retie her shoelaces. When she got up, she stood face-to-face with the remains of a poster: the fund-raiser poster, she realized. Tarcovich laughed. It had looked so fine before. The poor thing was pathetic now, hanging in gaudy shreds. She tore the rest of the poster down, putting it out of its misery.

By the time Tarcovich reached the courthouse, it was almost noon, and her stomach was protesting. Ignoring it, she greeted the clerk in the lobby with a placid smile. "That's the trick, Marc," she'd argued to Aubrion. "If you want someone to let you in where you don't belong, you must look like you don't care to be there."

"Hello," Tarcovich said to the clerk, sounding as though she'd rather be anywhere else. "I have an appointment with Judge Grandjean." She glanced at her watch. "For twelve fifteen."

The clerk consulted a pad of papers. "I apologize, madame, but Judge Grandjean was taken ill and has not come to the courthouse today. Can I take a message for you?"

Tarcovich declined, then proceeded to Andree's apartment. She did not dare believe that Andree's heartache had confined her to her flat; Lada could not afford to be so arrogant. If pressed, though, she would have admitted that a part of her hoped it was so—part of her prayed Andree could be struck dumb by her feeling for Lada, that she could be inspired to sit and wallow in her sweet anguish.

Lada knocked on Andree's door.

Andree opened it. "You?" she gasped, almost comically.

Tarcovich shrugged, as though she could not help it. "Me."

They went inside, regarding each other with fleeting glances. Though it was now past noon, Andree seemed to have just woken up. She leaned against a wall, watching Lada with wary eyes, while Tarcovich took a seat on the floor across from her.

"Going somewhere?" asked Lada.

"Why do you ask?"

"The place is a wreck."

It was true. Books lay in dust-covered mountains across the floor, scarves and trousers had been tossed onto lampshades, which teetered on their sides by blank shelves.

"I'd considered going on a trip." Andree played with the hem of her dressing gown. Tarcovich was faint with the sight of her. "But that's all. Just considered it."

"I see."

Andree mussed her curls. "Lada, why are you here?"

"Why am I here?"

"Do not do that."

Lada rummaged through a pile of Andree's books. She smiled at the titles: *Torchlight to Valhalla, Lady Chatterley's Lover, Poems of Sappho, We Too Are Drifting, Pity for Women, Songs of Lesbos.* The novels lay among the legal tomes and the encyclopedias and the reference books, open and visible like nude interlopers on a private beach. Tarcovich pulled *Torchlight to Valhalla* from a pile, sending two encyclopedias tumbling head-over-heels.

"I thought you didn't know," said Lada.

"I did not *know.*"

"They're beautiful."

"My books?" said Andree.

"I've never read most of those." Lada smiled mournfully. "For a long time, I did not even know that most of them existed. I'd heard whispers of books about deviants, sexual inversion, 'and that night, they were not divided,' Radclyffe Hall's trial. Women who made love to each other between the covers of their beds and these books, but never outside, never where

I could see them." Tarcovich's hands went to the shelf. "I *must* meet your smuggler."

"You already have. It's the Gestapo. Three-quarters of the material they deem obscene is burned. A quarter of it is spared. If you're good to the Reich—" here Grandjean shrugged an apology for being good to the Reich "—there are ways to get what you want."

Tarcovich walked over to Andree's bed, touched the woman's face on the cover of *Torchlight to Valhalla*. She took her notebook from her purse. "For you," she said to Andree.

Andree took it. "What is inside?"

"Stories."

"That you wrote?"

"Yes."

"You said you couldn't," whispered Andree. "That you could never bring yourself to write anything. Isn't that what you said?"

"Things changed."

"Oh, my God." Andree set the notebook atop *Torchlight to Valhalla*. Her voice had dropped to a whisper. She clutched a fistful of her hair as though in mourning already. She knew, she *knew*. "Something is about to happen. Isn't it?"

"Yes," said Lada. Her throat was dry. She tried to swallow, and the effort brought tears to her eyes. Lada repeated it: "Something is about to happen." The repetition was a promise, to herself and to Andree, that she would not leave here without telling Andree everything.

"With the FI?"

"I am not supposed to tell you—"

"Then don't."

Lada put her hands out to steady herself. "Do you mean that?"

"Christ." Andree laughed. The apartment smelled of her, of them. She laughed, and Lada laughed with her. It was a divine joke, the lot of it—whatever it was. "Of course not. Please, Lada."

And so, Lada told Andree everything. Andree Grandjean listened without moving or speaking.

YESTERDAY

The Scrivener

"I DO NOT know exactly what was said," the old woman murmured, "and I do not wish to know. This part of the story belongs to Tarcovich and Grandjean. It was written by them, and is theirs to tell or not." She leaned back, breathing slowly. Eliza's dark eyes were fixed on her. This room, the room in the back of the blue-doored building, had grown quieter since Helene's story began. Eliza wondered whether anything still existed, outside.

"This is not enough for you and your notebook, I know. You will want to know why Tarcovich went back. But I cannot tell you that."

"You don't know why she went back," said Eliza. It was half a question, half an admission on Helene's behalf.

"I can't know. I wasn't there."

"But can't you—"

"Can I guess?" Helene shrugged. The carelessness of the motion made her seem far younger than she was. "I don't know. Why do we do anything? Sometimes, there are no motives.

Other times, there are many. The important part is that she went back, and she told Grandjean everything—even though they'd quarreled, even though things seemed to have been lost between them. And when Lada had finished her tale, the church bells began to speak in her stead. They chimed and sang, and neither Lada nor Andree wanted to talk until they'd finished."

LAST DAY TO PRINT
AFTERNOON

The Smuggler

"THIS IS HAPPENING TOMORROW?" Andree said softly. "What you've told me? Tomorrow is the day?"

"It is," said Tarcovich.

Andree laughed. "My God. A fake newspaper."

"*Faux Soir* is what we're calling it."

"It's daring, I'll give you that." Andree shook her head, her eyes unfocused. Before now, Lada had never recounted the whole scheme from start to finish. It sounded absurd, horrifically absurd—not just absurd, but impossible, a caricature of some German comedy about those madcap Belgians and their daydreams. Lada watched Andree struggle to hold on to what she'd heard. "I apologize," she said, after a while, "but I can't quite—I can't quite grasp it, I suppose." She laughed shortly. "The Royal Air Force?"

"The Royal Air Force."

"And you will be arrested?" The way Andree asked the question—it was as though she was a child who'd just learned the word *arrested*. Tarcovich put her hand on Andree's knee, hoping she would not flinch. Andree did not. Perhaps she forgave Lada her sins, but perhaps she was only in shock.

"I don't know that for certain," said Tarcovich. "But we are printing the paper today and distributing it tomorrow, at four in the afternoon. The Gestapo is full to bursting with mindless arseholes, but even so, it should not take them long to figure out what is amiss." Lada took a breath. "Now that you know everything, I am going to plead with you again for the lives of my girls."

"Lada, no. I cannot."

"You cannot what?" It came out sharper than Lada intended. But she was furious at Andree for interrupting her when it had taken her so long and so much to say it. "You cannot listen to me?"

"I cannot *do* anything for them—for anyone." Andree stood, turning away from Lada, her posture hunched and impenetrable. "I cannot be seen with you any longer. I do not know what you want from me, or what you want me to do, what you think I *can* do. Whatever it is, I don't have it—I cannot do it."

Lada held out a hand. She did not frighten easily—she rarely panicked—and yet her heart pounded in her temples. Something was veering off course, but if Andree took her hand, the ship would right itself. Every muscle of Lada's body pled with her. "Andree, you *can*. Listen to me. Let Lotte and Clara go free, and then run—"

"Run where?"

"You can't stay here."

"This happened because of you." Grandjean's hands went to her chest. And there it was, exactly what Lada had feared. The cold shock of the thing had gone, and in its place, an impenetrable anger had filled Grandjean's body. "You *made* me."

"Made you what?"

"Fall in love with you." Andree's face was hideous with tears.

"You have known for weeks that tomorrow would come, and yet you did this anyway. *You* were all that mattered. I was nothing."

The weight of those words, *fall in love*, landed heavily between Lada's shoulder blades. It was true, it was not something Lada had made up. But the words were curdling in Andree's heart as Lada watched.

Grandjean held Lada's notebook out to her. "Leave me alone."

"Andree, please." Lada moved to push the notebook away. If she touched it, though, Grandjean would make her leave. "I don't know how to leave. I cannot live like this."

"You should have thought about that at the very beginning." Grandjean thrust the notebook into Lada's hands. "Take it."

Tarcovich tried to conjure a word or a feeling, but there was nothing left for her to say, nothing she could feel. She turned to go, dropping her notebook onto the pile of novels and tomes. It came to rest between *Poems of Sappho* and a volume of the *Encyclopedia Britannica*.

LAST DAY TO PRINT
LATE AFTERNOON

The Jester

WELLENS WAS BOUNDING about the factory floor like a schoolboy after the bell, his blue cape struggling to catch up. "You must see this," he kept saying. "You really must." He led Aubrion and me and the others to the loading dock behind his factory. There, workmen were unloading a pair of vans, carting away sheets of paper and barrels of ink.

"That's the lot of it?" Noël asked Victor.

The professor nodded. "That's everything the Germans gave us for our school, plus everything we purchased with the forty-five thousand francs from the auction, *plus* the five thousand francs Wolff gave us at the start of it."

Noël whistled. "Gentlemen, we have not done poorly for ourselves."

Aubrion peered into the van, his eyes widening. It was endless, the paper (bundled up in stacks of a hundred, tied together with string) and ink (packed in cheap, black-stained barrels that made seasick noises when the workmen lifted them) stretching on past what he could see. He was drunk with the smell of it. We all were. The ink caressed the clean, woody paper, and it all mingled together in the wind until Aubrion had to close his eyes with the power of it.

"It is," said Wellens, puffing out his chest, "more than enough for the fifty thousand copies we discussed, Monsieur Noël."

"Yes." Noël laughed, shaking his head like he'd just witnessed a miracle—which, of course, he had. "I suppose it is. Where the devil is Lada? She should be here for this."

Aubrion cleared his throat. "I think she went to see Grand-jean."

"Oh." Noël's expression could not quite make up its mind: hope, judgment, resignation. "Well, God save them."

Victor said, "Have your linotypists prepared the machines, Monsieur Wellens?"

"Hang on," said Aubrion. "*Linotypists?* Surely you have letter-pressing machines."

"Naturally." Wellens nodded at his factory floor.

"Then why aren't we using them?"

"It does not make sense financially," said Noël. "Letter-pressing would cost us around ten francs a paper."

"And so?" asked Aubrion.

"Linotyping, the modern way," replied Victor, "would cost around *one* franc per paper."

"I know how much these things cost."

"In that case," said Victor, "I do not understand the problem."

"The *problem* is that we have spent the past three weeks killing ourselves, sometimes literally, to create this paper." The workers started to look in Aubrion's direction. Noël motioned for him to lower his voice. "I know, René, but surely *you* aren't going to stand for this, are you? You have seen what linotype machines can do to a paper. It is rape, I say. Crooked text, fuzzy photographs—"

"Monsieur," Wellens said through his mustache, "my men are among the best in Europe."

Aubrion was insistent. "It does not matter how good they are. Don't you see? The equipment, Wellens. The problem is with the equipment."

"Shall we discuss this inside?" sighed Noël, so we filed into Wellens's office, shutting the door behind us. I sat on Wellens's desk. "Marc, listen. I understand where you are coming from. It is a matter of respect for our labors." The small room cramped the director's voice. "But, listen—if we use the cheaper material, we can print more papers. Surely that's more important than the quality of the stuff we've used to print it."

"Fifty thousand copies," said Aubrion, flatly.

"That's right. Fifty thousand people laughing at the *Fuhrer*... and more, really. They will give it to their families in the country, their friends in Flanders."

"Fifty thousand copies on bad paper, as opposed to what?" Aubrion calculated. "Five thousand copies on good paper?"

"That is accurate," said Victor.

"Quality is what matters here, don't you see?" said Aubrion, growing animated. "More than five thousand would be wonderful, of course, and I've dreamed about it, but—Christ, there is no way in heaven or hell we would be able to distribute *fifty* thousand fake newspapers before some chap at the Gestapo says, 'Gee, Hans, I wonder what those are.'"

"What has gotten into you?" said Noël, echoing my thoughts, for it alarmed me to see Aubrion this way. On Marc Aubrion, practicality was an ill-fitting suit.

He averted his eyes, and though I was not privy to Aubrion's feelings, I could see traces of them written in his hands and posture. He was thinking of Theo, I've no doubt. He could not decide whether Theo would've encouraged us to pull back, or to do as much as we could; he could not decide whether he would have listened. It hurt Aubrion, the callousness of not knowing.

"We have to do what is within our reach," Aubrion decided.

"But what if we *can* get fifty thousand copies out on the streets

before the Germans find out?" said Noël. "We have our distribution system figured out, we have a distraction—"

"If we can, they are never going to last, to survive time. Even
if people *have* them, the bloody cheap papers won't last longer
than a year. The text will fade. People will pass on the ghost of
our work to their children."

"Lord in Heaven," said Victor. "People are not going to be
passing this *joke* on to their children. It is a good thing we are
doing, an important thing, but for God's sake, Aubrion, be realistic. It only needs to last a day."

"A day for these people, yes, but also a day for their children."

Noël stepped between the two men. "The papers will last," he
said quietly, "if people want them to last. Think of the *knygnešiai*,
Marc."

"The book smugglers?"

"Weren't you going to write a play about them?" Noël looked
faintly disgusted with himself for remembering.

"I was." Aubrion pushed up his sleeves. "I'm surprised you
recall."

"Think of it, Marc. The stuff they brought into Lithuania
in the 1870s, the pamphlets and books they printed to defy the
Russians—none of it should have lasted. But it did, and it has,
and their language survived, their way of *living* survived. If people want *Faux Soir* to last, it will last. If they do not—" Noël
smiled. "We have done our job. The rest is out of our hands."

Aubrion thought for a moment. "Fine."

"Fine?" said Noël.

"Yes, fine. Have your linotypists prepare the machines, Monsieur Wellens?"

I have never smiled as broadly or openly as Ferdinand Wellens
did on this day. "They have, Monsieur Aubrion," he said.

At first the typesetters made an error, and in their haste to
correct it, jammed one of the linotype machines. Wellens's fac-

tory was immense, and at the echoing thunder of the machinery, we ducked, convinced it was to end there. But there was
no German rifle at our neck, no polished boots on the factory
floor. It was, as I said, simply an error. A few turns of a wrench,
a tightened bolt, and we set to work again.

Aubrion walked over to the linotypists' seats, standing nearly
on top of them as they labored. They kept looking up at him
with sweat and grimaces on their faces, but my dear friend Aubrion did not notice, or chose not to.

"For God's sake, Marc," said Noël, after this had grown in-
tolerable, "give them some room to breathe!"

So Aubrion gave them some room to breathe: half a meter, at
his most generous. There were two of them working their bleeding hands and chipped fingernails. I read their names in *Le Soir*
after they were caught: Pierre Ballancourt, the fellow on Aubrion's left, had worked closely with Noël for years, and Julien
Oorlinckx, the one on his right, was a typesetter renowned for
his calligraphy. Even though they moved quickly—they were, as
I said, the best of their age—we felt caged and impatient. Noël
and Wellens paced; Tarcovich, who had finally joined us, balled
up some scrap paper and tossed it against a wall; I drew shapes on
the dust on a window; Victor rolled an empty flask back and forth
between his hands; Aubrion had to take a walk, lest he combust.

I recall, from that time, that four roads converged in the parking lot of Wellens's factory; Aubrion picked the gentlest and followed it through downtown Enghien. I tailed him from a distance,
my desire to be close to him warring with his obvious need for
privacy. Though the trappings of the city—the Nazi patrols, the
shivering children—had not changed since the day before, or the
year before, Aubrion walked lightly. I noticed early in the occupation that people walk differently when they are free, and Aubrion walked *this* way, without care for how loud his boots fell
or whether he drew attention to himself. He walked as I did before the war, when I had candy in my pockets and knew nothing.

He stopped near the cemetery at the edge of town, the one in which he'd spoken to David Spiegelman ages before. After a moment's hesitation, he walked among the headstones, holding out his arms as though he were balancing on a tightrope. Aubrion's boots kicked clouds of dirt into the evening. There was a photographic quality to the place—a persistent stillness, a musty, old-book smell on the cool air—that made my scalp tingle. Aubrion did not remember a time when the cemetery didn't frighten him. "Death is for the dead," he used to say. Though we all mocked him for it, I later grew to understand the sentiment. To think about death was to admit defeat; that was how Aubrion felt. He avoided funerals and wakes, believing that if he shunned the company of death, it might return the favor. And if I'd asked how he felt the day we printed *Faux Soir*, when he was standing on tiptoe between the headstones of E. E. Berger and Tessa van Houst, he would have insisted nothing had changed, everything was the same. But Aubrion was a liar, bless him.

When he came to the northernmost edge, Aubrion turned to retrace his steps. As I've mentioned before, my dear Aubrion was not given to sentimentality, and while that was usually true, he broke with tradition that day. Aubrion was thinking, I learned later, of the war's start. He was sitting at a coffeehouse in Flanders when he learned about the new resistance paper, *La Libre Belgique*, worrying over a play he was writing with sixteen possible titles and no first line. Aubrion hadn't the money to buy coffee, but the barman played cards with him, so he let him stay. The FI's new press director, one René Noël, had sent letters to potential contributors for the paper. Though Aubrion had received no such letter, he wasn't about to let a technicality ruin his chances. He showed up to the writers' inaugural meeting with outlines and scribbles and drafts. "René wanted nothing to do with me," Aubrion was fond of saying. It was true. Noël agreed to let the wide-eyed, untidy man contribute only because he wasn't convinced Aubrion could sit still long enough to finish an article. To Noël's astonishment, though, Aubrion was the first of his contributors to turn in an assignment: a brilliant (though odd) exposé on how the Nazis extorted money for their Christmas dances. As Aubrion weaved through the headstones, he remembered, and he laughed, and he thought.

"Peter Jaan," Aubrion read, kneeling by a modest gravestone. "All that work, and Peter the Happy Citizen has been dead the entire time!" But what did it mean, that Peter had died? Aubrion knew nothing of this man, of anyone buried here, but if he wanted—if he was curious—he could walk to the records office and hold Peter Jaan's entire life in his hands. If he cared to do it, Aubrion could excavate the man's every disappointment, his children, his schooling, he could know the day of his birth and the time of his death, he could rebuild Peter's friendships from old journal entries and newspaper clippings, he'd know which mates he'd feuded with, he'd know Peter's secret loves, he'd know how much money the fellow made and whether he was satisfied with it, whether he'd tried to work other jobs and failed, or whether he was content in what he did, and if Aubrion wished it, he could stitch together the man's tastes from old ledgers and grocery lists and pocketbooks, what kind of wine he liked, whether he was a beer man instead—he could have all of it, he could resurrect this man, he could know everything Peter Jaan put on this earth before leaving it. And so, Aubrion wondered, what did it mean that Peter had died? He was no longer moving, but he still breathed; his body had gone, but his story lingered. And so, Aubrion no longer feared the graveyard. A graveyard was a bookshelf; a story was a beginning and an end.

It was growing late, Aubrion realized, and they'd want him back at the factory. He bid Peter Jaan goodbye, touching his lips to the damp stone; he turned to wave at all the others. Then he returned to the thin, dusty road, tightrope-walking among the dead.

LAST DAY TO PRINT
EVENING

The Pyromaniac

I WALKED BACK to the factory to wander among the machines. The expansiveness of the place—and the people, and the huffing machines—threatened to overwhelm me. Linotype machines, if you've ever seen one, are hulking, towering, cobbled-together things. They look, at first glance, like they should not be able to do anything, let alone the delicate work they *are* capable of doing. When I first saw one, I mistook it for a pile of tinkerer's scraps.

I found Noël staring absently at a printing press and shouted over the noise, "Can I trouble you with a question?" I said.

"I think I'd welcome the distraction," said Noël.

"How does the linotype machine work?"

Smiling, Noël beckoned me over. "It consists of four important parts," Noël explained, pointing. "The keyboard, magazine, casting mechanism, and distribution mechanism. See, the operators are pressing keys on their keyboards, and that horrible sound you hear is the matrices being released from the magazine channel. Each matrix is a piece of metal with a character in it, like a letter or a period or a comma, that corresponds with the characters on their keyboards."

"So, if they type a *K*, a *K* matrix is released."

"Very good, Gamin. Once they've finished a line of text, the corresponding line of matrices is sent over to a casting unit, where lead is injected into the mold. When *that's* done, the slug—that's what we call the piece, you see, after the injection is done—the slug is put into a tray. The original matrices are returned to the elevators where they came from. Look here."

Noël led me behind the linotype machines, where a woman was holding a tray of these matrices: squarish pieces of metal that were flat on three sides and toothed on the fourth. She laid the pieces out across a machine. The machine in question looked like a metal table, save for the crank mechanism in the belly, the rollers (like rolling pins, only massive and without handles) jutting out of one side, and the chunky nuts and bolts holding everything together. Noting my interest, the woman smiled at me.

"Hello, madame." Noël gave an apologetic wave. "I do hope we are not bothering you. I'm just showing the lad how it all works."

"No bother," she said.

Ferdinand Wellens materialized, looking a tad disheveled, but excited—God, I had never seen anyone so excited. "She is one of the best we have," he told us. "One of the best in Europe, no doubt. In the world! No one finer than she."

"Look here, Gamin," continued Noël. "This is the proofing area. She is locking the slugs into what is called a bed press, to print a draft of whatever line our friends typed out."

"Is this the final thing?"

"The final copy of the paper? No, not at all. As I said, it's only a draft. If there are any errors, the slug must go back to the linotypists and be recast."

"If there are no errors?"

"The slug is sent to the presses."

"It seems like a good deal of work, monsieur."

Noël and the woman laughed. "That's because it is a good deal of work, Gamin. Come, let me show you the presses."

"Oh, I've seen presses before, monsieur."

"These are much larger and more complicated than our presses."

He did show me the presses—all twenty-seven. And then it was back to the linotypists. Ballancourt had made another error, and as I watched, he quickly ran his fingers down the first two columns of the keyboard, typing ETAOIN SHRDLU to finish the line and start over. Noël told me that the letters on the linotype machine were arranged by letter frequency, so the most common letters—*ETAOIN* and *SHRDLU*—occupied the left-hand columns.

After that, I grew bored, and I wondered why the devil Noël was subjecting me to every sight and small wonder the factory had to offer. I now know: René Noël was trying to instill in me the idea that everyone in that factory was culpable. Think of it. *I* was culpable. The lads who brought Oorlinckx and Ballancourt sandwiches and beer after six hours of work—they were culpable. Producing a newspaper was not a one-man job, or even a hundred-man job. It was a breathless undertaking that required so many willing traitors.

HITTING THE STANDS
BARELY MORNING

The Jester

AUBRION WANTED TO scream at someone, perhaps him-self. He held himself rigidly, pacing the factory, opening and closing his hands. Aubrion's lungs felt leaden with the smell of oil and paper; he was breathing twice as fast as he usually did, though whether that was because of the quality of the air or his emotional state, he could not say. You must understand that Aubrion had been so occupied—so obsessed—with this paper for weeks, that it had become everything to him, his first wish and last wish and his only love, and now he'd handed it off to someone else. He was not a linotypist. He did not know how to calibrate distribution mechanisms. He could not fix broken machines. He had some working knowledge of printing presses, but only enough to get in the way. Aubrion's sole task until the paper's completion was to remain out of sight. The effort of not-doing must have been unbearable.

A lad brought him a cheese sandwich. Though he accepted it, Aubrion did not eat. He eventually handed it to me.

"You just refused your last meal." Smirking, Tarcovich punched Aubrion's shoulder.

Aubrion rubbed his eyes. "When did you get here?"

"Now."

"I thought you were with—"

"I was."

"Christ, what time is it?" said Aubrion.

"You have a watch."

"My eyes hurt too much to look at it."

"Two watches, in fact."

"And my brain hurts too much to remember which is the one that works."

"It's nearly three."

"In the afternoon?"

"In the morning, Marc."

"Already?" Aubrion listened to the groans of machinery. The curfew had hushed the world outside the factory, and exhaustion had quieted those inside. Only the languid creaks and grunts of well-oiled machines remained. He closed his eyes. "Did you know," said Aubrion, opening his eyes, "that most people die around now?"

"Around the time they decide to hoodwink the Gestapo? Yes, I did know that."

"No, no, at three in the morning. I knew a physician who used to watch all the worst plays, as I did. Really an interesting fellow. He told me he always sat with his patients until three in the morning, on the dot. If they made it to four, he said—well, that was it for them. The worst was over. But few of them ever did. They were fine at one, fine at two, but when three came along—" Aubrion put his thumb down. "Three was the axe-man."

Lada twirled an unlit cigarette. "Wellens says they're printing the last of the papers. He asked for you. A final inspection, or some nonsense. As though we have time at all to be choosy."

"How did you…" Aubrion let the sentence fade, then tried again. "How did you leave things with Grandjean?"

Tarcovich smiled. "I left things." Her cigarette broke in her hands. "We should go."

We'd all gathered around a printing press. Noël and Wellens were talking softly while Victor milled about nearby. When Wellens saw Aubrion approach, he brightened.

"Monsieur Aubrion!" he said, and before Aubrion had any say in the matter, the businessman had pressed him into an awkward hug. Unsure what else to do, Aubrion took a cue from the king and surrendered to the embrace. Wellens stepped back, grinning. "I am overcome, sir. I read your paper in its entirety."

"You did?" Aubrion said, dumbly.

"Yes! My God, my God, a finer piece of *zwanze* has never been produced, not in all my days. Look there. We are nearly finished with the last copy."

Aubrion steered his numb body toward the printing press. As he looked on, one copy, and then another, and then another, and then the last—four of them—separate copies, identical—each was ejected from the mouth of the thing. They rested together, like famished lovers, in the belly of the press. Aubrion slid one of the papers out of the machine; it took two tries, for his fingers were oversized, his body cold. He held it as though he'd never held a newspaper before, for the body in his hands was new, and he'd not yet learned its secrets. But then it came back to him, that familiar rhythm. Newspapers have a heartbeat; that's what Aubrion always used to say. Words have a pulse. And this paper—its heart had just started beating. The paper felt eager and fresh in his hands, the way young newspapers always did. Except that Aubrion had always read other people's newspapers, other people's books, pamphlets, leaflets, other people's posters, other people's magazines, their poetry, fiction, journals, other people's articles, other people's words, and these words were his, *his*, they belonged to him. Aubrion unfolded the paper with a *snap*, releasing the smell of ink. Oorlinckx and Ballancourt and that woman with the matrices—they'd done their jobs well. The text was even, the photographs sharp.

He flipped through the paper, searching for imperfections. The stamp on the front, to the right of the title—forty-eight cents for a copy—was a bit grainy. But Aubrion liked it. It was charming, like a bucktooth on a child. And the typeface of the title, *that* was good: brash and monumental, the way Aubrion wanted it. Satisfied with the look of the paper, he started to read. It was stuff he'd read before, of course; stuff he had memorized by now. He'd written it: he and his pen had agonized over it. But it was somehow new again, funny again. Aubrion laughed at the photograph of Hitler (the poor man had not wanted that!). He smiled at the editorials, the obituaries. He stood in the middle of the factory—I remember standing behind him, watching his shoulders tremble with laughter—and read it cover to cover, the way Peter the Happy Citizen might read it tomorrow after a long day at work. I have seen small beauties and great wonders all across this earth, but the shape of his back and neck and the paper in his hands are the most precious things I own. I watched him for ages, memorizing everything. And then Marc Aubrion folded his copy of *Faux Soir*, once across the top, once across the middle, and he looked at us with the eye of a man who'd seen God, or who'd created Him.

HITTING THE STANDS
MORNING

The Dybbuk

SOMEONE HAD TUCKED the newspaper under Wolff's door while he slept. A quarter of the paper was still trapped beneath the wood, so the *Gruppenführer* could see only part of the title, just *La Libre*, printed in a wavering typeface. He looked down at it. The printers would be working on the paper all through the night—that's what Manning had told him. And yet here it was already, sticking out from under his door. The *Gruppenführer* picked it up and held it away from his body, like it might burst into flames at the slightest provocation. He knew he should feel grateful the printers worked so quickly, proud the Reich was capable of such a feat, but the text was slightly lopsided, and some of the photographs had not come out well, and neither the printers nor the typesetters truly cared about what they were doing with their hands. There were no architects in the Reich, only builders.

He unfolded *La Libre Belgique*. This was the propaganda bomb of which he'd dreamed for years. But he felt nothing. It was far worse: he felt incomplete. Wolff considered summoning Spiegelman; for all his faults, Spiegelman had a competent eye, and the man was a craftsman. But summoning him would have been crassly unprofessional. And so August Wolff reviewed the paper alone. When he was done, he sent for Manning.

Normally punctual, even aggressively so, Manning arrived nearly thirty minutes after Wolff had sent for him. He knocked, then entered without waiting for the *Gruppenführer*'s permission. Breathing hard, he took the seat across from Wolff, then helped himself to a drink.

"Manning," said Wolff, with a nervous smile, "it's hardly ten in the morning."

"Is it?" Manning drank, smoothed his hair. "I beg your pardon, *Gruppenführer*. It has been a rather long night." He glanced behind him, hesitating. "There are rumors Himmler is about to conduct a comprehensive review of our records. Do you recall the last time that happened? He means to look at *everything*. At least, that was what he did last time. Communiques, notes, drafts, letters, personal diaries—"

Wolff thought of his memos, the thick folder at his elbow. "How interesting." His documents were cold and meticulous— and not handwritten. He had nothing Himmler could pick apart. "That should not be too much of an ordeal."

"It should not, no," said Manning, slightly defensive.

"Have you seen this?" Wolff tapped *La Libre Belgique*.

"The final version? No, I haven't had a moment."

Wolff slid the paper over to Manning, whose eyes moved across the first page.

"This is—" Manning shook his head, laughing. "This is excellent. I can hardly believe it." He turned the page. "It's even better than I thought it could be."

"A propaganda bomb for the ages."

"Yes, yes."

"I haven't yet met with Himmler, but I heard he's seen the draft and thinks highly of it. Goebbels, as well."

"The *Fuhrer* will adore it."

"I am not so self-important as to believe that the *Fuhrer* will read it," said Wolff.

"When are we planning to deploy it?" asked Manning.

"Our printers should have thirty thousand copies by this evening."

"Why stop at thirty thousand?"

"We are starting at thirty thousand," said Wolff. "The timing must be *just* so."

"This is unlike anything I've seen before." Shaking his head, Manning folded up the paper. "It's too bad Monsieur Aubrion will be living out his retirement in Fort Breendonk."

"I have been thinking about that." Wolff's sock had slipped down into his boot. He rubbed his leg, uncomfortable. "I'm going to ask for approval to offer him a position. Somewhat like what we've done with Spiegelman." Despite what Wolff had told Spiegelman, the *Gruppenführer* could not cast Aubrion aside after what he had done. It would be some time before he informed Spiegelman of his decision. Spiegelman needed to understand his pain and fear, to sit with it for a time. Pain and fear would turn his loyalty to iron. "Aubrion won't have a rank or a title," said Wolff, "and we will not pay him, but he'll have immunity and a place to stay."

"Do you think he'll agree to it?"

"Aubrion?"

"Yes."

Wolff played with his pen. "I can't decide," he said, truthfully. "Marc Aubrion is a singular character."

"He would have to be." Manning gestured at *La Libre Belgique*.

"And a selfish one, I believe. But I cannot decide *how* selfish he is. Enough to live for his work, or to die for it? Only Aubrion can tell us that."

HITTING THE STANDS
EARLY AFTERNOON

The Pyromaniac

FROM MY RECONNAISSANCE EFFORTS, I knew an abandoned ice cream stand lay on its side across from the *Le Soir* print factories. I ran the distance, just six blocks from Wellens's factory, and sheltered in the remains of the stand. The umbrella, faded to a paltry green, kept the rain off. I checked the wristwatch René Noël had given me, oversized on my arm. It was noon. I was not to set off the bombs until three thirty. But I'd thought to arrive early in case someone had discovered the bombs Nicolas and I made and removed them from the dumpster, or decided to park the vans elsewhere, or had placed guards around the buildings—none of which had occurred. To be honest, I was somewhat disappointed. In the absence of obstacles, I was forced to sit and wait.

I settled under the ice cream stand, pulling my battered coat over my face. I was shivering, not from the cold, but from the tremendousness of it all. It was not quite fear, you understand, but not innocent enough for excitement; this was an animal

I'd never met before. Rubbing my hands against my thighs to warm them up, I tried to focus on what was ahead. Before I'd left that morning, Aubrion and Noël had gone over my orders.

"At three thirty sharp," said Noël, "when the vans are loaded with papers, but they haven't yet left—"

"That is when you strike," said Aubrion.

"Remember, *Le Soir* hits newsstands at four o'clock, so the vans will be gone by then."

"He knows that, René."

"I am just reminding him."

"He used to sell the damned things, remember?"

"I am just reminding him!"

"Don't talk about the bloody lad like he's not there," Tarcovich called to them, talking about the bloody lad as though I were not there.

"Is this clear, Gamin?" asked Noël.

I nodded, too quickly. "Yes, monsieur."

"You can't strike too early, or the workers will not have finished loading, and you won't destroy enough of their papers," he continued.

"But you can't be too late, or the vans will take off before you have a chance to hit them," said Aubrion.

"Until you are ready," said Noël, "stay out of sight. If you are caught, it's all over."

"He won't be caught." Aubrion ruffled my hair. "Gamin is too good for that."

I'd puffed out my chest, trying to look every inch too good for that. In truth, I was not so confident. *Le Soir*, if you recall, was the most important Nazi propaganda mouthpiece in Belgium, the largest collaborationist paper in the country. The Nazi street patrols grew to twice their size while *Le Soir* was being loaded and delivered, and did not thin out again until nightfall. In other words, I was to bomb the vans carrying the newspaper the Germans valued most while the Germans were at their strongest. This is not the retrospection of an old woman. Though I was inexperienced in matters of planning and strategy, I knew these things *then*, too. Of course, I also knew that if I were caught, the *Faux Soir* project would not die instantly. The RAF could still bomb Belgium; the afternoon was young. And though our ranks had thinned, Noël could still bring in foot soldiers to stall *Le Soir*, if need be. On a less pragmatic level, though, I did not want to die. If the Germans caught me with a bomb in my fist, I would be shot. My youth would not spare me. I wish to God I could tell you that I did not entertain the thought of fleeing. No one would have known; if the bombs had failed to go off, Aubrion would simply have assumed that I'd fallen. But my thoughts turned also to the evils I'd done, the people I'd harmed, Leon and Nicolas and the fires, and I needed to do this mad thing more than I needed to live. That is the truth of it.

I closed my eyes, then shook myself, terrified I'd fall asleep. The rain had stopped, but the taste of it still hung in the air. I stuck out my tongue. Somewhere, a baby was crying. Perhaps I would leave my shelter briefly to steal a pastry or a bit of bread. That would be unwise, I knew. But I was bored, and hungry, and it was starting to rain again. And besides, it was a good day for unwise decisions.

The Gastromancer

The communications officers were beginning to think Spiegelman liked them. He'd gone into the office no fewer than twelve times that morning, and on the eighth pass, he'd heard their cruel whispering about that little queer and his eye for men with nimble fingers. Spiegelman's face was still flushed with the encounter. He paced the hall outside the communications room, cursing his misfortune. It had been two days now, and Spiegelman had heard no indication that the Royal Air Force was mobilizing. "No radio traffic?" he'd asked the comms offi-cers. "None," they'd said, snickering. "Are you tapped into the frequency that RAF pilots use to communicate? Are you mon-itoring government frequencies, as well? Churchill's office?"

"We've heard nothing." Again, the nudges and downward glances. "Why the sudden interest?"

Spiegelman had a draft of another letter, something from Churchill, that he was thinking of sending. But it could be too much. That was the risk. He stopped pacing, resting his head against the wall. David Spiegelman did not have the constitu-tion for waiting. He'd had a bad stomach since he was a boy. Every year, after his final examinations, there'd been a two-week period in which Spiegelman could not eat, could not sleep, and passed most of his time in the latrine or on his bed-room floor. His mother used to shake her head; "Have a bit of broth, David." Ruth Spiegelman never made soup, always in-sisted on trying her mother's recipes instead—huge, meaty por-tions, overcooked—except when David fell ill. Then there was soup everywhere. He'd quarantine himself in his bedroom just to be rid of the damn stuff.

Holding his stomach, Spiegelman dragged himself back to his quarters. The walk made him feel a tad better, so he was just well enough to truly internalize how unwell he was. After a few tense breaths, he took a pen to his latest draft of Churchill.

MY DEAR COMMANDER HARRIS,

Every moment since the first day of this Great War, I have seen heroic deeds done by heroic men, martyrs who do not dare shrink from that which frightens them. But I have too seen, every day, and will see every day hence, deeds just as great, at times greater, performed by men who do not carry banners, who instead sit be-hind those who lead and give their duties every bit of might the Lord gave them. You are such a man, Commander Harris. Your quiet strength and resolve shall prove an extraordinary lesson for all

*who hear of it. Even now, among the esteemed heads of White-
hall, I am engaged in an endeavor to produce a new propaganda
poster with your likeness upon it and the words "All things come
to those who wait!"*
      WINSTON S. CHURCHILL

Spiegelman could scarcely imagine how enraged Bomber
Harris would be upon learning his identity had been reduced to
"the man who waited." This would gall him beyond anything
even the Germans could do. Spiegelman pocketed the letter and
headed back to the communications room.

The Nazi headquarters, normally the organizational equiva-
lent of a clerk with well-parted hair and a polite cough, were in
disarray. Word of Himmler's impending inspection had spread,
and regardless of whether it was true, the consequences were
visible. Spiegelman, for one, doubted it was true. Over the years,
Himmler, Goebbels and Hitler had taken to whispering news
of "surprise" inspections or "loyalty checks" into their ranks.
The Germans rarely had the time or resources to inspect things
as often as they wanted, but these whispers had a way of revealing the disloyal anyway. Those who panicked were singled out
for interrogation. And those who fled were hunted down and
shot. Spiegelman dodged a frantic clerk who carried an armful
of clipboards. "Pardon me," the clerk said, forgetting to switch
from Flemish to German.

Spiegelman had timed his entry well. The communications
officers had left for their midday break. Though at least one
of them was supposed to remain behind at all times, the Nazi
headquarters in Enghien did not receive many important communiques, so they rarely abided by that protocol. Spiegelman
slipped into the office and closed the door behind him. He
spent a few minutes locating the codebook, which someone
had moved to behind a row of books, on a bottom shelf. "Got
you," he muttered, opening it to the relevant page. Spiegelman

flipped through the book, rubbing at his aching stomach. His hands shook as he translated his letter into the dots and lines of the telex tape. It was slow work, for he did not have code memorized, and had to rely on the ragged codebook. Heart pounding, Spiegelman keyed in the last of the letter and sent it off.

Something *clicked*: the door. Though the room was small, the *click* sounded far away, like a shout trailing after a man who'd fallen from a cliff.

And then there was a rush of air as someone opened it—someone *opened* the door—they opened it to find David Spiegelman at the telex, where David Spiegelman was not supposed to be. Spiegelman's heart stopped. He did not turn around, not immediately, because he knew what would happen if he turned around, and he was not yet ready. Aubrion still needed him; his brother and grandmother were not ready for him.

"Herr Spiegelman."

David Spiegelman turned around. For the second time in his life, August Wolff was pointing a gun at him.

The Jester

Fifty thousand newspapers, Aubrion soon realized, took up a great deal of space: to be exact, a dozen of Wellens's delivery vans, one extra van he had to borrow from his brother, the entire factory floor, and three enormous metal containers (each around nine feet high and six feet deep). Ferdinand Wellens's men loaded copies of *Faux Soir* into the delivery vans and then dumped the rest into the containers, where they would remain until the second and third rounds of distribution. Aubrion supervised—not that they needed his supervision, but Aubrion had nothing else to do, and he wanted to send off *Faux Soir*. He sat on the ground, drawing stick figures in Joseph Beckers's book of *Le Soir* distribution points.

Noël appeared and stood in front of Aubrion until the latter acknowledged him.

"Hello, René," said Aubrion.

Noël pointed at the workmen. "You could help them, you know."

"So could you."

"But I am not the one watching them sweat and toil over our paper."

"And I *am* the one watching them, which means I'm one step closer to helping them than you are."

Noël sighed. His clothes, Aubrion noted, were spattered in grease.

"What have you been fixing?" asked Aubrion.

"Oh." Noël wiped, futilely, at his shirt. "One of the linotype machines broke last night. I thought I'd lend a hand, since we were the cause of it."

"René Noël. A good Samaritan to the very last. Does that ever strike you as odd? That we refer to people that way, as good Samaritans? It implies that all the others—every single other Samaritan who ever lived a day on Earth—are bad. That's not very Christian-like, now, is it?"

"Since when do you care about being Christian-like?" Noël asked, in the tone of a man who did not wish to know, but who was about to find out anyway.

"This is precisely why I do not. Where is Martin? I'm certain he has an opinion."

"I think the poor fellow had an episode. He's been sparse."

"I beg your pardon for interrupting what sounds like a vitally important conversation," said Tarcovich, who was somehow impeccably made-up, "but I think I'm going to leave. If I don't, I think I'm going to run mad."

Noël nodded. "I understand. The waiting is terrible."

"Where will you go?" asked Aubrion.

"You'll remain in Enghien?" said Noël.

"No point in leaving."

"Do you have family here? I can't recall."

Tarcovich looked down, uncharacteristically shy. "I am trying to say goodbye to them right now, in fact. Be a good man and don't ruin it, René."

Aubrion got up, suddenly desperate for Lada to stay. "Surely you know people who—"

"I made my choice, Marc." Tarcovich's smile fluttered like moth wings. "I'll be fine, I promise."

"Where will you go?" repeated Noël.

"I used to frequent an old coffeehouse, years before the war. It's a cheap place, but the food is good, and the barman runs the tap every hour of the day. Apparently there's a lad with a newsstand right across from it—and I see no reason why I shouldn't have a front row seat."

HITTING THE STANDS
AFTERNOON

The Pyromaniac

AROUND TWO HOURS into my wait, I heard a shout from the streets. I remember that it startled me, and I suppose I must have dozed off. But I thought nothing of it, really, until someone echoed the shout. Both voices were hoarse from cigarettes and coal, but shrill with youth. I peered over the side of the ice cream cart.

A crowd of boys was approaching. They were lads I knew, Michael and Thomas and Jean, and Nicolas, twisting Leon's cap in his hand. Some carried sticks, others had crowbars, a few had stones, and Thomas had a pistol. Jean locked eyes with me.

"There!" he said. "She's over there! I seen her."

Saw, I wanted to correct him—my last rational thought before I started to panic. I am embarrassed to say so now, but the possibility that these boys might try to avenge Leon had never occurred to me. I huddled beneath the remains of the ice cream cart. My options were few. The boys clearly intended to do me harm, and if they got too close to the cart, I could make a scene, perhaps rouse the concerns of passersby. But the truth was—and is—that people don't care about lads with torn trousers and cut-up knees. They would likely ignore my cries. The other option was that I could run, and I might get away, but it wouldn't be like outrunning Germans. These boys fought and stole. They were alive because they could run faster and longer than anyone else. I'd run, and I would not get very far. After surveying these unattractive possibilities, I leapt over the cart and sprinted toward the factories.

"After her!" someone said.

I don't know why I did not hear it before, but I heard it now: *her.* I had only a second to wonder how the devil they found out, risking a glance behind me. The kids drew nearer with every step. Jean and Thomas were in the lead. Was Thomas's pistol loaded? That seemed impossible. He couldn't have afforded bullets. But he wouldn't have brought an *unloaded* pistol, now, would he? I pushed myself faster, scarcely breathing.

What I remember about this experience, most viscerally, is the stillness. The world had frozen. No one *saw* us. Shopkeepers went about their business, mothers quieted their infants, beggars held out their hands, dead-eyed refugees huddled in doorways. I was running through an abandoned photograph on the floor of the blue-doored building.

Then, of course, the boys caught up to me. Not thinking, I ran into the parking lot of the *Le Soir* factories. It was still early, so the workers hadn't begun loading the paper into the vans. Barbed wire fences surrounded the lot, and I did not have the time to climb them; they probably would have cut up my legs and hands anyway. As Thomas and the others advanced on me, I backed up against one of the fences. Even now, I can feel the teeth of the barbed wire and smell the rust.

When Nicolas and I were in the blue-doored building, I realized—why was I remembering it now?—I got up to relieve myself. I thought Nicolas was asleep. He must not have been.

And now these boys knew they had been taking orders from a girl. I am sure I do not have to tell you that in the minds of men, there is no deception more perverse.

"Hey, lads," I said, forcing a smile, "what's all this about?"

"We know what you done, Gamin." Thomas hefted his pistol. "What you *are*, too. No sense hiding it."

"Please, Gamin." Nicolas stepped forward, his eyes haunted. "I tried to tell 'em not to, but they had their minds set on it."

"Not to do what?" I stuffed my shaking hands into my pockets, partially so the boys could not see how scared I was, partially to see whether I had anything at my disposal. I cursed myself for abandoning my glass knife in the blue-doored photography lab. For once, my mischievous pockets were empty, save a few stray matches.

"We heard what happened to Leon," said Jean, slapping a crowbar against his palm. "You let him die. You liar, you let him die."

"I was not even *there* when he died. You want to know what happened to Leon? Ask Nicolas. It was him who was there, not me."

Nicolas shrank away from the eyes of his friends. "It was him who gave the orders—*her*, I mean! She tricked us all, said it would be easy. That's what Leon told me, too. But then I saw things, while we was together, she and me, and it's not like what she said at all—"

"Shut *up*, Nicolas," I said.

"You been hiding something, haven't you?" said Thomas, not quite a man, but leering like one.

"What are you going to do, Tom?" My ears pounded in time with my heart. "You're going to shoot me?"

"I might."

"And then what?"

"And then we'll see."

"You'll see nothing. The Germans hear a pistol, and they come running."

"I might not, if you show us what you been hiding."

I would realize, much later, what I should have said, what René Noël or Marc Aubrion would have said. "You're smarter than that, Tom. Come, let's work something out together. I have stuff you want. Let's cut a deal." That would have been Noël. Or: "We've known each other since the start of all this mess. I'll buy you a drink, and we'll talk about a job we can all do, something to make it up to you." That would have been Aubrion. But I was not thinking. A desperation had turned my bones to ash: I had to make off with the bombs *now*, or all was lost. I started to move toward the dumpster.

"Oh, come off it." Nicolas was weeping. "We know there aren't no bullets in that gun."

"Leon was my best mate," said Michael.

"We liked Leon just fine," said Nicolas, "but Gamin can't do nothing to bring him back."

I sidled closer to the dumpster. The boys did not notice. I was less than a meter from it.

"What's gotten into you?" Thomas raised his pistol as though he were about to strike Nicolas. "I never took you for a coward."

"One of us already got hurt! I don't see why another one of us has to."

"Because *she's* the cause of it." Michael jabbed a thumb in my direction.

Moving swiftly—like an animal, like my parents running from the trampling hordes in Toulouse—I scaled a pile of barrels near the dumpster. When I reached the topmost barrel, I leapt into the dumpster itself. I fell, suffocating in the stench. Outside, the boys were shouting. I found the sack of bombs, tossed it over my shoulder, and climbed out of the dumpster.

They went quiet when they saw me, perhaps wondering what on earth I'd fetched from the trash. I meant to use their confusion to my advantage, to make a run for it while they were still puzzling over what I had. And I tried, I swear to you, I tried. The blood pounded in my body as I started to run. But they ran after me, and my foot caught on something in the pavement, and I fell, I fell, dropping the sack as I tumbled to my knees.

The pain disappeared somewhere inside my body. I could hear the lads behind me, putting their hands on the bombs that Nicolas and I had made, the bombs that Leon died for, the bombs for Aubrion and *Faux Soir*. My fear slowed the world to an underwater pace. These boys were not fools. They knew what they had, what I'd had. A few matches had fallen from my pockets. I lifted my head to see Thomas striking a match, lighting the mouth of the pipe bomb, curling his arm like a javelin-thrower. I watched the gentle arc of the bomb as he threw it. The red in my eyes grew to multitudes.

The Jester

The vans drove away from Wellens's factory in single file, all thirteen of them, painted green like our military vans but stouter in the middle. They followed each other out of the parking lot and into the streets, parting a quarter mile away: to follow the road to Brussels, or to Flanders, or a hundred other places Joseph Beckers had listed in his book. Aubrion took in these facts clinically, like he was making a list based on secondhand information, not observing this event as it happened. When the vans were no longer in sight, he took a small, chipped bottle of something, maybe whiskey, from his pocket. Most people would have said a prayer, maybe, but Marc Aubrion didn't know any prayers. He was raised Catholic, meaning his parents walked him to a schoolhouse every Sunday where he snuck out a window to play marbles with the other boys. "For Theo Mullier," he whispered. And besides, Mullier (an atheist since he was a lad) would not have appreciated a Catholic prayer. Aubrion, who was pressed for time and out of options, recited one of the only lines of literature he'd committed to memory. It seemed appropriate. *"Mourir doit sacrément être une belle aventure."* Aubrion poured a drop of whiskey into the earth, and then sat on the ground and wept.

After a time, Noël, who had disappeared so Aubrion could sort through himself in peace, ran up to him. Even Aubrion, never a subtle figure, could see panic in the director's eyes.

"René?" Aubrion stood up, a tad dizzy. "What's gone on?"

"There's been a problem," he said.

"René, you're mad. I just saw the vans drive off."

"I didn't say there was a problem with the vans."

"You are not making any sense."

"I received word from one of our agents." René held on to Aubrion's shoulder, for support, it seemed. "Gamin set off the bombs."

Aubrion's body grew cold. "It's too early. We told him not to do it until three thirty."

"Something must have happened."

"Christ, we have to go—"

"We can't, Marc. You know that as well as I."

Aubrion jerked away from Noël. "We can't simply sit by while Gamin is in danger."

"There is no indication Gamin was harmed, at least according to our agent. And he did manage to cripple at least four of the delivery vans."

"Out of how many?"

"Seventeen."

"That is good, isn't it? *Le Soir* will not reach some of the newsstands at all."

"Not for a while, no."

"And the Germans will investigate," said Aubrion. "They will probably put a halt to all newspaper deliveries until they've cleared the area. That will delay everything, won't it?"

"Only a little. Here is the real problem—because of Gamin's timing, some newsstands will receive both *Faux Soir* and *Le Soir*, perhaps in rapid succession." Noël sighed, rubbing his eyes. "It's not good, Marc. It is not good at all. People will be spooked."

"They'll think it's some kind of damned loyalty test."

"Or they will know it is the FI. Whatever they believe, it will keep them from buying our paper—either of the papers, actually."

"What about the RAF?" said Aubrion, his voice wavering.

Noël's eyes softened. "They aren't coming, Marc."

Aubrion looked up at the pallid sky, white like arsenic skin. "Well," he said after a pause. "I suppose it was a long shot anyway."

Ferdinand Wellens interrupted them with a wave. He strutted across the parking lot, grinning through his beard. "How goes it, gentlemen?" he said.

"Not well, Monsieur Wellens," said Noël. He explained what was amiss.

Wellens, now considerably paler, said: "You know, Monsieur Noël, I have grown especially fond of you and yours since the beginning of this endeavor." He was oddly quiet. "I'll admit, I had my doubts, at the start of it all. I work for profit, and I saw no profit in this. But I've come to admire you, monsieur. You lot are doing things no one dares to do." Wellens's back straightened. "What I mean to say is that if there is anything you need—anything at all, to help you solve this problem—well, monsieur, you shall have it."

"Thank you, Monsieur Wellens," said Noël. "Your kindness is certainly appreciated. The larger problem here, I'm afraid, is that *we* do not know how to solve our problem. I suppose we can stop the vans—"

"We are not stopping the vans," said Aubrion.

"I had a feeling you would say that. It's probably not possible anyway." Noël sighed again. "I'm nearly terrified to ask, Marc, but do you have any ideas?"

Aubrion thought. "That depends," he said, "on whether you have any loose change."

The Professor

As the factory quieted and the workers put their machines to bed, Victor waited for the last van to leave. It rattled off, a trail of exhaust following it to the edge of town. He'd expected some great realization at the end of it all, some acknowledgment that he'd done his job well. It would not come. Any feeling about his work—any potential satisfaction—sat hollow in Victor's stomach. As a lad, Victor used to get a peculiar sensation every Sunday before church, as though the week's peccadillos had built a tremendous structure inside his soul. He felt that way now. The professor snuck out while the others were occupied and took a cab into town.

As Wolff instructed, Victor had brought all his belongings to an empty apartment in a secluded part of town. The apartment once belonged to a bookbinder, who fell out of favor with the Germans when he secured a contract with an American publishing company. Using the key Wolff had provided him, Victor let himself into the apartment. He walked the length and width of the place, as was his custom, to ensure no one was hiding inside. Though he did not *distrust* Wolff, he did not trust him, either. Killing Victor would solve problems.

Victor checked his watch. He had about six minutes of privacy. The professor lit a candle and set it atop one of his trunks. The apartment was small, and soon bathed in the smell of burning fat. He knelt before the candle with his hands clasped. Victor's grandfather taught him the Lord's Prayer when he was a boy. The words tasted like chocolate then; they tasted of whiskey now. "O, Heavenly Father," Victor murmured, "guide me with Your light." Smoke from the candle stung his eyes.

But Victor, whose students used to mock him for talking and talking without a moment's rest, could not summon another word. He had not prayed since Auschwitz. Though Victor still believed in God, to be sure, he was convinced He'd gone blind.

The professor was not a young man, and the effort of kneeling—with his back, and his knees—brought sweat to his brow. Still he knelt; perhaps if he kept kneeling, if he did it long enough, a prayer would come to him. His wristwatch ticked. Victor wanted to open his eyes to see how much time he had left, but he could not do so, not until God spoke to him. He cupped his hands, waiting for the words to fall into them.

"Guide me, Lord," he whispered. "Let my hands be Your hands, and my works be Your works, for You have not grown blind—I have."

Someone knocked at the door. "Professor?"

Victor stood up quickly. "Yes, I am coming."

They did not wait for him. The handle turned, and the door opened, emitting four men in uniform. They stood in front of the door with their hands on the butts of their pistols. The candle shone gold in their eyes, covering them with coins for the ferryman.

"Good afternoon, Professor. I am *Leutnant* Claus Huber." The officer clicked his heels together. His face looked as though it had been wiped clean of blemishes and expressions: pale eyebrows, light skin, a thin mouth. "Before we allow you to leave the country, we must inspect your belongings. I trust *Gruppenführer* Wolff has informed you—"

"Yes, I know," said Victor. "I am to take only what can fit into a small cart, plus manservants who will be provided to me."

"Very well. We will begin the inspection." Huber nodded at his men, who went to Victor's belongings with their hands outstretched. "Please stand against the wall, Professor."

"Here?" Victor indicated a spot.

"That's fine, yes. Since you are so very well-informed, I'm sure you know what will happen if we find anything that violates the terms of our agreement." Huber did not wait for Victor to respond. "You will be sent to Fort Breendonk immediately."

The professor had told himself he would close his eyes when it started. But now, he could not. Victor watched the Germans empty his trunks, putting their hands on everything he had. *What are you doing?* Martin's father had asked, seeing the boy at work. Martin had been so focused that he had not seen his father come in; he jumped, his legs hitting the bottom of his father's desk. *Making a treasure map, Papa. See? X marks the spot.* This was not *that* treasure map, but one of the many that came after. The Germans passed it to each other, puzzling over the odd names. Martin Victor's father had been an architect, a man of draft paper and ink, who took great pleasure in drawing maps with his son.

His parents were never rich, but they did well. By Martin's sixteenth year, they could afford to send him to one of the finest schools in Belgium. There, he learned the names of all the cities in the world, their languages, their histories; he traveled across Europe and drew pictures of things he saw and people he met; he made maps. After a year and a half of courses, Victor sold his first atlas. Then the war broke out: the First Great War. Shortly after Victor's eighteenth birthday, his profession was rendered obsolete. Europe had no need for maps any longer. In the apartment, the Nazis cracked open Martin's second atlas, the one that never sold. It was indistinguishable, that book, from the treasure maps Martin had drawn with his father.

A staunch pacifist, Victor was determined to avoid armed service. Weeks after the war broke out, he managed to secure his acceptance to Université Catholique de Louvain, where he studied ministry. The calling was good, but the work bored him. At the war's end, Martin Victor wrote a volume on the sociology of war. Rummaging through his trunk, the Nazi inspectors grew panicked when they found the draft, perhaps convinced they'd stumbled upon top secret FI information. As Claus Huber looked through it, the glory in his eyes faded to disappointment. "It is nothing," he said in German, echoing some of Victor's earliest colleagues.

Sofia Dufort had been one of the staunchest naysayers. Victor's advisor at the university told him that when Sofia first read his book, she pronounced sociology dead on arrival. Set on winning her over, Victor walked into her office unannounced and spent the afternoon making a case for sociology. And three years hence, Martin Victor and Sofia Dufort were married. His wedding ring was humble; it looked even humbler in the gloved hands of the Germans.

His wife Sofia had been ill for months when he received the assignment to Auschwitz. There was another war, and Martin spoke German, had traveled to Switzerland, France, Germany and America, had contacts in Berlin. Of course the *Front de l'Indépendance* sought him out. And of course he accepted. This was a different sort of war, or maybe Victor was a different sort of man. The *Comité de Défense des Juifs* had reported that the Germans were transporting Jews somewhere; Victor was to figure out where the trains went. Sofia begged him not to go—but it was such a simple assignment, and if he distinguished himself, there would be more work. In January, Sofia miscarried their child. She had been certain the child was to be a girl, and they would call her Eliza. "Eliza means Oath to God," Victor had translated. "What is our oath?" And Sofia had smiled and replied, "Don't be daft. It's just a name."

But Victor *had* sworn an oath, in that moment, to accomplish something beautiful—not just great, but beautiful—before he died. In February of 1940, Victor left for Katowice, and then for Auschwitz.

On his seventh day at Auschwitz, he had written a letter to Sofia. *My darling Sofia*, it began. *I will be brief. I do not wish to cause you any more anguish than I must.* According to the FI's records, he did not speak for forty-six hours upon his return to Belgium. *What shall I say to you that might justify what I aim to do?* On the third day, a young doctor who sat by his patient's bed was awakened by Victor's screams. *I have witnessed more sins than I thought the Lord our God would ever permit on His Earth. I am no longer the man you married, your husband, our Eliza's father.* After telling his story, Victor slept with such stillness they'd thought he had died. *Though my love for you is as it was on our wedding night, I feel we must part. Be safe and well, Sofia.*

Victor returned to Sofia with the letter in his pocket, never having mailed it. They used to laugh together, before Auschwitz. They used to cook together. But after, the house was quiet and smelled of forgotten things. Sofa died shortly after Victor's return, and Victor's letter to her remained unread—until now, until the Germans. The Nazis read it quietly, then folded it up without comment.

YESTERDAY

The Scrivener

ELIZA STOOD UP SUDDENLY—*volcanically* was the word Aubrion would have used—as though she'd had an idea that was too great for the world to contain. Her pen clattered to the floor, leaving her notebook friendless on the table. The old woman watched her. Eliza was not as young as Helene had initially believed. But the glint in her eyes and cleft in her chin played tricks. Once upon a time, Aubrion too had seemed ageless.

"That must be it," said Eliza. "My parents told me that was Martin Victor's request. That if either of them ever had a daughter, they would name her Eliza, that they'd help him accomplish something beautiful. But I never knew why."

"Now you do," said Helene.

"Oath to God."

"Or it's just a name."

"Nothing is *just* a name," said Eliza.

Helene smiled. "Indeed."

"I wonder when and how he asked them." Eliza returned to her seat, her forehead wrinkled. She stooped to get her pen.

"In the story, Victor betrays Aubrion and the others. Isn't that what you said?"

"It does seem like it, to be sure."

"He allies with August Wolff—there was that letter, and everything. It doesn't make any sense."

"Doesn't it?"

"You know something. Don't you?"

"I knew a few things."

"What do you know? How could Victor, a traitor, have asked my parents to name their daughter after the child he lost? Why would they listen to him?"

Helene sat back in her chair. She regarded Eliza without moving, a figure of wax and cloth, positioned like a display in the blue-doored museum.

"You never told me," said the old woman, "why you are here."

"I did tell you."

"Then tell me again."

"To write it all down. Don't you see?"

"I don't, no."

"This is the beautiful thing Victor promised to accomplish." Eliza placed her notebook and pen on the floor, so that only *Faux Soir* remained on the table. There, it breathed and took up space. Helene knew not how many copies remained. She wanted to walk the earth in search of them all, gathering them like lost children. The used-book smell was a third person in the room, ancient but bright-eyed. Eliza stopped just short of touching the old newspaper. "You've cared for the story until now, Helene, and you've watched over it, but it isn't yours to keep. The name 'Marc Aubrion' should not die with you."

The old woman's eyes were on the newspaper. "If you had one wish, what would it be?"

"What kind of a question is that?"

"An honest question."

Eliza spoke, the truest thing she had ever said. "I wish that

I could have met them. Marc Aubrion, Martin Victor, Theo Mullier..."

"Gamin."

"Yes. Gamin, too."

"Are you upset that you never got to say goodbye to them?"

"No." Eliza laughed sadly. "I'm upset I never got to say hello."

Helene nodded slowly.

"And besides," Eliza went on, "I've had this story in my family for so long, I had to know whether it was true. It's just..." Her laugh was far younger than Helene had ever been, even when she was Gamin. "This is a really amazing story. I know how that sounds, how juvenile that sounds, but it's how I feel. I had to know whether it was true, any of it."

"What did your parents tell you?" asked Helene.

"To look for Gamin."

"Why?"

"To finish the story. They had a piece of it, and they passed it on to me. I'm here to return it to you." Eliza's laughter seemed to lift a corner of *Faux Soir* so that the paper laughed with her. "But you must finish yours first."

HITTING THE STANDS
EARLY EVENING

The Smuggler

LADA TARCOVICH BOUGHT a large basket of pastries—
two chocolate rolls, one cheese bun, one slice of onion bread, all
warm—and a cup of coffee. People stared. They must have wondered: was she some governor's wife, taking bribes from the Germans? It seemed too unlikely: though she looked put-together,
her clothes were shabby. Smiling at the gawkers, Tarcovich took
her pastries and coffee to a table outside the coffeehouse.

Across the street, a newsboy was setting up his stand. Tarcovich checked her pocket watch. It was a quarter to four: about
fifteen minutes until *Le Soir* was due to go on sale. She settled
into her chair, watching the patched-up workmen queue by
the lad's stand. Bluish smoke from their pipes and cigars formed
halos around the lot of them, framing their defeated shoulders
and tired eyes.

Tarcovich studied their faces over the brim of her mug. She
felt breathless—not in anticipation of what was soon to occur,
but in fear of what might not—and she put down her cup too

hard, nearly shattering the saucer. Perhaps Tarcovich and Aubrion and Noël had misjudged their audience. These were not towering intellectuals. Lada watched one man wipe his nose with the back of his hand, and the back of his hand with his sleeve; the fellow behind him had the dullest face she'd ever seen, as if every bit of intelligence had been erased from his features; the man behind *him* seemed so exhausted he could barely walk; and so on. They bought the paper because their neighbors bought the paper, and they wanted to know who to blame for the bread shortage. Aubrion had worried that his readers would not find the material funny, but there was a chance, Tarcovich knew, they would not even realize it was a joke.

A horn blared. Lada turned around as a van rolled up the street. The driver jumped out, leaving the engine on, and took a stack of papers from the back. Tipping his cap at the newsboy, he deposited the newspapers on the lad's stand. As the driver climbed back into his car, the newsboy waved his thanks and started unwrapping the papers. The smell of ink—like the scent of rain, but sweeter—lightened the air.

That old clock tower in downtown Enghien chimed four times. In the still-life quiet that followed, the first man bought a copy of *Faux Soir.* He handed the newsboy his forty-eight cents, as did the man behind him, and they drifted away from the line. Tarcovich caught bits of their small talk: "—been ill for weeks now—can't remember the last time I saw him at church—his wife is doing fine, I gather—Henrietta saw her and the girls at market two days ago—" Six copies were sold, then eight. The newsboy was working swiftly. "—not certain how his farm's doing these days, what with the taxes—"

The first workman to buy the paper stopped, nudged his companion. Neither spoke. Their fingers traced out words—made adoring laps around the title, the columns on the front page—circled the photograph of Hitler and the American airplanes. Tarcovich's breath locked in her throat. The men looked, for an instant, as though they would throw their papers away. That was the danger: people were paranoid, in those days, always convinced the Nazis were testing them. But they held on to their papers. The workman turned to his friend as though looking for permission to do *something*, and then his friend doubled over and laughed. They both laughed, first quietly and then with abandon. All the while, they snuck guilty glances at the line. One of them made eye contact with another fellow, and a tense, wary second melted into wicked smiles. All across the line, people were gasping, laughing, then tucking the paper under their arms or into their sacks to consume in privacy. It was beautiful. Tarcovich breathed. It was everything.

News spread quickly. People talked; there was little else to do. The newsboy delighted as tens and then dozens of people ran to his stand. When it seemed he would run out of copies, Wellens's van returned to replenish his supply. Tarcovich soon lost count of the number of papers he sold. It was well over a thousand, for she'd stopped tallying at eight hundred and fifty.

At half past six, the crowd thinned. Tarcovich went inside the coffeehouse to buy another round. Upon her return, she found a throng of businessmen had joined the line. Tarcovich sat back with her coffee and her pastry, curious to see how *this* group would respond. Aubrion and Noël had a bet: Aubrion thought the "common man," as he called the workers and the civil servants, would find the paper funnier than the well-to-do, while Noël was betting on the latter. Tarcovich couldn't quite decide where she stood.

Toward the end of the line, a pair of women in cotton trousers were talking quietly. They had swastikas pinned to their lapels, as was required of everyone in the legal profession. One of them paused when she saw Tarcovich, but gave no other indication she recognized her. "*Le Soir*, please," Tarcovich heard, as she'd heard a thousand times that afternoon. Their pins— the swastikas on the women's blouses—were crooked. She felt a tearful smile growing inside her, threatening to break her in half, as Andree Grandjean purchased two copies of *Faux Soir*: one for herself, and one for Lada Tarcovich.

The Pyromaniac

The German response to the explosions was far slower than I'd expected. By the time I heard the first sirens, Jean and the lads had already thrown a half dozen of my pipe bombs into the parking lot behind the *Le Soir* factories. Nazi brigades rarely used sirens to announce their presence, opting instead to shock their victims in their last moments. And so, it took me a while to connect the sirens to what was about to occur: namely, my swift capture and execution.

"There! There!" a commander said in German, pointing at me. His face was apocalyptic with fury. I had hardly moved from where I'd fallen, knocked dizzy from the explosion, but the other boys had disappeared. As the Nazis opened fire, I got up and ran—fell again, jamming my shoulder into the concrete. The Germans could not see me in the smoke—or so I assumed, for I could not see them—and mistook several workers running out of the factory as their targets. They fired everywhere—lost, erratic—and I ran like mad. My shoulder did not hurt until I was halfway down the city block. I screamed at the pain, which radiated up and down my arm like some manner of infestation.

Biting back tears, I swerved down alleys and behind walls. The Germans were famed for their detailed maps of the streets, but maps were lies. I knew the city better than anyone: where to go, where not to go. I ran three blocks away from the factories, then doubled back. While I was fairly certain I'd lost them, I wanted to be sure. An arthritic church, centuries old and nameless, sat behind the factories. I ran into the courtyard and wedged my body into a well, covering myself in dirt and moss. Though I could still hear the sirens, I knew I'd lost them. The Germans would not find me there.

In the safety of my hiding place, I allowed myself to cry. The memory of this—the smell of peat, a faint rumble of thunder— still lives in me. But I cannot say what made me weep. I know I cried for Leon and everyone else who'd died because of me. I cried for failing Aubrion. I was in pain, and I feared for the lives of my family, the loss of my home. But more than anything, I wept for *Faux Soir*. This grand adventure was over. There would be no more schemes, no more capers, no more plots, no more escapes. The stories about it would become legends, and the legends would become myths.

And what would become of me? Where would I go, who would I be? I think many of us, the survivors, felt that way after the war. Those who were alive had to figure out how to live. Those who were dead never had to write the rest of the story.

The Jester

Noël parked his Nash-Kelvinator a block from the largest news-stand in the city, a shop owned by three generations of print-ers. A raucous line of customers snaked out the door, down the street. Aubrion got out of the passenger side of the car, stand-ing back to observe.

What struck him most was their *variety* of emotions. People were, at once, quietly terrified, anxious, curious, excited. Those in the back of the line, who faced a wait of an hour or more, had brought blankets and sandwiches. "Don't spoil it!" they said to the lucky ones who'd already bought a copy. "Keep it to yourself, will you? Give the rest of us a chance." Entire fami-lies joined the line; women swapped recipes; children played. A foreigner who visited Enghien on that particular day might have wondered about this strange holiday.

"Magnificent!" said Aubrion. Seconds after the word escaped him, an unmarked van pulled up.

The driver got out, allowing the engine to idle. He was a large man who looked, to Aubrion's eyes, like a farmhand. Indeed, he unloaded his papers the way one might unload a barrel of hay. The man threw his stack of papers to the ground and reached into the van to grab another. He froze, a cigar falling from his lips.

"Fuck," said Aubrion.

"Christ," said Noël.

His eyes on the queue and his cigar on the pavement, the driver marched into the shop. Aubrion beckoned to Noël. They listened outside the door. The man began shouting: "But I *am* the driver for *Le Soir*. Have been for two years." And then: "What the hell are you going on about? Run and fetch your father, boy. He knows me." Finally: "See what I told you? See what I bloody *told* you? Something odd is happening here."

Those in line began to sense it, too. They murmured to each other, their eyes and feet shifting nervously. "It's a test. A bloody test. I know it." Some of the men had sent their wives and children away. The businessmen, who had the most to lose, were the next to go. As the driver and the shopkeepers argued, the line dwindled to almost nothing.

"Pocket change." Aubrion patted Noël's trousers. The director pushed him away. "René, you said you had pocket change."

"Here, here, steady on." Noël deposited about two francs' worth of coins into Aubrion's hands. Aubrion started toward the shop, but Noël held him back. His eyes were low, his voice tight with fear. "Marc, are you quite sure about this?"

"You must trust me, René."

The would-be customers quieted down, fascinated by a new development. A lanky little man, stubbled, with scarecrow-trousers and wide eyes and handfuls of coins—this man was walking up to the shop. His shirt was too large, but he swaggered like a man dressed in silk. This fellow cleared his throat to get the shopkeepers' attention. Everyone watched.

"Can I help you?" asked the eldest shopkeeper.

"I would like to buy two copies of *Le Soir*."

The oldest shopkeeper glanced at his son, his grandson, and the driver, who looked rather like his lunch had been spoiled. "I am not sure how to put this," said the shopkeeper, "but we are not sure which version of *Le Soir* is the right version."

"I know that," said Aubrion.

"You know which version is the right one?" said the driver.

"No, no. In my mind, they are both the right one."

"How do you mean?" said the shopkeeper.

"They are both for sale, are they not? And that is what matters, isn't it?"

"Then—in that case—which copy would you like, monsieur?"

"As I said, two copies." Aubrion dumped his change on the counter. "One of each."

The Gastromancer

The eye of the pistol flickered between Spiegelman's face and body. Spiegelman guessed that August Wolff had never shot anyone. He gave the order; he did not pull the trigger. His body and the bodies of his victims were demarcated by someone else's gun. It was odd, almost sickening, to see the *Gruppenführer* tremble this way.

"You are under arrest," Wolff said, but he was not accustomed to saying such things, and the words sounded rigid, immobile, like he'd memorized a phrase in another language. The *Gruppenführer* tried again, speaking deliberately. "For treason against the Reich."

"What treason did I commit?" Spiegelman attempted a laugh. The sound was inhuman. "Is it a crime to walk about the base?"

"Why were you using the telex?"

"I was not—"

"Put your hands up, Herr Spiegelman."

Spiegelman complied.

The *Gruppenführer's* shoulders heaved. "I forgave you," he said. "You sinned, and I forgave you. I tried to protect you, don't you see? Your beautiful talent…"

Spiegelman's stomach twisted. In his time of servitude to the Reich, an older statesman once put his cold, clammy hand on Spiegelman's thigh. Wolff's compliment felt no different.

"This is protection?" Spiegelman nodded at Wolff's gun. "This is imprisonment."

"If I'd allowed you to wander free, you would have—"

"So you don't deny it."

"I am not here to defend myself."

"Just to shoot me."

"Keep your hands *up*, Spiegelman." Wolff shook his head, his eyes fraught with tears. A thrill of shock went through Spiegelman's body. "Such a waste. There is nothing I can do for you now, you understand. You will be sent to Fort Breendonk tomorrow, executed before the end of the month."

The reality of his fate had been no secret to David Spiegelman. Still, hearing it aloud—hearing it consummated by Wolff's words—that was something different.

"I am sorry," said the *Gruppenführer*. "I did everything I could, and yet I failed you."

Spiegelman's pulse quickened. "Do not feel sorry for yourself on *my* account. You have an inspection to worry about."

"What do you mean?"

"Himmler's inspection."

Wolff waved the pistol, an awkward shrug. "I have nothing to hide."

Spiegelman's heart was beating, harder and stronger than it

ever had, for Wolff, the *dybbuk,* was his: he belonged to Spiegelman and no one else. "You are a liar, August Wolff."

"What do you mean?" whispered August Wolff. "What have you done?"

"Your memos." Spiegelman went on: "Never a word of truth in them, was there? Never how you *truly* felt about burning those buildings, destroying those books. I know your heart, Wolff—and now Himmler will, too."

The *Gruppenführer* wore the expression of a man who was falling from a great height. "My memos." Wolff mouthed the words.

"I made them honest."

"You rewrote them." The sentence took on a life of its own, the way propaganda did.

"*November 6, —43,*" Spiegelman recited from memory. "*First of what promises to be many library fires this month. Library of the Covenant of the Three in Brussels. Managed by a man and his wife, family name Levant. Contained a wealth of perverse and illegal works: books on Jewish cultural thought, lurid poetry, several books on homosexuality and the mind of the cross-dresser, at least a dozen tomes glorifying deviant behavior. The fire destroyed all.* That is what you wrote. But that isn't what you *meant* to write, is it?" Spiegelman stepped forward, daring Wolff to shoot him before he was done. "*November 6, —43. First of what promises to be many library fires this month. Library of the Covenant of the Three in Brussels. Managed by a man and his wife, family name Levant. And so we continue to burn without reading, kill without learning. The work is lurid, perhaps perverse—as is everything before we open it up and peer inside to know it well. Our sword is blunt. We are blind.*"

Wolff lowered his pistol. "That is what you wrote?"

"That is what I wrote," said Spiegelman.

"You replaced my memos."

"That is how you truly felt."

Spiegelman spread his hands, and he knew Wolff must shoot him, this Jew, this queer, this traitor. And yet he could not. The *dybbuk* could not leave the body of his victim until his task was done. Spiegelman felt as though he could shout, as though the echo would outlive every man and woman on this earth.

The eye of Wolff's pistol searched the floor. Spiegelman had heard murmurs of strange pills the Nazis took to shed their fear and inhibitions, and he felt as though he too had taken such a pill, and had become hyperaware of everything: the veins in Wolff's hands, the crackle of a lightbulb about to burn out, a small hole in Spiegelman's left shoe. His heart had stopped, or it would never stop. David Spiegelman smiled—oh God, he *smiled*. He and his brother used to sit in a tree for hours, eating apples from the branches and making crude jokes about their neighbors, and he smiled like that, like he'd never climbed down from the tree. They would let their legs dangle from the branches as long as they liked, telling stories of heroes and poets and mythic beasts, of specters who walked among men.

The Dybbuk

Strange noises raged in Wolff's ears. Some were familiar, some were new. He did not try to understand them. Wolff lifted his gun and shot David Spiegelman twice: once in the chest, and once in the head. He waited for Spiegelman's body to fall. When it did, August Wolff turned the pistol on himself.

You now know this story as well as I do. You know, by now, that August Wolff was not a stupid man. He was a pitiful one, and a sad one, but not a stupid one. I cannot be sure of his last thoughts, of course, but I imagine that sometime between the first bullet and the third, Wolff must have understood what Spiegelman had done for him. By stripping away Wolff's lies to expose the trembling, honest voice beneath, Spiegelman had given him a gift: his last words.

HITTING THE STANDS
EVENING

The Jester

"ONE OF EACH!" became a rallying cry of sorts. No sooner had Aubrion stepped out of the newspaper shop than the next man in the queue made the same request. "One of each," he said to the astonished shopkeepers. "I'll have both copies of *Le Soir*, if you please." In minutes, customers started returning to the line. "One of each!" The driver who'd delivered the "real" *Le Soir* was distraught: "That's not the *right* one." The customers had an easy answer: "How are we to know that?"

"And that's the trick to it," Aubrion said to Noël. They'd climbed back into the Nash-Kelvinator to repeat the exercise at another newsstand. "If the Nazis come knocking, Peter the Happy Citizen can say he had no way of knowing which was which. Of course he wanted to buy the true *Le Soir*, but he had to buy *both* to do that!"

"It's bloody wonderful," said Noël.

"I don't do things that aren't bloody wonderful."

"But how are we to do it at every major newsstand in the country?"

"That, dear René, is the easiest part."

Aubrion and Noël found the same situation at *Rapide!*, the newsstand catering to Enghien's financial district. Smirking at Noël, Aubrion marched up to the stand and ordered one of each. When the queue had returned to its former health, Aubrion stopped a lad running messages through the city.

"How would you like to make a bit of easy coin?" he asked the boy, who looked wary. "I'll give you twelve francs."

"Twelve?"

"Are you a parrot or a boy?"

The lad huffed. "I'm a man!"

"Well, man, run to every newsstand within five kilometers of here and buy two copies of *Le Soir*. Tell them you want one of each—they'll know what you mean. *Le Soir* is forty-eight cents, so you will have forty-eight cents left over if you buy two copies at twelve newsstands." Aubrion caught Noël checking his math on his fingers. "These are the old francs, too. The good stuff, you understand? If you do your job right, you can keep what's left over."

"How do you know I won't just snatch it all up?"

"Because I am Marc Aubrion of the FI, and I have ways of knowing such things."

That was good enough for the lad. He took the money and ran off to do his job.

Aubrion found a small militia of boys to carry out this work, exhausting the money he and Noël had on them. It was a brilliant scheme. In newsstands across Belgium, *Faux Soir* sold out, and it sold out again when Wellens's trucks replenished their supply. As the sun set, and Wellens's drivers went into hiding, the news of the *zwanze* caper was on everyone's lips. *"I did not want that!"* people whispered between laughs. "Look at the bit on page four. It nearly killed me." Aubrion had not seen the people smile this way in years. He felt infected with their joy. It clung to him like perfume, and he could not run from it.

Nor could he run from the Germans. They talked about running, Aubrion and Noël did, but there was no sense in that. The Nazis would catch them, at the border or in town. "We should make something of the time we have left," Aubrion decided. And they did, until the Germans caught up with him and Noël at the sixth newsstand they visited that day. When Aubrion went inside to order one of each, a cadre of men in uniform were waiting for him. "What have I done wrong? I am a humble citizen, here to buy a newspaper." No one would speak to him, so Aubrion did what Aubrion often did: he threw a punch. He hit the commanding officer in the mouth, splitting his lips and painting his teeth red. Even so, Aubrion fought halfheartedly, and Noël did not fight at all. They knew how this story would end.

The people of Belgium watched as Aubrion and Noël were put in chains and loaded into armed vehicles. "This newsstand is closed," shouted the commander, "pending an official investigation." Everyone was ordered to disperse—which they did, lest they be shot as co-conspirators. Before Aubrion ducked into the back of a German van, he watched crowds of dirty workmen and children and clerks with parted hair and families—laughing, dancing crowds of them—carrying their picnic baskets to newsstands in other towns. They hurried; they had to. If they walked quickly enough, they could get there before the Gestapo.

The Smuggler

Andree Grandjean dropped a copy of *Faux Soir* on top of Lada's pastries. The paper sank a little, until Lada could see the greasy outline of the onion bread on the plate beneath. This was all so absurd that Lada felt she must have taken a bullet to the head already, that she must be hallucinating as she breathed her last on the grubby cobblestones. In short, Lada did not know what to say.

Grandjean spared her. "I liked your paper."

"Oh?" said Lada, with great effort.

"When is the next issue to be released?"

"Tomorrow at four o'clock," answered Lada, "but it won't be nearly as good." Andree laughed, and Lada had never heard anything quite so sad. Tarcovich nodded at the seat across from hers. "Join me, will you? I have some—well—" She extracted *Faux Soir* from her pile of pastries, wiped them off, and offered a pastry to Andree.

They admired the view with the quiet reverence of tourists. The fog and setting sun painted the alluvial clouds red and orange, illuminating a fantastic scene: eager customers who'd heard about this strange paper, newsboys plotting to spend their newfound wealth, workers who decided to take the rest of the day off to read, clergymen and butchers running to catch the last few copies before they sold out. Lada and Andree did not speak. There was far too much to say.

Only when the lad across the street began closing up his newsstand did Lada break the silence. "You realize you have doomed yourself by coming here, don't you?" She took a cigarette from her purse.

"I would have doomed myself if I'd stayed away," Andree said quietly.

Tarcovich lit her cigarette. "Why did you come back?"

"I don't know. I felt awful about Lotte and Clara—that I'd betrayed you."

"What does that matter? People feel awful about things, or they don't."

"That is true."

"And so?"

Andree gathered herself and said, "Lada, despite what you may believe about me, I entered this profession because I wanted to do something for people like them. That is God's honest truth. But I was so focused on getting through this, you understand, that I didn't think about what sort of person I would be when it was all over. I can't say exactly what happened. War makes beggars of us all."

"Christ." Lada exhaled smoke. "But does war have to make philosophers of us all?"

"Sorry."

"You bloody well should be."

"I also read the stories in your notebook." Andree looked at Lada. Her eyes smiled; the rest of her did not quite have the strength to do so. "They were glorious, Lada. The man who went out for a walk and lost his wife, the girl who built a tree-house to get closer to the moon, the pastry chef, the old couple with their dreams, the boy who wanted to be a dancer... It was wonderful, all of it. Like nothing I'd ever read." Andree reached across the table to take Lada's hand, stopping at the last moment. Lada's heart was in her throat.

"You came back," she said, "because you read my stories?"

Andree shook her head. "Because you were missing one."

Lada tossed her cigarette away. She was starving, desperate, her skin tingling and raw. "Hold me," she whispered hoarsely. "Hold my hand, please."

And they did. They held hands, Lada and Andree, in view of everyone in the coffeehouse. People stared and talked, of course. An older woman, her two children in tow, begged the bartender to kick the women out. Lada expected him to comply; the definition of love was narrow, in those days, with no room for people like her. But in a strange act of mercy, the bartender allowed them to stay, holding hands until the Gestapo came.

HITTING THE STANDS NIGHT

The Professor

IT WAS MANNING who opened the door, but Victor did not know that at first. The fellow was unrecognizable: his hair tousled, his clothes in ruins. He blinked at Victor for a long second—close to tears, it seemed. Then he said: "Oh, right. Come in, Professor."

Victor followed Manning inside the Nazi headquarters. The state of the place nearly took his breath from him. Clerks were running about, some of them sprinting. Papers, stamped in panicked footprints, lined the floor. Vases were overturned, paintings knocked crooked. The professor turned to Manning for an explanation.

Manning, however, seemed unwilling to provide one. All he would say was: "I apologize for all this."

"What on earth *happened*?"

"I will tell you soon, I promise."

"Are we in danger?"

"No, no. Not by any means. Please follow me."

Manning led Victor to a small room, about the size of a

closet. In fact, it looked as though it *had* been a closet until recently. Scuff marks streaked the floor where furniture once sat, and hastily-emptied filing cabinets still hung open. Manning gestured for Victor to stay put. He darted out of the room, returning moments later with a chair. It looked small and pitiful, sitting there by itself, as though this were the poorest, tiniest throne room in Europe.

"Have a seat, please," he said. "I'm afraid I will have to ask you to wait here while we sort everything out. You are technically a prisoner of the Reich until we release you—which we will, of course—so I will have to lock the door. I do hope you will not be offended. It really is a technicality. Well—ahh—" Manning put a hand on his forehead, struggling to think. "Can I get you something to pass the time? A book, perhaps? You do like to read, don't you? Oh, right, you're a bloody professor, of course you—"

"Herr Manning," said Victor, "would you do me the immense courtesy of telling me what is going on?"

Manning sank against a filing cabinet, his eyes rolling back into his head. Victor thought, for a moment, that he'd fainted. "August Wolff is dead," he said at last. "It appears he shot himself."

"Jesus, Mary, and Joseph," breathed Victor. "When?"

"Perhaps two hours ago. David Spiegelman—you know Spiegelman, don't you?"

"What happened to him?"

"He, too, is dead."

"How?"

"We believe Wolff shot him prior to taking his own life." Manning began to shake, like he was crying—but no, it was laughter. "It all happened—can you believe it?—in the bloody *communications* room. By the *telex*, of all things. I cannot imagine how they must have ended up there in the first place." He cleared his throat, wiped his eyes. "I beg your pardon, Professor. It has been an odd day."

"Do not apologize. I can only imagine."

"It keeps getting odder, too." Manning pressed his palms to his eyes. "We were due to release *La Libre Belgique* this afternoon, but there have been strange reports of newsstands receiving two different versions of *Le Soir*. Can you believe it? Naturally, that delayed everything. One of the versions is some sort of parody. *Swanzing*, I think the locals call it."

"*Zwanze*."

"I beg your pardon?"

"It is called *zwanze*." Victor tried to keep his expression neutral.

"I see," said Manning. "Well, I'm afraid you must excuse me for now. Is there anything I can do for you before I go?"

"No, thank you, Herr Manning," said Victor. "I think I could use a few moments alone. It has been, as you said, an odd day."

ONE DAY AFTER FAUX SOIR
MORNING

The Jester

THOUGH THE SET was the same, the players had changed between the first act and the last. Aubrion would have called it lazy writing. "Continuity is important in a play," he always said. "An audience is a disloyal bunch, so they must be given something to latch on to." This play was a woefully discontinuous one, Aubrion thought. It was the same brick-lined conference room as before, the same low, square table where Aubrion first met Wolff and learned of the propaganda bomb. But other than that, discontinuities abounded.

From the end of the table, Aubrion cataloged the characters' fates. Tarcovich was there, seated in the same spot as before. Her manacles rattled as she pushed in her chair. Grandjean sat next to her. Aubrion was surprised to see the judge there, but there was always some shocking romance in these cheap plays. Tarcovich looked mostly unchanged from last time, save a bruise over her eye and the absence of her scarf. And last time, Theo Mullier had sat between Aubrion and Tarcovich; his heavy absence made Aubrion's chest grow tight. After Tarcovich and Grand-jean came in, a man from the Gestapo led René Noël to the seat across from Aubrion. René had no part in the first meeting, and he looked as though he wanted no part in *this* one. He greeted Aubrion with a tense nod. Ferdinand Wellens trailed after him, the poor man; he looked naked without a cape. Martin Victor was the last to enter the room, his eyes never straying from his chains. Now *there* was a changed man, Aubrion thought. Victor's shoulders, always larger than Aubrion expected, bore the weight of some private defeat. As before, two soldiers with machine guns oversaw the whole thing.

But there were twists, too. Contrary to Aubrion's expectations, neither Wolff nor Spiegelman joined them at the table. Maybe Spiegelman had been spared all this business. If Wolff still knew nothing of his involvement, then Spiegelman was safe. And Aubrion thanked God, thanked anyone, that his dear Gamin had not been captured.

Manning entered, trailing behind a polite-looking man in the uniform of the *Schutzstaffel*. Aubrion felt the room tighten, as though all air had gone out of it. He'd seen photographs of the man, and he'd prayed that would be the extent of their interaction. But Heinrich Himmler was there, and he looked at them each in turn. He took his time, like a surveyor encountering a new map. Aubrion had never seen eyes quite like Himmler's: the intensity of a madman, the lucidity of a predator.

"Well done." Himmler lowered his head in a bow. "Well done, all of you. But the gentleman who did this will be shot with silver bullets."

When Himmler was seated at the head of the table, Aubrion replied: "With his humble slingshot, David killed Goliath. Rest assured, Monsieur Himmler, we will crumble the colossus with feet of clay."

Aubrion sat back, pleased with himself. His throat was a little hoarse, and that had affected his delivery, but all in all, it was a good line, one he'd prepared beforehand. Even so, Noël looked as though he wanted to punch him. At Himmler's nod, one of the guards *did* punch him—pulling out Aubrion's chair and planting a fist in his stomach. Aubrion doubled over.

"Any other comments?" asked Himmler. No one said anything. "Excellent. Let us proceed. Herr Manning?"

"Everyone here is a traitor to the Reich," said Manning, "guilty of sedition and propagandizing. Does anyone wish to deny that?" None of them did. "In that case, we will get straight to the point. Your guilt has been decided. All that remains is to sentence you appropriately." Manning was otherworldly with his sallow cheeks and hollow eyes. "As you might have guessed, we have files on each and every one of you. We know you occupied important positions in the FI. Therefore, we'd like to give you a chance to decide on your sentence with us. We are confident that, together, we can arrive at a punishment that is suitable for your crimes."

"Does anyone have any questions before we begin?" said Himmler.

"Yeah," said Aubrion. "Where is our pal Wolff?"

Himmler and Manning exchanged a glance. The former nodded.

"Wolff shot himself," said Manning.

Aubrion heard Tarcovich and Noël gasp. He sat back, blinking at his reflection in the table. It was strange, but he felt something—not quite sadness, and not yet pity—for the *Gruppenführer*. Wolff had seemed so very *incomplete*.

"And Spiegelman?" said Noël, haltingly.

"Wolff took David Spiegelman's life before he took his own." Disgust spoiled Himmler's clean features. "They were traitors, the both of them."

Aubrion was an empty sky after a hard rain. He'd suffered a universe of losses since this war began, but they were nothing at all. The world lost an undiscovered genius, a museum of wonders that would never be seen. It wasn't just the loss that pained Aubrion: it was that no one *knew*.

"Our intelligence reports suggest Spiegelman assisted you in your *Le Soir* endeavor," said Himmler. "And an examination of Herr Wolff's personal memos yielded some disappointing results." Himmler tapped a folder on the table.

A paper was sticking out of the folder, and though most of it was typed, a bit was handwritten. The handwriting looked, for the most part, like Wolff's, but Aubrion was certain—and here, his heart filled with the smallest joy—there was a touch of Winston Churchill there, too. Aubrion would have bet his right arm it was intentional. A smile came to him, warm and good, and slightly gawky, befitting David Spiegelman. Spiegelman was a fine jokester after all, and he'd saved his best work for last.

"David Spiegelman lived a great life," said Noël.

"Several of them, in fact," said Tarcovich, with a sad smile.

Himmler managed a tight-lipped nod. "Any other questions?" No one had any. "Good. Let us begin. Professor Victor." With some effort, Victor lifted his head. "You have been charged with the same crimes as everyone else. But, in appreciation for your service to the Reich, we hereby pardon you for all you have done wrong."

Aubrion tried to spring from his chair, forgetting he was chained to it. "What service? What goddamn service?"

"I bloody knew it," said Tarcovich.

"Martin, what have you done?" demanded Noël.

"The professor is a smart man," said Himmler. "He provided us certain information."

Victor closed his eyes. He used to recite a prayer in times like these, when he wanted the world to disappear. The words eluded him.

"However," said Himmler, "the Reich does not suffer traitors, and you are a traitor to your own kind. You have lost all privileges as a citizen, and you must leave the country."

"Does that strike you as fair?" asked Manning.

Victor nodded.

Wellens and Noël were next. Aubrion was so furious he missed the first part of Himmler's sentence. A crimson noise hummed in his ears. "—have used their labors for evil, they will be sent to a labor camp," he was saying. "Ferdinand Wellens, René Noël, and every member of the FI who remained in the print factory after Wolff's warning—you will all be aboard a train tomorrow morning. Do you find that fair?"

"I find nothing about this fair," said Noël, "but we haven't any choice, have we?"

"We can execute you or imprison you." Himmler spread his hands as though he were offering menu options. "All you must do is present your case. Our minds and hearts are open."

"We'll take your bloody labor camp," said Wellens, his eyes blazing.

"Do you feel the same, Monsieur Noël?" said Himmler.

"How many years?"

"I'm sorry?"

"In the camp."

"Fifteen."

"Fine. Your kind will not last that long anyway."

"Monsieur Aubrion," said Himmler. Aubrion forced himself to hold the man's blue stare. "You are the architect of this scheme, are you not?"

Aubrion tried to straighten his posture, but his torso was still sore from the punch. "Of course I am."

"Idiot," whispered Tarcovich, who'd started to cry.

"You will be executed for your crimes."

"Good." Aubrion struggled to keep his words from shaking. "The Nazis have yet to build a prison large enough to hold me."

Himmler looked prepared to spit at him. "You are a *child*, Marc Aubrion, and this is not a war for children. We have given everyone else a choice in their sentence, but not you. Children are treated as such." Himmler began organizing the objects on the table: Wolff's memos, a pen, an inkwell, a coffee mug. He did so idly, the same way he organized the country, Aubrion thought. "You owe us a debt of thanks. The Reich is doing you a great service by removing you from this *adult* affair."

"The problem with you German commanders," Aubrion said softly, "is that you don't have anyone around to tell you when you talk too much."

The Smuggler

When he'd finished with Aubrion, Himmler smiled in Tarcovich's direction. He did not know how to smile, Himmler. The man wore his smile like a carnival mask.

"This is especially unfortunate," Himmler said, but it was unclear which *this* he meant. "Madame Grandjean, until yesterday, your record was stellar." Tarcovich felt Grandjean tense in the seat next to her. Himmler's eyebrows descended. "We understand what it means to be corrupted by the perverse. That is why we take the measures we do, measures that some consider extreme. Even the noblest among us can be lured astray when we least suspect it. We have all heard the tragic stories of—"

"With all respect," said Andree, her voice clear, "my life has not been tragic. Please get to the point, Monsieur Himmler."

Shocked, Himmler sat back. He nodded at Manning, who said:

"As you know, the Reich has immense respect for those who make it their life's work to uphold the tenets of justice. We are therefore giving you a chance, Judge Grandjean, to show that you have not lost your way, and that you remember the nature of your life's work."

"You will preside over a trial tomorrow," said Himmler. "You will try Madame Tarcovich for the crimes of sedition, treachery, propagandizing, sexual perversion and prostitution. If you find her guilty, you may return to your position as a judge, and we will forget all this business."

Lada's heart stopped.

"And what will become of Lada?" whispered Andree.

"She will be imprisoned for her crimes."

"At Fort Breendonk?"

"No, no. A local prison, of your choosing. You can see to it she is well cared for."

"You will sign a document attesting to this?"

"Andree, no—" Lada tried to reach out to her. Her chains rattled against her seat.

"Of course. However, if you find her innocent, you will both be put to death." Himmler smiled, like a physician comforting a patient. "You need not make a decision now, Madame Grandjean. I understand this is difficult for you. We will give you tonight to think it over."

Lada could not look at Andree, could not stop herself. Andree stared down at the table, solitary and confused. And Lada tried to beg her silently—to do what? She wanted to be spared, of course she did, but even that choice was repugnant to her.

Himmler stood, motioning for Manning to do the same. "Well, then. I think that takes care of everything. This has been a productive meeting, hasn't it? I bid you all a good day."

As the guards chained Tarcovich and the other prisoners together, Noël quipped, "I think this has been the FI's problem all along. We don't have nearly enough productive meetings."

Tarcovich laughed, as did the others.

"Very good, René," said Aubrion. "You picked a hell of a time to develop a sense of humor."

ONE DAY AFTER FAUX SOIR
EVENING

The Professor

VICTOR PASSED THE night in the company of the dead. No one saw fit to tell him that these were Spiegelman's old quarters, but they did not need to. The professor had made it his business to know things that people did not say aloud. He *saw*: the walls were naked and cold, the desk bare, all the shelves and cabinets robbed of their intimate things. Victor sat in Spiegelman's chair, which sagged uncomfortably in the middle. He ran his fingers across the top of the desk. Spiegelman's hand, over the years, had tattooed the wood in a hundred tongues. In a glance, Victor could see Hungarian, Spanish, German, French, Cyrillic, English—cursive and print—labyrinths of paragraphs—honest, workmanlike letters—tiny sentences—vowels and consonants that dipped and spun with Machiavellian glee—huge, blind man's text—abandoned letters. Victor was dizzy with Spiegelman's work.

The minute hand paced the face of his watch. It was nearly midnight—but he could not sleep, not in Spiegelman's bed. Wasn't it bad luck to sleep in a dead man's bed? The professor had heard that somewhere. He'd done it before, though: in Auschwitz, in Cologne, in Enghien, in a French boardinghouse after the owner passed in his sleep. And he'd slept in his *own* bed, the bed Victor shared with his wife, after *she* died. Perhaps this explained his luck.

The professor knocked on his door to get the attention of the guard outside. The man in uniform put his head in.

"Would you send someone up to change the mattress?" asked Victor.

The guard nodded, closed the door. In no time at all, two Germans appeared, and Spiegelman's mattress disappeared. It was so easy to get things done in this place. If Victor had wanted a mattress changed back at the *Front de l'Indépendance* base, he'd have to fill out paperwork, put in a request, pay a bribe—and at the end of it all, someone would tell him they didn't have the funds. Victor knelt before the new mattress. Where did their funds go? Was it *all* used for mad ventures like *Faux Soir*? It bothered him that he did not know.

Victor knocked on his door again. The guard opened it, visibly annoyed.

"Do you know where they are holding Aubrion and his colleagues?" asked Victor.

"Downstairs, Professor. In the basement cells. Would you like me to escort you?"

"No, I don't think so."

Shaking his head, the guard closed the door.

The professor was, of course, an awkward man. He could never decide on matters of social appropriateness: an academic's curse. And, of course, Martin Victor was a brilliant academic, the kind of man who could argue his side of a problem for hours, and then mount an equally skillful argument for the other side. It turned decision-making into a tiresome exercise. Victor could make an excellent case for why he should go down to see his former colleagues in their cells, and a comparably excellent case for why he should not. He wondered whether he should apologize, or whether they were past apologies.

He sat at David Spiegelman's desk. Victor never had a relationship with the others, not in a friendly way. He took an oath when he joined the FI, and he was the sort of man who regarded oaths as sacred things. But an oath was really just a contract. The men and women of the FI had been his colleagues, and nothing more.

And now—and yet—there was something *here*, in this room, in his body, that Victor could not articulate. Something remained unfinished. Spiegelman had pressed his pen into his desk with such conviction that the wood recorded his words. It was a sin to envy the dead, but Victor was only a man.

The Jester

When Marc Aubrion was nine years of age, an aunt—in the midst of cutting a peach cake—pointed at the boy with her knife and said: "He's not a *quiet* lad, is he?" He had never been a quiet lad, not a day in his life. His parents could not recall his first word; only that he'd shouted it.

When he got to his cell, Aubrion asked the guards for writing materials. They refused him. And so Aubrion, who could not fill a paper with words, instead filled his cell with noise.

"My God," Lada said to Noël, who occupied the cell next to hers. "Did you have any idea he knew *every* line in *A Midsummer Night's Dream?*"

Noël's face was pressed to the bars. "I did not think anyone did. Not even Shakespeare."

"At least he's done singing."

Upon hearing her, Aubrion decided singing was a splendid idea. He embarked on a twelve-stanza Lithuanian folk song. When it was over, he fell silent.

But Aubrion could not remain silent for long. If he did—the

last time he did—he began to tremble. His cell smelled of burnt paper and antiseptic, and it was growing colder as the night aged. A square of brick, about a foot above his head, had been hollowed out and replaced with iron bars. The breeze still tasted of night. Soon, it would not. When the sun infiltrated his cell, the Germans would come back.

Death was not an easy thing to think about. The difficulty was not emotional; it was cognitive. To Aubrion, death occupied the same ambiguous category as God, heaven, hell, or what made a good joke. After one of his stand-up routines, someone in the audience had asked him over a drink: "How do you tell the good ones over the bad?"

"There are no bad jokes," replied Aubrion. "Only bad storytellers." In Aubrion's view, God was the worst storyteller of them all. "What kind of a writer makes characters in his own image?" he used to say. There was no fun in that, he said often: no risk. Predestination was a horrid plot hole. Death, though—that was a good final act. Aubrion tried to think of it that way: as a last bit of character development and nothing more. It did not help in the least.

Aubrion tried to sing again. He found, however, that his voice was gone. The Germans had left him a jug of water. He'd heard stories, though, about the Nazis poisoning their prisoners' water with whooping cough. Aubrion did not know whether the Germans planned to detain him at Fort Breendonk prior to his execution, but if they did, he had no intention of spending his last days holding the remains of his own lungs. So, he avoided the water.

"*Marc,*" Lada stage-whispered.

Aubrion dragged himself to the front of the cell to lean against the bars.

"How are you holding up?" said Lada.

To his left and right, a pair of guards looked at him as though waiting for his reply. Aubrion shrugged.

"Marc—" said Lada.

"That's enough talking in here," said one of the guards, as he did every half hour or so.

"What are you going to do?" taunted Aubrion, finding his voice again. "Shoot us?" To Aubrion's disappointment, the guard did not reply. "Lada?" he said, to fill the quiet.

"Yes, Marc?"

"Can I ask you something?"

"I don't think I have much of a choice."

"Would you have wanted children?"

"My God, really? All right, we can talk about this now. No, I don't think so." Tarcovich's words were doused in acid. "I fear for the children who are being raised in these times. What are they learning?"

"That the world is so ugly it can make a Hitler?" said Aubrion.

"It is not just Hitler," said Tarcovich, "but the fact that he was *elected*."

"What about you, Monsieur Aubrion?" asked Grandjean, from the cell next to his. "Do you wish to have children?"

"I don't know," he said truthfully. "I never thought about it until recently. There was something that happened the other day, with Gamin... I don't consider Gamin a child, you understand. But I did wonder, for a moment, how being a father might have been." Again, Marc Aubrion spoke the name of his friend. "Lada?"

"Yes, Marc?"

He wanted to say it aloud: that this was it, they were done. The rain on the prison walls was like the sky tuning up a cello. Lightning shattered the earth. Aubrion's tongue would not form the words. He was a broken linotype machine, stuck on some ill-used letter.

"Do you know what I'm going to miss?" he said, flicking a beetle's carcass off the prison bars. "The taste of good beer. My God, I'd kill a man for a beer."

The others laughed—even the guards—at the non sequitur.

TWO DAYS AFTER FAUX SOIR
EARLY MORNING

The Smuggler

THE GUARDS CAME for Andree first, removing her from her cell at the first yawn of sunlight. Lada whispered "goodbye, my love" as she walked past. To Lada's dismay, Andree Grand-jean did not respond.

"She did not hear you," Noël muttered through the bars. But if Noël heard her, surely Andree had, too. Lada fought to tame her panic.

The Germans came for her a few hours later. They opened Lada's cell—their pale faces and deep eyes swimming wordlessly in the dark—and motioned for her to turn around. When she obeyed, they chained her wrists and ankles together, so that her limbs felt alien and cold. A guard with plain features tugged her out of the cell. Lada nodded a farewell to Noël, who smiled; she turned to do the same for Marc Aubrion, but the poor man had fallen asleep, and Lada—who'd kicked her dear Aubrion awake after so many nights of revelry—did not have the heart to wake him.

And then the guards walked her through the building. Lada knew they must have been moving quickly, nearly marching, but her limbs felt carved from lead. Naturally, she saw faces she recognized—Himmler, Manning, the guards who'd been present the first time she met Wolff, a clerk who processed her paperwork— and yet their names stuck in Lada's throat. The world was a scab that had just been torn away, too raw and painful and sharp everywhere. Himmler supervised the guards as they took her from the base and loaded her into a vehicle, the same sort of vehicle, Lada realized with amusement, she'd stolen to meet Andree Grandjean.

It was a quick drive to Andree's courthouse. The car smelled of fresh leather, and the men smelled of old liquor. Lada had her eyes closed the entire time, so she only knew they'd arrived when the driver mumbled, "Fucking hell."

"What is it?" asked Lada Tarcovich.

"Bloody reporters."

Tarcovich strained to see out the window. Indeed, milling about on the steps of the courthouse, was a throng of bloody reporters. ("What do you think is the collective noun for reporters?" Aubrion once asked her. "A disappointment? A Biblical plague?") Most had cameras, which they trained on the car as it approached. Tarcovich laughed, for many wore the journalist's badge for *Le Soir*.

The guard seated next to her pulled on her handcuffs. "Is this your doing? These reporters?" Lada was amused to see terror in his eyes.

"It's flattering of you to think so," she said, "but I've actually been in a prison all night."

"Keep your head down as we walk inside," said the guard. "Do not say anything."

This proved a difficult task. As Lada and the guards mounted the courthouse steps, reporters shouted and pulled at her. "A word on your capture! Please, just a word!"

"Turn your head, you whore. Let us look at you."

"How many women have you perverted? Dozens? Hundreds?"

"How long did you think you could fool the Third Reich?" Lada shook their hands off her body, her chains rattling.

The guards kept her moving until she was in the courtroom. Andree Grandjean was already there, clad in her robes and wig. She arranged her pens and notebooks at the bench, avoiding Lada's eyes. Tarcovich stood on her toes to see Andree's face. But the judge did not wish to be seen. Tarcovich was preparing to cry out to her when the Germans grabbed her handcuffs. To Lada's surprise, they instructed her to sit in the back of the courtroom.

"Why?" she said. "Am I not being tried?"

Grandjean banged her gavel. The courtroom fell silent.

"Bring out the first two," she said. All the life had gone out of her voice. The courtroom air had been carved from oak and paper. "The prostitutes."

Lada's blood turned cold. A policeman dragged two girls into the courtroom: Lotte and Clara, their hair and eyes in ruins. Clara kept her head high, but poor, small Lotte searched the room in a panic. Tarcovich prayed the child would not see her. When she did, Lotte wept.

"Lotte and Clara Palomer," said Grandjean, "you have been accused of prostitution, forgery, and possession of false documents. Do you wish to make a statement in your defense?"

Lotte spoke. "We are sorry, so sorry for—"

"No," said Clara. "We do not."

"Then you admit to these crimes?"

"We do."

"Clara!" cried Lotte.

"I hereby sentence you to twenty years in prison for your crimes, to be served consecutively and immediately." Andree's gavel came down. "Next case."

The Germans prodded Tarcovich to the bench. Cameras chattered, like insects. They'd let a handful of reporters into the courtroom, the Nazis had. All wore badges proclaiming their affiliation with a collaborationist paper: *Volk en Staat, Le Pays Réel, De Gazet, Het Laatste Nieuws, Le Soir*. Lada recognized some of them. Jan Brans, the editor-in-chief of *Volk en Staat*, sat in the front, looking, as always, as though he'd just come to an unspeakable epiphany. Seated next to him, Paul Colin of *Le Nouveau Journal* made horrible scratches on a pad of paper. The courtroom reeked of camera equipment and hastily applied cologne. It was an extraordinary showing, to be sure. As she approached the bench, Lada Tarcovich had no greater desire than to be unimportant again.

"Lada Tarcovich," said Grandjean, looking above Tarcovich's head. Though her voice remained steady, Andree's lips trembled. "You have been accused of prostitution, sexual perversion—" The words were an abyss, and Lada fell in, tumbling into nothing. "—sedition, treachery and propagandizing." Andree's figure was unrecognizable in the solemn robes. Lada wondered whether she should hate her. "Do you wish to make a statement in your defense?"

"Look at me," said Tarcovich, for Andree still would not. She *should* hate her, Lada knew, for what she did to Lotte and Clara, for what she was about to do to Lada herself. Andree would save herself by locking Lada away, but maybe Lada deserved that. For imprisoning Andree behind the walls of her love, for exiling her to a land of wild schemes, Lada would have a cell of her own. "Please." Her body was still warm, somehow, from Andree's touch.

Grandjean forced her eyes to meet Lada's. "Do you have anything to say?" she said softly. "In your defense?" Around them, the courtroom sat still.

"No."

"Then do you admit to these crimes?"

"I admit nothing."

"If you confess, I might be able to arrange a lighter—"

"I am not going to confess anything."

Grandjean blinked rapidly. "Do you wish me to repeat the charges?"

"Why? Am I to defend myself?"

"The charges are prostitution, sexual perversion—"

"I know the damned charges," said Lada. "The only perversion here is that you dare call this a trial. This is a theater, not a courtroom, and I refuse to go on."

Behind her, the reporters began to stir, coughing and muttering like playgoers during intermission. Judge Grandjean stood, quieting them. "In light of this—this…" Grandjean held out her hand for a referent, but none came. "I will need to deliberate before sentencing. The court will reconvene in three hours." After a moment's hesitation, Grandjean slammed her gavel—but the reporters were already out of their seats, running to their pens and typewriters. Lada could hear nothing over the sounds of tomorrow's headlines.

The Jester

A cadre of eight Germans removed Aubrion from his cell and chained him to Wellens and Noël, but Himmler would have none of it. "No, we must be deliberate," he told the guards. "People will be watching. The prisoners should walk in a line, but not chained to each other. When they enter the van, I want them to do it one by one. If they are chained together, it will happen too quickly. This way, they will climb in slowly, their heads bowed." Himmler began to indulge in a bit of melodrama. "There is always a moment when prisoners realize, *truly* realize, their fate. The brain comprehends what the eyes are looking at. I want the people to see it when it happens."

So, as per Himmler's instructions, the guards unchained Aubrion and Wellens and Noël. The three of them walked in single file. It was a procession, of sorts, with four Nazis on either side and Himmler bringing up the rear. Aubrion could not help but admire the Nazis' showmanship. They parked their van—the van that was to transport Aubrion, Wellens and Noël to Fort Breendonk—in the middle of downtown Enghien, so all who'd come to buy their bread and eggs in the town square could see what had befallen the rebels. Wolff would have approved, Aubrion thought. Even his capture was propaganda.

When the parade was halfway across the town square, church bells chimed the end of morning service. Aubrion looked up, irritated. He found it an improper soundtrack: too joyful to be appropriate, too somber to be ironic. The bells carried on for ages, as though eager to drown out the prattle of chains.

In front of Aubrion, Wellens and Noël kept their eyes on the van. But Aubrion, being Aubrion, wanted to know his audience. Every five meters or so, he would strain to see around the guards. And that is when he saw me.

The Pyromaniac

The night before, someone (probably the Germans) had started a rumor that Marc Aubrion of the FI would be paraded through the streets the following morning. And so I'd ducked behind a butcher's stand to wait; there, I still sat. I did not move. Every bit of muscle and feeling in my body was directed toward a single task: memorizing the faces of my family. I never got to hear my parents' final words, and in many ways, this was a blessing; but I accepted the precious curse of playing spectator to my adopted family's death. Aubrion saw me, and the chains had not stolen his smile.

Even from that distance, I could see Aubrion was pleased with his audience. The people of Belgium were showmen, too, but terrible at it: though they pretended to go about the day's business, everyone was watching. Mothers hushed their children, businessmen took an early break, workers poked their heads out of their shops, lads sat together on street corners. The bread line *stopped*.

Those damned church bells were still chiming, though, so it took us a moment to hear the air raid siren. The wail paralyzed me, cutting straight to my gut. Everyone froze—even the Nazis, even Himmler—all their fears laid bare by the sound. Sickened, we looked to our old enemy, the sky.

I heard someone curse, or maybe I did it myself. I wanted to stay, wanted it more than anything, but old instincts won out, and I started to run, as we all did, even though running meant nothing. Two dozen bombers flew overhead, in a loose triangle, blocking out the sun with their bodies. I knew who it was immediately. It was the way they flew that tipped me off: the self-righteous perfection of the English.

Crouched in a gutter, I heard Himmler give the order twice: first in German, and then in French. "To the shelters! The *shelters*!" His men did not move. Perhaps they did not hear him over Aubrion's shouts.

"The RAF!" Aubrion whacked Noël on the shoulder, forgetting he was wearing handcuffs. "Would you look at them, René? It worked, it bloody *worked*."

"Marc." That was all Noël could say. He had tears in his eyes.

As the air raid siren wailed, the people of Belgium fled the streets. The Belgian government built shelters shortly before the occupation, and the Germans finished most of them. Every town had at least two; Enghien had six. But the shelters were not large enough for everyone, so the people ran and pushed, forgetting who they were and who they loved. I could not move. I could not look away from Aubrion.

"Hello there, Bomber Harris! You're late!" Laughing, Aubrion ran into the town square. The Nazi cadre, who'd turned to flee, looked back in time to see him climb atop the van. I remember this moment with everything that I am. He stood on the roof with his arms raised, as though he was trying to hitch a ride on one of the bombers. Though his hands were still cuffed at the wrists—they must have been; who would have removed the handcuffs?—I do not remember seeing them that way. The way I remember it, Marc Aubrion had no chains.

I never saw the German guards open fire. All I remember is that Aubrion was laughing, and then he was not—and then he was twitching, dancing with the impact of each bullet. They shot him over a hundred times before the air raid siren stopped.

In the sudden quiet, I tore my eyes away from my friend. Above, the bombers were beginning to dive. I clamped my hands over my ears as the Germans and Noël and Wellens ran for cover, as Marc Aubrion's body dropped to the ground. I was braced, ready for the unimpressive sound it would make when it fell. But Aubrion's timing, as always, was impeccable. The British dropped their first round the moment—the very *second*—Aubrion's body hit the cobbles.

My friend Aubrion was never a fearsome man. He laughed too high and too long, and he had a knack for the unintentional. He forgot to put his coat on in the rain. Still, when Aubrion fell, all of Belgium trembled.

TWO DAYS AFTER FAUX SOIR
EARLY MORNING

The Pyromaniac

AS IT TURNED OUT, Bomber Harris was not quite as upset as Aubrion and Spiegelman would have liked. The air raid lasted around three minutes, and most of the targets were on the outskirts of town. I watched the RAF strafe an abandoned schoolhouse a kilometer from Enghien. Then they peeled away from the city in a smug circle, disappearing like an afterimage.

People emerged from their homes, rubbing their eyes and holding their children close. I climbed out of the gutter, assessing the damage along with everyone else. There wasn't much. The RAF hit a church, but it was an ugly church that no one liked anyway. A shopkeeper noted that they'd made an obnoxious crater behind his apartment building. The Germans would patch it up in a day. I heard people speak of the air raid as though it were a mystery or a hallucination. Only I knew it for what it really was.

The town recovered, but the Nazis remained in their shelter. No one came to move Aubrion's body. I saw people approach him, murmuring, wondering at the identity of the man with the large, staring eyes. Word soon got out: it was Marc Aubrion of the FI. That was unremarkable; men from the FI died every day. And so I started whispering—it was *him*, it was the man responsible for the miracle of *Faux Soir*. The whispers grew louder. People wanted to know: Was it true? Was it Aubrion? The driver who delivered the "real" *Le Soir*, the man who first saw Aubrion buy one of each, *he* could confirm the body's identity; so, too, could the owners of the surrounding newsstands; so, too, could a handful of lads who Aubrion paid to buy two copies of *Le Soir* at every newsstand in the city. It was settled, then. This *was* Marc Aubrion of the FI, the man who'd laughed at Hitler.

It was Hans's first day at *Het Laatste Nieuws*, so his boss gave him the easiest job he had. "Stay here," he'd said, "by the courtroom door. We do not know when Judge Grandjean is coming back, but we want to have reporters in there when she does. As soon as those doors open, come get me." That was six hours ago. Hans didn't hear very well, truth be told, but he was fairly sure Judge Grandjean said she was going to deliberate for *three* hours. Six was at least twice that.

The air raid had probably slowed things up. Still, this was unusual. The other reporters noticed it, too. Outside the courtroom, the air was putrid with their restlessness: the stink of cigar smoke and perspiration. When seven hours passed, and then seven and a half, Hans's boss came to see for himself. Surely Grandjean could not be taking *this* long. She was notorious, Hans knew, for her quick decisions, and the evidence against that queer was overwhelming. And yet no one had heard from her. Exasperated, Hans's boss summoned the Germans.

Twelve Nazis divided themselves into two lines. They grabbed a bench from the lobby of the courthouse—*eins, zwei, drei!*—and slammed it into the courtroom doors.

Han was not sure what he expected to see inside. What he did know, however, was that he did not expect it to be empty. The Nazis swept the courtroom with their rifles up, in case, perhaps, Grandjean was hiding beneath a chair. They found nothing.

In the middle of their search, a shout went up in the hallway. "The prisoners! They are not in their cells!" Hans, the lucky man, made this important discovery, so it was he who led the Germans to the empty cells. Lada Tarcovich was gone, Lotte and Clara were gone, and, as the Germans soon found, Andree Grandjean was gone, too, having left her quarters without a trace.

As the Germans panicked and the Gestapo investigated and the reporters photographed it all, everyone missed an absurd detail. It took them ages to find it. When they did, the discovery caused quite a scene. The detail in question was a slip of paper—thin blotting paper, on which we printed the best and worst newspapers of our time—pasted to the judge's chair. The paper had a secret to tell, a verdict in Andree Grandjean's handwriting: GUILTY.

YESTERDAY

The Scrivener

"I CONFESS IT took me years to figure out how they did it," said Helene, answering the question in Eliza's eyes. She had not written in her notebook in hours. Had she breathed? The old woman couldn't tell. "In the end, it was simple, like the best of plans."

"Simple?" Eliza laughed.

"It had to be."

"Tell me."

"It began a few hours prior to the air raid."

"Aubrion's doing?" guessed Eliza.

The old woman shook her head. "Not Aubrion's. Not this time."

TWO DAYS AFTER FAUX SOIR
EARLY MORNING

The Professor's Witness

AS WOLFF PROMISED, the Germans escort Martin Victor to the Enghien courthouse. There, he will select a pair of convicts to join him as servants, to carry his belongings across the border. The Nazis flank Victor as he paces the rows of cells, his footsteps echoing like prisoners force-marched to the chambers, excited to bathe for the first time in ages, unknowing and unseeing but there is nothing Victor can do to enlighten them.

He selects Lotte and Clara, who he recognizes from Tarcovich's whorehouse. To Victor, prostitution is a wretched crime, and he feels no compassion for those who have engaged in it. But God no longer speaks to him about such things. He is a broken man, and he must find mercy in the ruins. The Germans give Lotte and Clara their freedom in exchange for their service. Victor signs the relevant paperwork. With that, the unlikely three set off toward Victor's apartment to gather what they need for the trip.

They have walked about twenty paces when Bomber Harris

arrives. Victor and the girls duck into a shelter, where the professor shuts his eyes against the terror. He expects the familiar cold sweat, the shaking. But he is oddly calm, even prepared, as the bombs fall and the sirens blare. At the air raid's end, Lotte and Clara—so young! Sofia was only a bit older when they met—leave the shelter and walk matter-of-factly toward the apartment. Victor follows, squinting up at the bombers.

The world *turns*—*turned*. When the grime and the bony hands and piles of shoes at Auschwitz first came to him, Victor had felt something similar: *this* piece of the world did not fit into *that* one, and Victor would spend the rest of his life in-between, sliding between the tectonic halves of these realities. And now Victor felt the same, but different. The Royal Air Force left a prim trail of exhaust in the sky. Each plane wore the little stars of Bomber Harris's division. "Stop me if you've heard this one. A *bouffon* with a telex tries to convince the RAF to bomb his country..." But it was not a joke; it was real. It was too absurd to be anything less. Like Auschwitz, like the death squads, this was the way of the world. As God was his witness, a *bouffon* with a telex could do wondrous things.

Victor stopped Lotte and Clara, pressing a dozen franc notes into Lotte's hand.

"If you are trying to buy us," said Clara, "I am warning you, we will die first. We have been through enough."

"I am not. This is a gift. I want you to run."

"What?"

"Run, now. Please."

"Come, Lotte." Clara grabbed Lotte's arm.

Lotte took Victor's hand. He let her. "Why are you doing this?" she asked.

The professor did not answer, only gestured for them to go.

Victor returned to the courthouse, which was in shock from the air raid. Reporters mobbed the Nazi soldiers on the steps, shouting for answers. Most of the Germans who'd been called to serve that day, to guard Tarcovich and her girls and ensure Grandjean did not leave the building, were new recruits. Some could not even shave; most were Flemish, pressed into service from their farms. They seemed paralyzed now, holding their rifles aloft, unsure whether they had the authority to shoot, and if so, whether it was advisable. The professor walked up to the man with the highest rank. He could not have been older than twenty-one.

"The prisoners you gave me," said Victor. "They ran away during the air raid."

"Christ," said the commander, forgetting himself.

"I am entitled to two servants. Those were the terms of my agreement with the Reich. If you do not supply two additional prisoners immediately, I will give your name and serial number to Herr Himmler."

The commander paled. "But I have my hands full here."

"You leave me with no choice."

"No, please! Go inside. Take two prisoners of your choosing."

Victor obeyed. He searched the courthouse for Grandjean, finding her seated by the window in her quarters. The door was open, so Victor went in. Grandjean jumped at the sight of him.

"Professor Victor?" she said.

"Do you have extra clothes here?" he demanded. "Rags? Something inconspicuous?"

"I do, I—"

"Get them. Hurry." He tossed her a set of keys. "We have no time at all."

"What are these?"

"The Germans are distracted. You must change out of those robes."

"Oh, yes." Grandjean's eyes cleared. "Yes, I will."

They took the stairs down to the prisoners' cells. The cells were unattended, as Victor had anticipated, for the Nazis had not yet returned from their bomb shelters. Tarcovich looked small and quiet in her cell, and her hands trembled on the bars.

"My God," she said, when she saw them. Grandjean tossed her a set of rags. She understood immediately, and changed without comment.

The three ran back upstairs and through the empty court-room. Victor could hear the reporters threatening to riot outside the door. They spoke Tarcovich's name, and Grandjean's, and they shouted Marc Aubrion's. Grandjean led the way to a back entrance, urging Victor and Tarcovich to follow her outside, assuring them no one would see their exit.

"Where are all the Germans?" asked Tarcovich.

"Aubrion's scheme worked," replied Victor.

Tarcovich laughed. "No, you can't be serious. The RAF?"

"We have to go while the Germans are still in the bomb shelters."

They were nearly free, the three of them, nearly out the back entrance and in the streets, when Tarcovich put a halt to the escape.

"Wait," she said, taking Andree's hand. The two shared a smile that made Victor's heart weep. "Andree, haven't you forgotten something?"

"What's that?" said Grandjean.

"You owe the people a verdict."

YESTERDAY

The Scrivener

"COME WITH ME," Helene said to her companion, rising from her seat.

The young woman tucked her leather notebook under her arm. "Where are we going?"

"To a coffeehouse."

They left the blue-doored building. As they walked, the city seemed to shrink in the abandoned quiet of evening. The cobblestones hurt Helene's feet. Sometime in the last decade, the city had paved over the old streets, masking the stones with concrete. But patches had worn away, baring the stubborn honesty of the city below.

"Eliza, let me ask you," said Helene. "Did your parents ever tell you why Victor did it?"

"All I know is what he told them."

"And what is that?"

"He said he couldn't grasp what he saw at the concentration camp. It was so illogical—the idea that people could *do* these things to each other—everything seemed to lose meaning, after that. You said it best. Victor thought it was his moral and intellectual responsibility to accept the new reality that the Nazis had created. But when he saw what Aubrion had done, he realized he'd been going about it the wrong way. The only way to deal with the absurdity of evil is with equal and opposite absurdity."

Helene allowed her laughter to carry her through the runaway streets. "Well said. There's hope for you and that notebook yet."

Eliza's features shifted in the dim. "Helene, there's a part of the story you don't know, an important part. My parents gave it to me. They made me promise to give it to you."

The old woman nodded. "I am ready to receive it."

"Lada and Andree thought they did not want children. It was like Lada said to Marc Aubrion—Hitler was elected, and what kind of a world is that? But they decided that was precisely why they should have children."

"Good," said Helene.

"Long before they adopted me, though, they came back."

"To Belgium?"

"To look for you, at the end of the war. They knew you must've survived it all. I heard so much about you, as a girl. My mother—Lada said they searched for months. But they ran out of money before they could find you. They made me promise to continue their search."

The old woman thought about that. "What else have I missed?"

"Neither Wellens nor Noël survived the camps. And Theo Mullier died in Fort Breendonk. The linotypists and printers, the men and women at Wellens's factory—they were captured and executed for their crimes." Eliza's eyes and face were delicate; they reminded Helene of those precious objects in the blue-doored museum, the bits of glass and obstinate little jewels that should not have lived through the war. "I'm so sorry."

"Never apologize for telling the truth."

"But Martin Victor fled to France, to Haute-Savoie. He

worked for the International Labor Organization until he died. No one knew who he was, in the end."

"It's all he wanted." The old woman stopped to lean against a wall. Every centimeter of her skin felt part of another time. "Thank you for telling me what became of them all."

"I've waited so long to give you that gift," said Eliza. "But what about you?"

"What of me?"

"What became of you, when the war ended?"

Helene shrugged, unsure what she was asking. "I returned to France."

"Is that all?"

"I did no great deeds, and I haven't died."

Eliza mirrored Aubrion's look of naked curiosity. "Does that sadden you?"

"The only reason I am alive," she said, and the gray and neon streets felt impossibly new, "is because I failed. Aubrion, Noël, Wellens, Spiegelman—their deaths were the product of their great deeds. I failed, I lived, and so I had to leave Belgium. If I'd stayed, everything would have reminded me of my failure, and of Marc Aubrion."

Helene kept walking, breathing in the jagged remains of her story. Eliza lingered for a moment, then ran after her.

"But that can't be *all* of your story," she said.

"I doubt you have room in your notebook for more. What are you going to do with it all, anyway?"

"Like I told you before. People should know."

"People *knew*."

She sped up to get in front of Helene. "There has to be more than failure."

"There's always failure at the end. René Noël used to say that."

"He was a pessimist. What about Marc Aubrion?"

The old woman kept silent until they arrived at the coffee-

house—the same coffeehouse, she told Eliza, where Lada Tarcovich sat to watch the people of Belgium give up their coin for
a farce, where Andree Grandjean came to sit beside her. Nothing had changed, except that everything was older. Helene ordered coffees for herself and Lada's daughter. They sat outside.

"You are right," she said. "There *was* more than that, at the
end."

"Wasn't there?" said Eliza, her face bright. This girl had picked
her pocket, Helene realized, rummaging around for tall tales.
She was a better thief than Gamin had ever been.

"I'll tell you the last bit." Helene warmed her hands on the
mug. "The Germans left Aubrion's body in the street for hours.
After a time, I went back for him."

TWO DAYS AFTER FAUX SOIR EVENING

The Jester and the Girl

AUBRION'S HANDS WERE COLD. I held on to them and dragged my friend behind the ruined church. I wasn't a weak child, not by any means, but I had not eaten in a good while, and my knees trembled. Looking at his face would have torn me up, so I struggled not to. After a good few minutes of work, I paused under a tree to rest.

I still had a few matches in my pocket, and as I said, my friend was cold. The first match, wet from my own perspiration, would not light. I had better luck with the second. In seconds, a tiny flame smirked at me from the tip of the match. I threw it into a patch of dry grass. It spread like water, illuminating everything.

The fire grew, and I let it, sitting back on my heels with Marc Aubrion. When the flame had expanded to three times its initial size, I said goodbye to my friend. Aubrion, as you now know, had a great deal of words in him. He was a loud character, my friend was. Every syllable he put on paper was a color I'd never seen, a musical note that had never been played. And so my farewell was wordless. He said all that needed to be said, in my view: enough for both of us.

We lay together in the shadow of the church, as comfortable as we'd ever been. I made up stories, to pass the time, about things that never happened. I fell asleep in the company of old friends. When I awoke, the Germans were still searching for him. Their torches died with the sun, but Aubrion's fire burned long into the night.

★ ★ ★ ★ ★

Author Note

I first "met" the original ventriloquist, Marc Aubrion, in my senior year at UC Berkeley. While doing archival research for my thesis on underground literature, I came across a document written by five women who worked for the Office of War during World War II. "The task of distributing [an underground publication]," they write, "poses special hazards. The [distribution] network may include a priest on his rounds or a policeman on his regular beat. A bundle may be smuggled aboard a steamer or concealed under the coal in the tender of a locomotive." They go on to mention a stunning exploit: "The patriots seem to take delight in including the Germans on their distribution routes. To get a wider public among the Germans, the patriots insert articles in the German-controlled press or manage to fake a whole edition. The Belgians sold sixty thousand copies of the Nazi *Le Soir* [*Faux Soir*] on the streets of Brussels on November 9, 1943." (In the novel, I changed the date to the 11th to correspond with Armistice Day.) Further research revealed that the Belgians wrote and distributed this paper in only eighteen days. A writer, Marc Aubrion, orchestrated the most elaborate feat of satire Europe has ever seen: the grandchild of Voltaire and the ancestor of *Improv Everywhere*.

Which characters were real?

Because the operation unfolded in secrecy, we know very little about Aubrion or his colleagues. However, we do have some broad character sketches. Marc Aubrion himself was a real person: a relatively minor journalist who wrote and edited articles for the resistance newspaper *La Libre Belgique*. He came up with the idea for *Faux Soir* on October 19, 1943, and wrote most of it in what his friends described as an "excited fury." René Noël, director of the *Front de l'Indépendance* (FI) press department in Brabant and Hainaut, did indeed supervise the project. Aubrion and Noël were assisted by Ferdinand Wellens, a flamboyant printer and businessman; Theo Mullier, a member of the FI who infiltrated the Nazi-controlled *Le Soir* factories; Andree Grandjean, a barrister; Pierre Ballancourt and Julien Oorlinckx, both linotypists; and at least one "youth partisan" who has remained nameless—or, rather, who I named *Gamin*. Professor Victor Martin (I switched his first and last names for the book) was a sociologist who spied for the FI and wrote one of the first investigative reports on Auschwitz, but he did not participate in the *Faux Soir* caper.

Though David Spiegelman, Lada Tarcovich and August Wolff are all fictional, they are echoes of real identities. It was rare, though not unheard of, that a Jewish or queer person would be granted immunity if they offered their services to the Reich. And prostitutes—queer or not—often operated smuggling rings with a variety of unlikely allies, from priests to farmers to children; the FI credited part of *Faux Soir*'s success to its network of smugglers, who made sure people all over the country, and then all over Europe, were able to secure a copy. Although Wolff the reluctant Nazi isn't based on anyone in particular, he is representative of a (sadly) common character: someone who could have given a voice to the oppressed, but didn't.

How many of these events actually happened?

Faux Soir is a story of everything going wrong in precisely the *right* way. Aubrion and Noël initially had trouble procuring the funds they needed for the project, so they enlisted the help of a barrister, Grandjean, renowned as a "puppet-master" who could get people to do what she wanted. While details of their initial meeting are hazy, we do know that the brash Aubrion alienated her at first. However, Grandjean soon came around, and she ultimately raised fifty thousand francs nearly overnight.

News of the endeavor made its way to businessman Ferdinand Wellens, who then requested a meeting with Noël. The FI made plans to abandon the operation, certain Wellens was going to demand a bribe in exchange for keeping quiet about *Faux Soir*. But as it turned out, Wellens was no friend of the Nazis, and he offered his factories to the FI.

After securing funds and printing materials, Aubrion and his colleagues wrote *Faux Soir* in only eighteen days—less time than it took me to *read* about the experience.

To disrupt the normal *Le Soir* distribution routes and get *Faux Soir* onto the streets in its stead, Aubrion conceived of two distractions. As part of the first distraction, a youth partisan would bomb the *Le Soir* vans before they began their daily route; the youth miscalculated and bombed them a day early. As part of the second distraction, the FI would convince the Royal Air Force (RAF) to stage an air raid on Brussels; the RAF miscalculated and arrived a day late. So, certain newsstands did in fact receive "one of each" version of *Le Soir*, and customers bought both. Despite these missteps, sixty thousand copies made it onto the streets before the Gestapo figured out anything was amiss.

How much of the book's Faux Soir *text is real?*

All of it! Everything—the text, the Hitler photographs, the German communique, Spiegelman's parody of Maurice-Charles Olivier's overwrought prose—was lifted from actual copies of *Faux Soir*. All of it is Aubrion's genius.

Did any copies of the paper survive?

For reasons I can't begin to imagine, the amazing story of *Faux Soir* has mostly been forgotten. But when the paper was first released, people cherished their copies and passed them down to their children. As such, multiple copies have survived.

Funny story: when I finished my senior thesis, I searched for a copy of the real *Faux Soir* and found that at least six still exist. I bought myself a copy from an antiques dealer as a graduation gift...the same day that my partner bought me a copy as a graduation gift, from the same antiques dealer.

Who survived the joke?

Sadly, most participants didn't make it out alive. "At the *Kommandantur*," one Nazi official wrote, "we pretended to accept the thing with fair play. 'Well done,' said an influential German officer, 'but the gentleman who did this will be shot with silver bullets.'" Within two months of the event, the Gestapo had captured everyone involved. As I mentioned in the book, Wellens and Noël were sent to labor camps from which they never returned. The printers and linotypists, including Ballancourt and Oorlinckx, received sentences of four months to five years in prison. Aubrion was either sentenced to death or fifteen years in prison; we can't say for sure. Only Victor Martin emerged from the war unscathed: he escaped from prison camps not once but *twice*, and retired to Haute-Savoie with his wife and children in the late 1970s. He died in 1989.

In January 1944, the secretary general of the FI memorialized *Faux Soir* with a brief eulogy in a resistance pamphlet: "We never forget that in the heart of the home front battles, we are men to whom nothing human is alien. Let us perpetuate a tradition of smiling during wartime. Not just that of Gavroche [...] but that of Peter Pan. With his humble slingshot, David killed Goliath. With a few well-guided blows, we will crumble the colossus with feet of clay."

Acknowledgments

Each book is a collection of stories—not just the ones on the page, but the ones behind every plot decision, every semicolon, every rejection, triumph, loss and obsession. I want to thank the characters in the story of this book.

This novel would not be in the world if not for my agent, Kristin Nelson. Kristin, "thank you" feels inadequate. Your tenacity and encouragement have made me a published writer—but more importantly, you've made me a better one. Every time I'm stuck on a plot point, I am grounded and guided by your refrain: that you're looking for a good story well told. Because of you, Kristin, I can keep telling stories. Here's to the next one, and the next.

Thanks also to the rest of the NLA family. Jamie, thank you for opening the door for a story about a newspaper heist. I'm forever grateful. Angie, thank you so much for your thoughtful, comprehensive edits and comments.

Thank you to my editor, Erika Imranyi at Park Row Books,

for your support and insight. Thank you to Natalie Hallak for incisive, thoughtful edits. This is a better book because of you.

Professor Ron Hassner read the novel when it was a paper about underground literature and rebellion that I wrote for his seminar; Professor Steve Fish read the novel when it was my thesis on the same topic. I think I've learned that the key to good mentorship is striking a balance between "That looks interesting and perilous! I'm going to wait and see what happens here" and "That looks interesting and perilous! I'm going to step in before it explodes." This novel would not exist if you two had not struck that balance. Thank you both.

Graham Warnken and Alice Ciciora were my first readers. They were in the trenches with me as I was writing the novel; they helped me work through plot and character problems; they endured the submission process with me. Though I am not a spiritual person, the best adjective I can use to describe their role is *sacred*. The only way I can thank you two for your role in this journey is by spending the rest of my life writing things you'd want to read. So I will.

Anna Flaherty read the book in one gulp. Your unbridled enthusiasm for the story was everything that I needed. Thank you.

Sherry Zaks was (and is always) my very first reader. Every morning when I wake up, Sherry asks, "Are you going to make me a book?" And every morning when I wake up, Sherry helps create a world so beautiful that I want to make her a book, and another, and another. Sherry, thank you. I love you. Let's keep making stories together.

The day that Park Row decided to buy my book, Sherry and I took a walk and stumbled across some graffiti. It was an image of a spaceship midflight, grinning with the words *The World Is Yours*. *The Ventriloquists* is based on a true story of people who realized the world *was* theirs, even if their country was not, who decided it was worth risking their lives for a joke that had never been told. We are still plagued by the forces of ignorance and oppression that took Belgium's typewriters—but the world is ours if we stand up and make it so. To that end, I extend my deepest gratitude to the real-life ventriloquists who inspired this story. Monsieur Aubrion, this book is yours.